Comes the Blind Fury

John Saul

Bestselling author of
Cry for the Strangers
and *Suffer the Children*

More than a century ago, a gentle, blind child walked the paths of Paradise Point. Then other children came, teasing and taunting her until she lost her footing on the cliff and plunged into the drowning sea.

Now, 12-year-old Michelle and her family have come to live in that same house—to escape the city pressures, to have a better life.

But the sins of the past do not die. They reach out to embrace the living. Dreams will become nightmares.

Serenity will become terror. There will be no escape.

A Dell Book $3.50   (11428-4)

LUCIANO'S LUCK

1943. Under cover of night, a strange group parachutes into Nazi occupied Sicily. It includes the overlord of the American Mafia, "Lucky" Luciano. The object? To convince the Sicilian Mafia king to put his power—the power of the Sicilian peasantry—behind the invading American forces. It is a dangerous gamble. If they fail, hundreds of thousands will die on Sicilian soil. If they succeed, American troops will march through Sicily toward a stunning victory on the Italian Front, forever indebted to Mafia king, Lucky Luciano.

A DELL BOOK   14321-7 $3.50

JACK HIGGINS

bestselling author of *Solo*

THE CLOSET DOOR STOOD OPEN.
THE BLACKNESS WITHIN SEEMED
TO PULSATE . . .

Outside her bedroom window, the moon was full and bright. The wind whined in the evergreens. Jenny shook with fear.

"Who's there?" she asked, her voice cracked and brittle.

She saw the eyes first . . . blazing out of the blackness within the closet. Then they started moving. Toward her. Wide eyes, reflecting moonlight. Dead, unseeing eyes glaring at her, burning through her, holding her hypnotically as they floated closer to her . . .

The marionette had come out of the closet. Suspended in air, it made no noise as it crossed the room. Now it hovered at the foot of her bed. It knew she was there! Its arms reached out for her. It was going to strangle her!

By Duffy Stein

THE OWLSFANE HORROR

GHOST CHILD

Duffy Stein

A DELL BOOK

Published by
Dell Publishing Co., Inc.
1 Dag Hammarskjold Plaza
New York, New York 10017

Dell ® TM 681510, Dell Publishing Co., Inc.

. ISBN: 0-440-12955-9

Printed in the United States of America

First printing—December 1982

for Debby—
her patience, her support, her love

ACKNOWLEDGMENT

Thousands of thanks to Coleen O'Shea, whose care and skill guided me from draft to book.

From our waking experience we are convinced that we produce our thoughts and that we can produce them when we wish. We also think we know where our thoughts come from, and why, and to what end we have them. If it should happen that a thought takes possession of us against our will, we feel as if something exceptional or morbid has happened.

—CARL JUNG

PROLOGUE

GLENDON, VERMONT, CIRCA 1900

The line of evergreens fringing the roadway cast long shadows across the yard and toward the house. A dark-haired woman stood hunched over, half hidden in the shadows. There was a vulnerability to her posture, and her hands played nervously against each other. Silently she watched the movers carry furniture up the porch stairs and the young couple, arm in arm, admiring their new home. It was the husband who first noticed the woman, and believing her to be a neighbor coming to welcome them to the town, took his wife's hand and approached her.

"Hello," he said, but quickly drew back his hand. His smile faded and instinctively he pulled his wife closer to him when he saw the face of the woman. She was young, but her eyes were small and sunken, tired, her skin prematurely lined.

"I lived in this house," the woman said—and her eyes rose to take it in—three stories with thick round classical columns supporting a sloping roof and a wide veranda running the length of the front and halfway along the sides. Nestled among evergreens and weeping willows, it seemed to be a peaceful house. But it was this house that had torn the woman's family apart, pitted brother against sister, father against son, her against her husband.

She let her glance linger on the open window on the second floor. An innocent room, a playroom, the *toy room* they called it. An attraction when they had bought the house, it was filled with costumed antique dolls, stuffed animals, and countless puppets and marionettes, the toys left by the previous owners. Even now, looking up at the window, she could picture the marionettes hanging from their pegs along the wall. The toy room—meant to be a play land for their daughter.

But it was in the toy room where so much had happened.

And she remembered the horror of the last night the family spent in the house. They had awoken to the screams and shrieks of their baby girl and found her in the toy room, tugging frantically at marionette wires wound tightly around her neck, choking her. Her husband had grabbed the knife and hunted for their son, chased him down into that room in the cellar . . .

Her body stiffened, and she slammed her eyes shut to block the unrelenting memory that had became part of her.

If she hadn't stopped him! My God! What could have happened? If she hadn't believed it all, her children might now be dead.

But they were all alive and out of the house, and the family was slowly becoming as they had been before. When there had been no screaming, no fighting, no terror. When her daughter had slept soundly and wasn't afraid of the night or sounds or *toys*.

"Do you have children?" she asked the young couple in a shaky voice that made them take a step back.

Mesmerized by this ghost of a woman, the husband answered dully, "No."

"Thank God," the woman said, and then repeated, "Thank God."

And then she turned and was gone.

CHAPTER 1

Mickie Talman put her hands against the dashboard, tensed her arms, and pushed for all she was worth, driving her body back against the seat. She felt the strain in her shoulders, the pain in the middle of her neck, but the stretch was wonderful.

"I can't take it anymore, Rufus," she yelled to her husband driving the Volkswagen Rabbit. "I haven't been in and out of as many houses since I was a kid trick-or-treating. I thought house-hunting was supposed to be fun."

Rufus leaned over and squeezed Mickie's knee. "We've covered a lot of ground today," he acknowledged.

"And last week," Mickie moaned, placing her hand over his, returning the squeeze. "Don't forget last week. After a while they all begin to look alike." She let her tongue fall out and her eyes roll upward. "And if I never see another real estate broker again, it'll be too soon. Did they really expect to palm off some of those clunkers on us? Do we look like we just got off the boat?"

"Just up from the city," Rufus said, smiling. "And that's probably worse."

Mickie rested her chin on the windowsill and stared out with round sad eyes. "You know, I was really hoping to find the perfect place the first shot out. March into a house, say 'this is the one for me,' and plop down the money." She rounded her chin, trying to remember. "What was the matter again with the third house we saw Monday? Or was it the second one yesterday? You know which one I mean—the house with that fantastic deck. That place had some nice things going for it."

Rufus remembered. It was an appealing house with enough room to convert into his office suite as well. And comfortably within their price range. But it had one key drawback.

"It was on a secondary road. Not a priority for the snowplows. In winter I have to count on getting out quickly in case of an emergency. After all, I'll be the only pediatrician in Glendon."

"We'll never find a place to live," Mickie said and pouted. "Let's convert the car into three bedrooms. What do you say? It'll be our own little condominium. Could have a resale value of eighty, ninety thousand."

Rufus Talman smiled and looked at his wife approvingly. It was almost as if she hadn't aged in the fifteen years they'd been married, looking today like she did at twenty. Her features were gentle, her skin smooth and girlish. Her light brown, almond-shaped eyes were soft and sensitive, easily misting when she grew sad. Always betrayed by those emotional eyes, she could never hide her feelings. Their children had the same transparent eyes, as well as Mickie's curly sandy hair. Rufus was a little hard pressed to find any of himself in Todd or Jenny. But that was okay; Mickie was much more pleasant to look at, although Mickie was quick to disagree. She had fallen in love with Rufus's deep blue eyes.

There was a pleasant stillness to the country air, as if city noise stopped at the state line. The sun was high in the sky and the soft breeze carried the summer smells and sounds, the sweetness of red clover, and the faint lowing of grazing cows in yards and postage stamp farms. They were passing through the older section of Glendon now, with large wood and brick houses and churches dating back to Colonial days, seemingly frozen in time. Mountains rose sharply beyond the town, the ski areas of central Vermont.

Suddenly Mickie frowned and looked at Rufus thoughtfully. "You realize all of our friends think we're crazy."

"I'd say it's more a lack of understanding," Rufus said. "What it comes down to is that there's not as much money to be made in Vermont as there is in New York. The simpler life is completely beyond their realm of comprehension. Mine, too, until not too long ago," he said and smiled. "But, in any event, I'd say they're more than just a bit envious. Not that they'll ever admit it." But then a flash of uncertainty crossed his face. "You don't think we're crazy, do you?"

Mickie thought a moment. She idly twirled her hair around her ear. "Probably," she said and laughed. "If for no other reason than giving up a fantastic two-bedroom apartment for only five sixty a month. They're going to raise the rent to eight hundred when we get out of there, and people will line up ten deep to get it."

But Mickie knew for certain they weren't crazy. The move was exactly what they all needed.

It was a combination of factors that had prompted the move. Rufus had a mild heart attack at the young age of thirty-eight, and his doctor ordered him to slow down his hectic schedule. And Todd was mugged on Central Park West a second time in less than a month. The first time the teen-aged muggers took a new ten-speed bicycle from him, the second time they dragged him into the bushes and opened a nasty cut above his eye. Rufus had to stitch it and the scar still remained.

And Jenny, their seven year old, deserved better than having to play indoors after school because it wasn't safe in the playground without supervision. Mickie couldn't always watch her and didn't want to be too overprotective with Jenny and Todd, walking the line that allowed her children to grow up safe, yet street-wise. Although deep down Mickie knew the truth about herself, especially where it concerned her children. She was an absolute alarmist, tending to see black instead of gray.

A ramshackle old wooden house peeked out from behind a row of feathered elm trees. A young girl led a horse out of the barn next to the house and waved at the passing car. It suddenly occurred to Mickie that none of them knew the first thing about country living.

"Oh, my God, Rufus," Mickie gasped. "We're not going to have a super anymore. What'll we do if the boiler breaks or the pipes freeze?"

"Not to worry," Rufus said and held up a calming hand. "You've never seen me in action. I'll just don my handyman coveralls, grab some tool or other, go right down to the cellar, assess the damage and"—he smiled —"come right back upstairs and let my fingers do the walking through the yellow pages." He patted Mickie's knee twice. "We'll do okay. I promise."

"I know," Mickie said, and leaned against him. Well, she had often wondered what kind of pioneer bride she would have made.

For a few months after the heart attack Rufus had slowed down, let the other doctors in his service do some of his work, and *actually spent his evenings at home*! But he had never been a person to sit back. If ever there was a type-A competitive heart, Rufus Talman had one, and soon the doctor's cautions were forgotten. He was back on his pre–heart attack routine of working twelve hours a day, followed by political dinners and meetings of the hospital and medical association. Mickie already considered herself a doctor's widow, because she saw her husband so rarely, but she resolved not to become one for real. After a particularly long day of one emergency after another, when Rufus's face was totally drained of color and his breathing was obviously labored, Mickie decided it was enough. The current pace would eventually kill her husband. It was time to establish a new pace.

On their winter vacation in Vermont they saw the sign on the billboard: Pediatrician Wanted.

Rufus jumped. This was what they were looking for: the great escape for him, healthy, country living for their children, and six months of winter for all of them. A fantasy life for a family of skiers. Inquiries were made immediately, and in less than the blink of an eye Rufus was ready to take the job.

Mickie, though, had been more cautious. The calm voice of reason, she liked to say. The only times she became analytical were when Rufus became impulsive. She, too, loved Vermont and enjoyed their ski vacations, when the family was all together, without nighttime phone calls and other distractions. But while Glendon was fine for skiing, might it not be too rural an area to actually move to? This was not just a move to the suburbs. *This is a move!* But the bug was planted in Rufus, and she had to admit excitement at the thought of a new adventure as well. But it was more than just fulfilling a fantasy. Those vacation weeks held such pleasant and magical memories for her, when Rufus devoted his total time to the family. She knew they would all be seeing so much more of him in the country than they had back home, and *they* would be able to spend more time together, like they had in the early days of their marriage before Rufus became so drawn into his career and the hours that medicine demanded. And that would be a very nice and important change in their lives.

And so she cast her vote as yes.

A freelance editor for a publishing firm, Mickie had initially been concerned that the move might hurt her getting work. But she had been assured by her employers that distance was not a problem. (How is mail delivered up there, Mick? By muleback?) So arrangements were worked out, and there was absolutely nothing standing in their way.

Except a place to live.

A truck lumbered slowly ahead of them, trying to take the incline. Exhaust fumes belched out of the diesel engine as the VW slowed down behind it.

"I thought pollution wasn't allowed up here," Rufus said as a blast of black smoke blanketed the windshield and blew into the car. "It's like New York all over again." He downshifted to try to pass the truck and almost missed the hand-scrawled For Sale by Owner sign. He quickly pulled back into lane and darted into the driveway.

It was an older house, much older than any of the houses they had been shown, and bigger too. Rufus estimated there might be a dozen rooms, maybe more, as well as an attic tucked under the eaves. A veranda ran the length of the house and thick, round columns held up a sloping roof. Under the veranda a brick base supported the house and hid a large cellar. Dirty, almost black storm windows lined the bricks. The house was set well back from the roadway, hidden behind a row of evergreens.

"What do you think?" he asked.

Mickie shrugged. It wasn't exactly what she had in mind, but then she realized she really didn't know exactly what she had in mind. She just suspected that when she saw *the house* it would jump up and hand her a deed.

"I think it has charm," Rufus offered.

"From the ivy crawling up the outside I think it has bugs," Mickie joked. "It's kind of old and dumpy-looking. Let's skip it for now. We've had enough for today anyway. We can always come back and look tomorrow. I just want to go back to the motel and dive into the pool." She stretched again and heard the snap of her neck and back muscles.

"Come on," Rufus pressed. "We're here. Let's take a quick look. If for no other reason than to chalk up another one. All we're going to blow is a couple of minutes."

They parked the car in the driveway and walked a slate path up to the house. The closer they got to the house, the more it showed its age. The roof needed work, the sides a paint job. The wooden steps which led to a side entrance were cracked and splintered, and on the open veranda several cane-back rocking chairs sat decaying, holes in their wicker backs. All of the windows were tightly closed and many of the rooms curtained, unable to catch the sweet summer breeze and fresh country air.

It was an old woman who answered the bell. She had silver-blue hair combed straight back on her head, coming to a bun on top. She was pale and Mickie concluded she didn't get out of the house all that often.

"Yes?"

"We saw your sign and thought we'd take a look at the house," Rufus said.

Another old woman shuffled from a room that opened onto the entrance foyer. "They're here to see the house. Let them in."

"I know, I know. I heard them too," the first woman growled and rudely pushed the other one out of the way, barreling them into the foyer. Mickie and Rufus exchanged glances.

The second woman took charge. "Welcome. I hope you like it here. I'm Penelope Benson. This is my sister, Hazel, but she's not important." Hazel glowered at her sister and Mickie swallowed a grin.

Rufus coughed into his hand and said, "Dr. Talman. My wife, Mickie."

Handshakes all around.

"Feel free to look around," Penelope said. "Go anywhere you want. Upstairs. Downstairs. Whatever we have you can look at." She opened her arms grandiosely.

"Thank you," Rufus said.

To the front of them a staircase headed up toward a landing before doubling back upon itself to the second floor. Off to both sides of the foyer were rooms lost in shadow. Mickie sniffed the air. There was a damp, musty odor that permeated the house. The smell of age. A sick room smell. The women had tried to mask the dankness with a flowered spray. But it just hung in the air and added to the mustiness. The house seemed to take on the smell of the old ladies and vice versa.

"Well, come on, come on," Hazel fluttered, trying to push them into another room. "Can't see the whole house standing there."

"They're taking their time!" Penelope snapped at her sister. "Don't rush them. Let them look at their own pace. Get the feel of the house." With obvious embarrassment, she smiled apologetically at Rufus and Mickie. "Please ignore Hazel. She has bats in her head. You just take your time. Ask any questions you want."

Behind her sister's back, Hazel made a face. Mickie restrained herself from laughing out loud.

Rufus rapped his knuckles against the paneled archway that separated one of the rooms from the foyer. It felt solid to his touch. "Oak," he said. "Nothing like the houses being built today or anything like the plasterboard on our walls back home. Come on—"

He reached for Mickie's hand and led her through the archway into a drawing room. The furniture was old, with overstuffed couches and Morris chairs resting on clawed feet. Covering many of the windows were heavy, dark curtains. Perfect for the winter to keep out drafts, but stifling for the summer months. Old photographs hung on the walls in chipped wooden frames. There were no light, cheery colors anywhere.

And no plants, Mickie realized. She remembered that window boxes sat under each window on the first floor, but they were all empty. There seemed to be no plants inside or outside the house and that saddened her. It was depressing to see how the women chose to live, yet she knew she had no right to be critical and impose her values on anyone else.

It was the fireplace, though, that made the room beautiful, even fantastic. It had a mantel of Italian marble and a decorative stone-and-brick face that ran the height of the room. Mickie had never seen a grander fireplace in any private home. Dusty porcelain figurines covered the mantel, and Mickie mentally substituted her own Waterford crystal. A showplace indeed.

"It's incredible," Rufus gasped and ran his hand up and down the smooth stone. He looked at Mickie and smiled, and she nodded in return, already imagining how their furniture would look in this room and what new things they might buy to complement it. She was suddenly feeling more excited than she had in days. This house, despite its run-down exterior, was beginning to capture her imagination. A definite maybe.

There were five large rooms on the first floor, all with fireplaces and all connected by sliding wood-paneled doors that disappeared into the walls when open. Rufus quickly pointed out that he could convert three of these rooms into his suite of offices; the others could be used for living. The kitchen seemed to stretch forever and was almost as large as their entire two-bedroom city apartment, Mickie thought.

"Do you have children?" Penelope asked her, suddenly sneaking up from nowhere, it seemed.

"Yes. A boy and a girl."

"Ah, you have a girl. Then this definitely is the house for you. Wait until you see what we have upstairs."

"Come on, hon," Rufus said and took her hand again.

Closed doors stretched along the second-floor corridor. At either end windows sparingly let in light and threw tree shadows along the tattered green rug. Gray, flowered wallpaper, water-stained in spots above the wainscoting, blanketed the corridor.

"Our rooms are this way," Penelope said, and led the way to the side of the house above the living room fireplace which would heat the bedrooms as well.

Penelope's room was spartanly furnished, with a four-poster bed, matching oakwood dresser, and a coatrack standing in the corner. A green-and-blue hooked oval rug covered the wooden floor.

"Forget the furniture, Mick," Rufus whispered. "Try to visualize it with our things."

He brushed aside one of the curtains. In the distance were mountains, and through a break in the trees he could make out a stream. "A hell of a view to wake up to, isn't it?" he breathed.

"Picture postcard Vermont," Mickie had to admit.

"And now for the pièce de résistance." Penelope smiled and wrinkle lines crisscrossed her face. She led the way to the far end of the corridor. "For your little girl, voilà, the toy room."

She pushed open the door and ushered them inside. Mickie let out a gasp of pleasure.

The room was a museum of antique toys with costumed dolls and furnished houses dating back to Colonial times, a rocking horse, stuffed animals, and dozens of tin and windup toys. And a wallful of marionettes and puppets, clowns, witches, ballerinas, Punch-and-Judys, their faces brightly, almost grotesquely, painted and their features exaggerated. On the floor was a calliope with a menagerie of galloping horses under a colorful canopy of red and blue. Rufus could almost hear the music playing, the horses rising and falling, racing each other. Mickie knelt down and fingered the tiny carved animals resting next to a wooden Noah's Ark. A smile played across her face.

"Jenny would love it in here," she said and beamed.

Rufus was the last one to leave the toy room, and before he closed the door, his glance fell on the shoe-button eyes and painted smirk of a clown marionette. He smiled and saluted good-bye.

When they got back to the first floor, Penelope wasted no time. "Well, shall we talk turkey?" she suggested.

"It's a bit soon," Rufus said, "although I do have to say you have one hell of a house here. Don't they, Mick?"

"It's nice," she wavered, instinctively playing the bad guy. "But I think we can be in touch if we decide. I'm sure the house isn't going anywhere."

"We're only asking seventy-five," Hazel sang.

Penelope shot her a look. "*I'll* do the dealing," she said huffily.

"Well, I thought you forgot," Hazel snapped back. "I was only trying to help."

"Well, I didn't forget and you can best help by being quiet."

Hazel started to respond, but caught Penelope's stern look and closed her lips tightly. In spite of herself Mickie couldn't help but smile. Rufus, though, had missed the whole exchange.

"Only seventy-five thousand, Mick!" he said excitedly. "We couldn't touch a one-bedroom condo back home for that."

"Rufe, I think we have to talk first," Mickie said. She took his arm and ushered him toward the door. She was interested too, but after all the time spent looking for the perfect house, she wasn't going to be rushed now. "Uh, Miss Benson?" she asked Penelope as the question occurred. "Why are you moving—if I may ask?"

"It's Hazel." Penelope scowled. "Her arthritis has gotten bad, and the doctor said she shouldn't spend another winter up here. We've lived in this house for twenty years and now we have to pick up and—"

"I feel fine," Hazel interrupted.

"You're not fine! You're old and you have to move to a warmer climate."

Mickie could see from the look on her face that Hazel disagreed with the doctor's advice.

"You've really got a great old house here," Rufus repeated, breaking into their conversation.

Penelope smiled graciously. "Thank you, Dr. Talman," she said. "And you'll be back, I'm sure of it. I see that this house has gotten inside of you the same way it did us the first time we saw it. Good-bye now. We'll see you soon, okay?"

"Thank you again," Mickie said hurriedly and waited until they were down the porch stairs and out of earshot for her laughter to ring full. "God, Rufus. Can you believe those two? And they say they've been happy!"

Rufus laughed as well. "To each his own. Some people enjoy fighting, but at least they care for each other. I just hope *we* don't grow crotchety with the years," he said. "Promise that you'll shoot me if I do."

"A suicide pact," Mickie said, smiling. "Shake on it."

They walked back to the car slowly, inspecting the outside of the house. As Rufus started the engine and backed out of the driveway, the house loomed large in front of them.

"So?" he started.

"It's tempting," Mickie said as they pulled back onto the highway. "As hideous as they kept it. But as much as I like it, I think we have to be practical. That kind of house is not for people like us."

"Define 'people like us,' " Rufus said.

"Inept," Mickie offered.

"I asked," Rufus said and they both laughed. But he knew she was right. He could envision how the real estate ad might read: "For Sale. Handyman's Special." Which meant don't come near it, unless you're a plumber, carpenter, electrician, roofer, and painter.

"And it'll probably cost a fortune to heat," Mickie added.

"It's by far the best house we've seen yet," Rufus said. "And we can close off the rooms we don't use. And burn lots of wood in all those fireplaces. Come on—" he pushed. "It's a fantastic buy."

"Yes, the price is reasonable. But you know why. Look at all the work that has to be done. The kitchen. The roof. A painting. Nobody's going to move into that house the way it is and they know it. We'd have to plow thousands into it."

"So we'll price it all out. And don't forget the town has agreed to chip in to help us too. I'm a VIP, remember?"

"You haven't even looked in the cellar. What if there's no boiler or water tank or whatever else a house like that is supposed to have. And how sound structurally is it?"

"I'm not going to do anything without thoroughly checking it out," Rufus said. "I might be inept but I'm not stupid. We'll hire somebody to look at it." He whistled. "Mick, didn't you ever dream of owning a house like that?"

"Of course. Who hasn't?"

"Well now we can have it. It's in our hands. That

fireplace. The toy room. It's all so absolutely incredible."

"But can we handle it?" Mickie asked nervously, excitedly, knowing that was the key. "Both of us are apartment born and raised. Neither of us has ever lived in a house before."

"I don't see what the problem is. A house is a house is a house. With three rooms or twelve."

"It's overwhelming, that's what it is. I'm afraid it might be too much house for Todd and Jenny." But her tone of voice begged him to disagree. He did.

"They'll love it. All that room to run around in. Mick, no house has really appealed to us before this one. And it's so much nicer than those tract houses or split levels we looked at. It's an old rambling country house with charm and history."

"Just so long as it doesn't ramble away in the first windstorm this winter."

Excitedly Rufus pounded on the steering wheel. "You know, I feel so strongly about that place. It's almost like there's a little voice inside of me saying 'buy me, buy me.' Let's think about it. Go back there tomorrow, stomp the place from top to bottom, block out everything that's there, and lay out our own stuff in it—plus whatever new things we think we can get."

"No bribery now, Rufe," Mickie said, already knowing she'd be disappointed if they didn't take the house. Penelope Benson was right—it had gotten inside of them.

"And I'll get Al Farrell from the Chamber of Commerce to recommend a contractor to come and walk the place with us. Tell us what's required, if it makes sense or not. And if it makes sense," he let his voice rise, "then we talk seriously."

"Deal."

Rufus pulled the car off the road, set the emergency brake, and pulled Mickie close to him. "It's going to be it, honey, I just know it is," he said and leaned over and kissed her.

There was new excitement to the kiss, and to their lives.

CHAPTER 2

Rufus's arm was draped around his son, his sweat dripping down onto the boy, mixing with Todd's. Their heavy breaths came out as animal grunts as they started their third mile of jogging. Todd was dressed in purple gym shorts, a U.S. Open T-shirt, and a red sweatband that held his hair out of his eyes. Rufus wore a sweat suit, which was oppressive in the heat of the muggy afternoon.

Mickie had designated Todd as watchdog over Rufus and his father's grunting sounds were beginning to alarm him. Even though he could have run more, Todd slowed to a walk.

"Had enough?" Rufus asked. He stopped in place and doubled over, trying to catch his breath.

"Yeah, Dad. Let's walk a bit, okay?"

"Won't argue with that," Rufus said. They pulled out of the jogging lane and into the grass-lined path under the trees. Around them were baby carriages, roller skaters, frisbee throwers, and an assortment of vendors that could have catered a six-course meal. Central Park in the summer.

The bench looked too inviting and Rufus collapsed on it, stretching his arms behind him and spreading his legs. He threw his head back and opened his mouth wide. The wheeze for air turned into a ten-count yawn. Todd bent at the waist and touched his toes a half-dozen times before sitting next to his father. He wiped his face with his sleeve.

Todd pointed through the trees to an isolated spot washed in shade near the stone wall that surrounded the park. Beyond the wall were the painful sounds of the midtown traffic.

"It happened over there," he said. "That's where those guys creamed me."

A baby sat on a blanket and played in the shade. The parents sat on lounge chairs nearby. It was deserted on the day Todd had been hit.

"Sons of bitches," Todd muttered angrily and remembered how they had opened a gash above his eye and the blood poured down his face, blinding him. It was only the sight of the blood that frightened the muggers away.

"One of the reasons we're moving, Todd," Rufus said softly and encircled his son with his arm. He saw Todd's anger and tried to break his mood. "And we're going to get everyone a season's ski pass. You'll be an expert skier in no time."

"Sounds really great," Todd said and his eyes sparkled. One ski week a winter had not been enough.

"And I'm going to have more free time to spend with you and Jenny," Rufus said. "I've been a little negligent lately, as I think you know." For a second he felt afraid that his children were growing up without him.

"Yeah," Todd said softly. "But it's okay."

"Well, I'm going to change all of that and concentrate on being a full-time father," Rufus said with just a little too much forcefulness in his voice that told Todd he was making a promise to himself as well.

There was an awkward silence between them as neither knew what to say. Todd didn't like to see his father apologize to him like that. Even though they were few in number, days like this alone with Rufus were cherished by Todd, who especially liked it when they

worked out and sweated together. It made him feel
more grown-up. More like his father. And perhaps because the days like this were few, they were all the
more special. There was a comfortable bond between
them, Todd felt, which could never be broken by distance or time apart. And he suspected his father felt the
same way.

"Deal, Todd?" Rufus held out his hand.

Todd took it. "Deal."

He got up from the bench.

"Come on, Dad. Race you to the ice cream guy.
Loser pays."

Rufus paid.

"Did you remember to pick up the pictures, Rufe?"
Mickie's voice challenged as they burst into the apartment. Rufus's sweatshirt was stained with chocolate
where he hadn't caught a drip in time; Todd had a simi-
lar stain on his face. They exchanged guilty glances;
they were bound together, accomplices. Todd swallowed a grin. They had forgotten the pictures.

Rufus nudged his son. "Create a diversion," he whispered. "I'll make a grab for my wallet, get some money,
and sneak out again."

Mickie entered the room. Rufus snapped his fingers.
"Caught," he said. A sheepish grin spread across his
face. Todd whistled nonchalantly.

"You did forget," Mickie said. "Aw, Rufe, I wanted
them for tonight."

"I lost the race," Rufus said. "I had to buy the ice
cream cones." He pulled his pockets inside out to show
he was broke.

Mickie glanced at the clock on their credenza. "It's
getting late and we have to be over at Lois's for dinner
at seven. We can pick up the pictures on the way. Now,
into the showers, both of you," she scolded and clapped

her hands together as Rufus and Todd ran off in different directions.

"And shave, will you?"

Todd ducked into the bathroom. "Sure, Mom."

"Wise asses." Mickie smiled and pushed her husband into the bedroom.

The cold water beat down on him, icy needles reviving him. Rufus vowed to get into a regular exercise program once they got to Vermont so that a two-mile jog wouldn't exhaust him.

Mickie came into the bathroom to apply her makeup.

"My mother will be here in a few minutes to stay with the kids," she yelled to Rufus over the rushing water.

Rufus stuck his head out from behind the shower curtain. "They don't need a babysitter anymore. Todd's almost twelve. You just told him to go shave."

"He's just turned eleven, and I know they don't need a babysitter. But you know how much Mother loves to be with them. How could I say no to her—we'll be moving in a couple of months."

Rufus flipped off the shower and reached for a towel. "Right. So I don't know why we're going to a going-away dinner tonight when we're not going away for another two months."

"Lois will be out in the Hamptons for the rest of the summer. This was the only time she could have us over. Besides, she's invited a lot of your friends over tonight. From the guest list it sounds like a mini-AMA convention.

"Good. I'll be the envy of everyone there," Rufus crowed. "Getting out of the rat race like I am. Let them eat their hearts out. Who's Lois's latest?" he asked.

"Rufus, be nice," she scolded. "She's had a tough go of it. She loved Dave very much, and it tore her up when he left her for that other woman."

"I know, I know, sorry," Rufus said and slapped the wet towel at Mickie. She tried to get out of the way, but he backed her against the sink. "Hey," he said softly. "Do we have time?"

A voice came from outside their door. "Mommy. Grandma's here."

Mickie smiled and shrugged innocently at her husband, grabbed her robe, and whisked out of the bathroom.

Mickie sat in the double-parked cab as Rufus dashed into the drugstore for the pictures. Most of the roll of twenty-four were shots of the house, the remaining ones were photos of the family during Todd's eleventh birthday party about six weeks before.

They got to the party early enough to greet their first guest in the elevator.

Lois Gardner, a petite woman with piercing dark eyes and a mouth that was always rounded into a pout, met them at the door. She hugged Mickie and Rufus warmly.

Within an hour the other guests had arrived, and the party was centering around the Talmans and—as one doctor put it—their maniacal move.

"The first time I met Mickie," Rufus said, with his arm draped around Mickie's shoulder and a toast glass in his hand, "she was struggling to lace up a pair of old-fashioned ski boots. The next time I saw her she was renting a pair of boots in the Stowe ski shop, and just last year she was *buying* a new pair of ski boots and sending the bill to me." Everyone laughed as Rufus finished up. "We love Vermont, we love the life up there. Neither of us is getting any younger, so we thought, what the hell? Call us crazy if you want, but we're going. Now eat your hearts out." He downed his drink in one take.

The call came from a balding doctor in a corner of

the room. "Hey, Rufe, you going to trade in your Rabbit for a horse and buggy?"

"No," Rufus shot back. "But I am going to change my license plate to read Dr. Bumpkin."

Milt Shapiro, an orthopedic surgeon, cleared his throat. "Actually I should be going up there with them. There's no way that a whole ski season is going to go by without this schlemiel breaking something."

As the joking continued, Lois grabbed Mickie's arm and whisked her into a corner, behind the hors d'oeuvres table. "So it's all a *fait accompli*, huh?" she asked.

Mickie nodded. "Held the closing last Thursday. We're now land barons in Vermont."

"No turning back then?"

"Well," Mickie hedged. "There's always turning back. Nothing has to be forever."

Lois's eyes were warm and moist and she looked genuinely sad. "I'm going to miss you, kid. You've been a good shoulder when I've needed it and I appreciate it. I just hope I never have to repay the favor." She indicated across the room to a tall, slender man talking with a group of doctors. "Isn't he gorgeous? Medical supply salesman from Montreal. I think he's over there doing business now."

Mickie smiled. "I wish you well with him."

"Thanks," Lois beamed, and then suddenly remembered. "Hey, you promised to bring pictures of the place."

"I almost forgot," Mickie said. "We've got them." She searched for Rufus. "Rufe"—she waved to him—"bring over the pictures, will you?"

He started to flip through the pictures with Lois and several of the others crowding to see. The first couple were interior shots, of the kitchen and living room, and finally a long shot which captured most of the house taken from the driveway.

Milt Shapiro gave a low whistle. "Certainly is big. Looks a little like the House on Haunted Hill to me."

"God damn it, Milt," Rufus snapped defensively, his face suddenly flushed red. "There is nothing wrong with that house, and I'm sure we're going to be very happy there."

Shapiro held up his hand in conciliation. "Joke, Rufe," he said. "I meant nothing by it."

Mickie looked at her husband, puzzled by his sharp reaction. He was usually the first one to roll with the punches.

"Yeah," Rufus said grudgingly. "Sorry. I guess I'm just a little sensitive about things right now. I like this house an awful lot."

"It's so wonderfully big," Lois said with a note of admiration. "You weren't kidding." The ringing phone pulled her away.

"And look at this," Mickie said, showing a picture of the toy room. "All these antiques. For Jenny it's going to be Christmas and her birthday all rolled into one."

"Mick," Lois called from across the room. "It's your mother."

"My mother?" Mickie frowned. Nervously, she reached for the phone. Her mother wouldn't be calling unless there was a problem.

"It's Jenny," Tessie Barrett said to her daughter. "There's something wrong with her."

Jenny was curled up in bed, her face buried in her pillow, crying hysterically. Mickie led the way into the room, followed by Rufus and her mother.

Mickie sat down at the edge of the bed, gently stroked Jenny's head, and turned her daughter's face to her. "Easy, honey. What is it?"

"I don't want to die, Mommy," Jenny sobbed.

Surprised, Mickie looked at Rufus who shrugged.

"Of course not, honey," she said to Jenny soothingly. "Why do you think you're going to die?"

"What happened?" Rufus asked Tessie.

Tessie shook her head. "I don't know. Right after you left, Mrs. Kingman asked if she could bring Sheila down to play with Jenny. I didn't see any reason why not. They were playing together for over an hour when all of a sudden I heard Jenny crying and I couldn't stop her. I didn't know what was wrong. Todd took Sheila back upstairs and I called you."

"Sheila didn't hit her, did she?" Rufus asked Tessie, not imagining the two seven-year-old girls could have been fighting.

Mickie cradled Jenny in her arms. In the safe comfort of her mother, the sobs were subsiding. Rufus walked over to the bed, knelt down, and looked at his daughter at her eye level. Her eyes were red from crying.

"What is it, honey?" he asked her and patted her face.

"Sheila said I was going to die."

"Why would she say that?"

"She said if we moved all the way to Vermont, I wouldn't have my friends anymore, and I'd die." Her eyes widened and searched her father's face fearfully. "I don't want to die, Daddy."

"You're not going to die, honey. That was a terrible thing for Sheila to say."

"I don't want to move," Jenny sobbed. "I like it right here and want to stay."

Rufus gently edged Mickie out of the way. "Let me, hon." He wrapped his arms around Jenny and rocked her back and forth. "It's time for Daddy to have a talk with his little girl." He nudged her. "Is that okay?"

Jenny nodded without conviction. Rufus winked at Mickie.

Mickie and Tessie closed the door behind them. Rufus held Jenny at arm's length and smiled broadly at her. "Now we seem to have a little problem here, don't we?"

Jenny nodded and the toss of her head almost brought tears to Rufus's eyes. His daughter was so small, so vulnerable, so defenseless.

"First of all," he said to her, "you have to know that Sheila is very wrong. You're not going to die if we move. You're going to make lots of new friends in Vermont. I think Sheila's unhappy because you're moving away, and she won't have anybody in the building to play with anymore. I wouldn't be surprised if she isn't in her own bed right now crying too. Before we move we're going to have a talk with Sheila so she won't be unhappy. Because I know for an absolute fact that you're not going to be. I promise you that in no time at all you'll have lots of friends."

A smile broke on Jenny's face. Rufus brushed her bangs off her forehead and with his handkerchief wiped the tears from her cheeks. "Feeling better now?" he asked.

Jenny nodded and threw her arms around him. Rufus's face glowed with love. "And now no more worries. What do you say?"

"I say no . . . more . . . worries?" Jenny repeated, punctuating each word with a shake of her head.

Mickie was stretched out in bed when Rufus came back from taking Tessie home. He slumped into the chair in the corner of the room. "Jenny still calm?" he asked.

"You've got the magic touch, Daddy. Right now she's looking forward to moving so Sheila can come and visit." Mickie smiled. "It all seems so official now, doesn't it?"

"Because we've told our friends?"

"No, not just that. I really think I'm beginning to feel

it now. It's not totally real because we haven't moved yet. But the ladies are out and the house is ours. I feel like I'm beginning to finally breathe Vermont."

"Any regrets?"

"Regrets? I'm absolutely delighted," she squealed.

"Good. Because I know things are going to work out great for us in that house." Rufus's eyes momentarily flicked away from Mickie, and they both realized what he was leaving unsaid. But nothing more had to be stated, no more apologies made. They knew they had somehow grown apart in recent years, when Rufus's career had clearly come first to all else, but this was a new life and both knew it was going to be different and better.

Mickie motioned for Rufus to join her on the bed. "Why don't you take your clothes off and get your ass over here?"

"Is that an invitation?"

"Invitation, hell. That's an order."

Mickie melted at his touch and readily received him. When they were finished he lay on top of her. She wrapped her arms around him, swearing to herself she would never let go. Just knowing they were moving was making her feel closer to Rufus than she had in a long time. And she suspected that he was feeling the same.

"I love you so very much, Rufus," she whispered into his ear and gave him a final squeeze.

And in the room next door, seven-year-old Jenny clutched her Snoopy doll tightly to her and remembered Sheila's words.

Jenny, if you move to that house in Vermont, you're going to die.

CHAPTER 3

There were different phases to her life, Mickie thought. From birth through high school under her parents' wing was one, leaving home for college and independence another. Then there was Rufus and their time B.C.—before children—and finally the arrival of Todd and Jenny. And now, as she glanced behind her to see the New York skyline disappear in the gray haze of the early morning, she knew she was entering yet another phase.

It was moving day, September 1, 1982. She would have loved to have been up in Vermont a month earlier to avoid a particularly brutal summer in the city, but there was just too much to pull together for that to happen—from closing Rufus's share of the New York practice, to getting the new house into livable condition. But now the hot summer was behind them and already forgotten, and a new life lay ahead.

She smiled at Todd and Jenny, who were strapped into the back seat, surrounded by necessities for the trip—a triple-A road map for Todd so he could follow along and his baseball mitt for a game of catch at a rest stop. Jenny held on to Snoopy, a doll now ragged with age that she had gotten on her fourth birthday and adopted as a constant companion.

"Well, this is it," Rufus announced for perhaps the fifteenth time since they had gotten up that morning. "Glendon, Vermont, here we come," and spontaneously

he broke into a chorus of "Country Roads" with everyone else joining in.

"We have a stream on our property so we can fish,"
Rufus said when they had finished singing. "And woods
so maybe we can build a tree house, Todd . . . and
there's certainly enough room in the yard for a game of
touch football or maybe even tackle."

Even though she had heard these words countless
times in the past two months, Rufus's exuberance made
them seem fresh and new. When they started to sing
"Don't Fence Me In," with Rufus's baritone voice
sounding less off-key than usual, Mickie let herself run
a mental checklist to see if everything had been completed in the house. There had been months of work,
and she knew that if Hazel and Penelope returned today, they wouldn't recognize it. Only the shell of the
house was the same; everything else had been over-
hauled.

They had spent the summer feverishly getting the
house in shape so they could move in by Labor Day
and in time for the start of the new school year. They
had done the work in shifts. First Rufus went up to lay
out his office area and go over the construction with
the local contractor. Walls were built, the parking area
paved, the outside stairs reconstructed, and presto: a
doctor's office.

Then Mickie and her mother had gone up to see
what had to be done in the living areas. In spite of the
amount of work, Mickie enjoyed it all. They had all
new appliances installed in the kitchen—refrigerator,
gas range, and dishwasher. Even the sink was new.
Yards of butcher block counter space were added, an
indoor barbecue for the winter months and a washer-
dryer so Mickie wouldn't have to run down to the cellar
on wash day.

Then they had the house scrubbed and painted top to
bottom, inside and out. The windows were left open for

a week to let the Vermont breeze blow through the house, filling it with smells of the country summer. When the painters were finished, Mickie had to admit there was a remarkable transformation. The musty smell was gone, the house felt newer, fresher.

Mentally laying out their furniture in the house, Mickie realized it wasn't going to go far. What looked like a lot in a crowded two-bedroom apartment would be quickly swallowed up by a house that size.

Hazel and Penelope were leaving behind a lot of furniture, and Rufus suggested they keep some of it to fill up the other rooms. Mickie vetoed the idea. She removed everything left by the women except for the toys. She wanted to sever any remaining connection with the house's previous owners. It was *theirs* now, and nothing in it would be old or gray.

They crossed the Vermont state line, and Rufus led them in a cheer.

"Aw riiight!" Todd exploded and whooped it up in the back seat. He was already the envy of all of his friends, and they had planned to spend Christmas week with him in the new house. That would mean at least a dozen sleeping bags, Mickie knew; her son had been voted the most popular boy in the sixth grade.

Mickie closed her eyes and curled her fingers in Rufus's on the seat between them. Even though they had spent much of the summer apart, she felt close to him. For the first time in a long while she felt they were really sharing something together.

The problems had come with Rufus's success at the hospital. As he got busier with his practice and spent more time serving on hospital committees, they began to see less of each other. And when they were together, Rufus only talked about his patients or his problems at the hospital and what could be done to get more money for a new hospital wing. There was less and less concern about what Mickie considered important—their feelings toward each other. It was almost as if Rufus didn't have time for her and her needs; as a result, she had felt used and taken advantage of. Yet she suspected he was oblivious to what was happening.

The few times she had broached the subject he had looked at her blankly. "We still talk, Mickie. We're talking now, aren't we?"

He just didn't understand what she needed from him, she concluded, realizing he wasn't aware of his insensitivity. For several days after their talks he was more attentive to her. But soon his work reclaimed him or a medical conference came up, and he slipped back into his old pattern. That was Rufus and she had to accept him or end it, and she would never do that. She loved him. But it was exasperating, nonetheless, and she was beginning to feel starved for his attention. Eventually, her own work became more important to her, to fill her time, to take Rufus's place.

Perhaps the heart attack was a blessing in disguise. It had brought them together for the recovery period and had led to this move.

Thinking about the brick-and-stone fireplace that awaited them in the house, and imagining it alive with flames, Mickie hoped they would recapture the feel of their early days together. She pictured them sitting hand in hand in front of the fire for long, uninterrupted evenings. A smile played across her lips and she squirmed closer to Rufus. They were being offered a new beginning, a fresh start, and how many people could boast that?

After a drive that seemed endless they were there.

Todd's eyes shot wide open as Rufus pulled into the driveway, and the house was suddenly visible. This *castle* was theirs. They had seen pictures of the house but no picture was as impressive as the real thing. "Wow!" was about all he could sputter as he unsnapped the seat belt.

Jenny held on tightly to Snoopy. She was filled with an uncertain mixture of excitement and nervousness. Out of the corner of her eye, Mickie watched her daughter, hoping that she would easily adapt to the house.

"Everyone out for pictures," Rufus ordered. He pulled a camera out of his travel bag. The roll of film was already half used with "after" pictures to show the metamorphosis of the house. They all posed together, and one of the moving men, who had arrived earlier, snapped a family portrait.

After a quick tour of the downstairs, they left Mickie in the kitchen to phone her mother to let her know of their safe arrival and went upstairs. Rufus showed the children the master bedroom, and then opened the door into Jenny's room.

It was a comfortable and cozy room for a little girl and for the first time she would not have to share a room with Todd. Todd's room was across the hall; the mirror image of Jenny's and he readily approved.

"And you're each going to be responsible for cleaning up your own room so Mommy doesn't have to do extra work, okay?" Rufus reminded. "This is a lot of house to take care of, and we don't want her to overwork."

"Okay," both children answered. The thought of having their own room after seven years of sharing dwarfed any problems a clean-up detail might cause.

"Let's go see the toy room now," Jenny said.

Rufus led the way and grandiosely opened his arms as they entered. He flipped on the light switch but it took several tries before it worked. The switch was obviously broken, and he made a mental note to take care of it so they could play in there at night as well.

Jenny's eyes sparkled as she stood in the doorway. The room was like the Children's Museum. There was so much here she didn't know what to touch first. Her eyes went from the puppets on the wall to the doll house to the wooden animals. It was all so overwhelming. "Go ahead," Rufus prompted. Nodding eagerly, she climbed on top of the hobby horse and with a wide grin threw her arms around the saw-toothed mane. The horse squealed as she happily rocked back and forth.

Todd looked sideways at his father. Rufus's face was glowing as he watched Jenny play and Todd felt a twinge of jealousy at this shared moment between his father and sister.

"Hey, Dad. You want to toss the football around?" he asked. "Try out the yard. I know where I packed it. I'll pull it out."

"Oh, not today, Todd, okay?" Rufus said, his eyes still on Jenny as she rode the horse. "I think I'm going to have my hands full setting up my office."

"Just a few minutes. Work up a little sweat."

"I said not today," Rufus repeated.

"Okay. Maybe tomorrow then. That yard looks really great for two-hand touch."

"*Maybe* tomorrow, Todd," Rufus said, a little irritably. "But you have to realize there's a lot to do, and I'm going to be busy."

Todd nodded, wondering why his father was suddenly so grumpy.

Rufus pushed open the door. "You staying up here, Jen?"

Jenny nodded. There was so much for her to get to know.

"I'm going to unpack my clothes," Todd said, and left with his father. "Really neat house, Dad," he added as Rufus started down the stairs.

"Isn't it?" Rufus beamed.

Alone in the toy room, Jenny climbed off the horse and listened to it squeal. She'd have to get her father to oil the runners. She knelt down to more closely inspect the ark animals and miniature furniture in the doll house. She picked up several of the dolls and ran her hands along the fitted costumes of silk, gingham, and cotton. She wound up the music box, listened to the happy carnival song, and watched the horses chase each other as the spring wound down.

Then she climbed back onto the hobby horse for another ride while all the marionettes looked on.

When she got off the horse, she thought she heard someone behind her, Todd coming back into the room, but the door was still closed. The wall was a silent jury of puppets and marionettes, their hands and feet held immobile in awkward, stiff positions by the wires attached to the wooden crossbars. Their sightless eyes trained on her.

She guessed she hadn't heard anything after all. Maybe only the final squeal of the hobby horse as it slowly rocked to a halt.

In his room Todd stood staring out the window, listening to the hollow creak of the horse. In the kitchen Mickie sorted through stacks of boxes, trying to organize the labeled cartons.

And in his office Rufus was unpacking his instruments. His cabinets were all arranged and he felt a warmth come over him that made him smile.

It was good to be in that house, good to be home.

He laid a stethoscope into a drawer.

The Talmans had moved in.

CHAPTER 4

Mickie was drying the last of the everyday dishes as Todd came back into the kitchen. There were still boxes of pots and good china that needed unpacking, but Mickie decided she had done enough for that day. She wanted to save some energy for fixing up her office after dinner. She dried her hands on a paper towel, looked around for a garbage bag, saw none, shrugged, and tossed the wet towel onto the pile of newspapers that littered the floor. The children laughed. Jenny had a soap bubble on her nose, and she cringed as Todd puffed it away with a flick of his middle finger.

"Okay"—Mickie slapped her hands together—"let's gather up all those papers, shove them into the boxes, and get the whole mess out of here. What do you say?"

Todd and Jenny scooped up armfuls of newspapers and began stuffing them into the empty packing crates.

From under a load that covered her face, Jenny asked, "Where's the 'cinerator?"

Mickie laughed. Her daughter had been apartment born and raised. "There is none, hon."

"Compactor?" She tripped over the word, uncertain if she was saying it correctly.

"No. No compactor either. We're going to have to take the trash outside and put it into garbage cans ourselves. But I've assigned that job to your father."

"And you have to be careful and put the lids on

tightly," Todd cautioned. "Otherwise the raccoons can get into the garbage cans and knock them over."

Todd was opening the cellar door when Mickie noticed him. "Todd—no. Don't go down there."

He stopped. "Why?"

"Daddy and I don't want any of us going into the cellar until he has had a chance to clean it out. Very strict orders. We should have told you before. I don't think anybody's been in the cellar in a very long time, and God knows what could be down there."

"Raccoons?" Jenny asked.

"Quite possibly." Or worse, Mickie thought. She wondered if there could be any rats in the cellar. Or bats even. "Now just promise me you'll stay out of the cellar until we sound the all clear."

She had never really been down there herself, just making it to the bottom step when Rufus and the contractor had ventured down. The cellar was man's domain she decided. The contractor had then pronounced the boiler and water pump sound, and Hazel and Penelope had argued about the cost of maintenance, but just hearing it was all in good operating order was enough for Rufus.

"Okay?" Mickie repeated.

Jenny nodded readily. The cellar held no particular attraction for her.

"Todd?"

"Yeah, Ma. I promise."

"Okay. Now who's hungry?"

Both children were.

"I am too. And I'm sure your father is." They hadn't eaten since lunch at Howard Johnson's in Springfield, Massachusetts.

Mickie looked around the kitchen. All they had brought with them were boxes of dry cereal and cans of soup. Nothing to make a dinner out of.

"What'll it be? Fried chicken or hamburger?"

"Chicken!" Jenny yelled.

Good. The Colonel was closer than the Burger King.

"Okay. Chicken it is. I'm going to run out and pick up dinner, and if I find a 7-11, some milk and paper plates." The thought of having to wash dishes tonight just did not appeal to her.

She picked up her purse. "I'll be back in about a half hour. Finish cleaning up while I'm gone, okay?"

The children went back to gathering the newspapers until they made the discovery that a balled up piece of newspaper was a pretty fair approximation of a snowball. They tossed the papers back and forth until deciding they had spent enough time scattering newspapers. Quickly they cleaned up the mess.

Todd's eyes fell on the cellar door: a slab of wood, a brass knob. He was curious. He wanted to go down there and poke around.

"Don't, Todd," Jenny cautioned. "Mommy doesn't want us to."

Todd bit on his lower lip, thinking. He didn't want to disobey his mother. But maybe he could get his father to take him down now. The cellar was ideal for exploration, a world of unknown, no doubt stacked to the rafters with treasure. "I'll be right back, Jen," he said, and scooted down the hall to his father's office.

Rufus was unpacking a scissors from its wrapping. His other instruments were all in place in the new stainless steel cabinet, which shined brightly in the overhead fluorescent lights.

The door to his office slammed open and Todd burst through. "Dad?" he said eagerly. "What about we go downstairs and—"

Rufus's movement was sudden, the sound sharp. He banged his fist down against the counter top, the handle end of the scissors striking the surface with a harsh metallic ring.

"I don't want you ever barging into my office like this again, Todd," he said angrily. "I could have had a patient in here. How would it look to have you coming in to play?"

"But I knew you were alone, Dad," Todd faltered, surprised, trying to make sense out of his father's reaction. Involuntarily, he took a step backward, bumping into Jenny who was behind him.

"I still want you to get into the proper habits. I have an office in this house. This is where I'm going to earn my living, and when I'm working, I need my privacy. Do you both understand?"

They nodded blankly.

"Good," Rufus said. "Now you're going to have to leave me alone, okay? I have things to do. I'll see you later."

Not knowing what they had done wrong, the children silently backed out of the doorway.

Rufus watched them go and immediately regretted scolding them. He could have handled that differently, he thought. But they had to learn that this was his office and not just another room in the house to play in. He got up. He would go after them, apologize. But then he sat back down on the stool. He would finish up what he was doing now and apologize later. He put the scissors in the drawer and closed it.

The children stood outside Rufus's door and looked uncomfortably around the foyer. The staircase loomed in front of them, the living room was off to the other side. Long shadows stretched across it; the sun was setting. The house suddenly seemed large and lonely and cooler. Only moments before there seemed to be so much to do; now nothing. The rooms upstairs were very far away.

Todd felt himself grow angry. His father had no right to yell at them like that. They didn't know the rules about his stupid office. And he knew what he wanted to do. "Come on, Jen," he said.

"Todd, don't," Jenny said when she saw where he was going.

"It's all right," he said, facing the cellar door. "It's nothing."

She shook her head. "No. Mommy said not to."

"Well, I'm going down," Todd said defiantly. He would fix his father, and go where he wasn't supposed to. "Promise you won't tell?"

Jenny shook her head tentatively, negatively, and Todd immediately saw his sister's dilemma. She didn't want to be put in a position to have to lie for him. He would make it easier for her.

"All right. If Mommy asks, you can tell her I went down, okay? But if she doesn't ask, don't say anything."

Jenny thought for a moment and realized that was probably okay.

"Are you going to wait here?" Todd asked.

"Yes."

"If you hear Mommy coming, call me and I'll come back up."

"Okay."

Todd grabbed the knob. It twisted easily in his hand. He pulled the door open wide, harder than he had intended to, and sent it all the way around on its hinges, banging it against the wall behind it with a loud thud— half expecting something to come falling through.

"Don't, Todd," Jenny said, suddenly nervous.

The cellar door stood open like a gaping mouth. Todd saw it too, and it was suddenly sobering. But having come this far already, he wanted to go through with it.

Why didn't his parents want him to go into the cellar? *What if there were things down there that could hurt him?* Nonsense, he dismissed the thought. What could be down there—raccoons? He wasn't afraid of raccoons. Certainly nothing else. No, he resolved firmly. There was nothing down there that could hurt him.

"I'll be right back," he said in a low voice, and only afterward wondered why the need to whisper.

He stepped through the door to the top of the stairs and flipped on the light switch. The naked bulb went on at the foot of the stairs. The wattage was weak and the bulb was layered with dust; the light it offered was dim. Beyond it, the cellar seemed washed in a haphazard mix of gray and black.

Todd walked slowly down the stairs, his hand skimming the rail, picking up the cellar dust. His sneakers made no sound on the wooden boards as he took them carefully one step at a time. He stopped at the bottom, one hand still holding on to the banister. The plasterboard walls were gray from their cover of dust with openings and archways leading into hidden dark rooms.

It was cool and damp and an unpleasant musty smell permeated throughout. Todd felt prickly all over from the dankness, and he shivered involuntarily as goose bumps took a Sunday stroll across his body. He looked around, wary and tensed against anything coming at him from out of the shadows.

Perhaps going down there alone wasn't such a good idea at that, he thought suddenly, as the cellar beckoned to him. But still he kept walking.

Weak light struggled in through clear gaps in the dirt-streaked windows. The sun was setting low in the sky. There were workbenches of rusty, dust-covered tools such as nails, screwdrivers, and vises. Bundles of old books and newspapers were tied together with rope and securely knotted. The papers were yellowed with age, water-stained, and heavily coated with dirt. Packing crates, waiting to be opened and explored, were randomly strewn about the cellar.

He tripped over a pair of lace-up shoes and stopped himself from falling into a pile of furniture—tables and chairs with broken or missing legs, exposed dowels, or seats splintered and worn through—all in a delicately balanced heap. To move one item would send the whole pile crashing noisily to the floor.

He backed cautiously away from the furniture and gasped as he bumped into a headless dressmaker's mannequin sporting a green felt hat with a fake flower stuck in its brim. The mannequin teetered back and forth and Todd, swearing that he could almost see a head under the hat, steadied it.

He moved farther into the cellar, and saw a labyrinth of rooms. He turned quickly around to get his bearings. He knew where he was. He could almost see the staircase around a bend and the patch of yellow light beneath the bulb. He could easily retrace his path if he had to. But he didn't want to yet. More cellar stretched ahead of him. It ran the length of the house, and he estimated he was somewhere under his father's office. He would go until he could go no more and only then come back. He would prove to himself he was not afraid of being down there.

But it was so easy to imagine things crouching behind the mounds of cellar junk, eyeing him through broken table legs, charting his progress, waiting for the right moment to reach out and grab him. As he walked deeper into the cellar, farther away from the light and the stairs, he had no proof that something like that wasn't happening right now. No proof at all.

He passed through a doorway and turned around. The stairway beacon was completely gone and the only light came from the last of the sun's rays, which he sensed was barely above the horizon.

At the far end of the room there was a closed door and something intuitive told Todd that that was where he should go.

It was a wooden door, flush with a wall of brick. A skeleton key dangled out of a coffin-shaped keyhole. He looked at the door with mixed emotions of curiosity and fear. His throat was suddenly dry with a flour-and-water taste in his mouth. *No, nothing down here that could hurt me*, he repeated to himself. His lips thinned as he stared at the door, suddenly wary of this closed door, suddenly frightened without knowing why. His senses were switched to overdrive, ready to discern the slightest smell, sound, movement.

He turned the key and pushed the door open a crack. It was dark behind the door, the thin sliver of darkness broadening as he opened the door even more. He strained to see into the room beyond.

Common sense and creeping fear told him to go no farther, to wait for his father before entering this room. But morbid curiosity made him push open the door a little wider, although not yet wide enough to see in.

Then suddenly he made a conscious decision to do it and get it over with. He inhaled deeply, summoned strength, tensed his arms, and started to push. The voice startled him.

"Todd!" It was Jenny, a mixture of excitement and fear in her voice that echoed loudly in the cellar.

Todd pulled his hand off the doorknob as if he had been caught.

"Mommy's coming. She just drove up."

The door was suspended—not open, not closed—mockingly inviting him to open it more. He tried to think quickly, but Jenny made up his mind and perhaps it was best.

"Hurry, Todd," she called. Her voice was nervous. Why wasn't Todd answering her?

"Coming," he called and darted back through the cellar. He almost caught his shirt on a metallic edge but only felt a slight tug against the cotton. Brushing his jeans free of dust he climbed the stairs two at a time.

He beat his mother by seconds. He tried to control his breathing so it would not seem like he had been running. Mickie came into the kitchen, her arms filled with bags, and dropped them on the table.

"What have you two been up to?" Mickie asked as she opened the buckets of chicken.

"Nothing," Todd answered, perhaps too quickly.

"And you too?" Mickie asked, turning to Jenny. "Also nothing?" She ripped the cellophane wrapping off the paper plates and plastic forks. "Well, okay, Mr. and Miss Nothing. Let's eat this gourmet meal before it gets cold. Go wash up for dinner. I'll call your father."

When Jenny and Todd were upstairs, Jenny whispered to her brother, "What was down there, Todd? What did you see?"

And Todd, now back in the light, answered easily. "It was no big deal, Jen. There was nothing down there. Nothing at all."

But he knew that wasn't so, and he knew he'd be down there again and go into that room.

There was strain during the meal of chicken, potato salad, and diet soda, and Mickie didn't know why. The children ate in silence and never took their eyes from their plates. Rufus, too, was quiet. And that was odd. She expected him above all to be overflowing with energy.

Todd and Jenny went upstairs as soon as supper was over. They wanted to unpack, they said. But Mickie saw that they couldn't wait to leave the table. They didn't look at their father, just darted out of the kitchen. Something had obviously come between them and Rufus.

"What happened?" Mickie asked when they were out of earshot.

Rufus seemed to be expecting the question and answered perhaps too immediately. "Nothing happened." There was a defensive note to his voice.

"Rufus, what upset the children?"

"They came barging into my office," he said, and then stopped, ashamed. He appeared to hide behind his coffee, his eyes in the cup. "I was putting things away. I guess they startled me. I—I raised my voice. I'm sorry," he shrugged.

"Don't apologize to me, Rufe. In fact I'm surprised you haven't apologized to them yet. Letting something like this carry through dinner just isn't like you."

"Mick, please don't tell me what is or isn't like me, okay? It's been a long day. I'll apologize to them. When I tuck them in later." He rubbed his eyes. "But you're right," he said when he met her glance. "I shouldn't have let it go through dinner the way I did."

Mickie stood to the side as Rufus perched on the edge of Todd's bed.

"It was a busy day," he explained. "The long drive up here. The unpacking. I was overtired, I guess. Then when you came into my office like that, I was so wound up, I snapped."

Todd nodded, pretended to look away, pretending to still be hurt. But he melted and smiled and his eyes lit up with relief. He didn't want his father to be angry with him.

"*I* was wrong, Dad," he insisted. "I should have knocked. I shouldn't have barged into your office like that."

"We were both wrong," Rufus said and patted his son's back.

Jenny was in bed reading a Bobbsey Twins book when her parents came in. Rufus sat down on the edge of her bed and reached for his daughter. He pushed the bangs off her forehead, but her hair flopped right back.

He smoothed it down. This was Rufus's moment with his daughter as he reestablished contact.

"Sometimes we say things we don't really mean, honey. Forgive me?"

The little girl's eyes sparkled. "Yes, Daddy."

"Good," Rufus said with a smile. He tapped her knee. "Hey—do you like it around this place? Shall we stay?"

Jenny bobbed her head up and down. This was the first night she was going to sleep in her own room.

"And now bedtime," Mickie said, as she collected the book and put it on a shelf. "Remember, we're right next door if you need anything. Just come and get us."

"But knock first," Rufus whispered to Mickie as he nuzzled her neck. Mickie smiled.

She flipped off the lamp on the night table, plunging the room into darkness, and opened the door into the hallway where the night-light was ablaze. "We'll keep this light on all night so you can find your way to the bathroom if you have to." She closed the door to her daughter's room, hearing it gently latch. Rufus slipped his arm around her waist and led her quickly to their bedroom. At the door he scooped her up in his arms.

"You're not going to carry me over the threshold, are you?" Mickie asked.

"You bet your ass I am," Rufus said. He kicked the door shut behind him and plopped Mickie down on the bed.

"Now that was painless, wasn't it?" she asked him.

"What?"

"Apologizing to the kids."

"Oh, that. I had forgotten about that already. Hey, want a little country air? This is stuff you can breathe with no side effects." He opened the window and let the night breeze pass through the room. The cricket sounds were surprisingly loud.

"Sounds like they're holding a convention right below our window," Mickie said. But at least the crickets were more restful than the all-night drone of traffic on Central Park West. She walked to the window and inhaled deeply, filling her lungs with pure country air. She looked out at the Vermont night, toward the dark lines of trees that fringed their property. Rufus joined her at the window and circled her waist with his arm. She leaned against him and asked, "So how does it feel to be land baron of this glorious estate?"

Rufus laughed. "With what we're paying in interest, I tend to think of this more as my little tax deduction."

"Did you remember to put out the garbage?"

"Done."

"Lock the doors? Windows?"

"Nobody steals in the state of Vermont," he said, "but yes, everything is locked. God, there's a lot to remember when you're a land baron." He puffed out his chest. "But it feels good. Ownership. After a lifetime of renting, it's going to be great not to have to mail the rent check in on the first of the month. Although the mortgage is due on the tenth, and the property taxes. And the fuel bill," he reminded himself, ticking off a mental checklist. "And the water bill. I think I miss renting already," he joked. "But tell me, Mrs. Land Baron, how does it feel to you?"

Mickie turned and faced him. "It's a wonderful house, Rufe. It is. With everything I can possibly want. But it really doesn't change anything for me. I could live anywhere, I think, as long as we're there together."

Rufus hugged her tightly and stroked her hair. "Tired?" he asked softly.

"Mmm-hmmm," she answered a little dreamily.

"*Too* tired?"

"God, yes!" she gasped.

"Okay, you owe me," Rufus said. They were silent for a moment and then he asked, "What are you thinking now?"

Mickie shrugged and smiled. "A silly thought. I'm trying to commit this moment to memory. Hold on to it because it's so special. I wish I could just bottle it and have it if I'm ever feeling down."

Rufus tilted her head up and looked warmly into her eyes. "Why should you ever feel down?"

"People do feel down."

"Not people around here," Rufus said. "I promise."

Jenny heard the crickets too. She was alone in her room in the dark listening to the unfamiliar sounds. She had never before spent a night alone. There had always been somebody else there with her—her parents, Todd, friends. And now the excitement of moments before was replaced suddenly with childhood fears of darkness, of the unknown, of shadowy things that come out of the night to creep and crawl and moan and scare. Her eyes started to slip closed, then they opened wide to the distant, baleful call of a lone hoot owl that chilled her with its eerie cry.

But then she thought about the toy room and all the fun she would have playing in there. She drifted off to sleep, hearing the squeal of the hobby horse as it rocked back and forth, back and forth, blending with the sounds of the owl and the crickets.

CHAPTER 5

The next morning was warm and clear, hovering in the mid sixties. Almost sweater weather as the day hesitated on the brink of autumn, although not quite ready to lose its grasp on the waning New England summer. The early September air was trying to hold on to summer smells, but the faint ripple of breeze brought with it the first touch of fall. A flurry of migrant birds, told by the length of days that winter was coming soon, were starting the annual trek southward.

Mickie was making French toast when Todd and Jenny came down for breakfast. They were dressed in jeans and play clothes, ready for a day of adventure.

"How did you sleep?" Mickie asked.

"Great!" Todd said. "I think they put something in the air up here."

Yes, Mickie thought. *Air.* "Jenny?" she asked.

Jenny shrugged. "Okay." And Mickie understood. "The crickets keep you awake, hon? You'll get used to them in time."

Rufus came bounding into the kitchen. "French toast!" he said excitedly. "My favorite country breakfast."

"Just don't expect it too often," Mickie warned. "It's a treat for today. First morning in the new house and all of that. Tomorrow, though, it's back to corn flakes. Oh, you can still have French toast," she added slyly. "But you're going to have to make it yourself."

"Tyrant," Rufus said with a wink at Jenny and sat down at the table. Mickie dished out the breakfast.

"Hey, Dad," Todd said eagerly. "You want to do something this morning? A little football maybe? Or fishing?"

"That's a good idea," Mickie said. "I've got to get my office in some kind of shape and finish up an editing job I started last week. I hope I can find the stuff in those packing crates," she added. "Then I'll join you later on, okay?"

"Oh, I thought I'd run out and get the car looked at this morning," Rufus said. "It was straining a little on the uphill grades yesterday. It wouldn't look too good for the doctor's car to break down on the way to a house call."

"That's okay, Dad," Todd said. "Can I come?"

Rufus laughed. "And stand around in a garage for half the morning breathing gasoline fumes when you've got all this great country air! I'm sure you can find something better to do than that. Get out, poke around the neighborhood, see if you can make some new friends before school starts. Maybe later when I get back, we'll be able to do something."

"Sure, Dad," Todd said, his father's words sounding too vague to be much of a promise.

"Good," Rufus said. He wolfed down his cup of coffee and zipped up his windbreaker. "See you all later."

"Bye, Daddy," Jenny said, wiping syrup off her chin.

"Yeah. Bye," Todd said.

Thinking he really could have taken Todd with him, Mickie watched Rufus slam the kitchen screen door. But she knew there'd be plenty of time for them to play. Then she got up. "Think you can handle the dishes while I run upstairs?"

"No sweat," Todd said and started to stack the breakfast plates.

* * *

An office all to herself, Mickie thought happily. Another fringe benefit of the move. She was used to doing her work on the kitchen table, which meant having to clear it all up at mealtimes and then start again afterward, a lot of unnecessary shifting of papers, not to mention the proximity to the refrigerator. It was just too easy to reach out and grab something. She pinched an inch of flab and cringed. She had put that on in the last two years. But it could have been worse, she realized, and prided herself on *some* self-control. Rufus, though, had never worked at home, and she'd have to watch him because he tended to put on weight.

She spread the manuscript on the table in front of her. A desk had been ordered weeks ago from a local distributor, and it was expected to arrive soon, so she was temporarily working on a bridge table with one leg a half inch shorter than the other three. From across the hall she heard the squeal of the hobby horse. Jenny was obviously in the toy room; they must have finished the dishes. Then Todd's door closed. She hoped he would get outside, the day was too nice to spend indoors.

The fall day kept drifting through the open window, and she couldn't keep her mind on her work. The manuscript was interesting enough—a self-help book for people whose marriages were threatened because one partner was straying. What were the divorce statistics now? She tried to remember. At least one out of three couples split up, probably more. Many of their friends had broken up, couples whose husbands were doctors, men with God complexes who felt they could rule the world and any women they wanted. That's what had happened to Lois, whose husband left her for a younger woman. It was a cliché, but it happens, Mickie realized. But not to her and Rufus. They were among the lucky ones; their love was strong and only for each other, and now with the strains of recent years behind them she suspected that nothing could ever pull them apart.

She got up from the desk and walked over to the open window. She did feel a little like a land baroness, she thought with a stitch of pride. Their house was so much larger than the surrounding ones, with more land in front and back. And how could she feel anything other than a thrill at the view that opened up in front of her. Glendon was a valley town, and beyond grazing fields, mountains rose regally skyward. Soon winter would descend and the ski trails would be visible as wandering ribbons of white against a sea of evergreens.

She had met Rufus in the ski shop in Stowe, Vermont. His poles had been stolen over lunch, and he was trying to glom a pair from the shop for use that afternoon because he couldn't afford a new pair. No go. She had been struggling with her lace-up boots on a bench off to the side. He offered his help. They spent the day together and the rest of Christmas vacation as well. Both from New York, they were attending school in Boston—she was graduating from Boston University with a degree in English, he was finishing medical school, ready to intern at a Massachusetts hospital the first of July. She had stayed in Boston after graduation. It was a difficult decision, one she would not have made unless her mother had supported her as strongly as she did. Her father had recently died and Mickie knew that Tessie would have preferred her closer to home during the transitional period. But Tessie, seeing real strength in her daughter's relationship—and genuinely liking Rufus—insisted that she remain in Boston.

After marriage they settled in New York.

And still skied in Vermont where it had all begun.

And now they lived there.

Mickie saw a woman walking up the stone pathway toward the front door. The woman caught her eye and waved. She was carrying a cake plate.

"Be right down," Mickie shouted.

She opened the door to an attractive, although slightly overweight, woman of about her own age.

"Hi," the woman said pleasantly. "I know that moving day or the day after is a dreadful time to barge in, but I live just next door, and saw you arrive yesterday. So ready or not, here I am." She held out her hand. "Nina Wallace."

"Mickie Talman," Mickie said and smiled. "But I suspect you already know that."

"No secrets in Glendon. Besides, it's been on your mailbox since July." She offered Mickie the cake. "For you. Angel food. Sweet enough but higher in cholesterol than calories."

"As if you were reading my mind," Mickie said. "Come in." She led the way into the kitchen. "I think I remember where I put the coffee. I've never had this much shelf space before."

"Oh, you'll need all of it. Possessions tend to expand to fill the space allotted to them."

"You sound like an expert."

"I do a little interior decorating." She quickly held up her hand. "But I'm not here soliciting business. Purely a social call." She took in the kitchen. "You've done a fantastic job in here."

"Thank you."

"You know I haven't been inside this house in *years*. Not since the old ladies bought it. They were crazy, you know . . ." She circled her temple with her index finger. "Certifiably."

"I suspected," Mickie said. "But they seemed harmless enough."

"Oh, they were. But the fighting that went on between them. It was comical. In public as well where you'd expect them to exercise a little restraint. But not the Benson girls. If one said black, the other automatically and invariably said white. They must have thrived on their arguing. But you know all of this."

"I've seen them in action," Mickie said.

"I've lived in my house for fifteen years, but was born only a couple of blocks from here, so I've known them for almost forever, it seems. This was the house we used to throw eggs at on Halloween." She winked at Mickie confidentially. "The kids still do."

"Oh, no," Mickie said. "I guess we should put up a sign—Under New Management. I don't want to get splattered this year."

"Just treat the kids well during trick or treat and you won't have any trouble. But with two of your own that goes without saying."

"Do you have children?" Mickie asked.

"Yes. A little girl about your daughter's age. Cara. She's down with a sore throat, so I don't want to bring her around until she's better."

"Oh, I'm sure Jenny will love to meet her. And Cara's going to flip over what we have upstairs."

"The room with the toys?"

"Yes," Mickie said, surprised. "How did you know?"

"I've played up there myself," Nina said. "I used to have a friend who lived in this house. Oh, I'm going back years and years before the old ladies lived here." She smiled, but then her face seemed to fall as she looked into herself. "We were both seven when Essie died."

"No—" Mickie said.

"I went over to play with her one morning. Her mother came out. She was very very upset and said that Essie couldn't play anymore, that Essie had died. Then we watched the people come and take her away. And the family moved out very soon afterward."

"How sad."

"But if you want to look for good in something, I guess you can find it. It wasn't a happy house. The parents were always fighting with each other. I remember my own parents talking about it. Maybe Essie found peace in death."

"How did she die?" Mickie asked tentatively. "I shouldn't even be asking but—she wasn't sick, was she? From what you said it seemed so sudden."

"No, I never remember Essie being sick. It *was* sudden. I don't know of what. I don't know if anybody ever did, and I was really too young to ask questions. It was just a very sobering experience for me, that's all. But that was all a long time ago and, except for people like me who knew her, forgotten."

"Were there other children?"

"A boy, but I don't remember his name anymore."

"Tragic," Mickie said. "To lose a child." But she brushed the thought aside and smiled warmly at Nina. "And after that the old ladies moved in?"

"Not right away. There were other people before them, but they didn't stay very long. Then came the Benson girls, and they've been here for God knows how long. If anybody was going to die in a house, I would have sworn it would have been them." Nina smiled. "And now they're gone, but I can't say I miss them. It'll be so much more fun having you next door."

"Thank you," Mickie said. "That's very nice of you to say. And now teach me everything I have to know about survival in Glendon. All the local gossip."

"Do you have a week?" Nina asked. "You come from the city. You don't know about small towns. We tend to absolutely thrive on gossip. I've got as much as you can absorb."

"Shall I take notes?" Mickie asked, and they both laughed, the somber mood of a moment before behind them.

* * *

Todd had been in his room for half the morning and was bored. At first he had been excited at the thrill of having his own room after seven years of sharing with his sister, but there was just so much he could do there all alone. He didn't want to take out any of his books; with school starting in less than a week, he could imagine all the reading they'd be piling on him then. He missed his friends and was feeling a little lonely. But his father was right—he had to get out and meet some new guys or else he'd die a hermit or something.

Through the window he saw the boy next door. He seemed older than Todd, but still he was male and flesh and blood. Worth checking out, Todd thought. He slid down the banister and picked up his new bicycle in the garage.

He aimed it down the driveway and made a right onto Route 17, staying in the graveled shoulder of the road. He turned into the dirt driveway of the house next door. There was a car parked there, and when Todd was abreast of it, the front tire of the bike got caught in a driveway rut. The bike went out from under him and crashed into the parked car, the pedal angrily scratching the paint with a metal-on-metal screech. The bike fell over to the side and toppled Todd to the soft, just watered grass.

The boy shot out of the car where he had been sitting. He was taller than Todd, with wavy black hair, a spotty mustache, and a mean look across his face. He inspected the scratch; it was about two feet long.

"Look what you did, asshole!" the boy screamed.

"I'm sorry," Todd mumbled as he raised himself to his feet. His jeans were wet from the lawn and clumps of grass clung to him.

"It's a new car," the boy sputtered. "My father just got it yesterday. We didn't even drive it yet."

Todd studied the boy. His back was tense, his fists

clenched. He was angry, no mistaking that. Unconsciously, he moved away from the older boy who blocked his path.

"What are you going to do about it, dipshit?"

"We'll get it fixed," Todd said. "My father will pay for it. It was my fault."

"Who are you, anyway? I never saw you around here."

"Todd Talman. We just moved into the house next—"

"Oh, yeah. The doctor everyone's been talking about? Must think you're hot shit, don't you, being a doctor's kid?"

Todd hadn't really ever considered himself hot shit before.

"Well, I'm going to knock the crap out of you, hot shit."

Todd sized up the boy as he started to circle him, feigning punches. With a stubby index finger he pointed to his chin as if daring Todd to bop him on it. Todd wished he could but doubted his arms were that long or could get through the web of the boy's arms. The boy must have had three years and thirty pounds on him. He didn't think he could take him in a fight.

"Hey, I didn't mean to scratch your car. Really."

The boy lunged at him suddenly with an open palm catching his face. It stung. He pulled his arm back and with a wide grin went back to circling and toying with Todd.

"We'll get it fixed. I swear it."

The boy advanced again. Todd saw him coming and side-stepped out of the way. This infuriated the boy all the more. He charged, arms swinging, fists balled and ready. Todd protected his face and took the next punch in his stomach. And then a direct hit to his right shoulder, which registered all the way down to the bone. A clean jab to the stomach, and he doubled over with nausea. He couldn't straighten up, couldn't catch his breath. In an instant the boy had Todd on the ground. He hunched himself fetally, instinctively protecting his mid-section, trying to swing back wildly at the bigger boy. He kept on rolling side to side so as not to let the boy get on top of him, because that would be death. He landed very few of his punches, while the other boy scored again and again, rubbing Todd's face in the dirt, breaking skin, drawing blood.

It was then that Rufus came driving home. He saw his son go down under the other boy. He swung the car into the neighbor's driveway and was out in one motion. He pulled the boy off Todd, held him by the arm, and shook him.

"What's going on here?" Rufus boomed.

The boy was heaving, trying to break away from Rufus who tightened his grasp on him.

"I said what's going on?" He shook the boy with each word.

The boy pointed toward the car. "He did that."

"My bike skidded, Dad," Todd said, trying to swallow his tears. "It was an accident."

"A new car. My father just got it yesterday."

Rufus immediately understood the situation. He loosened his hold on the boy's collar.

"Something like that happens you get the car fixed. You don't go around beating up children smaller than you. I could either tell your father or call the police about what you were doing," Rufus threatened. "But because we're going to be living next door to each other, I don't think I'm going to do either. That's my son, Todd, over there, and I want you two to be friends. What's your name?"

The boy hesitated, but then seemed to decide it didn't cost him anything to say it. There was a sneer across his face. "Rick Webb."

"Well, Rick Webb, why don't you shake hands with Todd Talman?"

Todd held his hand out first. Rick was slow to take it, but finally did. Rufus let Rick go.

"You tell your father I'm going to call him later and settle the damage. Name's Dr. Talman. Let's go, Todd."

Todd lifted the bicycle from the grass and with his father still watching him, rode off the Webb property and onto the road. Rufus followed in the car.

When they were back home and Rufus had pulled the car into the garage, he asked Todd to tell him again what had happened.

"Just like I said, Dad," Todd explained excitedly, rubbing his face and smearing the dirt. "It was an accident. And boy—if you hadn't come along, I would have been beaten up for sure. They should put that guy in a cage somewhere and throw away—"

"The problem as I see it, Todd," Rufus said, "is that these things are not accidents."

"It was. There was a rut there and the bike fell. I didn't do it on purpose."

"No, I'm not saying you did it on purpose. What I am saying is that perhaps you didn't do all you could to prevent it from happening."

"Huh?"

"If you're careful, Todd, accidents don't happen."

Todd was confused by his father's tone, not knowing why he seemed so annoyed at him. "Yeah, Dad," he said uncertainly.

"If you were careful, you would have seen the rut. You have to anticipate things. Be observant. The times you were mugged you weren't careful. You called attention to yourself, announced to the world that you had a new ten-speed bicycle. And even after they took that you went back to the same place again. You might as well have worn a sign saying Mug Me. We create things for ourselves, Todd. We attract trouble. I want you to remember that. Do you understand?"

"Sure, Dad. I promise," Todd said, not understanding at all.

"Now go upstairs and get cleaned off, okay?"

"Yeah, Dad. Okay." And Todd couldn't wait to get away from his father. Maybe it would have been better if his father *hadn't* shown up when he did.

Mickie and Nina were walking downstairs as Todd and Rufus were coming in. Todd's head was down to hide his dirty, tear-stained face.

"Hey, what happened?" Mickie asked, motherly radar drawing her to her son's face. She cupped his chin and wiped away some of the dirt with a tissue. There was some dried blood on Todd's upper lip, and he struggled not to look his mother in the eye.

"Just a little disagreement with the boy next door," Rufus said. "But nothing to make a federal case out of." Mickie backed off. She understood Todd's embarrassment. Todd darted around the landing and up to the bathroom to wash up and cool down.

"Rick Webb is a bit of a troublemaker," Nina said. "It's too bad Todd started off with him on the wrong foot. By the way," she said, holding out her hand to Rufus. "I'm Nina Wallace. I've just finished taking the grand tour of your glorious mansion here. I live in the cottage next door. Cottage is such a good euphemism for small house, isn't it? Hey, you two have got to come to dinner. When are you free?"

"Almost anytime," Mickie said. "We don't really know anybody yet."

"We've got the reception tomorrow night at the school," Rufus reminded. He smiled sheepishly. "The welcome Dr. Talman fete."

"Don't scoff," Nina said. "I helped organize it. My PTA duty for the year. So let's keep the date open. I'll see you at the school and then we can set something up for later on. And now I think I've imposed long enough."

"Not at all," Mickie protested.

"You have work to do, I know, and"—she pointed up the stairs—"a wounded child up there. See you tomorrow night, okay?"

"Hey, nice meeting you," Mickie called after her. Then she turned to Rufus. "Was Todd hurt at all?"

"No. Just shook up, I guess. And a little overpowered."

"And to think we moved up here to escape all of that."

Rufus shook his head. "No. It wasn't a mugging situation. It was one on one, although somewhat uneven. He wasn't after Todd's money. Todd scratched his father's new car and the boy overreacted. Todd should have been more careful, that's all."

"Well, I hope that's the end of it," Mickie said. "What we don't need is for one kid to turn the others against Todd."

"From what Nina said I don't think we have to worry. Seems like the others might be happy to band together with Todd against Webb."

"I just don't want anything to mar this new life of ours, Rufe. Am I being selfish?"

"No, of course not," he answered with a smile. "Just a mother."

"Just a mother," Mickie repeated and rolled her eyes. "Who's got to finish editing sixty pages *and* put on the roast. Will you go upstairs and see to Todd?"

"Leave him, Mick. He'll be okay. I'm sure he doesn't want to see either of us right now. Let him grow on his own."

"You're probably right, Rufe," she said, and then smiled.

"Kids are my business," Rufus said and kissed her lightly. "Now just leave Mr. Todd Talman to me, I'll make a man out of him yet."

"Not too fast, Rufe, okay?" Mickie said.

* * *

Upstairs Todd held tightly to the sides of the sink as he dunked his head under the cold water and let it rush over him. He shivered involuntarily as the water poured down his neck, and then raised his head and shook it from side to side like a dog trying to dry off. His hair was plastered to his forehead and the water trickled down his face and back and spotted the mirror in front of him. His stomach was still tender, his chest sore from the pummeling he had taken. Rick Webb was nothing but a bully, no better than the boys who had mugged him.

He hated Rick Webb, and decided he wanted to kill him. But not an easy death. He would have to suffer. Todd mentally conjured up the things he would do to the boy, the pain he would cause him. He envisioned Rick advancing toward him, his fist clenched, his expression mean, out for blood. But instinctively Todd knew what to do. If he concentrated on stopping Rick Webb, he wouldn't be hurt. So he concentrated, and suddenly the bigger boy's tough expression was replaced by one of surprise. Then his face twisted as pain shot through him. His hands flew to the sides of his head as Todd concentrated and brought him pain. And in that one moment Todd sensed he could make Rick Webb experience anything, any kind of pain, as long as he concentrated. Because Todd had the power to do it!

The horn of a truck startled him. He exhaled, unknotted his forehead, breathed in deeply, and freed the sudden stiffness in his fingers where they had tightened and curled around the edge of the sink.

It was only a daydream, he knew, just his imagination. But it was pleasing.

The calliope music played hoarsely and gaily. Jenny watched with fascination as the speckled horses bobbed up and down, and the platform revolved clockwise un-

der a counterclockwise moving canopy, a flow of color.
She had fitted some of the smaller dolls onto the saddles and was sending them for a ride, wrapping their
hands around the leather reins. There was so much to
look at. She marveled at the detail on the horses—
sculpted and gilded saddles and stirrups, teeth champ-
ing at painted bits, lips parted happily so she could almost hear the horses whinny. Their wooden manes and
tails were curled smartly, their front hooves were raised
and bent at the knee; the carousel horses were galloping.

She lifted the clown marionette off its wall hook and
manipulated the cross bars to make it dance. Its cheeks
and nose were brightly painted red with a border of
white surrounding rose red lips and bushy eyebrows
above shoe button eyes. Swirls of reddish brown yarn
served as hair. Its teeth were jagged, with uneven
spaces between them. Perhaps from far away on a stage
the clown's face might be seen as happy, Jenny thought
as she put the toy back in its place, but up close its eyes
were pained, its grin a taunting scowl. There seemed to
be nothing funny about this clown; it was almost a little
scary. The witch too, hanging limply on the wall in her
gown of black silk and a cone-shaped hat of velvet,
looked odd. Her face was pale, sickly, accenting the
hellish blackness of her piercing eyes, sunken deep into
her face like dark pools.

Suddenly she felt a prickliness against her skin, as if
fingers had lightly, almost imperceptibly drummed
against her.

Jenny giggled. It must be Todd, sneaking up on her,
trying to scare her.

She waved her arms in the air. She would scare him
instead. "Boo!"

But Todd wasn't there. No one was.

She tried to figure out what she had felt. The windows were open. A breeze must have brushed across

her, tickling her neck. The carousel had ground to a stop, and she was suddenly aware of how quiet the room was. She was at the far end of the hallway, away from the other bedrooms, away from everyone else.

The carousel started again. It was moving by itself; she hadn't wound it. She watched as the platform crept slowly around its axis once. The music rumbled. It was low pitched, the notes long and drawn out, like a record playing at the wrong speed. It almost sounded like moaning.

The spring had not completely wound down, that was it. And now it had and that was why the music box was silent again, the horses locked in time, motionless.

It was late in the evening and the children were sleeping. Neither Mickie nor Rufus was tired enough to go to bed, and Rufus suggested they not spend the night in front of the television. They pulled two beach chairs out of the garage and set them up on the porch where they sat in their ski parkas in the cool air and toasted each other with an *amaretto* on the rocks.

"Day two." Mickie smiled as they clinked glasses.

The beach chair shifted under Rufus. He caught his balance. "I don't think these chairs really constitute acceptable Vermont veranda furniture," he said, as he tapped out a tune on the aluminum.

"I think the only acceptable furniture up here is at least a hundred years old," Mickie answered. "But I wouldn't mind getting a couple of those big wooden chairs with the tombstone-shaped backs. Make us look like real country old-timers."

"And maybe I could take up whittling," Rufus joked.

They sat in silence for a moment looking at the star-laden sky, identifying constellations of the northern hemisphere.

"Nina seems very nice," Rufus said. "Do you like her?"

"She'll make a good friend," Mickie agreed. "You know, she used to be friendly with a child who lived in this house. The child died when she was seven. Sad, isn't it?"

"Of course. But I would expect the mortality rate among children years ago to be high. The winters up here can be very cruel."

"No, apparently this was nothing like that. The child's death was sudden. An accident perhaps."

"Well, I wouldn't be surprised if lots of people have died in this house."

"Why do you say that?"

"It's a very old house. It's bound to have its ghosts."

"I guess." They fell silent, each locked in thought. Then suddenly Mickie said, "Did you think Todd was unusually quiet at dinner tonight?"

Rufus shook his head. "No. Not any more or less quiet than he normally is."

"I hope he's all right. I thought he seemed a little nervous."

"You mean because of what happened today? Don't worry. He's already survived two muggings; Rick Webb's not going to bother him. He's a street kid. A trouper. With a little meat on his bones he'll be able to knock the hell out of any kid."

"That's not my aspirations for him, Rufe." Mickie smiled. "To have him knock hell out of any kid. I just wouldn't want him to sour on this house before we even got started. He shouldn't start out here with a bad taste; it wouldn't be right." She dismissed the thought. "Maybe I worry too much."

"Well, if you're going to worry," Rufus said, "why don't you worry about something really important?"

"Like what?"

"Like me making a complete jackass of myself at that dinner tomorrow night. You know I'm terrified of talking in public. What are we going to do if I fall flat on my face out there?"

"If you do fall flat on your face, Rufe," Mickie promised, "I'll be right there to catch you."

CHAPTER 6

The reception in Rufus's honor was sponsored by the Glendon Chamber of Commerce, organized by the PTA, and held in the school cafeteria. It was attended by over a hundred people. Command appearances to welcome Dr. Rufus Talman to the town. The guests included everyone who had anything to do with children or the county payroll.

The organizer of the evening and hostess was Mrs. Maguire, the head of the school board. She was dressed completely in purple with shoes dyed perfectly to match. She was stationed next to Mickie and introduced her to the people when they came up to take a closer look at the new doctor's wife. Dr. Green, the local general practitioner, shepherded Rufus around the room. He had a full head of white hair with aged, chiseled features and had spent his life growing up and practicing in Glendon. He had been overworked since the last pediatrician died and was more than grateful that Rufus was going to be relieving some of his practice.

"Just the opposite in New York," Rufus said, "where any new doctor on the block is competition."

In between meeting the guests he and Dr. Green talked about the general state of health in the town. "These people are tough and usually hearty," Green told him. "But if they really need you, they expect you to be there. Because they'd be there for you. That's the way it works here."

It was after Mickie had shaken hands with at least fifty people, she estimated, that she felt the tap on her shoulder. She turned around. "Oh, thank God, a familiar face." she exclaimed.

Nina smiled. "I tried to get here earlier, but Bob got stuck in the store. How are you holding up?"

"I'm doing okay," Mickie said. "But I think the kids peaked a half hour ago." She waved at Todd and Jenny who were seated in the corner at a cocktail table piled with food. For the first half hour she had kept them next to her, but in the roomful of grownups she had seen the fear on Jenny's face and felt her edge closer and closer to her until she was practically clinging to her leg. It had been wrong to bring them. But they had been specifically invited, and Mickie didn't yet know a babysitter in Glendon, and was hesitant to leave them alone until they got to know the house better.

"It's a little overwhelming for them," she told Nina. "But they're little troupers." Then she added, "I think it's a little overwhelming for me too. I have never been the center of anything before. But the people seem so nice. How's Cara?"

"Coming along. Almost a hundred percent. But I'm still keeping her indoors. My mother's watching her tonight."

Mrs. Maguire was gently tugging Mickie's arm to bring her to another group.

"See you later," Nina said. "Or tomorrow. Hang in there, kid."

Todd and Jenny were the only children present and were feeling very conspicuous and out of place. There was something unsettling about being in a school at night. Todd suspected that the people were just trying to be friendly, but still he was tired of answering the same childish questions over and over again.

The little hotdogs and egg rolls were turning out to be the only saving grace of the entire evening. But soon

Todd and Jenny were full and tired of eating and took
to giving the people names based on obvious physical
characteristics. The woman with the bump on her nose
became the witch, and for a few minutes they charted
her progress through the room. The man with the excep-
tionally wide grin they called shit eater, and the fat man
became pork face. Todd wished that his friends from
back home were with him now because he'd have a better
time making up names with a bunch of guys than with
his sister.

"*Oink, oink,*" he said under his breath as pork face
passed by and Jenny laughed.

After the introductions were over, Mrs. Maguire left
Mickie and drifted into the crowd to create her own
little power circle so as not to be eclipsed by the Talmans, and Mickie found Rufus. Tired of standing, she
shifted from foot to foot and took a second to lean on
his shoulder.

"A political barracuda, isn't she?" Rufus whispered
to Mickie when Mrs. Maguire was out of earshot. And
then he added, "God, I wish this evening was over."

"You sound like Todd now." Mickie smiled. "But
admit you're loving every second of it. Absolutely rev-
eling in the attention."

"Maybe," Rufus agreed with a grin he couldn't hide.
"But why does my stomach feel so lousy? Is the food
greasy?"

"It's your speech that has you terrified. Relax. You'll
do okay."

"Thanks. I wish I weren't so worried about it. Want
to duck out the back?"

Through teeth locked in a smile Mickie answered,
"No way. With the mortgage we've got, you're going to
give that speech and love it. Hey, we'd better go rescue the
kids."

"Yeah, one sec," Rufus said as Dr. Green motioned
for him to join him across the room.

When Mickie came over to the table with another plate of egg rolls, Todd made a sour face.

"Full, huh?" Mickie asked.

"I'll say," Todd answered and held his stomach. "I'm beginning to feel like pork face," he whispered to Jenny.

"How much longer?" Jenny asked, a bit of a whine to her voice.

"Not too much. The evening's half over. Just dinner and then we can get out of here."

"Dinner too?" Jenny made a face.

"And Daddy's speech," Mickie reminded. "Don't you want to listen to Daddy?"

Jenny nodded uncertainly.

"Are we going to have to sit at the head table?" Todd asked.

"I'm afraid so, dear. After all, we are the guests of honor here."

Rufus was bringing over a man to meet them: a portly man wearing a gray suit with a watch chain hanging from his vest pocket. He was followed by his own mini-entourage, including Mrs. Maguire. Mickie hadn't met him yet but sensed his importance and flashed a broad smile.

"This is Mr. DeWitt," Rufus said. "He's with the State Education Council. He came all the way from Burlington tonight for the dinner."

"Pleased to meet you," Mickie said graciously. She extended her hand which the man took.

Rufus beckoned for Todd and Jenny to stand up and greet the man. Todd didn't know where Burlington was and didn't really care.

"My daughter, Jenny."

"Hello." Jenny's voice was small and she was embarrassed in front of all these people.

"And my son, Todd."

"Hello, there, Todd," Mr. DeWitt said.

It suddenly occurred to Todd that he had had enough of this evening—the phony attention, all these people, and he had missed *Dallas* on TV. And now here was this new guy, the heavy one with the perpetual five o'clock shadow and sweaty right palm, whose breath was strong from too much liquor and cigars. Todd took an instant dislike to him.

"So are you enjoying yourself tonight, Todd?" the man asked.

"No. If you want to know the truth, I'm having a lousy time and I wish I was home watching *Dallas*."

Todd heard the words as he was saying them, and he was unable to stop them.

There were noises of surprise from Mrs. Maguire who had personally invited Mr. DeWitt. At first Jenny smiled but then realized that nobody else was laughing and quickly swallowed her grin.

Todd didn't know what he was doing. It wasn't *him* saying those words; it was someone else. He wanted to crawl into a hole and die.

Mickie recovered first. She knelt down next to Todd, put her hand around his waist, and asked loudly enough for those around them to hear, "I'm sure he's only joking, aren't you, Todd?"

The urge to answer truthfully was suddenly strong. No, he wasn't joking. In a strange, hollow voice that didn't sound like his, he answered, "Yes. I was only joking."

Mickie smiled and Mr. DeWitt, obviously uncomfortable, turned to talk to a woman on his left. The crowd slowly broke apart, leaving the four of them in a tight circle.

Todd saw that his father was furious, justifiably so, he knew. He spoke in a harsh whisper as he pointed his index finger into Todd's chest.

"Look, buster. Don't be a smart ass anymore, all right? This evening means a lot to me, and I don't want you lousing it up. I don't care if you're having a bad time, but you keep it to yourself. Do you understand?"

Mickie moved in, aware that several people were watching them. She brushed Rufus's finger away from Todd.

"Okay. It's enough. We were wrong to drag them here tonight."

"Wrong or not, it doesn't matter. They're here and they can be polite and dignified."

"I'm sorry, Dad," Todd said in a small voice.

"You just watch yourself, you hear me? Sit down and don't say anything to anybody for the rest of the evening. Understand?"

From across the room Mickie saw Mrs. Maguire signaling that dinner was about to begin, and relieved, she ushered the children toward their table. Rufus made his way over to Mr. DeWitt to apologize for his son.

Mickie put Todd and Jenny in their seats and knelt down between them.

"Just eat quietly and we'll soon get out of here, okay? I don't like it any more than either of you, but it's for Daddy's job, and we have to make the best of it."

"Okay," Todd said glumly.

Rufus came back and sat down next to Mickie.

"It's all squared away with DeWitt," he said.

"That's good," Mickie said. She pointed to Todd, who sat silently, with a long, unhappy face. "But I'd rather you squared it away with your son. You reacted a little sharply back there, wouldn't you think?"

"No, I wouldn't think," Rufus answered under his breath, smiling over her head and waving at someone else. "And I don't really want to talk about it anymore now, okay?"

"Okay, Rufe," she said pointedly. "But just calm down, okay? He didn't mean to say it." She rubbed her hand gently on Rufus's leg. "Feeling better about your speech?"

Rufus crossed his fingers tightly. "No, but here's hoping."

"Don't forget, hon. You're the expert here. They're here to listen to you. It doesn't really matter what you say."

"Thanks, but I still want to be somewhat coherent." He grabbed his stomach. "Butterflies. A whole tribe of them."

Under the table Mickie grabbed her husband's hand, encircling her fingers in his, lending support.

During the after dinner speeches Todd had to go to the boy's room. He pushed open the swinging doors and was out in the hallway. The air was cool and fresh. No cigarette smoke. No perfume. And it was suddenly quiet, the principal's voice not carrying through the closed cafeteria doors.

Still upset at Rufus, Todd made a decision. He had no friends in this town, his father was too busy to play with him and always on his case, it seemed, so it was obvious he was going to have to make it on his own. Look for his own fun, his own excitement and adventure. And he knew just where he was going to start: spooky or not, allowed or not, he thought with defiance, he was going down into the forbidden cellar.

Jenny fell asleep in the car on the way home and was curled up on Mickie's lap. Todd was stretched out in the back seat. Mickie didn't know if he was asleep or only pretending, to avoid Rufus. She was a little annoyed at her husband. After the incident, he had not spoken two words to his son, even though Todd had tried to break the ice. She quickly glanced behind her and saw him looking very small and vulnerable, his cheek flush against the seat, bouncing with the car. His eyes were closed. She would talk to Rufus because she knew her son was hurting.

But Rufus was high, talking nonstop about the evening, the people, his speech, his plans for the town, how he knew for certain they had made the right move by coming here.

Mickie stared out the window, her hand idly stroking her daughter's face. The Vermont blackness was strangling. Evergreens lined the road, arching over it in shadowy canopies. Only an occasional house was lit. Except for the people at the school, the town of Glendon was asleep.

With Rufus still talking, unaware that Mickie wasn't listening, they pulled into their driveway. Todd rubbed his eyes and shivered as the night air closed in on him. Rufus hoisted Jenny from Mickie's lap and carried her into the house.

Todd hurried up the stairs. Midway up he stopped and turned around.

"Night, Mom. Night, Dad."

"Good night, honey," Mickie said and then looked at her husband.

"Good night, Todd," Rufus said softly and then added, "it's okay, isn't it?"

Todd smiled and Mickie could see the weight that had been lifted from him.

"Sure, Dad," he said.

Thank you, Rufus, Mickie said silently as she watched Todd round the landing and disappear from sight.

Rufus carried Jenny into her bedroom. Mickie gently woke her and managed to pull off her clothes and slip on her pajamas. She handed Jenny Snoopy and tucked her in. They tiptoed out of the room. Jenny was back to sleep before the door closed behind them.

Mickie got undressed and flopped down on the edge of the bed. Rufus was still excited about the evening and there seemed to be no containing him. "I actually spoke to a hundred people. Without quaking. Without one slip up. I've never done that before." He took off his shirt and pants. "I was terrific tonight!" he decided and dove onto the bed next to Mickie, encircling her with his arms, rolling over with her, kissing her. "Maybe I should go on the lecture circuit. What do you think?"

"It was one speech," Mickie reminded. "You're not Lowell Thomas yet. One career at a time, okay?" She jabbed him playfully. "You've got responsibilities to this town now. Especially after what you promised them tonight."

"And I intend to keep all of them."

"Do my back, Rufe?"

"Sure. Roll over." He pushed himself up and straddled Mickie as she slipped off her bra and rolled onto her stomach under him. She tossed her pillow out of the way and laid her head down on folded arms. Rufus's fingers played at her neck, expertly searching out the muscles, catching them between thumb and middle finger, easing them back and forth, snapping them, slowly, gently, sensing their loosening and kneading them rhythmically between his fingers. Mickie sighed deeply, her eyes closed, a smile across her face, as she luxuriated in the massage.

"You're so tense," Rufus said softly, as he worked in deeper and deeper. He could sense her pleasure. He leaned back and rocked with the massage motion, working his fingers faster, pressing harder, feeling the muscles move under his touch, until Mickie gasped and he stopped. "Feeling better?" he asked.

"Oh, yes," she answered dreamily.

Rufus settled himself comfortably next to her. His arms drew her close. She buried her face in his neck, her body snuggled tightly to his. Her tongue slithered against him. His breath quickened. His body came alive. She felt herself responding. She swung her left leg over his and tried to draw herself even closer to him.

"Make love to me, Rufe," she said, and helped him on top of her.

He smoothed her hair down afterward. It was warm under the blanket and the closeness was comforting. They were lying together on his pillow, his arm supporting her neck, his breath passing lightly over her. She breathed softly. She felt safe.

"Tired?" he asked.

"Relaxed." She squirmed in closer to him. "This is so nice."

"Isn't it?" he whispered.

She lay quietly next to him, images of the reception passing through her mind. Suddenly bothered by the uneasy tension of the evening between Rufus and Todd, she rose and rested on her elbows.

"What is it?" Rufus asked.

"Don't you think you were a little harsh on Todd tonight?"

Rufus rolled back onto his pillow, his hands clasped under his head. "Oh, that. It's all squared away, Mick."

"I know, Rufe. But the way you treated him at the dinner. That wasn't you."

"Don't you think I have a right to be upset with him? Look what he did."

"What did he do, Rufe? Really?"

"He embarrassed me."

"He did no such thing. If anything he embarrassed himself. You saw him after it happened."

"What kind of a son will those people think I raised?" Rufus asked.

Mickie spoke softly. "Todd's a good boy. But this move is putting him—all of us—through a lot of fast changes. We have to be a bit more patient. Besides, does it really matter to us what Mrs. Maguire or that Mr. DeWitt think? You can stop playing politics, Rufe. You *are* politics around here. Your job and our life here is very secure. It's what *we* want that's important. Those people have to cater to you—not the other way around."

"He's got to learn," Rufus said, but now his anger of the evening appeared excessive, and he regretted what he had done. "But you're right, Mick," he added softly. "I don't want him to be terrified of making a mistake." He laughed shortly. "I guess I'm not always right when it comes to kids."

"You're right enough," Mickie said. "Okay?" She let her eyes drift shut. "Night, hon."

"Good night," Rufus said and felt the gentle pressure of her next to him. Within moments she was asleep.

The house was silent around him as Rufus lay awake thinking. He had been too short with Todd over the last several days. He'd have to watch himself. They had a good father-son relationship, and he didn't want anything to louse it up.

And then he was asleep as well.

. The hoarse, tinny music woke Jenny. The room was dark; she didn't know what time it was. All she knew was that the carousel music was playing, and until it stopped she wouldn't be able to fall back asleep. The repetitious tune was distracting, hypnotic.

A minute passed. Two minutes. The song ran through her head. The carousel was not winding down.

She could almost see the doll riders strapped in the saddles, the horses running in their endless circles.

She waited. The music persisted.

She would go into the toy room and stop the carousel. She would wind down the key herself.

The night-light snuck in under the door guiding her to it. She stepped out into the hallway and shielded her eyes against the sudden flood of light. But the corridor was long and the far end near the toy room was gray and dimly lit. Jenny swallowed. That was where she had to go. She slowly walked toward the shadows, her left hand brushing the wall. The hallway was cold and she shivered in her cotton pajamas.

The music continued to play and Jenny walked toward it.

Drawn to the music.

Drawn to the toy room.

She neared the staircase that led to the first floor. It was a dark hole, a pit full of monsters and devils ready to reach out and snare her. She quickened her pace.

She thought about getting her parents to come and investigate, but dismissed the idea. She was a big girl with her own room! She could take care of herself. So after only a second of hesitation she reached out and touched the cold doorknob. It twisted easily to her push and the room opened to her. She stepped inside, letting the door slip shut behind her. She heard the sharp click of the latch.

The room was washed in yellow moonlight, the toys silhouetted and steeped in shadow. Something undefined made her skin start to crawl. She felt uneasy, as though she were intruding where she shouldn't. Her eyes darted rapidly about her, searching out the dark corners of the room. Her breath quickened.

The eyes of a ghoulish marionette reflected the moonlight and shone brightly, weirdly, its ebony body lost in a shadowy gray. The dolls were watching her, she thought. They had been waiting for her. And now she was there.

She fumbled for the light switch next to the door, but it didn't work. The only light was the eerie glow of the moon. But then a cloud drifted in front of it, lengthening the shadows that suddenly seemed to have life of their own, patches of darkness crisscrossing the walls. Her hands were moist. She heard the rapid pounding of her heart and felt the quiver of her stomach.

And then she noticed that the carousel wasn't moving, and the room was silent. She didn't know when the music had stopped.

Something was very wrong in here.

The warning came intuitively from deep within her.

She brushed against the hobby horse and its sudden rhythmic squeal made her jump. A breeze whipped through the room chilling her in her thin pajamas, fluttering the gowns of the puppets and giving them life.

She had to get out of here!

But her feet were frozen to the ground. She couldn't respond. She couldn't move. Fear had locked her in place.

Now!

With her breath caught high in her chest she charged for the door. At first she couldn't find the knob and palmed the wall frantically. Then her fingers closed around the brass. She pushed and pushed, but the knob twisted continuously, uselessly through her fingers.

She couldn't get out!

She was locked in!

Above her on the wall the shadows danced. Out of the corner of her eyes, at the very limit of her vision she saw movement.

A marionette coming off the wall.

Moving by itself!

Moving toward her!

To kill her! her mind shrieked.

Their daughter's screams brought Mickie and Rufus running. As Rufus pushed open the door, Jenny raced out, burying herself in her father's legs. Rufus wrapped his arms around her; she was shivering uncontrollably, her body shaking.

"There, there, baby," he said as he stroked her back. "Everything's all right."

"It isn't!" Jenny insisted. "It's all wrong. I heard the carousel. But nobody wound it! And then I got locked

in and couldn't turn on the light and then the marionettes—they wanted to hurt me!"

"No, honey, there's nothing wrong here," Rufus said
gently. "And the door doesn't lock."

"It *was* locked!" Jenny almost screamed.

"No. See," Rufus said. He opened and closed the
door several times. "Were you trying to push the door,
Jenny? Because from the inside you have to pull it
open."

"I don't remember," Jenny said with a teary voice.

Rufus entered the room and flipped the light switch.
It took several trys before the connection was made.

"Damn!" he said out loud. "I was meaning to fix
that." He shook his head, angry at himself. They all
stepped into the toy room, with Jenny holding tightly to
Rufus's hand. "Now honey, what's wrong. Show me."

"I heard the carousel, Daddy," Jenny repeated. "I
came to stop the music. I couldn't sleep."

Rufus frowned and looked at the music box. The
horses stared straight ahead, silent, motionless, oblivious to the scene in the room.

"But the carousel couldn't have turned itself on," he
said. "You have to wind the handle."

"I heard it!"

"Don't you think you might have dreamed you heard
the music, Jen?" Mickie asked.

Jenny looked at her mother and shook her head. It
wasn't like that. She had heard the music and the carousel *could* turn itself on.

"It's a familiar tune and you've been listening to it
for several days now. I think you like it so much that
you just took it to sleep with you."

"And the marionettes. They wanted to kill me. I saw
them coming. They were moving!"

"No, hon," Rufus said softly. "None of them have
moved at all. See?" He turned her to show her the wall
of puppets. They were all on their pegs. "It was some-

thing else that you saw. A shadow perhaps. Passing headlights. But the marionettes never moved. You shouldn't be afraid of them."

Jenny buried herself in Rufus's arms. "I am afraid, Daddy," she said, her voice cracking.

"I know you are, honey," he said and patted her hair softly, locked eyes with Mickie. "Coming in here in the dark, and then the light not working. It was spooky and you were frightened. You thought you saw something, but you really didn't. Now you can see that everything's all right and you're perfectly safe. Can't you?"

Slowly, Jenny looked around the room again. At the wall of puppets, the hobby horse, motionless, the carousel silent, and shook her head.

Mickie held out her hand. "Come on, Jen. Let's go back to bed. Do you want to sleep with us for the rest of the night?"

Jenny shook her head no. It wasn't necessary. She had only dreamed about the music, she decided. And the marionettes couldn't move by themselves. There was nothing that could hurt her. Nothing at all.

Rufus stood in the toy room door and let his eyes linger on the wall of marionettes. And after he switched off the light, he understood how the row of faces could frighten his daughter. He would get the switch fixed first thing in the morning, he resolved.

He lifted Jenny and carried her into her bedroom and laid her on the bed.

"You're sure you're all right now?" Mickie asked.

Jenny nodded. "Yes, Mommy."

"Do you want us to leave the light on?"

"I'll go to sleep now, Mommy." She decided she wasn't really afraid anymore.

"That's my big girl," Rufus said and bent down and kissed her on the forehead. "My big, brave girl."

"Good night, honey," Mickie said.

"Good night, Mommy. Good night, Daddy."

Jenny turned over on her side. She looked so tiny in the bed, so defenseless, that Mickie didn't want to leave her. She was aware that she was still shaking for her daughter. But Rufus gently led her from the room.

When they got back to their bedroom, Mickie flipped on the lamp and sat down on the edge of the bed. She looked at the clock on her dresser. It was almost 3:00 A.M. She ran her hand through her hair.

"My God, Rufus. What do you think happened in there?"

"Just what she said, Mick. She dreamed the carousel music. It woke her up. She thought she was still hearing the music, went down the hall to investigate, and—" he shrugged. "It was frightening. The room was dark, the house is still unfamiliar. She doesn't know its sounds yet. But she'll be all right," he said strongly. "We know she was nervous about moving here. It's a very large house for a very little girl to get to know. And it will take time for her to adjust." He met Mickie's eyes and said pointedly, "But she will adjust."

"I know she will. I'm just upset. But what do we do until then?"

"Nothing. I don't think we should even refer to what happened. If she brings it up, fine, we'll reassure her. But if she doesn't, then treat it like it never happened, all right?"

"All right," Mickie said reluctantly.

"I know!" Rufus said suddenly as an idea formed. "I'll learn to manipulate the marionettes and put on a show for her. She'd love that. And it'll help her get over her fears of the room. A private show. Just for her." He smiled broadly, pleased with the idea.

"A puppet show?" Mickie asked thoughtfully. "It might be a good idea." She looked puzzled. "But why exclude Todd? He'd enjoy it too."

"No. I think it should just be me and Jenny." He got into bed and closed his eyes.

"Okay, Rufe," Mickie said. "Whatever you think is best." She flipped off the light and crawled under the covers, ready to sleep. "Good night," she whispered, and searched for her husband to kiss him. But he was already asleep, snoring gently.

CHAPTER 7

The move to Vermont was slowly sinking in. They were really there, Mickie realized, with a sigh of relief or a stitch of fear. But either way, it had happened, it was real. As Lois had said, a *fait accompli*.

She was in the Rabbit, driving through Glendon, seeing it through different eyes. When they had been there on ski vacations, almost all they had to think about was the location of the best inns and which service station had the lowest price gas. Now she was looking for dry cleaners, drugstores, bakeries, a barber for Todd, and anything else that would fall into the realm of everyday living.

It was a mere three months from their ordered lives on the West Side of Manhattan, and little more than a year from Rufus's heart attack. The motivating factor, she realized. If it hadn't been for the heart attack and Rufus's subsequent inability to slow down, life would have continued exactly as it was, and they would no doubt still be living in New York talking about a move they would probably never make. But here they were and their lives had turned 180 degrees. She wondered if they would start voting Republican.

Mickie yawned. She was tired this morning. After the incident with Jenny last night, it had taken her some time to fall asleep. But this morning had gone smoothly enough. Jenny did seem to forget what had happened, as Rufus had said she would, or if not forgotten, she had put it behind her. Mickie was tempted to bring it up, to make certain everything was *really* okay, but she sensed it was wrong. *Let sleeping dogs lie*, she warned herself. Jenny had always been very open with them, and if she was still frightened, or wanted to talk, she would come to them.

She had given Jenny the option of coming with her this morning, but Jenny chose to stay home and play with Todd, and Mickie agreed, thrilled that the children were so close. Even back home Todd carefully watched over his little sister, especially after the muggings when he wouldn't let her go anywhere by herself. Well, Mickie thought with a surge of pride, he's playing "big brother." She was just looking forward to the start of school so the children could make some friends, because they couldn't be entirely happy until that happened. There was Cara Wallace right next door for Jenny, as soon as she got over her cold, and Todd would make his own friends quickly enough—he always had.

She stopped for a light in front of the town hall, a white-domed building set back behind a grassy mall dotted with benches and a bandstand. Old people, looking relaxed and comfortable, sat on the benches, free of the fears of the elderly back in New York where they were prey to violent street crime. Small town America was the only way to live, Mickie decided.

And she was glad they were part of it, she told herself with a forceful nod of her head. A woman crossing in front of her car thought Mickie was nodding to her, smiled pleasantly, and waved in return. Mickie laughed. She felt an excited warmth spread over her, a glow.

She breathed in deeply. If she let her imagination run away with itself, she could just about smell winter and the skiing she loved. She had to laugh to herself, though, when she thought about what really were the smells of skiing—gasoline engines that ran the chair lifts and hamburgers grilling in the base lodge. But there was no feeling she had ever experienced that was as exhilarating as racing down a ski slope with the wind at her back. Her mother still couldn't figure out what the family saw in the sport—getting up at 6:00 A.M. to go outside in minus 10 degrees to ride a freezing chair lift directly into a northern wind, all for the privilege of falling down a mountain? But, as Mickie said to her, skiing cannot be explained to the uninitiated. It has to be experienced.

The whole move was a dream experience. Although nothing was forever, she hedged. If it didn't work, they could always junk it. Sell the practice, try somewhere else. They could always move to a larger city if Glendon felt too confining. But not New York. She never wanted to return where uneasy concern for her children was a daily habit, and Rufus would be placed under a pressure that could be killing. She didn't even want to think about the possibility that Glendon would not work out. *No negative thoughts,* she scolded herself.

But even with all her positive thoughts, Mickie couldn't help but feel a twinge of nervousness at what they had done. She was thinking exactly like a mother, she knew, because the only real question was whether they had made the right move for the children. Time would answer that.

She had only two hopes and prayers—that her family would remain together in health and happiness, and that they could afford to pay their fuel bills during the long New England winters.

Something caught Mickie's eye and she turned off the road.

Maybe Penelope and Hazel didn't have any plants in the house, but Mickie Talman certainly would!

Fifteen minutes later she carried boxes of houseplants out to the car.

* * *

They had been putting together a jigsaw puzzle—Todd and Jenny and Snoopy—when Todd remembered that last night he had promised himself to return to the cellar. He sensed he *had* to see what was down there, had to explore the unknown. The curiosity was overwhelming. His father was working, his mother was out. Now was the time to do it so he wouldn't get caught.

He stretched and shadow-boxed the wall. "I'm going out for a few minutes, Jen."

"Where?"

"Just out. Do a little running or something. Are you going to stay here and finish the puzzle? We'll show Mommy what we did when she gets home."

Jenny looked a little disappointed at not being included in the new plan, but she nodded affirmatively anyway. The puzzle was fun and she was good at it. "Okay, Todd. See you later."

As Todd neared the cellar door, he had second thoughts. There was no getting around the fact that the cellar was a very spooky place. Fear chased through his mind and jockeyed with his curiosity for prominence as he opened the cellar door and stepped onto the landing. Curiosity won. The cellar drew him in, committed him, to his plan. He knew where he had to go.

He stood in front of the door. It was partially open, just as he had left it. Mocking him. Daring him to push it wide and enter. *Come into my parlor said the spider to the fly*, he thought. Why was he thinking *that* now; that saying always made him nervous, the image was so terrible.

Involuntarily, he shivered. Why had he come down here? he questioned himself as he warily eyed the door. Nobody had made him. *Except himself*.

He inhaled sharply. It was age he was smelling. The smell of decay. Disintegrating newspapers. Rotting furniture. Decomposing bodies?

He thought he heard a moan and jumped. But it

wasn't a human sound he was hearing; rather the squeal of a floorboard above him, the whine of a settling house crying out with a gasp of pain. He suddenly wished he wasn't alone and wished his friends were there. Nothing bad ever happens in a crowd.

But he couldn't force himself to turn around. Not until he found out what was down here, why *he* was down here—and it was now or never.

He reached out and touched the door, ran his hand along the rough wood. He tensed and slowly edged the door open, while visions of every horror movie he had ever seen kaleidoscoped through his head. He was half expecting to be met on the other side of the door by a chalk white face with piercing, burning eyes or a sheeted ghost, body stiff and bound or mummified with outstretched arms. A ghost with a face burned by acid. A ghost who likes to eat children—

He shoved the door open wide and closed his eyes. Silence. Nothing. Only heartbeat and breath.

One eye opened. Then the other. And there was the room.

It was a bedroom and wasn't that odd? A bedroom at the end of the cellar. But no ghost or dead body, and it was apparently safe to enter. Feeling embarrassed by his ridiculous fears, he boldly stepped forward.

The room was darker than the rest of the cellar. On the opposite wall, high up near the ceiling, a small window heavily layered with dirt sparingly let in light which shrouded the objects in the room in shadow—a chest of drawers, a bookcase full of books, a bed.

The room was even colder than the rest of the cellar and lacked any feeling of human warmth. If it had really been used as a bedroom, no care had been given to it. It was a place to sleep, that was all. Little more than a cell. Not a room to live in.

Something happened in here.

Something he should know about.

The thought pricked at his mind, but he brushed it away.

Then he saw a rumpled mound of covers was on the bed as though someone had just gotten up.

Or—the thought came to him—*someone or something was still under them.*

He brushed his hair back and made himself take a step. It was now much more than curiosity.

A trick of light suddenly gave the covers life. Did they really move? He thought he could see a head.

No, he told himself. Nothing had moved under the covers.

His stomach suddenly heaved and threatened to turn itself upside down. His muscles tightened. Adrenaline surged through his body.

There couldn't be anything, couldn't be anything, couldn't be anything, he decided. As if wishing it would make it so.

Another step forward.

His palms were wet and he wiped them on his jeans. He never took his eyes from the bed. He sucked in his breath.

There could be something at this very minute creeping up behind him, ready to grab his leg, something snaky, something terrible. But he dared not shift his eyes from the bed. Because in that fraction of a second it would spring out and get him. Nor could he turn away for the same reason—he was trapped. Oh, God, why did he come down here?

He was within reaching distance of the bed. He could just lean over and touch the covers—

Whatever was there could reach him too!

A floorboard creaked. *From upstairs,* his mind yelled madly at him. *Where? Get out of here, Todd.*

He spread his legs apart in ready position, balanced equally on both feet. He could go in either direction; he could run like hell if he had to. Cold perspiration layered his body like slime. His right arm twitched nervously, and he tried to quiet his heart; it was shockingly loud, announcing his presence.

He reached out with his thumb and middle finger and touched the covers.

Nothing happened. Nothing fell out from underneath.

Bolder, suddenly, in one motion he did it. Grabbed the blanket, lifted it up, and tossed it high and far aside.

He heard the noise from behind him and the sharp touch on his shoulder that felt like human nails. *It had been behind him all along.*

With a yelp of horror he wrenched himself free from the hand that held his shoulder. Air blasted through his nostrils as he turned around to confront the being that had grabbed him, his fists balled and ready.

It was a toss-up as to who was more frightened—Todd, hunched in fight position, or Jenny, who had frozen in fear at the sudden, violent reaction of her brother.

"You scared the hell out of me!" Todd screamed at her. "What did you do that for? What are you doing down here?"

Frightened by Todd's voice, Jenny backed away from him.

"I thought you were going to work on the jigsaw puzzle."

"I was," Jenny stammered. "But I decided to come with you. I saw you go down here. I called you."

"I didn't hear you," Todd cut her off.

"I know," Jenny said, her voice small and quivering, trying to get all of her words out before Todd chopped them off. "So I followed you in here. I only wanted to play with you, Todd. I didn't mean to scare you. You came in here, and you looked so strange." Tears started to flow down her face. "I'm so sorry, Todd . . ."

"Hey," Todd said, suppressing his own strangling terror, again the big brother. "Stop that, will you?"

Jenny shook her head and cried louder. She knew she had done something terrible, touching Todd like she did. She knew how she would feel if Todd ever frightened her like that.

"Come on. Stop." Todd took Jenny's hand and smiled warmly. "It's all right now. There's no harm done. So I was a little scared. No big deal." He wagged a cautionary finger at her like he had seen his mother do so many times. "You'd better stop crying now or the tears are going to freeze on your face." He knew that usually worked on Jenny, and sure enough a smile broke through. She sniffed back the tears and rubbed her nose with the back of her hand.

"You're sure it's all right?" she asked.

"Sure I'm sure," Todd smiled.

"Good," Jenny said softly, and then asked, "What were you doing with that blanket, Todd?"

Todd glanced over to the blanket, which was now crumpled on the floor next to the bed, where he had tossed it. The bed was empty. There was nothing on it except for a faded yellow sheet. His breathing eased and his old confidence returned. There was nothing frightening down here after all. But how could he tell Jenny what he had thought? Instead, he shrugged. "I don't know. Fooling around, I guess. Exploring the cellar. I found this crazy room here."

Jenny took in the room and made a face. "A bedroom in a cellar? That doesn't make any sense."

Todd had to agree with her. "It doesn't."

"Who would ever stay down here? It's so cold and dark and creepy." She wrinkled up her nose.

"Maybe a criminal," Todd said. "Or a crazy old relative that they didn't want anybody to see." Jenny nodded. That seemed to make sense. "Hey," Todd said suddenly. "We better not say anything to Mommy and

Daddy about our being down here. Not yet anyway. I don't think they'd like the idea."

Jenny shook her head up and down strongly. Todd was right. She had forgotten her promise not to come down here. She looked around quickly, expecting her mother to magically appear, a disapproving look on her face, an accusatory finger pointing at her. "I think I'd better go upstairs," she said, suddenly feeling very uneasy about being down there.

"That's a good idea," Todd agreed. "I'll be with you in a minute. Then we'll play again. I just want to look around a little more."

Jenny ran off. Todd heard her footsteps on the stairs and the slam of the kitchen door. He was alone in the room.

But now the spell was broken, the fear gone. He moved around the room taking it all in, inspecting the corners and under the bed. He picked the blanket off the floor, folded it, and put it back on the bed in a flat heap. He sat down on top of it to flatten it even more. He would never think there was anything under those covers again. He was ashamed of himself for being so afraid.

But who would ever stay down here? he questioned. It was a bedroom with rumpled covers, and that meant it must have been used by somebody at sometime.

He ran back through the cellar without looking behind him, back up the stairs to the kitchen where he closed and latched the cellar door, and up to Jenny on the second floor. Jenny was standing up on a chair, taking a game box out of her closet. "You want to play with the Ouija board, Todd?" she asked. "Check out the new house for any spirits?"

"No," Todd said. "Let's finish the jigsaw puzzle."

CHAPTER 8

Kids were kids, Rufus thought, as he ushered another one into his examining room. Whether in New York City or Glendon, Vermont, their illnesses and ailments were the same. Tonsils. Sniffles. Broken bones.

"And here we go," he said to the little boy in front of him as he lifted him up under the arms and set him down on the examination table.

He was happiest when he was taking care of children, and he had never minded the long hours. Early morning hospital time for operations, afternoon rounds, office hours. The long hours came with the job, all doctors knew that. And their wives should as well.

But he knew Mickie only grudgingly accepted the hours, wanting more of him than he could give her. Their needs were different; hers more personal than professional. But he had responsibilities, to his partners who had taken him in, to his patients who loved and needed him, and to his family. He didn't want his children to lack anything or have to work their way through school as he did when growing up. There was a trade-off; no question of that.

"Now let's see what the trouble is, Mark," he said pleasantly. He prided himself on his bedside manner, but Mark just wasn't responding. He sat with his arms folded tightly in front of him, his lips curved downward in a frown. He wasn't letting this new doctor anywhere near him.

"Well," Rufus said, shrugging and stepping back. "I guess we can't make you better then, can we?"

"Nope," the boy grinned. He had won.

He watched curiously as Rufus put away his stethoscope. "Shall we talk about something else then?" Rufus asked. "Do you like baseball? Who do you think will win the pennant this year?" Within minutes he had Mark jabbering away happily about baseball. Before he knew it, Dr. Talman had looked into his ears, nose, and down his throat, and had listened to his chest. *He was good with kids,* Rufus knew.

At lunch Mickie suspected that something was up. Jenny did not meet her glance and kept looking at Todd and suppressing a giggle. They were guilty of something, she knew, but she wasn't going to press it. It was all right for the kids to have their secrets.

She was just finishing up the dishes when the doorbell rang.

"Hi," Nina beamed.

"Come on in," Mickie offered.

"Look who I have with me."

Mickie looked down and there was a small girl of Jenny's age. Her dark hair was braided. "And who's this?" she asked.

"Say your name," Nina prompted.

"Cara," said the small voice.

"She's a little shy. Give her a day or two and she'll warm up to you."

"She's very pretty," Mickie said cheerily, and Cara blushed and tried to hide behind her mother's skirt. "Jenny," Mickie called. "Company. Can you stay?" she asked Nina.

"Hi," Jenny said uncertainly from the stairs.

"Jenny, this is Cara," Mickie made the introductions.

"Hi, Cara," Jenny said excitedly. This was the first person her own age she had met up here.

"I've been telling Cara about the toy room, and she's all ready to go upstairs and play, aren't you, Cara?"

Cara nodded eagerly. "Can we, Jenny?" she asked.

Mickie noticed the flicker of hesitation across her daughter's face. The events of last night were not completely forgotten. But then Jenny nodded and motioned for Cara to join her.

"Upstairs. Come on." The two girls scampered up the stairs. "It's really a neat place," Jenny said as they rounded the landing and disappeared from sight. "With puppets and dolls and a rocking horse!"

Mickie smiled at Nina. "Friendships form fast at that age."

"At our age too," Nina said.

Later, they watched from the doorway as the girls played in the toy room. For Nina memories came flooding back. She saw herself in her daughter, thirty years before, playing in this very same room with her friend, Essie and the marionettes, making them dance with each other.

And then suddenly one day Essie had died.

Todd and Jenny were in the living room reading when the adults finished the dishes and came in to join them. Rufus ducked into his office for a second. Todd's eyes widened in pleasure as Rufus handed him a gift-wrapped box.

"A little peace offering," he said sheepishly. "For my—shall we say?—uncalled-for behavior at the school last night."

"You didn't have to do that, Dad," Todd said, a little embarrassed, still thinking he was the one at fault.

"Okay," Rufus said and made a grab for the box. Todd spun around and pulled it out of his reach.

"But as long as you did—" The wrapping paper quickly littered the floor—"A microscope! Thanks,

Dad! Thanks!" He ran to his father and threw his arms around him. They kissed. Rufus hugged his son to him. He felt good about himself.

It was a very nice gift, Mickie noted. Rufus could have gotten away with less, but she was pleased he had gone all out. He was apologetic. He cared. And now Todd knew it.

"Thanks, Rufe," she whispered under her breath.

"How about we build a fire tonight?" Rufus asked.

"It is getting kind of chilly," Mickie agreed. "Although if we need a fire now in early September, how cold is it going to be up here in late January?" She shuddered to herself; as a skier she knew. She picked up a sweater she was knitting for Todd that she hoped to have finished by Thanksgiving.

Rufus stacked the wood pyramid fashion. Todd handed him the kindling. The wrapping paper was crumpled and placed under the wood. Rufus lit the fire.

Mickie looked up from her knitting as the first pieces of paper caught. Within minutes the starter sticks at the bottom of the pyramid were red and glowing.

"My little woodsmen," Mickie said, smiling. This was really the first time since they'd been in the new house that they were all comfortably together with no strain between them.

Then the fire started to burn full. Fingers of flame lapped at the top of the hearth.

"Great work, Davy Crockett," Mickie said. "Hey— let's all give Daddy a round of applause."

The children clapped. Rufus stood and took a bow, and then held out his arms toward Todd.

"Couldn't have done a thing without my able-bodied assistant here. Come on, able-bodied assistant. Stand up and join me in the spotlight. Or should I say firelight?"

Everyone groaned as Todd stood. Rufus put his arm around him and pulled his son close. Nothing further had to be said. Their pose in front of the fire was confirmation enough that all was squared away between them.

For a few moments they stared contentedly into the fire watching the flames crackle and wave. Suddenly Todd's thoughts drifted to the room downstairs and the strange feelings he had experienced in the cellar.

"Dad, can I talk to you for a minute?" He took a deep breath and brushed the hair out of his eyes. "I did something today I shouldn't have," he started slowly. Mickie put down her knitting and quietly watched her son. "And some things happened which I don't understand, and they got me kind of worried. I know I promised Mommy I'd stay out of the cellar, but I went down there anyway—"

"Oh, Todd, I told you not to."

"Two times," he continued hurriedly. "The first time when you yelled at me because I went into your office, Dad, but I didn't get to see too much then, and the second time today. I got really curious about what's down there."

"Go on," Mickie said gently as she noticed he was squirming to avoid her glance.

"Well, I felt kind of strange all over. Creepy. Like there were spooks watching me or something. And there's this room down there. A bedroom. Why would there be a bedroom in the cellar? Did anybody stay in it? What do you think happened down there, Dad?"

"I don't know what happened down there, Todd," Rufus said slowly, evenly. "But I do know what's happened up here. We have a case of a broken promise, don't we? Well, I think you've learned a very valuable lesson today. When your mother tells you something, it's for a reason. You were specifically told to stay out of the cellar until I cleaned it. And you promised you would. But then you went and immediately broke that promise. Well, promises are worth a little more than that. I would punish you, but I suspect you've been punished enough by being scared down there today. Now I want you to apologize to your mother."

"I'm sorry, Mom," he said, and Mickie saw the hurt in his eyes.

Jenny, silent throughout the discussion, suddenly felt compelled to rush to her brother's aid. "I went downstairs too!" she said and Mickie noticed there was almost a note of pride in her voice. She was sticking up for Todd, deflecting the attention from him by offering her own head on the chopping block.

"That's okay, darling," Rufus said. "*Todd* was responsible for you, and he should have known better than to take you down there."

"I went on my own!" she persisted.

"Just don't do it again, okay?" Rufus asked.

Jenny nodded readily. "Okay."

"But what about the bedroom, Dad?" Todd asked excitedly. "It's a mystery, isn't it? What do you think happened down there? Do you think they kept a guy locked up in it or something?"

"Todd, we don't know if anything happened down there. Maybe it's only a playroom."

"I don't think so, Dad," he said, and Jenny shook her head negatively as well. The room didn't look like anybody's playroom.

"Well, I don't have any other ideas," Rufus said with finality. "It's just a room, that's all. And I'm certain that nothing ever happened down there. Nothing that anybody here has to worry about."

"Yeah, Dad. Okay," Todd said. "I won't go down there anymore."

"Me either," Jenny said readily.

Todd turned his attention to the fireplace and lost himself in the alluring patterns of the flickering flames. He was mad at himself for having been afraid down in that room, and for getting himself yelled at. All that

creepy-crawly bullshit. His father was right—there was
nothing down there that meant anything to him. But
something deep within Todd told him that just saying it
did not make it true. He stole a glance at Rufus, who was
reading a paperback book, and wondered if he'd ever do
anything that his father approved of again. "Well, I
guess I'll go upstairs and play with my microscope," he
said and shrugged, but there was no enthusiasm in his
voice.

"I'll go too," Jenny said.

"Okay," Mickie said. "We'll be up later to tuck you
in."

When the children disappeared up the stairs, she
turned to Rufus. "You didn't have to speak so severely
to Todd. You could see he was upset."

"He was upset because he was frightened. And we
knew he'd be frightened by the cellar and that's why we
told him to stay out of there."

"But your yelling at him didn't help—" Mickie
started, then asked, "Do you know anything about that
bedroom down there?"

"It's just a room, Mick. I saw it the first day we were
here when I went downstairs with the contractor. I
didn't think anything of it then or now. I don't know
what it was used for and don't really care."

"Okay, Rufe, have it your way," Mickie said. But
that room in the cellar had frightened Todd, and
Mickie resolved she'd go take a look at it herself in the
morning.

CHAPTER 9

The next morning Mickie went into the cellar. The air was cool, the corners lost to dusty shadow. She could see why her children had been frightened, and suddenly she didn't feel any braver than they.

The room was as Todd described it. A bedroom in the middle of the cellar. Little more than a cell, really. But her eyes were drawn immediately to the bookcase against the wall and the dust-covered old volumes. Her background was literature, as was her profession, and the books interested her.

She went back to the kitchen, got one of Rufus's old T-shirts, which had been demoted to dust rag status, and wiped as much of the accumulated dirt off the books as the rag would absorb. She read through the titles now faded with time. Books by American masters, Hawthorne, Emerson, Whittier, and English writers as well. And a whole shelf of children's books! She gently opened up the pages, yellowed and brittle from dampness and years of neglect.

It took about a half-dozen trips to transport the books up to the kitchen and then up again to her office where she could read and examine them in comfort.

In a collection of poetry by Longfellow she found a folded piece of paper. It was crushed between the pages, not sticking out on top or bottom. If she hadn't been flipping through the book, she would have missed it.

The writer was unmistakably female, the words shaky as if a quivering hand had written them. The paper was discolored as though water had spilled on it and dried—no, not water, Mickie decided. Tears. The ink was faded and Mickie almost didn't bother with it, until she saw it was addressed to God. She started to read the letter, her breath quickening as she realized it was a suicide note.

Dear God:

My guilt shadows me like darkness. There is no escape from my constant dread companion. He sees me to sleep and is waiting for me when I awaken. He preys on me at night and haunts my dreams. I pray I could bathe my soul in light and cleanse myself of the enormous weight I carry as my burden. I am responsible for so many deaths. My daughter. My son. The others. Had I known all that was to happen, how could I have prevented it? I would have sacrificed myself instead.

It is now less than a year since the death of our darling daughter Sarah and without her Jonas has no one to offer his love. He has become more bitter than ever. He screams at me, he beats me. But I accept my punishment silently because I am at fault. If only I had been stronger with Jonas, perhaps none of it would have happened.

My own death has become the only path for me. I think of little else. I look at the knife beside me, cradle it in my hands, and wonder what it will feel like when it finally slashes me, as it must. I want to experience the pain my children did. There is already a mark on my wrist where I have touched the knife to it. I fight my terrible urges, I struggle not to commit the ultimate sin against You, God, but I can fight no more. He has returned for me as he had for Sarah.

God rest his troubled soul, and I pray it will all end with my death. But I fear his hatred is still too strong, and God forbid, he will return and kill again.

Mickie read and reread the letter again until the ink blurred on the paper and she had to shut her eyes. She could almost feel the pain of this woman as her own, share her guilt. Every sentence in the letter was filled with self-condemnation and terrors Mickie prayed she would never have visited upon her family. She regretted disturbing what she prayed was final peace for a hopelessly troubled woman. She put the letter back into the book and shut it, rested her hand on the book of poetry as if it were a Bible upon which she was taking a solemn oath, swearing that the death of the woman would remain a closed chapter.

But she couldn't stop thinking about the dead woman in her final, painful days, when she tortured herself with guilt and struggled against the urges to kill herself, and finally was consumed by the desperate act of suicide. Mickie pictured the frail woman cutting into her wrists with the knife. She twisted her own hands and looked at the undersides of her wrists, where the slashes would be made, at the pale pink flesh and folds of skin that ran across it, at the thin bones and narrow blue veins pulsing with blood. She imagined slicing through those veins with the sharp edge of a knife and watching the blood spurt forth and her life flow from her.

She shuddered. No thoughts of death, Mickie cautioned herself. Let the dead remain undisturbed. She freed her thoughts and shook her head. She slipped the volume of poetry into the bookcase. She turned to the other books and tried to focus her attention on the new discoveries.

The suicide letter had no meaning to her life, and she swore she would not disturb it again.

* * *

That night, in sleep, Mickie heard her daughter's
voice. It was faint, shaky, laced with fear.

Help me, Mommy. Help me, the child cried and
Mickie could hear the trembling in her voice.

She struggled for consciousness, to raise herself out
of sleep, like a diver swimming frantically upward,
through dark, murky water, finally bursting through the
surface, gasping for air—

Her eyes opened.

Had she really heard her daughter's voice? she questioned herself.

Help me, Mommy.

My God! Mickie said and sat up in bed. She tossed
off the covers. *Jen?* she called, then louder again. *Jenny?*

He wants to kill me, Mommy. The words came
through the wall, faster now, more desperate, thick with
tears.

Rufus! Mickie screamed at her husband asleep next
to her and shook him to wake him up. But he didn't
respond.

Hurry, Mommy.

I'm coming, Jen, she called out. *Where are you?* She
looked frantically around her, disoriented in the black
shadowed bedroom.

I'm here, Mommy. Over here. Come find me.

I'm coming, Mickie yelled and bolted from the bed.
But suddenly her feet felt like lead weights. She
could barely lift them.

She staggered from room to room, frantically searching for her daughter.

She was moving in slow motion. Terrifying frustra-
tion overwhelmed her as she struggled to another room
in the endless second-floor corridor.

Too many rooms, too many rooms, she told herself.
I'll never get to Jenny in time. She felt the helplessness
of being lost in quicksand.

Mommy! Here I am, Mommy.

The end of the hallway. Mickie knew where to go.

Jenny was in the toy room, backed into a corner of the room, hunched fetally, her eyes staring wildly, cringing from—*her*? No—there was someone else. She felt it. She smelled it.

There was a boy.

She couldn't see him clearly. He was robed in shadow in a far corner of the room. In his hand he held a knife, the tip of the knife pointing directly at Jenny.

No, Mickie hissed. She tried to rush toward the boy but she couldn't move. She was paralyzed. She watched the boy take a step forward. He was still in the gray light; she could not yet see his face.

Don't, she whispered huskily, her eyes brimming with fear. *Don't hurt my daughter.*

The boy didn't answer. He took another step forward.

What do you want? Desperation in her tone. She still couldn't move. Tears streamed down her face. Quickly she looked at Jenny, folded into herself, staring at the approaching boy.

Please, Mickie begged. *Leave my daughter and take me. Let me sacrifice myself for my daughter.*

The words freed her, and Mickie sprang forward, lunging toward the shadowed figure, throwing herself against the tip of the knife, taking it in her stomach. She reeled backwards. Her body shuddered and chilled as the blood pulsed out of her. She watched with horror and fascination as the front of her nightgown stained red and blood flowed down her legs and pooled on the floor.

Run, Jenny, she whispered to her daughter. *Get up and run out.*

She grasped her stomach and fell to her knees in her blood. She felt herself losing consciousness and knew she was dying. *Run,* she repeated urgently. *Get away now*. But Jenny remained stock still in the corner, too terrified to move. She would die, Mickie knew, not knowing if she had saved her daughter.

The boy walked out of the shadows, stepped over her, and started toward Jenny. With her final strength Mickie raised her eyes to look at her killer.

She woke up trembling, her body soaked with perspiration, her hands clutching tightly at her stomach. Her mouth was chalky with fear, and it took her long moments to reorient herself. She was in bed; Rufus was asleep next to her. Her heart was pounding wildly, her stomach tender where the knife had plunged in. She brought her fingers to her mouth wondering if she would taste her blood.

Jenny!

It was a dream, she knew, but nonetheless she threw the covers off her and raced across the hall to her daughter's room.

Jenny's room was peaceful, a sudden shift from the fury of the nightmare. But still, half frantic from the dream, she had to lean over her daughter, watch the covers rise and fall, listen for the faint wisps of breath as Jenny took in air. After long moments of holding her own breath and struggling to see her daughter's form from the dim hallway night-light, Mickie accepted that Jenny was alive and all was as it should be.

She wanted to remain in Jenny's room longer, but she knew there was no danger here. She was just over-reacting to the terrible dream. And, she thought to herself with the slightest ironic curl to her smile, she had to believe what she had taught her children when they were plagued by nightmares—*dreams can't hurt me, dreams mean nothing*. She walked out of the bedroom, let the door close behind her. She looked down toward the end of the hallway, and the toy room shadowed at the other end. She fought the urge to go down there and look in. Instead, she threw cold water on her face.

But the dream was so frighteningly real. She stared at her image in the bathroom mirror, trying to forget it. Her face looked drawn, tired, pale. She shuddered as water trickled over her breasts.

So real.

Rufus stirred as she got back into bed. She patted him to lull him under again.

That damn letter, she almost cried. She thought she had forgotten about it, but that must have been what brought on the dream. The words from the suicide note: *I would sacrifice myself instead* ran through her mind—and chilled her flesh.

She breathed slowly trying to calm herself. But when she finally settled back under the covers and allowed her eyes to drift closed, the final moments of the dream returned unbidden.

She was lying in a pool of her blood. She knew she was dying but strained anyway to hold her eyes open to see the face of the boy as he stepped out of the shadow, still grasping the knife, walking toward Jenny . . .

But there was distortion and grayness in the shadowed light, and she couldn't see his face.

CHAPTER 10

It was a little past eight thirty when Mickie drove the children to school to register. Buses were pulling up, students pouring out, and others arriving by foot or bike. An excited buzz filled the air.

Jenny stole glances at the other children. She held her mother's hand as they waded through the crowd, not quite ready to assault the second grade. Todd walked ahead of his mother, pretending he wasn't with her. His head was high, his chin forward and set, trying to look mature. He certainly didn't want anyone to think that he needed his mother to take him to school.

He didn't notice Rick Webb anywhere in the crowd. So far so good.

He received his program from the guidance counselor. Seventh grade was departmentalized; he had English first period, then math, French, lunch, history, earth science, and gym. Last period gym was the favorite, he was told. If he was involved in an exciting game he wouldn't have to break it up early to change and go to another subject.

"So you're all set," Mickie said to him as he pocketed his program card.

"I guess."

"Good. At the end of the day I want you to meet Jenny in front of the building and take the bus home together. It's a little too far to walk until you know the way. It's the Number 5 bus. It goes right past the house. Got that?"

Todd nodded. Number 5 bus. Got it.

He looked at his sister. Her eyes were sad and searching. She was scared. Todd didn't want to leave her alone, but he knew she had to face the day on her own, as he did.

"Right in front, Jen. Where we came in. I'll be waiting for you."

"And now for Jenny," the counselor said. "You'll be in a different wing of the building . . ."

Todd found his homeroom with no problem. The teacher took the pass and indicated he should sit wherever he wanted. He took a seat at the end of the first row and nodded to the boy sitting next to him.

"Todd Talman," he said, holding out his hand.

The other boy took it. "Jeff Westmore. Just move here?"

Todd nodded. "Last week."

"You like it?"

"I guess."

"Yeah, it's okay. Where you from?"

"New York."

Jeff looked impressed. "I was in New York once. My family went down for a week." He made a face. "Didn't like it. Too much noise. Too crowded. We were afraid of getting ripped off."

"I was mugged once," Todd said.

Jeff's eyes widened. "Really? What happened?"

Around them students were filing into the room.

"Four big guys jumped me when I was getting off the bus."

"Jesus—" Jeff gasped. "What did they get?"

"Five dollars and some change. No big deal."

"Did they beat you up at all?"

Todd nodded. "Pretty bad. I needed stitches over my eye."

Someone was walking by the desk. Jeff grabbed his arm. "Greg, meet Todd Talman. He comes from New York and was mugged!"

"Really? Wow!"

He pulled up the chair in front of Jeff and turned to be included in the conversation.

As the room filled, Todd recounted in detail the events of the afternoon he was mugged, from his stepping off the bus, to being hustled into the bushes. He was thrilled he was already talking to two other boys, making friends at last.

Jenny's teacher was a tall, slender woman with brown hair that tucked inward at the neck. Jenny looked around the room and searched for Cara and saw her in the front row. She smiled to her, then took her assigned seat in the third row. Then Miss Kitchen asked her to stand and tell everyone a little about herself— where in New York she came from, why her family moved to Glendon, who her father is, where she lived now.

Reluctantly, Jenny stood at her place, but Miss Kitchen directed her to the front of the room.

There seemed to be a thousand children in the class, instead of the thirty she knew were there. But she met Cara's eyes which were warm and encouraging. So talking directly to Cara, Jenny tried to offer the teacher what she seemed to want. The next several minutes were a blur, and before Jenny knew it she was back in her seat, only remembering having spoken her name.

"Wasn't that awful?" Cara asked her. "Miss Bathroom—that's what we call her—does that to everyone. We all had to do it last year. She thinks she's helping us. It's just harder when you have to do it alone."

"Cara," Miss Kitchen scolded gently.

"There are so many other girls for you to meet,"

Cara whispered to Jenny. "But we'll talk at lunch, okay?"

Jenny nodded and smiled. She knew she had made a good friend. And there were many other children she would get to meet. And she would invite all of them to play in the toy room.

She felt very happy.

It was cold in the gym when Todd arrived for last period. His legs were goose bumps under the purple gym shorts, and his arms were folded tightly in front of him to try to keep warm. The beginning of the period was free time and the gathering boys were shooting hoops, rappeling up and down the ropes, and playing on the apparatus—the parallel bars, the horse, the high bar. Todd stood to the side, searching for familiar faces. He saw one.

He met Rick Webb's eyes.

Rick was halfway up the rope. He had stopped for a breather when he saw Todd. Effortlessly he hoisted himself up the rest of the way, palmed the ceiling fiercely, then quickly dropped to the mats. He puffed out his chest, tightened his arm muscles, and started toward him. Todd tensed and steeled himself for another fight.

The whistle blew. The boys dropped to one knee in place as the formal part of the class began.

They met again in the locker room.

Todd had just slipped off his gym shorts when he felt eyes on him.

Rick was leaning comfortably against the row of lockers opposite Todd's. Todd looked at him briefly, his face a mask. He was trying to hide his fear. Perhaps if he ignored him he would go away.

"Hello, Todd."

Todd pulled on his pants. He didn't respond.

Rick Webb slammed a locker shut. The metallic ring was loud. Todd absorbed the sound with his body. Other boys turned to look. With stiff shoulders Todd faced Rick. The bigger boy smiled, but his lips twisted into a mean curl.

Todd's voice was low, and he tried to hold it steady. To show fear was definitely to invite trouble.

"I don't want to fight you, Rick," he said.

"Why not?" The voice dripped with sarcasm. "Don't have your father with you, Todd-y?"

"That's not what I mean," Todd said. He reached for his shirt, aware of each motion he made.

"What *do* you mean, Todd-y?"

Todd pulled the shirt on. "Nothing." His fingers flew through the buttons, and he wasn't certain if he got them all right. But he didn't take the time to look. He wanted to get out of there fast. There was a clock on the far wall. It was almost three. He thought of Jenny. She must be outside waiting for him by now. The locker room was emptying as the other boys raced out to make the buses. Todd threw his T-shirt into the locker, pulled on his shoes, hastily tied them, slammed the locker shut, twirled his combination lock, and picked up his books to leave. Rick Webb blocked his path.

"Excuse me," Todd said.

Rick didn't move. Behind him two other boys came up.

"Hey, Todd-y," Rick said easily. "Meet my friends. Riley and Biff."

"What's up?" Riley asked. He reached into his locker and pulled out a towel. Rick stood casually with his arms folded in front of him. Wordlessly, he jutted his chin to indicate Todd. The situation was suddenly interesting. "What are you going to do, Rick?"

Todd's eyes shifted to Rick. Pretending to think, Rick ran his fingers lightly over his upper lip. He finally spoke.

"Nothing."

"Excuse me," Todd said again and tried to brush past him. Rick moved in front of him, once more blocking his path. He broke into a broad grin.

"Yeah, I ain't gonna do anything. If old hot shit here wants to make the school bus"—he glanced casually behind him at the clock, which was dangerously close to five past three—"he's going to have to do something about it." He turned to face Todd directly. "Aren't you?"

Todd knew he was going to have to fight his way out. With sinking realization, he also knew that the school bus was going to leave without him, and he thought of Jenny waiting for him outside. What would she do now that he wasn't there and the buses were leaving? But then his thoughts shifted back to his own predicament. The locker room was empty except for the four of them.

"I'm not going to fight you, Rick," he said, looking the bigger boy square in the eye.

"Too bad." Rick shrugged. "Then I guess you aren't going to get home. I've got all day." He grinned at his friends. "I think I'll do a little rearranging on the kid's face." He took a step closer to Todd, torturing him and enjoying it. The fight was inevitable. Rick wanted to continue what his father had interrupted.

He hated Rick Webb.

Concentrate.

The word came to Todd, and suddenly he remembered the daydream of a week ago.

Where he had concentrated.

And stopped Rick Webb in his tracks.

"Hey, I'm tired of waiting, hot shit turd face," Rick said and stepped closer. Unconsciously, Todd took a step back.

Concentrate.

Rick Webb squared his chin and balled his hand into

a fist. Behind him the two other boys closed in to watch. Todd was backed against the wall. He dropped his notebook to the floor and made two fists, his hands small and puny compared to the bigger boy's.

The word came to him again.

Concentrate.

And Todd did. He furrowed his brow and stared hard at Rick Webb. Concentrated on him and tried to will him to stop, to fall. Just like he had in the daydream.

Then the absurdity of what he was doing hit him. *Concentrate,* he thought to himself glumly, as Rick Webb advanced toward him. In fact, with the one small portion of his mind that wasn't concentrating on stopping Rick, Todd thought he probably looked rather silly to the three bigger boys with his shoulders rounded, his brow furrowed as marks of concentration etched his face.

No, concentration alone was not going to stop this boy from beating him up. He clenched his fists and awaited the inevitable. If he was going to go down, he'd go down swinging. But Rick Webb wasn't ready yet. A smile played across his face. He took practice swings at the air, slaps, and punches. Todd saw that he was milking the moment for all it was worth, delaying the beating.

The noise from behind startled them all. The heavy footsteps entered the locker room.

"Todd Talman. Are you in here?"

Eyes on Rick Webb, Todd hesitated. But his hesitation lasted only a fraction of a second. This was his opportunity, and if he didn't grab it now, he'd be pummeled for sure.

"Here," he called out.

Rick backed off. He opened a locker and pretended to look into it. The man appeared at the end of the row of lockers. Todd looked at his benefactor. He was carrying a marking book, and Todd knew he was one of the teachers. In a moment the teacher understood the situation.

"I'm Mr. Ferber," he said. "I've come to take you to your sister. She's been waiting for you outside. You're running a bit late, son."

Todd edged out of the locker aisle, careful not to meet Rick's eye nor brush against him. Once freed, he raced down the hall toward the front door.

"Shit!" Rick spat out when he and his friends were alone again. "I'm going to level that little son of a bitch. Hot shit because his father's a doctor and everyone's out protecting his ass."

His friends nodded in agreement. They wanted to watch Rick level the kid. But the moment had passed, and they all knew it.

Todd found Jenny outside. Her face lit up when she saw him.

"Where have you been, Todd? The teacher came out and found me. We missed the bus."

"I know. But we'll get home okay." He looked behind him into the dark school corridor. "Come on," he said and took off down the steps. He wanted to put distance between himself and Rick Webb.

He double-timed it down the road with Jenny running to keep up with him. A fat lot of good concentrating did. He was just lucky that that guy Ferber was around, because by now Rick Webb would have done a good job rearranging his face.

CHAPTER 11

Mickie parked her car on River Street. Out of habit she locked the door, although she had been assured at the reception that no one else did. In fact, several of the people there didn't even bother to lock their houses, a habit Mickie didn't think she'd ever get into. Overnight you just don't wash away years of New York living.

The afternoon sun was still strong on this early September day, just starting to dip in the sky, letting a chill rustle the air. Late summer tourists strolled in shorts and sandals trying to fill their lungs with enough Vermont air to last until their next country vacation. They would soon be replaced by other city people, very much like themselves, coming north to watch the leaves changing. Already the nights were brisk. The ski areas were starting to think in terms of the coming winter season, closing down their summer mountain slides, interviewing personnel, testing out the generators that would blow artificial snow across the slopes as soon as the temperature dipped below freezing and promised to stay there.

Mickie walked past the antique shop on the corner of River and Elm, wares displayed across the sidewalk. She swore that the same Sale sign had been taped up the previous winter when they had been there skiing. She waved to the owner (feeling a satisfying closeness to her—she was now *one of them*), a white-haired woman with more wrinkles than years, creaking on a rocking chair in front of the store, knitting and smiling at people who busied themselves among her merchandise.

Mickie headed toward a pleasant-looking shop sandwiched between an old-fashioned ice cream parlor and a needlepoint store with colored yarns in the shapes of flowers dressing the window.

The wooden sign above the entranceway was handlettered in peeling black paint and said simply Books, the *s* a little crowded. Stenciled on the glass doors were the words Southern Vermont Historical Society. Inquire Within.

The nightmare had stayed with her. And like a vision that takes firm hold and refuses to let go, she saw again and again the terrifying finish when the boy had stepped out of the shadows, plunged the knife into her, and headed toward Jenny. Just thinking about it made her shudder and shut her eyes.

She knew she could easily dismiss the nightmare to a subconscious reaction to the suicide note, projecting the dead woman's guilt and fears onto herself; she didn't need a psychiatrist to explain that to her. But there were so many unanswered questions left by the letter, and curiosity was prodding her to learn more about the past of her house.

She pushed open the door to the airy tinkle of Chinese bells. The air conditioning hummed loudly, but it was still stuffy in the shop with the westerly sun beating down on the untinted glass. Dust particles danced in the rays of light, and shadows splashed across the floor.

There were paperback racks running the length of the store with a broad selection of gothics, mysteries, sagas, and romances, all neatly stacked by category. The hardcover books were limited mostly to the recent best sellers and shelves of special interest books on farming, cheese-making, weaving—the local industries—and several books on diet and exercise. Mickie was pleased to notice two of the books she had worked on recently.

"Hello?" she called tentatively, looking around. "Is anyone here?"

"Yes, yes, hello," a voice came back.

An elderly man shuffled out from behind a curtain in the back of the store. He was adjusting his glasses and peering out over them at Mickie. As he drew closer Mickie noticed crumbs on his shirt, as if he had just finished eating. He looked almost comical, an absent-minded professor, the type one would expect to own a small bookshop in Vermont. He was slender, and his wrinkled pants held up by light blue suspenders seemed a little too large for him. He had a full head of white hair and his pale face was stubbled with a gray beard. His skin was lined and weatherbeaten, but he sported a natural smile that lit his face and his eyes were friendly and warm.

"Yes?" he asked pleasantly. "Can I help you?"

"Is this the Southern Vermont Historical Society?" Mickie asked tentatively.

"Actually, no," the man said. "This is the Glendon Book Shop."

Mickie frowned. "The sign on your door—"

"Ah," he said and pointed to the back of the store from where he had come. "Historical Society is right through there." He stuck out a leathery hand. "My name is Stoneham. Nice to meet you, Miss—"

"Mrs. Talman. I called."

"Yes. Mrs. Talman." He seemed to sift the name through his mind and Mickie saw it register. "The lady with the house."

"That's one way of putting it," Mickie said with a smile.

Stoneham chuckled. "That's how we have most things catalogued, so I guess that's how I think." He extended his arm to indicate she should lead the way to the back of the store. She parted the hanging gray curtains and found herself in a windowless room little larger than a child's bedroom. It was stacked floor to ceiling with file drawers, boxes, folders, and newspaper clippings. A desk and chair were crammed against a wall.

"The Southern Vermont Historical Society, I presume," Mickie asked.

"None other," Stoneham said proudly.

"I apologize for my filing system," he said with an embarrassed grin. "But as you can see we're not yet computerized. Not that we have any plans for that matter. This is a rather low-budget operation. Little more than a labor of love. The state pays for the subscriptions, all the other expenses are mine." He winked at her confidentially. "Although deductible."

"I didn't really know what to expect when I phoned," Mickie said, glancing uncertainly around the room. "Or whether you could help me or not." What she had expected were neat rows of file cabinets and local crafts on display. The room was warm and confining.

"Well, then, let's just see," Stoneham said. He offered her a swivel-back chair, the only one in the room, but Mickie saw that it was covered with crumbs and declined.

"We have clippings and records dating back at least two hundred years. My great-great-grandfather had a strong sense of the future about him. He passed his love of data to my great-grandfather, who passed it on down the line to me. I grew up among these clippings and learned to love the role of historian. Unfortunately, my son doesn't share the family interest, and I wouldn't dream of letting my grandson take over once I'm gone, but I think the state has some plans for it then. Make it part of the library system, I believe. But by then," he winked, "I'll have my own little file somewhere in here and frankly I won't give a damn. Would you like some tea, Mrs. Talman?"

"Oh, no, thank you."

"Please," he said with a sad smile. "I really hate to drink alone."

Mickie didn't have the heart to decline.

There was a small hotplate on which a kettle of water was steaming. Taking two cups from a shelf, Stoneham made the tea.

"Sugar?"

"Please. Two spoonfuls."

"Sweet," he said, and then smiled at Mickie. "Like you."

Mickie accepted the tea and met his eyes over the steaming cup. "Why, Mr. Stoneham," she said in her best Scarlett O'Hara imitation, "if I didn't know any better, I would say you were flirting with me."

"And I would say you're right," Stoneham answered. "It isn't often we get such an attractive young woman in here. Mostly grizzled old farm folk wanting the latest weather almanac." He lifted the cup in toast. "Here's to friendship."

"To friendship," Mickie agreed and clinked teacups with him.

"Now I realize I'm probably taking up a lot of your valuable time, and you didn't come here on this lovely afternoon to sip tea with an old man like me, so what can I do you for?"

"Actually I am in a bit of a rush, but I don't want to appear rude. I have two children, and this is the first day of school, and I'd like to get home before they do."

"I understand. The first day in a new school can be quite traumatic at that. I remember back to when—" he broke off. "I don't think you really want to hear what I remember back when and"—he added with a smile—"I don't really remember it anyway. So down to business. What can I look up for you?"

"As I said on the phone," Mickie started. "We've just moved to Glendon—"

"Right, right," Stoneham said, remembering. "You bought the Cuttings House."

"The Cuttings House?" Mickie questioned.

Stoneham nodded. "That's how it's filed. Ethan Cuttings built the house in the late twenties. *Eighteen* twenties, that is. I'm familiar with most of the old houses in the area." He winked. "Saw a lot of them go up myself."

Mickie laughed appreciatively, but her tone abruptly changed as she pulled the letter out of her pocket.

"I found this in our basement. A suicide note. It was hidden between two pages of a book of poetry in an out-of-the-way room. Almost like whoever wrote it hoped it would never be found."

"Or whoever found it first," Stoneham said, looking at her sagely over his bifocals, "hoped it would never be found again,"

Mickie nodded. A possibility.

Stoneham took the letter from her. She watched his eyes as he read it. He seemed to be examining the paper as much as the words. He clucked twice to himself.

"Interesting. And undoubtedly authentic."

"I first went to Glendon Library, hoping they could help me find some background on our house, and they referred me here. If you've got a file on the house, maybe I can understand what this suicide note means." She hesitated, but felt she could take this man into her confidence. His eyes exuded trust, compassion. She lowered her voice. "It frightens me."

"Yes," Stoneham murmured. "I can see your being disturbed by this letter. Sooooo," he said almost in singsong, and let a smile break across his face to ease the moment, "let's just see what we shall see."

He moved to a file cabinet nestled in the corner of the room. He knelt down to the lowest drawer, his knees cracking audibly. He rummaged through the cabinet for several moments as Mickie's eyes swept the room. In contrast to the immaculate bookshop out front, this room seemed as if an earthquake had struck. Folders were strewn around the room, some sticking haphazardly out of file drawers; tattered and yellowed newspapers were in piles on the desk and floor. It seemed as if files hadn't been put away in years, and she hoped that the file on her house—if there was one—would be in its proper place. Stoneham straightened up, a thin folder in his hand.

"Eureka!" he said, smiling. "Your house does have a file." And his face clouded a little. "Which means, I'm sorry to tell you, that something untoward once happened there. My family has always had a bit of a gruesome streak, and we tend to save the sensational. But then how is history measured except by wars and deaths?"

He opened the file and read what was in it himself. He frowned. The lines on his face seemed to grow longer, deeper; his eyes lost their sparkle.

"Yes, your house has had its share of tragedy."

"What?" Mickie asked, leaning toward him. Her fingers tightened around the suicide note until the paper started to crinkle.

"Let me take that from you," Stoneham said, afraid she might damage the valuable old testament. "I'll make you a copy, if that's okay?" Without waiting for an answer he took the suicide note from her and moved toward the photocopy machine across the room.

"Yes, fine," Mickie said, a bit numbly. "Please let me see the file."

"Yes, yes, of course," Stoneham said. "Sorry. You have every right to see it. The house is yours now."

Mickie knew that the old man meant nothing by his words or tone, bur she shivered nervously in spite of herself.

She looked into the file. There was a small newspaper clipping from the *Burlington Times,* dating back to November 13, 1861.

Tragedy struck the town of Glendon Friday when six girls were killed during a children's party. An unidentified assailant broke into the house owned by Jonas Cuttings and murdered the children. Cuttings, alerted by his daughter, raced up the stairs, but was not in time to save any of the others. Cuttings reports that he chased the man out of the house with a knife but was unable to catch him. Examination of the house showed no doors or windows had been tampered with and no one knew how the assailant got in. Description of the man was sketchy.

Local officials believe the assailant was insane because of the horrible ways in which the children were killed. One was burned, one stabbed, one . . .

Mickie couldn't read anymore and looked up from the article in horror. She met Stoneham's eyes.

"You see?" he asked gently. "I'm sorry."

"Yes," Mickie mumbled, tight-lipped, numb. She was aware her hands were shaking.

There was a second item in the file, another clipping a year later. Mickie skimmed it quickly. It told of the accidental strangulation death of the daughter of Jonas and Laura Cuttings. *Laura* Cuttings, Mickie noted. The woman who wrote the suicide note had a name.

The words from the note jumped back at her.

He has returned for me as he had for Sarah. Had the madman returned for Sarah? she questioned. And then for Laura as well? Did that make sense? No—because Laura committed suicide. And why did Laura feel she could have somehow prevented the deaths? *Did any of it make any sense?*

The file also contained the birthdates of Jonas, Laura, and Sarah, and the dates and causes of their deaths. Jonas succumbed to pneumonia three years after Laura's suicide.

Something was missing.

"Is this all there is to the file?" Mickie asked.

"All that there appears to be."

Mickie looked around the room, at the piles of papers and manila folders. "Would there be anything else?"

"I wouldn't think so," Stoneham said. "Most of what is unfiled is recent material. From around nineteen fifty," he added with a smile. "My ancestors were a bit more tidy and conscientious than I am. I tend to get a little too absorbed in what I read. I've spent lots of time going back through the old files for a sense of history, and I'm afraid I've fallen somewhat behind in my current work—like a whole generation." He let his eyes roam the room. "But, no, I wouldn't think anything unfiled here would belong to you. And there's no recent history of the house that should concern you. At least not in my lifetime."

"There's no mention of the son," Mickie said.

"Excuse me?"

"The son," she repeated and pointed to the suicide letter. "The whole family is accounted for—Jonas, Laura, Sarah. But not the son. This letter says he died too."

"Hmm," Stoneham agreed. "It's possible the records are sketchy from back then, that a clipping was overlooked. Although great-grandfather was rather thorough—eighteen sixty—yes, that would be the time great-grandad was officiating at the Society. As soon as a house was identified and flagged as something worth remembering, he was very careful about keeping his eyes open. I don't think he would have missed another death in that house—sorry, just speaking professionally, of course. No," he shook his head with assurance. "It's possible that nothing was ever written about him. Or he died before the file on the house was opened. What you can do is check the county records bureau at the courthouse. I believe they go back that far. Or very close. It's possible that you can at least get the birth and death dates of the boy."

"Yes," Mickie said. Suddenly substantiating the boy's death seemed very important to her. It was a gap and she wanted it filled. And then she remembered something else. "Another girl died in our house. An Essie—" She searched for the last name but didn't remember if Nina had mentioned it. "It wasn't too long ago. About thirty years."

Stoneham shrugged. "Nothing in the file. But that might be an item that hasn't been filed yet." He indicated the mounds of unfiled clippings. "Somewhere here." He noticed Mickie's face and smiled warmly. "I don't want you leaving here with a frown, okay? There's nothing so bad that a smile can't make it better." He took his thumb and middle finger and tugged at his lips, bringing them up into a smile. Despite herself, Mickie matched his grin.

"Thank you, Mr. Stoneham. Those are lovely words."

"And true ones. Remember that. And my thanks to you for brightening up what would have been a rather dull and ordinary day. I'm only sorry that your day couldn't have been as good as mine. Let yourself out, why don't you? I think you've stirred me on to do some catching up back here. I don't think great-great-grandfather would be proud of this mess."

The courthouse was across the town and, hoping the MD license plates would keep her from getting a ticket, Mickie left her car in a no-parking zone. The records bureau was on the second floor, at one end of a Tshaped hallway. The director of records, Bob Greeley, was a young man, dressed in a three-piece charcoal gray suit, a contrast to Mr. Stoneham. He politely listened to her request to examine the records, asked the proper questions about why she was inquiring about the birthdates of people who had died a century and a half before, allowed how they were public records and she had every right to see them, but she had to understand that those records were kept down in the basement, and begged her to please come back another time when he wasn't so busy.

But Mickie persisted and a flash of fear deep within her eyes convinced Greeley he should help her.

The courthouse basement was almost as damp and dusty as her cellar at home. They had to step over cartons that littered the hallways to finally reach the record section they needed.

The appropriate drawers were opened, papers pushed, records pulled.

There was a listing for Jonas Cuttings (1820–1865); his wife Laura (1821–1862); and Sarah (1852–1861). That was all. No other children. It was the end of the family line. No mention of a son, no listing of a birth or death.

"Can there be anything else?" Mickie asked, confused. Why wasn't there a record of the son anywhere?

"What is it that you're looking for?" Greeley asked.

"There was a son in this family. I'm curious about his death."

"Can you tell me why?"

Mickie tightened her lips and answered honestly. "I don't know why, but for some reason it's important to me. That's not answering your question, I know, and I apologize. You've been so helpful to me . . ."

She turned away from him, preoccupied. He noticed her intensity and had an idea.

"One suggestion. It might be a bit unpleasant and perhaps time-consuming."

"What?" Mickie hung on his words, willing to grab at anything.

"These people lived in Glendon, right?"

"Yes."

"You might consider paying them a little visit then." He smiled at her puzzled expression. "We might not have the records, but a cemetery is sure going to have the bodies. If you knew which church they attended, that's your starting-off point."

"Thank you," Mickie said, suddenly brightening. "An excellent idea."

They climbed back up to the first floor. Bob Greeley wished her the best of luck and bade her come back and tell him if she ever uncovered anything. He blushed suddenly, acknowledging it was indeed a poor choice of words.

Mickie ran back to her car.

As she drove home with the afternoon sun glaring off the windshield dazzling her eyes, she had the time to fully comprehend the material in the Cuttings file. It was horrifying, truly incomprehensible. Dear God! Six girls killed by a madman. And then a year later he returned for little Sarah Cuttings, the one child he had missed. And then again for Laura and caused her suicide? She shook her head. It couldn't have happened.

A layer of clouds drifted across the sun and a breeze swept through the car chilling her.

As she passed the Union Christian Church, a one-room country wood-and-brick church, she eyed the cemetery to the side and rear of it. Rows of ordered tombstones stood at attention in some sections, in others the stones were set into the ground randomly, seemingly without thought to placement or design. Several stately mausoleums towered over the headstones, grim reminders of the inevitability of death. She'd search the cemetery tomorrow. The Cuttings graves would not be hard to find.

She pounded her fist against the steering wheel.

Damn it! she almost shrieked out loud. *Children were killed in my house!*

She went through the house making certain all the windows downstairs were closed and locked, the back door as well, as if her actions could blot out the tragedies that had happened there. Then she thought about the old ladies and how tightly shut they had kept the house.

Rufus didn't come in from his office until dinner was already on the table and the children in place. He rubbed his hands together as he sat down.

"One week of work and I'm already two weeks behind in my paperwork. I'm going to spend the rest of my life trying to catch up." He moaned. "Can you believe it? Even on the first day of school I saw twenty kids. No—make that twenty-one. There was a set of twins with colds."

Todd smiled weakly at his father's joke. He was still angry at his father for scolding him for going into the cellar, and he didn't feel like joking; he wanted to punish his father, to make him feel bad for yelling at him.

Then Rufus added, "I don't know whether to bill them for one visit or two. What do you think, Todd?"

At first Todd didn't answer, but then he realized that his father was trying to be friendly; the incident was forgotten, so it seemed, and that was really what he wanted as well. He thought a moment longer. "What's going to help my allowance, Dad?"

Rufus laughed. "I'll send them a bill for two." He looked up at Mickie, who was standing at the stove stirring a pot of spaghetti and meatballs. "You think, hon?" he asked, trying to draw her into the conversation. He was surprised that Mickie was so quiet.

"I guess so," she said, distracted. Then added, "Rufe, I have to talk to you after supper."

"Sure. What's up?"

"Nothing that can't wait." She tried to make her voice sound casual, but there was an underlying note that rang out: *important*.

"You're sure?"

Mickie waved him off. "After we eat. It's okay."

Rufus served up the spaghetti and addressed the children. "Well, we must have some news around here. How was the first day of school?"

Jenny chatted happily about her day. Todd was more reticent, having reached the age where his parents didn't have to know all of his business. Except for what happened in the gym, the day had been passable. He thought about mentioning the incident but decided that wouldn't be a good idea. The last time he had had contact with Rick Webb, his father had gotten annoyed with him. It was best to lay low now, he analyzed, and say that everything was fine. He knew he still had to deal with Webb tomorrow. He shrugged noncommittally. "It was all right, I guess. I met a couple of guys." As he lowered his head to eat, his hair flopped into his eyes.

They were barely finished eating when Mickie stood up. "Okay, everybody upstairs for homework. I haven't seen Daddy all day and want to talk to him a little." She tried to smile but found it difficult. "And then later we can make another fire." Rufus eyed Mickie strangely but said nothing. "I assume they give homework in Vermont," she asked Todd with a forced smile.

Todd rolled his eyes and pushed himself away from the table. "Do they ever?" Homework in six subjects was going to be something. What did they expect from a guy up here?

"We'll call you down later for dessert in the living room."

The children got up and ran out of the kitchen. Rufus, still silent, watched them go. Mickie almost collapsed back into her chair.

"What was that all about?" Rufus asked.

Mickie quickly filled him in about the suicide note, her day, everything. Rufus listened, stone-faced, interested. Then when she was finished, what had been bottled up inside her for the afternoon suddenly sprang out. "How could something like this come as a surprise to us, Rufe?" she asked. She rubbed her eyes and covered her face with her hands.

"I understand, Mickie," he said gently. "But it was a long time ago." He reached across the table and touched her hand, pulled it away from her face. She looked at him. "None of this has anything to do with us. None of this can touch or change our lives one bit. You've got to know that. Just strip away the gut reaction, the horror of what happened, and when you start thinking clearly, you're going to see that what I'm saying is correct. It just doesn't matter."

"Such terrible things have happened here."

"It was all a long time ago," Rufus breathed, almost in a whisper. "Remember that."

Mickie's eyes darted around the room. Her house suddenly looked so different than it had before. A suicide. Murders. And then there was the little girl, Essie. Everyone who came into this house seemed to die!

"We check out the entire house, top to bottom, inside and out. Foundation, plumbing, wires, roofing, termites." She started to laugh, but it was laughter mixed with almost panicky tears. "But nobody bothered to check out its past. I guess now we know why the house was so cheap, don't we? Because nobody else wanted to buy it. There's always a catch, isn't there, Rufe? You never get something for nothing. Well, this is a hell of a catch, isn't it?"

She got up from the table and walked over to the sink, leaned against it and stared into the drain. Then she quickly turned back to Rufus as the new idea formed.

"Do you think we can call off the deal? Get out of it somehow? Get our money back?"

Rufus's voice was low. "No, hon. We own this house."

"What if we say we bought it under false pretenses? Withheld information?" She was grasping, she knew.

"Do you want to move, Mick?" Rufus asked quietly.

She shrugged. "How can I answer that?" Then quickly she added, "Of course I can answer. No! Besides we have everything we own tied up here. No, I don't want to move, Rufe."

"Then listen to me." He got up and walked over to her, cradled her face in his hands, tilted it up to meet his. He looked directly into her eyes and held her hypnotically. "I don't want you making yourself crazy over this. It's not healthy for you or any of us. Let's not look for anything more, okay? Don't go to that cemetery tomorrow. We're starting clean in this house. Yes, there were deaths. It's an old house. I just want you to understand, hon, that what happened in the past has no meaning to us." His eyes were wide and compassionate, his face warm and sure.

"I'll try to see your point of view," she said distantly.

"That's all I can ask." There was silence for a moment. "Where's the suicide letter?" Rufus asked softly.

Mickie hesitated, her eyes flitting from him to the corners of the room, then back to him. "Mr. Stoneham at the Historical Society kept it."

"Good. So you won't be bothered by it."

"No."

Her eyes dropped to the floor. She had lied to Rufus, she knew. She still had the photocopy in her office, put back between the pages of the poetry volume. For some reason she didn't want to give it up.

"So we're in agreement then?" Rufus asked gently.

She nodded imperceptibly.

"No more worries?"

"No." Her voice was small.

"No traipsing around in cemeteries?"

"No, Rufe. No traipsing around in cemeteries." And suddenly her voice was a little stronger, her eyes a little brighter, as she felt his strength pass on to her. Perhaps this talk was what she had needed all day. A fresh viewpoint, a calm, rational look at the facts without the complications of a mother's fears. What was she worrying about, *really*? That a threat hung over her house, that a madman was coming back a century later to kill again? She felt a feeling of relief flood through her. She was being silly, jittery; perhaps allowing herself to be gripped by the remnants of her insecurity about giving up their New York lives for unfamiliar ones.

"I'm sure you're right, Rufe," she said softly. "Nothing that happened can touch our lives."

"Good!" he said with a wide grin and pulled her to him, hugging her tightly.

But her eyes were still glazed, still distant, her voice not as full as either of them would have liked. She had put herself through too much anxiety to do a complete reversal. But she was feeling better than she had felt all afternoon. She had shared this with Rufus, was no longer carrying it alone, and his advice was good, his words what she needed to hear. Like Jenny, when she had been afraid to move here and just needed the confirmation that all was okay.

"I'm going to go upstairs now and play with Jenny," Rufus said. "You'll be all right?"

"I'm fine now, Rufe. Really. Hysterics are over. I promise."

"Good," he said. "But if you decide to get another bout, call me. I'm not far."

"Go. I'll finish up down here." And she shooed him out of the kitchen.

But having freely voiced her feelings of ease, she was suddenly fearful that maybe she had inadvertently called upon the evil spirits to come into their lives and do their worst.

It was a damned if you do, damned if you don't situation, she analyzed, but yes, Rufus was right. She did have the capacity to make herself certifiably crazy. A little like the old ladies, she thought with a humorless smile. And she vowed she would not let it happen.

Rufus and Jenny were in the toy room, and it was difficult to tell who was having a better time.

For Jenny there was nothing spooky about the carousel when her father was there to wind it up. The horses bobbed happily and the calliope music was peppy and pleasing. The puppets weren't frightening when he lifted them off the wall and slipped his hand inside their cloth bodies or worked the marionette strings in performance for her. Jenny sat on the hobby horse and clapped as Rufus put on a show and tried to manipulate two of the marionettes at once and get them to dance. It was a mess of spastic arms and legs, and that was indeed why Rufus labeled their dance "the jerk."

"What's that you say?" Rufus asked suddenly.

Jenny looked at him curiously. She hadn't said anything.

"Shh." Rufus raised a finger to his mouth. He put his hand to his ear, cocked his head, and listened. "Don't you hear it?"

"What, Daddy?" Jenny asked.

"The clown," Rufus said, pointing to one of the marionettes. "It's talking."

Jenny frowned. "I don't hear anything," she said, suddenly a little nervous.

Rufus leaned in toward the clown marionette. He bobbed his head up and down, listening, understanding. He repeated the words of the marionette, slowly, as he was hearing them. "You say you want to go for a ride on the rocking horse, but you can't because Jenny is on it?" He smiled and Jenny relaxed. Her father was only fooling around. The marionette wasn't really talking.

Rufus put on a hurt face and looked at his daughter. "You hear that, Jen? You want to give the clown a chance to ride?"

Jenny laughed. "Okay. But I want to push." She hopped off the horse. Rufus danced the marionette over to it. The clown tried to swing its left leg over the horse. One try. Two.

"Alley-oop," Rufus said and plopped the marionette square in the saddle.

"That was good, Daddy," Jenny said. "This is fun." She started to push the hobby horse and give the marionette a ride.

"Isn't it?" Rufus smiled, suddenly feeling a closeness to his daughter like never before. And then it hit him. This was really one of the few times that he could remember being all alone with Jenny, and now that he thought about it, wasn't that odd? He was usually out with the family all together or with both of the children at the same time. He felt a twinge of regret and shame. My God! Had he been *that* busy that he had never really gotten to know his daughter? Mickie was so much closer to Jenny than he was, and he immediately resolved to change that.

He smiled at Jenny, who happily smiled back. She had Mickie's smile, full, round with all teeth showing, although two of her front ones were missing, dimples at the corners of her mouth. He was so proud of his little girl. She was pretty, articulate, intelligent. A straight-A student, unlike Todd, who wasn't really a student at heart and was struggling to maintain his B-minus average.

"Do you like it up here, Jen?" he asked.

"Oh, yes, Daddy." She opened her arms to hug him.

"Do you want to stay here for ever and ever?"

"And ever!" she finished happily.

"That's my girl." He beamed and kissed her cheek. "I love you so much, Jenny," he said. "You're the absolute best daughter in the whole world."

"And you're the absolutely best Daddy," she said.

"What do you want to do next?"

"I want to ride on the horse again."

"Okay, then. Let's just get this guy off and you on. One, two, three, alley-oop!" he sang. He swung the marionette off the horse and Jenny jumped on. The door opened.

"Hi, Todd," Jenny said cheerfully.

"I got tired of doing my homework and came to play too."

"Did you finish?" Rufus asked.

"Most of it. It's all bullshit," he shrugged.

"Watch your language, Todd."

"Sorry."

"And I'm sure it's not all bullshit, so I think you'd better go back now and finish up everything, okay?"

"I'll do it later, Dad. It's not much. What are you guys doing?"

"*Now,* Todd," Rufus said. "You're in the seventh grade, and you'll be getting lots of homework every night. You can't let yourself fall behind. Besides, *I'm* playing with Jenny now."

"But I'm tired. I need a break."

"Todd, please go back to your room," Rufus said. Jenny stopped pushing the hobby horse and looked curiously at her father. Todd didn't move. "*Todd, I want to be alone with Jenny now!*"

"I just wanted to play a little too," he whined.

"Todd! I said something to you!"

"This is my house too!"

"Todd!" Rufus's voice was sharp. He looked up and saw Mickie opening the toy room door.

"All right then," Todd said angrily. "Who needs any of you!" And he turned and slammed past his mother and out of the room.

"Rufe?" Mickie questioned.

"I sent him to finish his homework, Mick," Rufus explained and then turned his attention back to Jenny. "Let's keep playing, okay?"

But for Jenny the magic was gone. She went through the motions of rocking the horse while Rufus danced a marionette around her. She liked being all alone with her father, but she wouldn't have minded if Todd had played too.

Todd sat hunched over his desk, angry at being excluded. But he had too much homework left to worry about not playing with a bunch of dolls. Although that wasn't the point, he knew. He was memorizing French verbs when suddenly his stomach flipped. He knew immediately what was making him feel this way. Tomorrow was only a few short hours away, and he'd have to see Rick Webb again.

He could almost see the leering smiles on the faces of Rick and his friends, the jabbing of his hand against the lockers. By luck, and only luck, he hadn't been beaten up today. But how long would his luck last? He knew he couldn't live his life in fear of Rick Webb.

Concentrate.

Yeah, right, he thought. A fat lot of good that did him today.

But he remembered when he had concentrated on Rick and stopped him cold, made him grovel and beg for release.

Todd continued to copy his French verbs, but his mind was suddenly elsewhere, as the visions performed for him. He could concentrate and make anything happen. He was Super Todd and he had *the power*.

They were in the gym and Rick was coming toward

him. But Todd let him advance because he knew he could stop him. It was just a question of how.

Behind Rick the rope started to twitch and move and come to life because Todd willed it to. It grabbed Rick by his ankles, tripped him to the gym mat, and then slowly snaked around his neck, choking him, hoisting him high into the air, hanging him.

Todd felt a stiffening in his fingers.

Or, if he wanted, he could make Rick pick up a knife, hold it at arm's length in front of him, and force him to plunge it into himself and commit hara-kiri. But Todd would let him struggle, trying futilely to keep his arms from pushing the knife into his body, strain and terror written all over his face. But he would never defeat Todd's commands.

Todd looked down at his right hand, detached, as if it didn't belong to his body. His fingers were slowly curling inward. He threw down his pen.

Or he could drown Rick, forcing him under bathtub water until his lungs filled with water and his eyes bulged.

What was the matter with his hand?

His fingers were tightening, bending stiff at each knuckle, locking in place.

With all his effort, Todd forced his fingers straight and worked out the stiffness. In seconds they were flexible again. He exhaled and wiggled his fingers freely and massaged his right hand with his left.

Writer's cramp, he thought. Too much damned homework.

"Todd, Jenny, are you coming down for breakfast?" Mickie called. "It's late. You're going to miss the school bus."

But Todd was still upstairs, not at all anxious to get to school, worried about bumping into Rick Webb and what would result. He was in the bathroom, killing time, rubbing Rufus's shaving cream onto his face.

"Hey, Dad," he said, when he heard his father passing outside. "Can I borrow your razor?"

"What are you doing, Todd?" Rufus asked.

"Shaving. I think it's about time. I'm in junior high school now and all."

Jenny came out of her room, all dressed and carrying her books. She saw Todd and laughed. "You look like Daddy, Todd."

"Todd, why don't you wipe off your face now," Rufus suggested with an edge to his voice. "If I heard Mommy correctly, it's getting late, and I won't be happy if you miss the school bus."

"I was just playing, Dad," Todd shrugged.

"If you want you can play tonight."

"Like last night?" Todd said sourly.

"Todd, I'm not going to argue with you," Rufus said. "I just want you on that school bus. And clean your room. I don't think you've thrown any of your clothes in the hamper since we've gotten here."

"Yeah," he said and disappeared into the bathroom.

"And how's my little girl this morning?" Rufus asked Jenny.

"I'm a big girl," Jenny protested, and Rufus lifted her off the floor and swung her around.

Todd had to run for the school bus but made it. As he got aboard in front of the house, he saw his father looking at him through his office window and wondered why his father was leaning on him so much. But now he had bigger things to worry about, although happily the bus sailed past Rick Webb's house without picking him up. Maybe he was sick, Todd hoped. Or dead. But he couldn't count on that, and still had to get through the day and last period gym. He carried the fear with him all morning, his entire body on a tension alert.

"Hey, what's with you today?" Jeff asked in the cafeteria at lunchtime. "Jeez, you're jumpy."

"Been having trouble with a guy."

"Who?"

"Rick Webb. I scratched his father's car, and he started beating me up. My father stopped him. I have gym with him, and he cornered me in the locker room yesterday with two friends of his."

"Yeah," Greg interjected. "They run around like the Three Stooges."

"He would have killed me if a teacher hadn't shown up."

"What are you going to do about it?"

"Watch my ass," Todd said, and then laughed shortly. "Got to thinking last night, you know, that it would really be great to have a certain power where you can just wish somebody dead. Make things happen like that." He snapped his fingers. "All I'd have to do is concentrate and make anything happen to Rick." He smiled weakly. "You think things like that when you're scared."

"Yeah," Greg nodded. "You wouldn't have to be afraid of anything if you had that kind of power."

"Too bad it didn't work yesterday in the locker room." Todd laughed, mostly at himself. "I tried concentrating but nothing happened."

"But something did," Jeff said. "That teacher came in and broke up the fight."

"I guess," Todd shrugged, unconvinced.

He stared past his friends at the rest of the cafeteria, the other children and noise becoming a blur. "Just to concentrate," he said, "and have anything happen at all. I could go around the school and flatten every bully. And then I'd go back to New York and take care of those goons who mugged me." He beat his chest with his fist. "Hey, just call me Super Todd."

"Hey, Super Todd," Greg said. "If you're not going

to eat the rest of your sandwich, can I have it?" He pointed to the cafeteria hot lunch of roast beef. "This stuff's going to stunt my growth."

Todd passed him the remaining half of his tuna sandwich. He wasn't really all that hungry. He still had the rest of the afternoon and the gym class to get through, and in reality he wasn't Super Todd, and he was afraid.

He asked for a new locker and got it. It was in the first aisle right near the door. He was changing into his gym clothes when Rick and his friends came in. He stiffened. Rick saw him, but said nothing, hardly even glanced at him. And then in the gym he moved right to the high bar, as if Todd didn't even exist. And then as still nothing happened between them when Todd was changing into his street clothes, he breathed easier. And for a wild fraction of a second he thought maybe it was his concentrating that had put a stop to the boy.

But he found out differently on the bus going home. They were nearing their house when Todd felt a tap on his shoulder. He turned around and met Rick Webb's eyes, peeking out from behind his seat. A smile opened on Rick's face. "Hi, Todd-y," he said.

"Hi, Rick," he said tight-lipped.

"And who do we have here?" Rick looked down at Jenny.

"That's my sister and you leave her alone," Todd said.

"Sure," Rick said. "I don't have business with your sister."

The bus pulled up in front of their house. Todd ushered Jenny into their driveway.

"Hey, Todd," Rick called as he started to walk toward his house.

Todd stopped. "Keep walking, Jenny," he whispered, then faced the boy, trying to summon some strength. If it was going to happen, let it happen. "What, Rick?"

"Just thought I'd tell you," Rick said, smiling easily. "To sort of keep you on your toes. I may not get you today, Todd-y. And I may not get you tomorrow. But when I do, it'll be a fate worse than death. Bye bye, sucker."

Todd took off and ran into the house. He was scared and needed his father, but he suspected that his father would only tell him he wasn't observant or careful, or had done something wrong like not cleaning his room.

Well, he thought with a hollow laugh. He could always practice concentrating.

CHAPTER 12

Mickie checked her rearview mirror. Traffic was piling up in back of the car. She was driving much slower than the posted speed limit, taking the bumps easily. At an antique shop in North Milford, she had found a gilded oval-shaped mirror that cried out to be bought, and she didn't want to break it on the trip home. What the house didn't need, she suspected, was seven years of bad luck.

It had been a week since the discovery of the suicide note and her talk with Rufus. Neither had mentioned it again, and she knew that Rufus considered the subject closed. She had resolved not to let what she had discovered about the house bother her again.

But as she neared home she drove past the Union Christian Church and noticed that the churchyard was filled with cars, and more were parked along the shoulder of the road. Unusual for a weekday afternoon.

The wooden doors to the Union Christian Church swung open and out of the corner of her eye Mickie caught a glimpse of the casket being carried out by six dark-suited pallbearers. She hit her blinker signal and pulled off the road. She silenced the engine and turned to watch the funeral.

A line of mourners left the church, walking down the brick steps, turning up the path, following the casket. The burial was going to be in the churchyard cemetery.

Mickie got out of the car. This was the cemetery

where she suspected the Cuttings family was buried. As her eyes fell on the rows of tombstones, Rufus's words came back: *No traipsing through cemeteries, Mick.* And she had agreed with him. Yet here she was.

But it was as if this funeral were an invitation she could not pass up, and besides, Rufus wouldn't have to know about it.

She waited for a break in the traffic and crossed the road.

The pallbearers were carrying the casket up the cobbled path leading to the crossbar cemetery gate. The mourners were lined up behind. Judging from the crowd in attendance, Mickie could only conclude that the deceased was a person of importance, a church elder perhaps. She thought she recognized one or two of the people from the reception, although no one acknowledged her.

She felt conspicuous standing on the roadway outside the low stone cemetery wall, so blatantly watching the funeral, a gawker at a spectacle. She hesitated momentarily. She knew Rufus would be furious, but she entered the churchyard anyway and joined the procession of mourners.

She felt exposed, out of place; she did not belong there. Her reasons for being at the funeral were not pure, and she felt the mourners would turn to her in accusation, in judgment. She felt uncomfortable, sensing disapproving eyes on her.

But still she walked with the processional. She was drawn to this cemetery and had a feeling it was more than just curiosity.

The pallbearers turned away from the road, heading beyond the rear of the church to the burial plot. The cemetery was much larger than it had appeared from the roadway, stretching a good distance behind the church to a pasture and farmhouse beyond as the land sloped deeper into the Glendon Valley.

The pallbearers stopped before an open grave. They laid the casket on top of taut burial straps, which would lower the coffin into the hole. The people fanned out in a half moon to get closer to see. Mickie stayed on the fringes of the crowd as the burial began with the reading of the Twenty-third Psalm.

"The Lord is my shepherd, I shall not want," the minister intoned.

Above them birds called to each other in cheerful song, a travesty during the funeral service, but drawing attention nonetheless to the continuation of life.

Mickie started to drift back, away from the burial site. Her eyes went from grave to grave, hoping she might see headstones marked Cuttings.

"He restoreth my soul."

The minister's voice was softer now, more distant, as she wandered behind a small thicket of trees which blocked the sound. The air was quiet, eerily still. There was no whine of cars, no rustle of breeze. The peacefulness of a country cemetery.

She strolled along the cobblestoned paths, eyeing the tombstones, glancing at the names on the stately mausoleums, telling herself she wasn't really looking for the Cuttings stones, just strolling through the churchyard cemetery. But she wasn't fooling herself.

There were hundreds of tiny, sagging tombstones, many adorned with artwork. These must have dated back to the early days of the church, Colonial times, she thought. She knelt down to more closely inspect the tombstones. Lichens covered many of the older, uncared-for stones, but she was still able to make out their designs: etchings of skeletons, hourglasses with funneling, dripping sands, father-time figures with scythes and scenes of the resurrection, all leaving no doubt in the minds of passersby about the certainty of death.

She tried to decipher some of the faded, weather-worn inscriptions but found them blurred, unreadable. She ran her hand over one of the stones, trying to clean out the lettering with her nails. True American art, she thought to herself, and marveled at how beautiful they must have been when first cut. Some stones of quarried marble seemed quite expensive, while some of the poorer grave markers were made of wood, rotted and decayed from the passage of time and the cruelty of the Vermont winters.

The dates on one tombstone caught her eye: 1913–1917. A four-year-old child was buried there. The stone was clear, surprisingly so compared to the others, and Mickie knelt down to see it more closely. The child's name was Rose Jenkins. The stone sported a cherub resting on a cluster of grapes, badly rubbed away by the elements. Her eyes misted over as she thought of the little girl who had barely started life before death claimed her.

She didn't hear the sound behind her, but saw instead the shadow cross over the tombstone.

With a start she stood up. Embarrassed. A little frightened.

There was a man there. He was elderly, with white hair and a gray beard mottled with brown. He was dressed in a rumpled suit and bow tie. His eyes were sad, his face lined and tired, but there was warmth around his mouth. He carried a brown cane.

"I'm sorry," he said in a voice hoarse from years. "I didn't mean to startle you. I came around that mausoleum and saw you kneeling here." He looked down at the gravestone and frowned. "Family?" he asked.

"Oh, no, no," Mickie said, recovering. "Just . . ."

"Browsing?" the man asked and a smile tugged at his lips. He held up his hand. "Only joking. I have no right to question your being here."

"Were you attending the funeral?" Mickie asked.

"The funeral?" The man looked confused a second

and then quickly said, "Oh, no. I was watching from behind those trees. I don't know whose funeral it is. They're almost finished now. Lowering the body in. That's the saddest part as I see it. The true finality. Lowering the body. Tossing clumps of earth onto the casket. As if until that very final moment it's still possible for the deceased to spring the coffin lid wide, step out, and do a jig. But once it's covered," he mused, "well, the dead must remain dead." He smiled at Mickie. "I guess you must be wondering what I'm doing here?" he asked.

"I have no right to ask," Mickie smiled, realizing she was being charmed by this old man.

"I'll answer anyway," he said, "because I'll bet you don't know many people who take their afternoon strolls through cemeteries now, do you?" He winked at her confidentially. "There's a special serenity here that's missing anywhere else, a stillness in the air as if even the elements have respect for the dead. Where I can be alone with my thoughts, the songs of birds, and"—he surveyed the stones around him—"with some of my friends."

"I'm sorry," Mickie stumbled.

"Oh, don't be. They all lived to ripe old ages, and God took them peacefully. No. None of them should have any complaints about their deaths. Although where they all are now," he added with a devilish twinkle in his eyes, "well, that's of course something else altogether."

Mickie wasn't certain how to respond. She looked out into the distance where sheep grazed as they might have a century before, seemingly untouched by the passing of time. Beyond, above the valley, the mountains of the ski areas rose regally skyward in a wall of evergreens, nudging low drifting clouds.

The man smiled warmly at her. "Come. Let's walk a little. Do you have time?"

"Well," Mickie hesitated.

"Indulge an old man who makes a habit of walking through cemeteries." He winked. "Might find it educational."

Why not? Mickie decided. She could look through the cemetery and perhaps this man could even help her.

"Sure," she smiled.

"Good." He pointed ahead of him with the cane. "That's one of my favorite spots over there." There was a circle of rhododendrons surrounded by a ring of neatly mowed grass. A stone bench perched off to the side.

"Wonderful spot to catch the afternoon sun. Of course there won't be too much more of that once winter comes in. Are you from around here?"

"Actually just up the road. We've recently moved here."

"To escape the hustle and bustle of some city, I presume?"

"In a way, yes."

"Good. A wise move. Wise. You'll live longer here than anywhere else." He winked at her suggestively. "Love longer too." Mickie smiled appreciatively, wondering if everybody in the town was going to flirt with her. "The winters are cold and long, but you'll develop a heartiness about you that will scare away any disease. Soon minus ten will feel like thirty. Of course you'll have to put some meat on your bones first."

"Oh, no." Mickie laughed. "I've had to work hard half of my life to keep this figure."

"Ah, yes. Younger people and their resolve to remain slender. Never could understand it. But then I haven't been young for quite some time, and I guess my mind works a little differently these days, tending to creak more." The man drew a breath and surveyed the headstones as if they were his.

"I'll bet you'd be surprised to know that in the early

days of this country a lot of people did what we're doing right now," the man said, almost lecturing. "Took long walks through the local graveyards. Today it's looked on as a bit odd, but back then everybody did it. On the way to church, after church. There wasn't much else to do and"—he winked again—"they never really knew who might be next. Sort of making friends here, you might say."

Mickie felt an involuntary shiver spiral up her spine.

"The funerals were much more elaborate in those days too. Some of them were shows, attended by everyone for miles around. A good funeral was talked about for months. After the burial there was a funeral feast where people drank wine and liquor. In fact, the drinking often began before the services. Me," he sighed, "I'll settle for a simple wooden box and a few people who knew me to shed a tear or two." He looked sad for a moment but then brightened as a new thought occurred. "I've already got my spot picked out. Right through there." He directed her vision with the tip of his cane to a cleared area where graves had just started to be dug. "That way I'll be able to catch the afternoon sun and remember what it was like here."

"You must know the cemetery well, then?" Mickie asked.

"I would say."

"Do you know where the Cuttings are buried?"

"Lots of Cuttings buried here. Very old name. Even have a Cuttingsville north of here aways."

"A family," Mickie prodded. "Jonas Cuttings. His wife, Laura. A daughter. Sarah."

The man thought for a moment. "Wealthy family?" he asked.

"I don't know."

"I think yes. Come. Walk with me."

He led her to a mausoleum near the back fence of

the cemetery. Above the bronze doors in simple lettering was the family name: Cuttings.

"I think this is who you're looking for."

"Thank you."

"May I ask why?" The question was asked quietly, out of friendship. The man wasn't prying.

Mickie hesitated but then answered. "We've just moved into what had been their house. I've found some things which have made me curious about the Cuttings family."

"Ah, a search for roots. Well, you are at the source, or rather, the termination point."

Mickie did not respond. She was looking at the mausoleum: grim, foreboding, more ominous than the humble tombstones of clay or slate that dotted the graveyard.

"Am I to leave you here then?" the man asked softly.

"Please," Mickie said, although still uncertain what she really wanted to do.

"That is fair enough. It's been good speaking with you; or rather, I should say, having you listen to me. I look forward to seeing you again here very soon. But only with us both among the living," he qualified.

Mickie smiled and extended her hand. "Thank you, Mr.—"

"Jenkins."

Mickie seemed to recognize the name.

"That was my sister's grave you were kneeling by when I first came upon you."

Mickie reacted with shame and horror. "I'm sorry. I didn't know," she fumbled.

Mr. Jenkins held up his hand. "No. Don't be. That's why I spoke with you. Anybody with as much compassion as you apparently have is a person I'd like to get to know better." His eyes grew sad and distant as he lost himself to a long buried memory. "Barely four when she died. Influenza."

"I'm sorry," Mickie whispered.

"A beautiful little thing. Do you have children?"

"Yes."

"Take care of them. Watch over them and they'll grow." Jenkins dropped his eyes. "Only four when she died."

"Yes, I will watch my children," Mickie said firmly, assuring this man, assuring herself.

"Good. They will thrive then. Because they have a mother who is warm and loving."

Tears came to Mickie's eyes.

"But enough today," Mr. Jenkins said. "You have your thoughts, I believe." He looked at her wisely over his glasses. "And I have mine." He looked into the sky and rubbed his eyes. "Good. Another hour of afternoon sun. I think I'll catch it back over there. Good day."

He turned and without another word started back up the graveled path. In the distance Mickie was able to see the funeral breaking up as people shook hands and walked back toward the churchyard and their cars. She was alone in the cemetery, in front of the Cuttings mausoleum.

Just where Rufus didn't want her to be.

The mausoleum cast a long shadow across the ground, a black shroud over the smaller stones nearby. It was eight feet high and as many wide. Sculpted angels played across the ebony doors as if to indicate the pleasant peaceful sleep of the dead, instead of the disquiet that must be inside.

My own death has become the only path for me now. Laura's words from the suicide letter sounded within her.

What a poor, troubled family, Mickie thought pitifully and prayed that they finally found their eternal rest.

A breeze rippled, swirling about the first of the dying leaves, rustling through trees in a faint *whooshing* sound that rang eerily through the deserted cemetery. The harsh *caw-caw* of a blackbird in flight disrupted the silence.

There was a bench to the side of the mausoleum and Mickie sat down on it, envisioning Laura on the same bench, coming to visit her children.

She knew she should leave the cemetery, but her curiosity was still strong. She had found their graves; too easily she had been brought here. The question surged through her: Was the son in the mausoleum? But now she wasn't ready to pull open the mausoleum doors and look inside, not quite ready to open up a Pandora's box that still remained sealed.

She thought about the death of Laura, and in her mind's eye she saw her—she had her image now. She was a slight woman with light brown hair and a drawn look on her face, lines etched into her forehead and around her eyes. Deep, frightened-looking eyes filled with remorse. Cold eyes that no longer held love. Sad, sunken eyes destined for death.

Within her she imagined the poor woman's final moments on earth. She saw Laura reaching for the knife, her eyes narrowing and staring at the blade, her emotions battling with each other, guilt and terror fighting against reason.

The fantasy held Mickie as she saw Laura touch the blade to her skin, bend back her hand and expose her wrist, and cut across it. A thin line of blood immediately appeared, trickling from the open wound. A quick change of hands and the other wrist was slashed. The wounds opened, blood bubbled and flowed. The knife fell to the floor as Laura stared at her hands. She lifted her arms high above her head in supplication, asking heavenly forgiveness. The blood ran down her arms in streams of red.

Laura weakened and fell to the floor in an ever-widening pool of her own blood. Her face touched the floor and stained dark with blood. Suddenly her hand grabbed spastically for the knife. She grasped the handle and struggled to lift it as blood trickled from the corners of her mouth.

It was a moment of cold realization as Mickie saw she was offering the knife to her.

"Here, Mickie," the woman said in a voice lined with death. "If you don't leave that house, you'll be next."

Sudden blackness.

The vision ended.

Mickie opened her eyes. She looked directly into the sun and was caught by a blinding stream of light. She had to close them quickly. Color circles danced in front of her eyes. For a second she was disoriented. Then her eyes opened again and she saw where she was. She rubbed them and shook off the daydream. She fought to warm her body. It was only a vision; there was no danger.

Fantasies, she thought ruefully. The most common one being envisioning the death of self or loved ones.

She got up from the bench and quickly walked away from the mausoleum, back toward the road and her car. Rufus was right, she told herself. She did have the capacity to make herself crazy, and the daydream she just had was proof positive of that. She would forget it. It was only a daydream, nothing more. Product of her own imagination.

But she turned back for one last look at the Cuttings mausoleum. The tomb was lost in the glare of the sun that hovered over the mausoleum, about to dip below it.

As she reached the churchyard again, the parking area was empty. The funeral was over. She quickly crossed the road and climbed into her car. She started up the engine and glanced at her wrists. Her eyes widened in horror.

For a second she thought she saw blood tracing down

her arms. Then she realized they were only streaked brown with dirt from where she had been leaning against the bench.

Fantasies . . .

CHAPTER 13

Rufus hung the mirror in the second-floor hallway opposite the top of the stairs. It was a good addition to the house, he agreed.

Mickie didn't mention her visit to the cemetery; it would have angered him, she knew. But she could still see the knife being offered to her like a coiled snake, the anguish and warning written on the woman's face.

Fantasies, she scolded herself again, *that was all.* But still, it took two hands to lift the saucepan. She was afraid she might drop the pot if she used only one. She steadied herself and vowed that she wouldn't let it get to her.

"Well," Mickie said at the table, when they had finished talking about the day in school. "Isn't anyone around here going to ask me about *my* day? I'm beginning to feel a little left out."

Rufus put his finger to his mouth and winked at Jenny. Nobody should ask Mommy. But Jenny couldn't contain herself and blurted out the question anyway.

"Well, first I bought some new curtains for the kitchen, which Daddy will help me hang tomorrow." Rufus groaned. "And of course you saw the mirror upstairs." Todd eyed his mother in a so what? "And—" Mickie paused dramatically, which made the children start paying attention. "I found a store that has some terrific preseason ski sales going on now. Boots. Bindings. Skis. Everything. And since we have a new house in the mountains, and we'll be doing a lot more skiing this year, Daddy and I have been talking about getting you both some new equipment."

"Great!" Todd said. "Burt bindings too?"

"Whatever you want," Mickie said. "So one day next week we'll go shopping after dinner. You guys up to it?"

"Am I ever!" Todd whooped.

Jenny jumped up and down and clapped her hands. She had had a pair of baby skis until outgrowing them last year. This was going to be her first pair of real skis.

"And that's what I did today," Mickie said. Then she thought, *And attended the funeral of a person I didn't know and sat in front of a mausoleum.* A perfectly normal way to pass a day.

Todd shot her a thumbs up. "You did good, Mommy."

"Somehow I thought you'd say that."

"Hey, Dad," Todd said. "I finished up my homework before dinner. You want to do something later? Teach me to shave or something?"

"No, Todd, I don't think you're quite ready to handle a razor yet."

"Almost, Dad," he said proudly, pointing to his upper lip. "I think I got a couple of hairs growing here."

"Where?" Mickie smiled.

"Well, you gotta look real close but they're there."

"When you don't have to look so close, then we'll talk about it," Rufus said.

"Okay. But you want to do something else? Some Monopoly? Risk?"

"I really have to work tonight, Todd."

"Oh—"

"You've been working every night this week, Rufe," Mickie said. "Take a couple of hours off. Play a game with him."

"No can do." Rufus shrugged with a helpless smile.

"It's been an awful week, Mick, you've seen that. Seems like every kid within a radius of fifty miles has been in to see me. I'm surprised the schools aren't empty. And I've been interviewing nurses in the afternoon. The only time I have to do my paperwork is now. As soon as I get someone to do the transcribing, billing, and making appointments, then my time will open up."

"One night, Rufe," Mickie said.

"Mick—" he said, and the discussion was closed.

"It's okay, Dad," Todd said. "I understand."

"I knew you would, son."

"Yeah." But his voice was laced with disappointment.

"I'll play with you, Todd," Jenny said. "Maybe we can try out the Ouija board."

"Sure, Jen," he said and then addressed his mother. "Can we be excused?"

"Sure," Mickie said, and when they were out of earshot, moved closer to Rufus. "Rufe, it's just like it was back home, you know?"

"*This* is home," he corrected.

Mickie exhaled. "Back in New York then, but you know what I'm saying. You've been in that office every night this week. Todd wants to play with you. *I* haven't even seen you."

"Mick, it's been a particularly bad week. I'm sorry."

"Make an effort. That's all I can ask. For them."

"I'll make an effort," he said automatically.

"It should be tonight. They're so happy about the skis."

"I'll try, okay? I promise I will try."

"That's all I can ask," she said. "That you try."

They finished the meal in silence, but then Mickie said, "Rufe, correct me if I'm wrong, but I don't think you and Todd have exchanged two words since we've been up here."

"I've been busy, Mick. You know that."

"Not too busy to yell at him, though? I've been watching, Rufe."

He looked at her for a second before answering. Then he said, "You watch, Mick. And you can think what you want." Then he disappeared into his office.

Mickie rubbed the tears from her eyes, immediately regretting what she had said.

They hadn't played with the Ouija board for quite some time. The last couple of times out absolutely nothing happened. They asked their questions and sat back quietly until someone got bored and pushed the planchette to the desired letters. They had decided there were no spirits in their West Side Manhattan apartment. Nor in any of their friends' apartments.

"It's all a crock," Todd had said. But in this new house they really could put it to a test. Jenny clapped her hands expectantly. "But we've got to do this right," Todd said. He turned off all the lights except for the Tensor lamp on his desk which he aimed up at the ceiling. Their shadows loomed large on the wall behind them, grotesquely dancing across the ceiling and walls everytime they moved. Jenny giggled involuntarily, nervously.

They balanced the Ouija board on their knees and rested their fingers on the planchette. They were set.

"What shall we ask it?" Jenny whispered and swallowed her giggle.

"How about, Is there anybody here?" Todd said. "I have a feeling about this place." Jenny nodded. Todd inhaled, relaxed his body, and made certain his fingers were lightly on the indicator. His voice went low and deliberate. "Is there anybody here?"

Once asked, the question hung between them waiting for an answer. Todd felt a tingling in his fingertips. Was there a real spirit in the room or just wishful thinking on his part? Power of suggestion? He wanted something to be in the room, and he felt it suddenly in his finger-tips. But it was only a false alarm; the planchette wasn't moving. He wondered how many times wishful thinking had moved Ouija boards.

The children concentrated on the board between them.

For two minutes nothing happened, a very long time to sit quietly, patiently. Disappointment was written across Jenny's face as she stared intently at the board. She looked up briefly at Todd and then redirected her attention back to the planchette in front of them, brow furrowed, as if trying to force a presence to reveal itself. Still nothing.

Then Todd's fingers pressed against the planchette and eased it forward. It moved slightly, barely noticeable to the eye, but Jenny felt its push against her own fingers. Uncertain at first, but hopeful, she said nothing. When it happened again she could not contain herself.

Her eyes widened. She sucked in her breath.

"It's moving, Todd," she said. She had never before seen the planchette move on its own. Had they really invaded the spirit world?

"I know," Todd said softly, a note of awe to his voice. The planchette skidded across the board. It pointed to the letter *H*.

Todd's fingers applied pressure again. The planchette nosed toward the letter next to it.

"*I!*" Jenny exclaimed. "It's saying Hi." Her hands trembled. She almost lifted them off the indicator.

"Don't break it, Jen!" Todd said excitedly. "We've got something here. Total concentration," he repeated and then in a low eerie voice said, "Who are you? What do you want from us?"

The planchette began to move again. Jenny's fingers, lightly resting on her side of the marker, traveled with it. She looked at her brother, her eyes wide now with uncertainty. Todd stared down at his fingertips, concentration etched on his face. The planchette scudded across the board, coming to rest at the *B*.

Then there seemed to be no stopping it as it skidded across the Ouija board, alive with movement, pointing to letter after letter. Jenny was too intrigued to notice Todd's subtle pressure on the marker.

"Don't lose it, Jenny!" Todd said excitedly as he called out the letters already formed.

It was from B-E-N-J-A-M that Jenny put it together.

"Benjamin!" she called out triumphantly, as if she had broken a code. She looked at her brother wide-eyed, suddenly a little frightened, and then at the shadows behind her on the wall. Had they gone too far?

But it was then that she saw the tension in Todd's fingers, felt his push on the planchette. The mood was broken.

"You're moving it, Todd!"

"I am not," he said defensively. "The spirit is doing it."

"I saw you move it!" She lifted her fingers off the planchette.

Todd laughed. The jig was obviously up. "I had you going, didn't I?"

"No fair," Jenny pouted. "I really thought there was a spirit in the room."

"That's because you wanted to believe there was," Todd said. He waved his arms mysteriously but Jenny sloughed him off.

"I thought you said you were going to play honestly," she said, not happy she had been duped.

"I was," Todd said. He put the Ouija board back into its box. "But then I saw you wanted something to happen, and I thought it would be fun. Too bad you caught on. Almost got away with it."

As Todd hoisted the game up onto the shelf in the closet, he realized he *had* intended to play the game honestly and to really search for spirits in this big old house. It was only when they started to play and nothing was happening that he decided to push the planchette and spell out Benjamin.

But then another thought occurred to him.

He remembered his fingers had already been applying pressure to the planchette when the idea came to him. He was pretty certain that he had *first* pushed the planchette—then thought of fooling Jenny.

But that didn't make sense so it couldn't be right.

Nor did he know why he had chosen to write the name Benjamin.

But he dismissed it all. It was just a goof and had worked well; he had really had his sister going. And then he noticed the stiffness in his fingers. They were tight from pushing the planchette. He worked the tension out of them.

When he turned back from the closet, out of the corner of his eye, he saw the ghostlike figure coming at him—white sheeted as he had always imagined. He drew in his breath sharply and swung around to face it.

"Hi, Todd," the figure said in a deep, throaty voice, and then his sister dissolved into laughter, ripping the pillowcase from her head. "Got you, didn't I?"

"Yep." Todd managed a grin.

"Good. Then we're even."

"Not quite," Todd said. He threw up his arms and screamed at her. Jenny shrieked in delight and ran out of the room. Todd raced after her, chasing her across the hall. She beat him to her room, ran inside, slammed the door closed, and leaned against it. Giggling all the way.

The sounds from down the hall brought Todd up from sleep. He rubbed his eyes and strained to hear the noise through the closed door.

There were the sounds of a party. A party? He lay in his bed letting the sounds come to him—faint giggling, happy voices, children's calls. It was a children's party, he realized.

Then he heard his sister's voice. "Come to the party, Todd. Come."

He threw off his covers and his feet found his slippers. He walked to the door and opened it a crack. The sounds were louder, little girl sounds of playing games and having fun.

"Come, Todd," Jenny insisted. "We're waiting for you."

Curious and confused he walked down the hallway to the toy room. He opened the door a crack and peeked in. He saw them—a half dozen girls, all Jenny's age. His sister was blindfolded. She held a pin and was walking toward the picture of a donkey. The girls were trying to direct her.

Todd walked into the room. The fire was full in the hearth. He wanted to join the party.

The first girl who saw him screamed. It was a scream of terror, of revulsion.

The party stopped. The other girls turned to look. His sister removed her blindfold. And when they all saw him they also screamed. Their hands flew to their mouths, their eyes.

Monster! one of them yelled suddenly, loudly, her voice shrieking, cracking. The call was taken up by the others.

Todd froze. In fear. In surprise. In confusion. Why were these girls screaming at him, calling him names, hating him?

The first apple that was thrown hit him square in the chest. He winced from the sudden pain. The apple fell to the floor and rolled away from him. More came. Apples. Party hats. Garbage.

The girls were throwing things at him, staring at him, calling him names. *Monster. Devil. Monster. Devil. Stay away!*

Todd ran out of the room, down the hall. The girls spilled out into the hallway. Todd stopped where the staircase met the second-floor hallway. He was breathing hard.

Then he saw it: The reflection of his hand in the oval-shaped mirror his mother had bought. He stared in amazement. In fear.

It wasn't *his* hand he was seeing. It couldn't be. The hand in the mirror was a distortion, a fraud. Was there anyone else there that the mirror was capturing? No— There was no one behind him.

He stared in horror at the image of his hand and twisted it in front of him to make certain it was real. It was misshapen, his fingers elongated and stiff, like an animal's claw. That was what the girls had seen and made them scream.

At the end of the hall he saw his sister. A look of revulsion was splashed across her face and the word was on her lips: monster. The other girls took up the terrible cry.

Todd flew back to his room, the words of hate echoing in his ears.

As Todd rose up from sleep, his right hand lay under his stomach. He had been sleeping on it and now it was numb; he had no feeling in his fingers. He massaged them with his other hand, and it took ten minutes for the blood to flow and for him to regain feeling.

And as his breathing eased, Todd's thoughts went to the words he knew so well: *Dreams can't hurt me, dreams mean nothing.* He hadn't said that in a long time, not since he was a kid! But there was comfort in them and soon he was asleep again.

CHAPTER 14

'Why didn't you tell us you lived in *this* house!" Jeff said excitedly when he and Greg came over after school to play. "This is where the crazy old ladies lived! Jeez! I don't think anybody's ever been inside here."

"It's a pretty neat house," Todd said, happy to be the center of attention. He led his friends into the kitchen. The house was quiet. His father was working, his mother was out shopping somewhere, and Jenny was next door playing with Cara. "You want to see my room?" he asked proudly. He hadn't cleaned it up, but he didn't think his friends cared.

"Nah," Jeff said. "Later. Let's go see the cellar you told us about."

"Why?" Todd asked. "Nothing down there except old junk. I just got a new microscope. And Monopoly."

"Who knows what we might find down there," Jeff pressed. "I hear the old ladies practiced devil worship or something. Maybe we'll find an altar down there. Or a dead cat! We've tried to look in the cellar windows under the porch, but they're all streaked with dirt and we couldn't see in. This the door?" he asked.

"Yeah," Todd said uncertainly.

"Hey, what's the matter with you?" Jeff asked. "Not chicken, are you?"

"Chicken?" Todd said, hoping his voice didn't give away his fear. "It's my cellar."

"What's down there?" Jeff asked.

"Nothing much. Just a bunch of old junk."

"Well, that's for me. Let's take a look. Okay, Todd?" he asked with a whisper of challenge.

"Sure. I don't give a shit." He opened the cellar door, grateful his parents weren't around to catch him. He indicated his friends should lead the way.

"Not me," Jeff said with a mysterious smile on his face. "I once saw a movie where a guy ran down into the cellar. But somebody had sawed away the stairs and he fell onto spikes that were standing vertical on the floor where the steps should have been. Impaled the guy right on 'em!" He clutched his stomach and let his head roll to the side to mime the dead. "You go first, Todd."

Todd stepped through the cellar door. He hadn't been down there in almost two weeks. He shivered as he remembered standing in the bedroom when Jenny touched his shoulder. He must have jumped four feet into the air, not knowing what *thing* had grabbed him.

He led his friends through the cellar maze. Jeff saluted the mannequin, joking that it was a patient of Dr. Talman's who didn't pull through. Greg tried out a rocking chair with a broken runner.

Then Jeff saw the door. "Hey, what's behind there? That where they keep the bodies buried?"

"Nothing," Todd said. "Just a bedroom."

"A bedroom? Down here?" He pushed the door open as Greg made sound effects with his mouth of a door being inched wide on rusty hinges. The boys stepped inside.

"It *is* a bedroom," Jeff shrugged. "No big deal." He didn't know what he had been expecting.

And when Todd looked at the room now, with the afternoon sun passing through it, and his two friends with him, that's all he saw too: just a bedroom. No big deal.

Greg tried the bed and made a face. "Ugh. Hard. Wouldn't want to sleep on this bed. Wouldn't want to sleep down here at all. Looks like a place you'd put a guy if you wanted to punish him or something. Or hide him."

"Maybe they kept a guy locked up down here and starved him to death," Jeff offered excitedly. "Or maybe an escaped criminal holed up in here. Or a runaway slave."

"There were no slaves in Vermont," Todd said. But something *had* happened down here, he was certain, a tingly feeling told him it was so.

Todd was the last one out of the room and let the latch click shut behind him.

"Hey, neat!" Jeff called. "Would you look at this!"

Todd followed his friend's voice, aware that he had never been in this corner of the cellar before.

"What in the hell is it?"

The statue was sitting on the floor. It was made of iron which was cold to the touch. It had the head and wings of an eagle and the body of a lion. Its front talon was raised, poised, seemingly about to strike, its nose haughty, high in the air. The eyes were dark and painted with enamel. They were shiny and almost seemed to glow.

"That's one mean mother," Greg observed. "I wouldn't want to meet that thing in a dark alley. But I'll bet you've seen worse in New York, huh, Todd?"

The boys laughed. Jeff inspected the statue more closely running his fingers in between the claws of the animal. "Maybe it's some sort of devil," he said seriously.

"I think it's called a griffin," Greg said. "I once saw a picture of it in a mythology book."

Todd only saw the knife because of the way the sun was struggling into the cellar, past the dirt-stained windows. A fine beam of light caught the blade and illuminated it. It was wedged between a support wall of the house and a wooden workbench.

With his friends still poking around the griffin, Todd crossed the room and picked up the knife. This was a find! The blade was long, ten inches, he estimated, or longer. The handle was wooden and ornately carved in a crisscrossing pattern of X's. He looked closely at the knife, carefully holding the handle lightly in his fingers, turning it from side to side. He ran his index finger along the flat of the blade. The dirt came off on his fingertip. Beneath the layer of dust he saw the gleam of the metal. He ran the knife crosswise against his pants, cleaning first one side and then the other.

There was something strangely familiar about this knife. But he was sure he had never seen one like it before. Then his thoughts about the knife shifted to the fantasy thoughts of being Super Todd. *He could do anything he wanted if only he learned to concentrate.* It made him smile.

Jeff looked up from the griffin at Todd's back. "Hey, what have you got there?" he asked. He started walking toward Todd with Greg following. "Todd?" he repeated, and when he didn't get an answer, he whistled. "Yo, Todd?"

The thoughts held Todd, excited him. *He could have the power to do anything he wanted.*

Greg noticed Todd's right hand. It was down at his side, his fingers twisted and stiff.

"What's with your hand, Todd?" he asked.

But Todd didn't answer.

"Todd!"

They saw what he was holding.

"Hey, a knife!" Jeff squealed, and pulled up in back of Todd. "Let's see it."

He didn't expect Todd to turn at that moment. The knife blade was pointing outward. The tip caught Jeff on the arm, slashed a thin line across the skin. Blood surfaced.

"Jesus Christ, Talman!" Jeff jumped backwards. His hand went to his arm. The blood was trickling down. "You trying to kill me or something?" He pulled out his handkerchief and clamped it over the cut.

Todd looked at his friend. Then at the knife. His head cleared. Then he exploded. "What are you doing sneaking up on me like that? Why didn't you say something?"

"Say something! I've only been screaming at you for the last half hour. You could have killed me! Didn't you hear me?"

"I didn't."

"Then you're deaf, Talman."

"How's the cut?" Greg asked.

Jeff peeked under the handkerchief. It was only a superficial cut. The blood was already stopping. Todd put the knife down on the workbench.

"I'm sorry, Jeff," Todd said, frightened at what could have happened.

"It's okay. Let's just get out of here."

"You guys want to see my room?" Todd asked when they were back in the kitchen. "Look over the rest of the house?"

"Some other time, okay, Todd?"

"Hey, I'm sorry—"

"It's okay," Jeff repeated. "It was an accident."

"Can I get you a Band-Aid? Have my father look at it? He's pretty good with blood," Todd tried for a joke. But he knew he didn't really want that. *He* would catch it for sure—playing with a knife, not being careful. So he was somewhat relieved when Jeff waved him off.

"I'm okay. No sweat. Look, see you in school tomorrow, Todd." And he was out, with Greg following.

Todd closed the kitchen door behind his friends. He watched them pick up their bicycles and ride off. When they were out of sight a feeling of loneliness came over him like a veil. He had almost hurt his friends and they had left him.

But he thought again about the knife and swelled with ownership.

It was *his* knife; he found it. He didn't want to leave it lying around so his father could stumble upon it and take it away from him.

It seemed very important to hide the knife so his father wouldn't find it.

He went back down the stairs. The tip of the knife was red with Jeff's blood. He wiped it carefully, almost reverently on his pants, cleaning it.

Where to hide it?

He knew.

He walked back to the cellar bedroom, opened the bottom drawer of the dresser, and pulled it all the way out. He put the knife behind the drawer and slid the drawer back in. No one else would ever find it. He hoped his friends weren't mad at him, but as he climbed the stairs to his room, he realized he really didn't care one way or the other.

He was Super Todd. He had the power.

And his feelings of loneliness had passed.

The sun was low over the Cuttings mausoleum, almost ready to duck behind the mountain peaks. Mickie's lips were tight and dry as she gazed at the black doors of the burial tomb. She was sitting on the bench across from it. She had been there for the last half hour, racked with indecision. She had watched the sun dip lower and lower in the western sky until it nudged the tips of the mountains. A closing, mocking eye.

She had come to investigate the interment of the Cuttingses' son. But she couldn't bring herself to pull open the mausoleum doors.

She had tried for days to run away from the nagging

feeling that she had to return to the cemetery and know for certain. But know what? What difference would it make if she found the grave—or not? She couldn't answer that, at least not yet, and maybe the question could never be answered.

But she needed to know more about the tragic past of her house and the need extended beyond curiosity, beyond the facts—the deaths of the children, Sarah, the suicide of Laura Cuttings. Something within her was prodding her on. The whole thing had happened more than a century before, generations ago, yet there was still a bizarre, unsettling feeling shrouding her mind.

She had taken Nina into her confidence, showed her the suicide note, and filled her in on the first trip to the cemetery. She also swore her to secrecy.

At first Nina's reaction had been identical to Rufus's.

"Forget it, Mick," she had put it simply. "It's all a long time ago, water over the bridge, or under the dam, or wherever water goes, and it's probably better anyway that you stop right here and don't find out anymore."

"But what would you do if you were in my spot?" Mickie asked.

And Nina had to smile. "If the tables were turned, Mickie," she said, "I'd probably be doing exactly the same thing you're doing, and like you, I wouldn't know why."

Mickie's heart was beating rapidly. She tried joking to herself, but it didn't have its usual calming effect. Her defenses were refusing to help her out. She knew she had to do it or put it out of her mind, walk away from her fears, imagined or otherwise, and stop her foolishness.

She got up from the bench, squinted against the sun that was tucking itself down below the mountain line, throwing long shadows across the ground. She walked toward the mausoleum and was swallowed up by a dark splash of shade. Her fingers touched the brass ring handle and gave a gentle tug, not enough to budge the doors, but to establish she was there. She looked quickly behind her. To see if Mr. Jenkins, anyone, was there and watching her.

But she had perfect right to enter the mausoleum, she told herself. People did it. To visit loved ones. To pay respects.

But that was not why she was there.

An image suddenly flashed within her. There was a girl who had lived in the nearby town of Owlsfane, Vermont, a century ago and was tragically interred alive in the family mausoleum. They discovered her at the next funeral when the mausoleum was opened. She was on the floor by the door where she had crawled from her coffin. Her arms were outstretched above her, fingers bent and twisted in a paralyzed claw, desperately trying to dig into the cold door and pull herself up to the knob. Her nails were broken, streaks of blood ran to the floor, her mouth was open and contorted, tongue stiff and dry, her eyes frozen open wide as silver dollars. She had tried to claw her way out of the mausoleum but had lacked the strength and died.

But that was not what Mickie wanted to think about right now.

She pulled open the door.

There was no body on the floor or affixed to the door, no girl buried alive. But then there wasn't supposed to be.

Light quickly streamed in where it had not been for more than a century, rushing to fill a vacuum. She hesitated on the concrete steps. The air inside was damp and cold, colder than the day, filled with the presence of death.

There were coffins on either side of the mausoleum. Small brass plaques were affixed to the wooden shelves upon which the coffins rested. Her eyes quickly went from one to the next. She muttered a prayer for the dead, although later on she would not recall what she had actually said.

She saw where Jonas was buried.

Laura.

Sarah.

There was a fourth coffin. It was pushed against the back wall of the tomb, wedged in behind Jonas's. Mickie hesitated, then knelt down to more closely inspect it.

It wasn't really shocking to see what was written on its plaque; if anything, it was anticlimactic. She knew she had been expecting it, but what it meant and why there was no other record were still the unanswered questions.

The boy's name was Benjamin. He had been born March 16, 1848, and died thirteen years later on November 13, 1861.

It came to her suddenly. The date of the first newspaper clipping, the date the madman had mutilated and killed those girls. The same date. November 13, 1861.

Mickie frowned.

If Benjamin had also been killed that day—presumably by the same person—why was there no mention of him in the article or anywhere else?

Closing the doors behind her, she stepped out into the graveyard. She took a deep breath of the crisp air to cleanse herself of the touch of death.

It wasn't rational that this should worry her, she kept repeating to herself. If anything she should now be feeling calmer. *She had solved the mystery. The son was dead and buried. Like he should be.*

But she couldn't rid herself of the feeling that something was still missing, still wrong.

She wondered if vibrations could remain in a house for a century.

CHAPTER 15

They returned from the ski shop a little after eight. Todd and Jenny went the distance with complete packages of skis, boots, bindings, and poles. Rufus picked up a half-priced parka and Mickie a new pair of boots, guaranteed by the shop to be both warm and comfortable and not to pinch her toes. Mickie didn't think that combination of ski boot existed anywhere and would have to see for herself. And she noted that the salesman did not offer her a money-back guarantee in case she wasn't satisfied.

They made a fire in the living room. Rufus brought in work from his office and laid out his patients' files on the couch. He was still working but at least they were all together. He was trying, Mickie realized, and again felt bad about what she had said to Rufus. On the floor in front of the fire the children were lying with their chins resting on their hands. Jenny was reading a Bobbsey Twins book and Todd was rereading a Superman comic book for perhaps the twelfth time.

Rufus noticed and expressed his dismay. "Why are you reading that, Todd? I thought you mentioned you had a history test tomorrow."

"I do," Todd said. "And it's called social studies up here."

"Whatever it's called, shouldn't you be doing a little studying for it? Or do you have the answers written on the bottoms of your shoes?"

Todd smiled. "Nothing like that, Dad. But I know all the stuff. We did a lot of it last year. They're repeating some things I learned in New York. Besides, it's essays and I can bullshit my way through anything."

"Language, Todd," Rufus cautioned.

"Sorry."

"And your B-minus average doesn't really indicate that, does it? Maybe with a little more work you can be getting marks like Jenny."

Todd shrugged. "I guess." And he looked at Jenny who turned away from him in embarrassment. Her good grades came easily; she knew Todd had to struggle for his.

"Did you ever consider that?" Rufus pressed.

"Sure. And I'll study when I have to. But don't want to overdo it. Don't want my brain to get soft." He caught Jenny's eye and she smiled at his joke. "Don't sweat it, Dad," Todd dismissed it. "I know it cold."

"*I'm* not *sweating it*, Todd," Rufus said. "It's not my test. But I hope for your sake that you do know the material *cold*." And Todd didn't like the emphasis his father put on the word.

He felt a stab of uncertainty and considered maybe he should go upstairs and peek at the books again, but he knew he'd become too bored. He'd been through the stuff last year and now this year again and enough was enough.

"I know it, Dad," he said and turned a page in the comic book. Then he remembered something else. "Got the first playoff game tomorrow night. We going to watch?"

"You bet," Rufus said.

"Who are you rooting for, Dad? I'm sticking with the Yankees."

"We're supposed to be Red Sox fans now," Rufus said. "Up here everybody is."

"Maybe next year. And I'll just lay low in school if the Yankees win it. Or then again, maybe I won't."

"Okay, son," Rufus said, and turned his attention back to his files. They were finished talking and Todd lost himself in the comic book and the planet Krypton.

After the children were in bed, Mickie and Rufus snuggled in front of the fire. Mickie's head rested on Rufus's shoulder, her arm comfortably around his waist as they watched the last flames sputter and die. Except for the dim glow of the firelight, the room was dark. For the first time all day she felt relaxed. She sighed easily. "This is so nice, Rufe."

"Isn't it?" Rufus cupped her chin and lifted her mouth to his. He kissed her gently, tenderly. She squirmed closer to him. He looked into her eyes. "Happy?"

"Um hmm."

"What are you thinking?"

Mickie smiled. "I was thinking about when we first met and went skiing together. We've spent a lot of winter evenings in lodges with fires like this one."

"I remember."

"The only difference was back then there was usually thirty or forty other people around. This is a lot nicer." He slipped a finger under her blouse and started to tease her nipple. Mickie giggled.

"Not here, Rufe."

"Why not?"

"The children." But she made no move to brush his hand away.

"What about the children?"

"Oh, Rufe."

"They're asleep. You tucked them in yourself." He started to undo her buttons.

"They might wake up." She let the pleasure of his touch pulse through her.

"They might not," he said and nuzzled her neck, breathing in her smell. Her hand caressed his cheek.

"What is it about fires that brings out the romance in you?"

"Not just the fire. It's everything. The house. Our happiness. *You*."

"I feel like we're a couple of teen-agers making out on the sly hoping our parents don't come down and catch us." She nervously checked behind her at the stairway, concerned that the children might be there. "Talk about role reversal."

"Would you be happier if we went to bed?" Rufus asked. "It's just so much more illicit this way."

Mickie smiled. "I don't think I could make it up the stairs, without my knees buckling. They're rubbery already. Oh, Rufe, don't stop," she sighed as his hand played against her. "Don't ever stop."

"Let's go into my office then," he said. "I've got a couch there I've been saving for moments like this."

"You got it," she breathed huskily.

Rufus scooped her up in his arms, kicked open his office door, and carried her inside. He turned on a weak lamp on his desk, laid her down on the couch, and kissed her. She responded eagerly.

Rufus was taking off his clothes when Mickie opened her eyes. Her glance fell on the zebra plant she had bought for the end table in his office.

She remembered a conversation she had had with Hazel and Penelope Benson during the closing, when the papers were being signed.

"Why don't you have any plants in the house?" she had asked. She had not wanted to pry, but now that the house was finally theirs, felt free to ask anything.

Penelope had dismissed it. "Plants just refuse to grow in this house," she said. "And believe me, we've tried. But never had any luck."

"If you planted them right, they would grow," Hazel had snapped at her.

"I can't make plants grow and I've tried!" Penelope answered with finality.

Mickie had smiled weakly and muttered thanks.

And now the leaves of Rufus's zebra plant were dry and drooping, the plant dead.

As Todd slept the thoughts came to him: he was special, he was Super Todd, he could do anything he wanted if only he learned to concentrate. Did he want to learn? Yes, Todd's sleeping mind responded, and he was allowed to awaken.

The room was cold, and Todd's body temperature was at its lowest. It was late; closer to dawn than to midnight, the pit of the night. He pulled the quilt up to his neck and lay awake in the darkness. He let his eyes patrol the room. With no cars passing outside, the Vermont silence was formidable. He could hear the beating of his own heart, the click of the digital clock as a minute ticked by.

Then he thought he heard a voice. But it wasn't really a voice. More like a sense that he should get out of bed.

His feet dangled over the edge of the bed, and he shivered from the chill in the room. He slipped on his moccasins and reached for the bathrobe that was thrown over the back of his desk chair. He looked at the digital clock. Four twelve. He heard the click. Four thirteen. *It wasn't a dream*, he said to himself.

Faint moonlight seeped through the window, enabling him to discern outlines of the familiar objects around him. A baseball was sitting in the mitt on his desk. Without lifting his eyes from the baseball he sat down at his desk and stared at the ball, concentrating on it.

He concentrated because he sensed he was supposed to concentrate.

Because he *had* to concentrate.

Concentrate and make the ball rise into the air. He could do it.

That was the power!

Excitedly he stared at the familiar ball, with its scuffed, gray-white surface, the black thread stitches that wound around the ball in a never-ending pattern. His mind was totally fixed on the ball, his body tensed, straining, working with him. He saw only the ball and envisioned it rising. His head hurt but he ignored the pain. That was part of it, he understood.

Concentrate.

His eyes burned. They wanted to blink. He strained to hold them open.

The digital clock clicked but Todd didn't hear it.

Nothing was happening. The ball wasn't moving.

But then he hazily sensed a presence in the room with him. A boy. Helping him concentrate.

And then he saw movement. The ball left the glove. It was hovering inches in the air. He willed it to rise higher. He was able to make it happen merely by thinking it.

He had the power! He blinked, and when he opened his eyes, the ball was back in the glove.

It was broken.

He suddenly felt strange. And more than a little frightened. It wasn't the feeling of someone who had the power.

The baseball was still sitting in the glove. He stared at it, trying to remember the position of the stitching. Had it changed? Had the ball really levitated and spun around? Or had he only fallen asleep at his desk? He didn't know the answer to any of these questions.

Whatever it was, it was over. The show was over.

He was suddenly exhausted and staggered across the room. His eyes were heavy, demanding rest. There was a leftover throbbing in his head. He took off his robe, lay down, and pulled the quilt tightly under his chin. It offered some security against bogeymen in the night. And once again he was a little boy in a dark room and he let his eyes comb through the blackness.

He fell off to sleep seeing the baseball rise above his closed eyes. And he wondered if he would remember, come morning, the strange midnight awakening and the events of the last several moments.

Click.

CHAPTER 16

Morning came gray and dreary, and the rain slanting loudly against the window woke Todd. His eyes opened for only a second before shutting again. He felt as if he hadn't slept at all. He couldn't remember ever having been this tired in the morning before. He struggled to hoist himself up on his side, resting on his arm. He shook his head to try to clear it. It was cloudy, like the day.

He went to the window. The inside was all fogged over, and he cleaned a circle with his fingertips and looked out. The rain was falling heavily, the ground muddy and wet. Water rushed down the driveway.

Then he saw the baseball and remembered.

Had it really happened? He shivered involuntarily. From the breeze sneaking into the room? From the possibility that it had? He heard the click of the digital clock, faint, almost imperceptible. He knew he had gotten out of bed in the middle of the night, knew he had sat at his desk and concentrated on the ball.

And he thought the ball had risen.

But deep down he knew that nothing had happened. That was impossible.

Why not try it again?

He shrugged indifferently, but sat down at his desk anyway.

He looked at the ball, a mixture of curiosity and uncertainty across his face.

It hurt him to concentrate. There was a stabbing pain behind his eyes. He heard no sound. Not the tumble of the clock, not the persistent tapping of the rain against the window glass.

At first nothing happened. He was ready to stop, rub his eyes, and mark this whole thing closed when he sensed it: an extra push, *help*, someone working with him.

The ball rose from the glove. An inch. Two inches. It was happening. Todd flooded with excitement. He reached out and touched the ball. The door to his room opened.

"Are you up, Todd?"

From off in the distance Todd thought he heard his father.

"I don't want you to be late for your test today. Knock 'em dead, okay?"

He did hear his father. He blinked and looked at his hand. It was wrapped around the ball. He twisted in his chair and looked up at Rufus.

"Yeah, okay, Dad."

He gently laid the ball back into the glove. It had happened again!

The ball had risen. Because he had concentrated.

The school bus smelled like wet children. Pools of water were in the aisle and everyone was dripping on everyone else. Todd took a window seat and stared out, tracing drops of water with his finger as they ran in rivulets down the glass.

He thought about what had happened in his room, and wondered if he had only imagined the ball rising out of the glove, if he only thought it happened because he really wanted it to. But then he realized with a flash of understanding that the boy taught him how to raise the ball. He reviewed how he had fixed his mind on the ball, saw it rise within him, and held it with his eyes, his body.

His mind suddenly clouded. What boy? He thought he remembered a boy somewhere, a boy who had helped him, but he wasn't certain. He furrowed his brow, tried to remember.

"We're here, Todd," Jenny said. She tugged at his raincoat.

The bus drove up to the school. Todd was pulled from his thoughts. All around children were stirring, buttoning slickers, gathering books. Todd hauled himself out of his seat.

He filed out of the bus, thinking about *the power,* and even though he still didn't really believe it, he couldn't help but toy with the fantasy of trying it again.

Mickie dropped her pencil, raised her arms high over her head, stretched. She yawned and rolled her head around her neck to ease out the tightness. She had been working for three straight hours. The work was compelling, editing the new thriller by a best-selling novelist. But if she didn't take a break soon she would stiffen up.

She stepped out into the corridor. The rain had stopped, but the sun still hadn't managed to fight its way through the clouds, and the hallway was washed in gray.

Not wanting to raid the refrigerator she found herself in front of the toy room door and stepped in. She met the wide, unblinking eyes of the clown marionette. Two nails supported its arms and from the way its head tilted limply forward, Mickie thought of a crucifixion. She scanned the wall, observed the others, like gargoyles on display. She bent down to finger the tiny animals surrounding the Noah's Ark and saw the small brass plaque affixed to the wooden ship: Made Especially for Jonas Cuttings, July 1859.

She turned the thought over in her mind. She had

known the toys were old but had no idea they had belonged to Sarah and Benjamin Cuttings.

The madman must have killed those children *here*, she realized. In the toy room. And suddenly the tragedy of that party, the deaths of the children, seemed so much closer. Etched, perhaps, into the faces of the marionettes.

But she grew annoyed with herself. She had known the tragedy happened in the house. Why should it bother her more to suspect that it happened in the toy room. But the answer came easily: because her children played in here.

She couldn't help but think of Laura Cuttings and wondered if the woman had ever stood where she was standing now, watching *her* children play.

Her children, Mickie thought coldly.

Benjamin. Sarah.

A boy and a girl.

Todd. Jenny.

No! she said strongly to herself.

She was leaving the room when the new thought came to her. There had been so many owners of this house since the Cuttings—why was the toy room still intact? Had it become a tradition in the house when children grew up and families moved to leave the toys for the next owner? The old ladies mentioned nothing when they passed the house on to them. Or, like Essie, had children died and the parents left the toys so they wouldn't be constant reminders of their loss.

Either way, these toys seemed to be a permanent fixture in the house. Like the fireplace. Or the cellar.

She turned to leave the room. Her fingers rested gently on the knob and she remembered the night Jenny tried frantically to open the door, terrified of the marionettes.

She felt them staring at her as well—the puppets and marionettes.

With her back stiff, she yanked the door open.

It was an odd thought, but Mickie didn't want to give them the satisfaction of turning around and looking at them.

The teacher passed out the mimeographed test papers. Todd scanned the questions. Good. Just what he had studied. Around him papers rustled and students coughed as they settled in, and quiet fell over the room. In seconds he was writing furiously.

Midway through, Todd grew tired. He had been writing feverishly and felt the strain in his fingers. They were wrapped tightly around the pencil as if glued to it. Almost clawlike, he thought ruefully, and smiled. Flexing his fingers, he let the pencil fall to the desk as he took a momentary break. Then he had an idea.

He didn't have to hold the pencil. He could concentrate on it, make it stand on its own, and write the answers without touching it. With a flush of excitement he knew he could do it.

He hunched his shoulders over the desk, narrowed his eyes to slits, and trained himself on the pencil. The room became a distant blur. The pain started behind his eyes, throbbing, a pulsing. But he accepted it, welcomed it, because the pain was necessary.

Then it happened. Like the ball. Like it should.

The pencil rose into the air, hovered in front of him almost seductively, and then settled on the paper and started to write in Todd's familiar scrawl. His hands were balled in his lap; the pencil was writing on its own. He had done it!

He felt the presence next to him. Then he heard the voice. It was deep, familiar.

"Staring at your pencil, Mr. Talman, is not going to give you the right answers."

Todd blinked, his concentration broken. He looked up. His teacher brushed past him, walking down the aisle. *What?* he mouthed in hazy confusion. He shook his head, stung, as if hit by the flat of a hand. He wiped his palms across his forehead and rubbed his eyes. Then he looked down at his paper and his eyes widened in momentary panic. There was nothing on it except what he had written himself. Confusion raged through him, as he quickly searched for another sheet of paper— there had to be another sheet—the one the pencil had written the answers on. Where was it? But there was no other answer sheet, and with a sinking feeling in his stomach, he knew. The pencil had never left the desk. He hadn't willed it to rise; he had only imagined it. None of it had happened.

He swallowed nervously. His throat was dry. He checked his watch. Only ten minutes left to the period. And he had barely started the test. Had he fallen asleep? Blacked out? He didn't know. All he knew was that the pencil hadn't moved.

The boy . . . His memory jogged and Todd's eyebrows arched closer to his nose as he fought to remember. The boy who had helped him. Where was he, he wondered. He couldn't do any of this on his own.

But he would deal with it all later. Now he had a test to complete and barely enough time to do it.

He returned to the test. He read the next question and reread it again. He blinked in confusion, shook his head, and inhaled sharply. Quickly, he read the rest of the test. His eyes widened with the sudden realization that he could not answer any of the remaining questions. He looked at his watch. Nine minutes until the bell, and he had written only four of the ten answers. His mind was a blank. He couldn't summon a thing. But he had known it all when he started. Think!

He looked at the teacher. He was standing in front of the class, arms folded, surveying the room. Todd's eyes searched out his, pleading for understanding, for more time. He knew the answers.

The teacher clapped his hands together once. "Leave your papers on my desk on your way out."

As if on cue the bell rang. The class relaxed. Murmuring began. The test was over. Todd remained in his seat as the others filed out of the room.

"You, too, Mr. Talman."

Reluctantly, Todd handed in his paper. He wished he could drop into the earth. He had never handed in a test like this before. The teacher scanned it quickly.

"I would say you really didn't allow yourself the opportunity to pass, Mr. Talman."

Todd shook his head. "I knew the answers, sir," he said in a small, frightened voice. "My mind just went blank."

"I'm sorry, Todd, but you haven't proved you studied. I expect you to do better next month."

Todd didn't move, hoping the teacher might excuse him from the test, say it didn't count, and tell him he could take it again. But instead the teacher said, "You'd better run along to your next class, son. You don't want to be late."

"No, sir," Todd said and opened his mouth to try to explain to the teacher what had happened. But words failed him, as had the answers. He hoped he would meet Rick Webb in the gym that afternoon. He was feeling so down he prayed Rick would kill him and put him out of his misery.

Rufus picked up the phone and automatically reached for his appointment book. He prayed it wasn't an emergency. He had been forced to make one house call already today, and the waiting room was backed up. He hadn't yet found an acceptable nurse and was considering just hiring a temporary receptionist to keep the traffic flowing smoothly.

"Dr. Talman? My name is Mr. Stevens. I'm your son's social studies teacher."

Rufus was instantly alert. "Yes. Is anything wrong? Is Todd all right?"

"Oh, nothing's the matter at all, Dr. Talman. Please don't worry. I just wanted to have a word with you. I usually wait until open school week to speak to parents, but that's still many weeks away and since Todd is new to the community and school I decided it was better that we talk now."

"Yes, Mr. Stevens. What is it?"

"Perhaps you'd like to make an appointment to come in and see me?"

"You said you wanted to talk to me *now*," Rufus said. "Please let's do so."

"On the phone?"

"That's fine."

"Well—" he gathered his thoughts. "There is a little problem. Nothing serious although something I would like to try and nip in the bud. I had the chance to look at Todd's academic records before he entered my class, and I looked at them again just before I made this call. Todd seems to have no major problems academically. His grades could be better but so could most."

"Yes," Rufus said. "He does all right. But . . . ?" He trailed off questioningly, hoping Stevens would get to the point.

"I gave a test today. A relatively simple test, I thought. More for my benefit than for theirs to see how well I'm communicating the material to them. Most of the class did well. Your son, however, did not. In fact he failed rather badly."

"Yes, I knew about the test," Rufus said. "Todd assured me last night that he was well prepared for it."

"Apparently not. He only answered four of the ten questions and parts of the four that he answered were incorrect."

"I see," Rufus said.

"At one point he seemed completely lost. He was

staring into the air, as if searching for the answers. Well, the purpose of this call was only to make you aware of what happened in school and to say that I hope your son applies himself more. The tests will be getting harder after this one."

"Thank you for calling, Mr. Stevens. It won't happen again, I promise you."

"Not at all, Dr. Talman. I hope I have been of some help to the boy."

"Yes," Rufus said, and hung up the phone.

CHAPTER 17

After school Todd raced home. He took the stairs two at a time, went into his room, and closed the door behind him.

Things were beginning to happen, and he wanted to sort them out.

The day was behind him. Failing the test was unfortunate, but at least he knew why the pencil hadn't levitated. Because the boy hadn't been helping him. He still wasn't certain who this boy was, but Todd knew that he needed him to fully exploit the power.

He tossed his jacket onto the bed, rubbed his hands together expectantly, and uttered the words, "I'm ready. Are you here?"

The words hung strangely in the air like a too loud whisper, and Todd was a little frightened by them. It was like summoning the devil, he thought briefly. He also thought the words were superfluous, certain the boy already knew he was there. He sat down at his desk and stared at the baseball. "Come on," he hissed. To the ball. To the boy. He glanced over his right shoulder, wondering if he would see anybody there. The wall was awash with sun.

Where was the boy?

Todd trained himself on the ball and concentrated. But nothing happened—except the pain in his head that the concentrating brought on.

But then a shadow played across the wall. Faint. Indistinct. His breath caught. He strained to see it. The silhouette of the hand, the fingers gnarled and curved, animal-like. Like the hand he had seen in the mirror in his dream. *It was the boy!* Todd realized triumphantly and was no longer afraid. The boy was his friend. And then suddenly he sensed now was the time. He was to do it now. He stared at the ball and concentrated on it, willed it to rise from the glove.

And it did. Into the air. Two inches above the glove. Four. A foot in the air. It hovered below the ceiling. Todd whisked it around the room merely by thinking it. The ball flew like it had wings and a mind of its own. But Todd was directing it, commanding it to fly.

But it wasn't him alone. It was—

Todd broke his concentration.

The ball fell from the ceiling to the floor where it landed with a dull thud and rolled to a stop next to the leg of his desk.

He stared at the ball, then down at his hand. His fingers were tense, stiff, and bent. Maybe it was only his *own* shadow he had seen across the wall, projected by the sunlight. Slowly he opened his hands, massaged his fingers, and worked out the stiffness, the numbness.

He looked at the ball again and knew: it had flown. With the help of the boy he had done it! And there was no question of his being awake!

He heard the voice from far away. "Dinner, Todd." His mother.

Surprised, he checked his watch. It was already suppertime. He had spent three hours in his room. And he had accomplished what he set out to. A wide smile exploded on his face, and light-headed, he skipped out of the room.

He met his father in the hallway, and from the look on his face, Todd knew it spelled trouble.

"I got a call from Mr. Stevens today," Rufus started sternly.

"Mr. Stevens?" Todd was blank for a moment. "My social studies teacher?"

"He marked your test paper. Perhaps you'd like to give me an explanation."

"You know I failed?"

"I know you failed very badly. What I don't know is why. Since you assured me you knew everything. Since you took the time last night to read a comic book and laugh at me when I suggested you do a little more studying."

"I didn't laugh at you, Dad."

"You also didn't study enough, it seems."

"I knew the answers," Todd said, his voice filled with fear at his father's reaction. "I knew all that stuff."

"Then what happened?" Rufus's voice was getting louder, angrier. "If you knew everything, why did you only answer four of the ten questions and even make mistakes on those?"

Jenny's door clicked open. She stood at the entrance, watching, listening. Her father was frightening her; she was afraid to come out of her room.

"I don't know, Dad. I swear. When I started the test, I knew all the answers. It was a breeze. I answered some of the questions, then I thought I would do this thing with the pencil—" He broke off—try to explain *that* to his father. "Then when I went back to the test, I forgot everything. I must have froze. But I knew it all—"

"Rufus—" It was Mickie from the bottom of the stairs. "Dinner's on. Children—"

"We'll be down as soon as we can," Rufus called back to her. "We have a very serious problem up here." He turned back to Todd. "You know, Todd, I just don't accept freezing on a test as an answer. If you study and know the answers, you just don't freeze. Jenny doesn't freeze. She gets straight A's because she works! Why can't you work like Jenny?"

Todd looked at Jenny, and she saw the sudden flash

of anger in his eyes. She shrank back more into her room and let the door slip shut.

"Because I'm not like Jenny!" Todd yelled back. "And you don't know anything about what happened today!"

Mickie came up the stairs. "What's all the screaming about? They can hear the two of you back in New York."

"This is no time for jokes," Rufus said pointedly. "Todd very badly failed a test today after he had promised us he studied. Well, it turned out he didn't study nearly well enough."

"So he'll study for the next test," Mickie said easily. "Won't you, hon?" Todd nodded quickly, and Mickie's eyes tried telegraphing to Rufus: *enough.*

But Rufus wasn't yet ready to let it go. "I'm sorry, but that's just not good enough," he said. "It doesn't correct the situation here."

"And yelling does?" Mickie asked him.

"My profession, Mickie—Todd," Rufus said, "is with children. And I am not going to have them think in that school, where most of my patients come from, that my own son is a failure. Do you know how embarrassing it is for me to receive a call like that from a teacher!"

. . . "How embarrassing it is for me," Todd muttered under his breath.

"Rufus," Mickie said softly. "Todd failed. You didn't."

"Todd is my son! A reflection on me! What kind of a doctor are they going to think I am if my son can't pass a simple—"

"You're being irrational!" Mickie flared. "One has nothing to do with the other."

"Well, I guess we just see things differently, Mick." He turned back to Todd. "Todd, I am going to punish you. For lying to me about studying."

"I didn't lie, Dad," Todd protested.

Rufus continued as if he didn't hear him. "You will stay in your room and you will study the entire night. Without any supper. And how will I know if you've studied? Because I'm going to ask you questions myself."

"Rufe, you can't punish him or starve him into getting better grades."

"Well, I have to try something. Letting him study by himself doesn't get us anywhere. Let's just see what happens if he stays in his room all night."

"Why don't you just lock me up downstairs in the cellar?" Todd challenged, and immediately knew he had gone too far. He watched the flare of anger in his father's eyes, the rise of his hand.

"Don't you ever get fresh with me, young man!" Rufus said. "I have never taken the strap to you, which doesn't mean I can't start now."

"All right, that's enough," Mickie hissed.

"Dad, I knew everything," Todd pleaded. "I swear it. The boy didn't let me answer, that's all. He made me forget the answers."

"Todd, I just don't want to hear excuses from you anymore. Now into your room and crack those books."

"But the playoff's on tonight," he said in a small voice.

"Well, I'm very sorry. You should have thought of that last night."

"He's got to eat supper," Mickie protested.

"He's got to study," Rufus said. "Now are we going downstairs to dinner?"

Mickie looked from Rufus to Todd, torn, not knowing what to say. She whispered to Todd, "Into your room. I'll bring you a tray later, okay?" Todd numbly nodded yes. Mickie knocked on Jenny's door. "Hungry, hon?"

Jenny opened the door and stood in the threshold.

She was still afraid to come out. But she nodded to her mother.

"Well, come on downstairs then."

"Is Todd coming too?" Jenny asked.

"I think Todd is better off staying in his room for a while, don't you?"

Supper was fast and silent. Rufus was tight-lipped and Mickie glowered at him. Jenny ate with her head in her plate and couldn't wait to leave the table. Another habit that seemed to be forming, Mickie thought as she watched Jenny pass through the swinging kitchen doors. This time she didn't even move closer to Rufus.

"Rufe, I swear to God I do not understand you sometimes."

"Mick, I'm tired. I don't want to talk about it."

"Yes, you're tired," she repeated. "You're tired, I'm upset, and Todd is upstairs and probably doesn't know what to make of you anymore, and I can't say I blame him. Maybe you should be confined to your room too."

"You heard him last night. He said he completed his studying. He sat there and read that idiotic comic book for the umpteenth time when he could have been upstairs reviewing his material."

"He said he froze. If he had memorized the entire book, he still might have frozen. He's new in the school. There may have been distractions we don't know about. Who is this boy he mentioned? What did he do to Todd? You didn't even give him a chance to speak before you were down his throat."

"I have said this to you before," Rufus said. "And I'm going to say it once again and tell you exactly how I feel. When I am disciplining our children, I expect some support from you. If you don't agree with me, that's okay. Tell me later. But just don't contradict me in front of them. Don't undermine my authority here. If I say he can't have supper, don't tell him you'll bring him a tray. If I say he has to be punished, don't say he shouldn't be punished. Don't make me out to look weak or bad, okay? And I don't want him watching the play-off game tonight."

"I hear you, Rufe," Mickie said softly.

"But you don't agree with me."

"I hear you," she repeated. "And I'll try to accede to your wishes. But I want you to hear me as well. You can be a little more tolerant too. Todd is not Jenny. He's not an A student; he may never be an A student, and you know that. Locking him in his room, making him go without eating will not make him what he isn't. But that isn't even the issue. You didn't give him a chance to speak. You could have listened to him before jumping with both feet down his throat. It even seemed to me like you were *looking* to jump on him.

"There may have been extenuating factors here. Todd may not have been totally at fault. That's all. I don't want to say anything more about it except that I *am* going to bring him up something to eat—and tell him that you sent it."

She pushed her chair back from the table. It scratched against the floor with a grating squeal, almost as if in punctuation to her statement. She stood for a moment, waiting for Rufus's reaction.

He nodded slowly and said, "Okay." Mickie was pleased that his voice was softer; her words seemed to have their effect. "Maybe I do expect too much from him, Mick." And Mickie couldn't read into his tone of voice. Was it acceptance? Or resignation? But she didn't want to continue the discussion now. They had each said enough.

She let Rufus go into his office. Then she fixed a tray and brought it upstairs to Todd. She found him at his desk reading his social studies book. His cheek rested on his palm. He looked tired, bored. Mickie smiled. "This is from Daddy," she said.

"Is he still angry?" Todd asked.

"No. He's calmed down." She set the tray on the desk, helped Todd off his chair, and led him to the bed where she sat down. He stood facing her at eye level. His eyes were red, bloodshot; he must have been crying.

"I didn't mean to be fresh," he said.

"I know you didn't, hon."

"Why did Daddy yell like he did?" Todd's voice cracked. He rubbed his eyes.

"Daddy expects a lot from you, and I guess he was just disappointed, that's all."

"I try."

"I know you do."

"Is he ashamed of me?"

"Of course he isn't ashamed of you. But he wants so much to be proud of you. Both you and Jenny. And maybe a little more of you because you are the first-born."

"He hates me. Because I'm no good."

"Now where did you get that idea from?" Mickie scolded. "He lost his temper, that's all. Didn't you ever lose your temper?"

"Uh huh."

"Well, let's all use this as a lesson then because we can see what happens when tempers are lost. You're not happy, Daddy's not happy, nobody is. And Daddy and I both know that you're doing the best you can. And that's all we want from you."

"Okay," Todd said numbly, but Mickie didn't suspect that her words penetrated his wall of hurt.

"And I think we can forgive Daddy, can't we?"

Todd shrugged in uncertain acceptance. Mickie brushed the hair out of his eyes, pushed it off his fore-head, made physical contact with him to show she cared. She saw a single tear escape and slide down his cheek. She caught it with her index finger and smiled.

He was hurt, but he would get over it. What Mickie

couldn't understand was Rufus's behavior. His outburst was so totally uncharacteristic, and as she had observed, it seemed like he'd done little else in the way of communicating with Todd in weeks. Since the move.

"What happened today?" she asked. "Want to tell me?" She made room for him on the bed next to her. Todd shrugged and sat down. "You mentioned a boy to Daddy. Did someone at school do anything to you? Was it that Rick Webb?"

"No. He doesn't bother me too much now."

"Okay, but if you ever want us to do anything, just tell us. I can call his parents. Or the principal. Whatever you want."

"You don't have to do anything."

"So what happened on the test?" Mickie repeated softly.

Todd thought for a moment. He thought about the boy and knew that he had made him freeze. But he didn't want to say anything to his mother. He didn't expect her to believe him. He shrugged. "I froze, Mom. That's all."

"Okay, Todd. I'll come back for the tray later." As she stood in the doorway, Todd looked up.

"Tell Daddy I want to make him happy," he said. "But I don't know how."

"We'll patch things up, hon," Mickie said and gently closed the door behind her. "I promise," she added under her breath.

She went into Jenny's room to find her daughter sitting at her desk copying words from a spelling list.

"Will Daddy yell at me if I fail too?" she asked in a shaky voice. "I don't want to fail, but what if it happens?" Mickie could see how much Rufus's outburst had affected her.

"We all fail sometimes, honey. That's human. Nobody's perfect and nobody expects you to be perfect either."

"I study hard, Mommy."

"I know you do."

"I don't want ever to fail."

"But it's okay if you do," Mickie said.

"I want to be perfect so Daddy will love me."

"Daddy will love you even if you're not perfect. And he loves Todd too. He's just been tired lately and he blew up. Like everybody does."

"Is Daddy perfect, Mommy?"

Mickie smiled sadly and shook her head. "No, Jenny. Daddy isn't perfect either."

Jenny met her smile. That made it easier on all of them.

Todd looked up from his books. His shoulders hurt from being rounded over the desk and his neck was stiff. The food was only half touched on the tray next to him. He wasn't really hungry, just hurt and upset.

He wanted to get back at his father, hurt him, make him feel really bad for yelling the way he did. Todd knew what he would do and smiled to himself. He would sit up all night without eating, study really hard, have a heart attack, and die! His father would come in in the morning to yell at him again, and he'd find him dead at his desk.

The daydream widened. Todd saw himself dead and in his casket, an observer at his own funeral. He watched them lower him into the earth. Tears were streaming down his father's face. Rufus was feeling terribly guilty; he had killed his son. That's how he would fix his father!

Suddenly he grew frightened. He didn't want to be dead. He prayed that God had not been reading his thoughts just then. As though wishing he were dead would make it happen. He didn't want to punish his father by making him suffer, because he was afraid the punishment might be visited back on him. His face flushed red with shame and a touch of fear.

And loneliness.

He would call the boy. His friend.

"Where are you?" he whispered to the empty room, and sat back and waited for the boy to come to him.

Mickie was reading in bed when Rufus came upstairs at eleven. "Finished for the night?" she asked.

Rufus smiled. "I hope you're not being sarcastic, hon."

"I wasn't," Mickie said. "But I'm glad you thought I was."

"I am finished for the night," Rufus said. "And I am calm. And civil. And embarrassed."

"Does Todd know any of this?"

Rufus shook his head. "He's sleeping. I didn't want to wake him. I'll tell him tomorrow."

"Please make sure that you do, Rufe, and"—she broke off—"I think you know exactly what I want to say, so there's no reason to continue."

"Let me hold you, Mick," he said softly. "I think I need a friend now."

"You want me to side with you, is that it?" Mickie asked. "And I meant that with a little bit of sarcasm."

"I deserved it," he said.

"Just apologize to Todd and I will hold you and be your friend."

"You got it. I promise."

"Rufe—" She took his hand and pulled him down next to her, reached up, and circled his neck. "Todd said it—and he's right because I've seen it too. You've been so short with him lately."

"Nah," Rufus said automatically and looked away from her, knowing she was right.

"He's confused. He wants to please you, but he

doesn't know how. I don't want him to be afraid of you."

"No," Rufus said. "I don't want that either."

"Is there something the matter, Rufe? I'm here. I want to help you."

"Nothing's the matter. It's just me, I guess. I'll watch myself. I promise. Really."

"I'm here, Rufe. If you ever need me. By the way, who won the playoff?"

"I forgot to watch," he said. "I was working. I guess that subconsciously I knew it wouldn't be any fun without Todd."

"Good." Mickie smiled. "I'm glad."

"Open wider now . . . wider," Rufus instructed as he pressed the depression stick down against the child's tongue and looked down his throat. There was no mistaking what he saw. The tonsils were red, inflamed, they'd have to come out.

The boy gagged and fought against Rufus. But Rufus, certain of his diagnosis, had already pulled the stick out. He'd schedule the operation for within the week.

The boy watched as Rufus opened up the garbage pail with his foot and dropped the stick in.

"Do you like ice cream, Tommy?" Rufus asked.

But Tommy already knew the score.

"My tonsils, right, Dr. Talman?"

Rufus smiled. "Afraid so."

"Sure," Tommy grinned ear to ear. He already knew that it meant ice cream and missed school. What he didn't yet know, Rufus realized, was that for three days his throat would be too sore to swallow even ice cream without pain.

Rufus helped him off the examining table and into his office where Tommy's mother paced restlessly.

"I'm going to have my tonsils out, Mommy," Tommy

sang happily. The boy's mother looked quickly to Rufus whose nod confirmed the boy's words.

Rufus consulted his schedule. His hospital days were Tuesday and Wednesday. A quick call reserved an operating room for early Wednesday morning.

"And nothing to eat for supper the night before," he cautioned.

"Thank you, doctor," the woman said as she ushered her son out of the office. Tommy wore a broad smile. Rufus knew what was going through his mind: Tommy Johnson was going to be the envy of all his friends.

Children, Rufus thought, as he beckoned the next one into his examining room, a boy with a skin rash he was trying to treat without having to send the child to the nearest dermatologist in Rutland. There had never been any question in his mind once he started medical school as to what would be his specialty. There were the usual jokes during the first year about specializing in obstetrics and gynecology when the only way many of the overly busy, sex-starved freshmen could even dream about getting close to a woman was clinically.

But Rufus wanted pediatrics.

He had always loved kids and, he thought, was born to parent.

Early in their relationship he knew that Mickie shared his love of children as well. He had come right out and asked. He had stopped seeing perfectly loving and seemingly warm women who had put their careers in front of family life and had expressed no interest in having children. Thankfully, Mickie was able to comfortably combine career and family, even in Vermont.

Rufus knew that his actions smacked of hypocrisy. He had never really given the children the time he would have liked, the time they deserved. Being a doctor and taking care of other children had always come first. He knew his own children understood, Todd especially, who was already ingrained with the instinctive drive of caring for women, supporting a household, and taking care of children.

Todd, he thought miserably, remembering what had happened last night. He hadn't been able to speak to him this morning, having been called away on an emergency. Tonight, he resolved. He made a solemn promise to himself.

"Do I have to put the oinkman on again?" the boy in front of him asked. "It gets all sticky."

"Only a little longer," Rufus said as he closely inspected the boy's arm. The rash was responding to the corticosteroid he had prescribed. A lucky break. Skin diseases were funny and unpredictable. No telling what might bring them on—from a reaction to medication, to psychosomatic stresses—or what might clear them up. But the boy was responding. A few more weeks of application and he'd be all right.

"Only a little longer," he repeated and looked into the boy's eyes. But instead of his patient he saw his son and felt a twinge of shame. Regret.

Things had certainly not been going the way he had thought they would—or expected them to.

Ever since they had moved to Vermont he had been riding his son hard, and he couldn't imagine why. He had been short-tempered with Todd and Mickie both. More so with Todd. He had been snapping at him without provocation. He was being unfair to him. Unreasonable.

And unless there was an immediate change he knew he was putting distance between himself and Todd.

But nothing was irreversible.

He let his eyes patrol the office, see through the ceiling to the bedroom upstairs. His house. He liked this house. And his family would be happy here, he knew.

CHAPTER 18

He had been cataloguing ten years of newspaper clippings in as many days, getting up early, working well into the night. As though he were being driven, Simon Stoneham thought. To complete a life project before he died? No, he didn't want to think of it that way. But at the pace he was going, he certainly would have all the back clippings filed in no time, the Southern Vermont Historical Society would be up to date, and he would keep it that way, he vowed, until the public library took it over and relieved him of his recording responsibilities. He had almost neglected the bookshop, though. Shipments had come in and remained unopened, special orders went unfilled. But Stoneham was having a good time reading the clippings, cataloguing them, and keeping the records.

When he had found one more clipping that belonged to the Cuttings file, he thought about Mrs. Talman—the reason, perhaps, for his sudden burst of ambition. A pretty woman, starting a new life. He wished her well. She had moved into a house of tragedy if indeed there ever was one. But she was strong; she would overcome the fear that had driven her to his shop.

She had asked about the death of another girl—Essie Webster—only she hadn't known the last name. The clipping was short, only a half column in the *Burlington Times*. The little girl had met her death accidentally, he read. Marionette wires had been twisted around her neck. She had run out of a playroom on the second floor of the house, obviously terrified of the wires wrapped around her. She had tripped over the stairway railing. The marionette caught on the other side, the wires tightened and broke her fall, and held, and choked the little girl. Essie Webster had been accidentally hung in her house.

Simon Stoneham's eyes watered over, and he took off his glasses to wipe them. After years of reading and cataloguing news events, mostly dealing with tragedy and death, he thought he was immune, desensitized to the worst that life had to offer. Not so, he realized; the death of the girl had moved him deeply.

He had promised Mrs. Talman he would call her when he found the clipping, but he tucked it away in the folder. With children of her own, this wasn't something she should see; she had seen enough about her house already. Then he thought again and removed the clipping from the file altogether and tossed it away, something he had never done in fifty years at the Historical Society. He had destroyed a testament, and nobody would ever see that clipping, nobody would ever know what happened to Essie Webster.

He poured himself a cup of tea and tried to wipe away the image within him—the little girl hanging over the stairway balcony, her eyes bulged wide in final terror, arms limply at her sides, while a marionette held fast to the other side of the railing. A tragedy. A waste.

When he finally sipped the tea it was cold.

"Rufus, hurry, will you—" Mickie called from the kitchen as she heard Rufus come into the house from his office. "I'm going to feed the kids, and then we've got to get out of here."

"Damn, I forgot!" he said.

The day had been a long one. It was six forty-five, and they were due at the Wallaces for dinner at seven.

Rufus ran his hand over the back of his neck and rolled his head all the way back. His muscles cricked audibly. He figured he needed about an hour in the shower to become human again, but he only had five minutes.

He was halfway up the stairs when he met Todd coming down. They tried to pass each other on the same side and danced back and forth in an attempt to avoid touching the other. Todd eyed his father uncertainly, trying to read his unpredictable mood, gauge what was behind his eyes. Rufus immediately saw Todd's mistrust and understood.

"Hey, how's it going?" Rufus asked in an overly friendly voice. Any other time the words would have sounded genuine; now he was pushing.

"Okay," Todd answered neutrally, without enthusiasm.

There was an awkward moment between them. Rufus knew he should say something. "I'm sorry about last night, Todd. Sorry I yelled . . ."

But Todd cut him off. "It's okay, Dad. Really. I'm not mad anymore. I stayed late at school and studied. I won't fail anymore."

"I just want the best for you, Todd."

"I know, Dad."

"Hey, tomorrow is Saturday. After my office hours, why don't the two of us do something. Alone, without the girls. Toss the football, go to a movie. Anything you want."

"Sounds good, Dad," Todd said.

"I just want you to know, Todd," Rufus said slowly, carefully, "that anything I do is only for your own good."

"I know." Todd's voice was strained with emotion.

Rufus looked up. Mickie was standing at the bottom of the stairs, nodding silent thanks.

Todd turned and saw her too. "You got to get going,

Dad," he said and took off up the stairs. Rufus knew he didn't want him to see that he was crying.

"Give me five, Mick, okay?"

"Sure." She smiled.

Rufus turned the shower water on as hot as he could stand it. To cleanse his body. To cleanse his spirit.

It was the first time Jenny and Todd were staying alone in the house at night, and Mickie gave them final instructions while waiting in the front hallway for Rufus to knot his tie. Then she and Rufus stood on the front porch until they heard the snap of the door lock.

Inside the house Todd smiled at Jenny and said, "Well, kid, it's just you and me." He let his voice grow mysterious and his eyes roam the ceiling. "And anyone else who may be in here."

And then he flew up the stairs and out of sight, leaving Jenny in the entranceway. Through the window she watched her parents enter the house next door, the small patch of light spilling out into the night, and then the door closing. Her parents were gone.

And she and Todd were alone in the house.

A sudden gust of wind swirled leaves against the window.

Later Jenny was in the bathtub. The bubbles were warm and fluffy, and she liked blowing them off her hand and watching them scatter through the air. She soaped up the sponge and lathered herself. She was rinsing herself off when she heard it.

It was the music box tune that had snuck into her head and was playing within her. Continuously. Annoyingly. She didn't like the carnival song. It reminded her of the time she was so badly frightened in the toy room.

There was movement.

Out of the corner of her eye she thought she saw a reflection of a boy in the mirror above the sink. Someone was watching her bathe. Quickly she looked around the bathroom. There was no one there. The music box tune had suddenly ended, and the bathroom was eerily quiet. Even the splashing noise she made with the tub water wasn't comforting, echoing strangely in the empty room.

She swallowed, suddenly frightened.

She started to call for her mother, but neither her mother nor her father was home. And Todd had never seen her bathe; she knew it would be wrong to call him.

She was alone.

The thought came to her: *He was in the mirror.* That's why she didn't see him now. *Somehow he was in the mirror.*

But that wasn't possible.

From the low angle of the bathtub she looked up at the mirror. There was the reflection of the closed door but nothing else. Not the towel rack or the line of blue towels. Just the silvery sheen of the mirror.

He was hiding below the mirror line. And when she got out of the bathtub and looked into the mirror, he would spring up from where he was hiding and get her!

She lifted the drain plug. The gurgling sound was loud as the water whirlpooled down the pipes. As the water level dropped, her body grew cold and she shivered. She held on to the sides of the tub and slowly lifted herself up, careful not to look into the mirror. If she couldn't see what was there, she couldn't be hurt.

Still wet, she hurried into her pajamas and grabbed for the bathroom door. At the limits of her peripheral vision she thought she saw a face in the mirror. Frightened, she jumped. "Todd—!" she yelped. But then saw for certain that the face was her own. But still in a flash she was out of the bathroom, into the cold hallway, her hand on the bathroom door, holding it shut, not knowing who else was in the mirror. "Todd!" she called again. But there was no answer. "Todd—?"

The house was silent. She felt it breathe around her. Settle. Moan. The hallway was drafty. She shivered. Her teeth started to chatter.

Where was Todd?

Did anything happen to him?

Did anything get him?

She inched away from the bathroom and stood poised outside her bedroom door. The hallway was long and lonely. She wasn't brave enough to go and look for Todd. She'd wait in her room. Her parents would soon be home, and it would all be all right. They were only next door; she could even call to them if she wanted to.

She flipped on the bedroom light and with a flash the bulb blew. The door slipped shut behind her.

Outside her window the moon was full and bright. Shadows from the glowing moon spotted the wall. The wind whined through the evergreens. Jenny climbed into bed. It was the safest place she could think of.

Not safe enough.

The closet door swung slowly open, squealing loudly on its hinges.

It was in the closet!

Jenny looked to the direction of the sudden noise. The door was half open, the closet a black hole.

Who is it? she mouthed. *Who's there?* But fear blocked the words.

No one answered. Only another squeal of the hinge. Grating.

The door stood open. The blackness seemed to pulsate.

Jenny's eyes widened and she searched the shadowy darkness, strained to see. She sat up in bed and the covers fell from her. She thought suddenly of the face she had seen in the bathroom mirror.

It was here!

"Who's there?" she asked out loud in a voice cracked and brittle.

The clammy feeling grew, walked over her. The darkness was strangling. She couldn't turn on the light; the bulb had blown.

She saw the eyes first. Blazing in the closet.

Caught in the moonlight like twin spotlights in a horror play, they glowed brightly, inexorably at her.

"No," she whispered sharply. "Go away."

Her skin iced over. She was too terrified to move, too frightened to call out. She was aware of nothing but those eyes.

Then the eyes started moving. Out of the closet.

Moving toward her.

Wide eyes, reflecting the moonlight. Dead, unseeing eyes glaring at her, burning through her.

She hugged herself tightly, afraid she might wet her pajamas.

The marionette came out of the closet. It made no noise as it crossed the room, suspended in the air, its arms and legs flopping loosely. But Jenny didn't see the arms and legs. She only saw the eyes of the clown marionette trained on her, holding her hypnotically as it floated closer to her. It was too late to burrow under the covers. It knew she was there. It hovered at the foot of her bed. Its arms stretched out toward her, hands stiff. It reached for her neck. It was going to strangle her!

She jammed her eyes shut, opened her mouth, and tried to force sound from deep within her. She wasn't aware if she had screamed out loud or not, but when she opened her eyes, Todd was standing next to her bed. The marionette was draped casually over his arm, its arms, legs, head hanging limply. The marionette was lifeless.

"Boo!" Todd said with a broad grin and lunged toward her suddenly. "Scared you, didn't I?"

The scream escaped from her involuntarily.

Todd was laughing.

Jenny struggled to catch her breath. She wanted to lash out at her brother for scaring her like that. She started to cry.

"That was a terrible thing to do, Todd."

He smiled. "Come on, Jen. It was only a joke. I thought you'd laugh."

"It wasn't a joke," she cried and shook her head from side to side. "I was scared."

"Well, I meant it as a joke," Todd said. But when he looked into his sister's eyes, swollen with fear, it suddenly didn't seem so funny. He knew he shouldn't have done it, and now he wondered why he had. "I'm sorry, Jen. Really." He wrapped his arms around her. "Are you all right?"

She nodded uncertainly.

"I'll put the marionette back in the toy room. I'll never do it again." He opened the door. The hall light streamed in. "I'm sorry," he repeated. The door closed behind him.

Jenny lay back in bed and decided to forgive Todd; he thought it was a joke.

But the closet door was still open the way Todd had left it, the blackness of the closet a scrim wall beyond which lay terrible things. Jenny got out of bed and closed the door. She didn't want it open all night. She didn't want things watching her. Faces. Puppets. It was a long time before her heart slowed and her breathing eased.

She burrowed under the covers and coughed, testing her voice, seeing if she could still make sound, to scream if she had to, and know that Todd would hear her and come.

She had one final, puzzling thought before she fell asleep. How had Todd manipulated the marionette across the room without being seen?

* * *

The feeling brought Jenny up from sleep. Her eyes opened uncertainly, not knowing what she would see in the dark of the bedroom.

Her throat was dry and scratchy, and she wanted a drink of water. But she hesitated. The bathroom was out in the corridor, past the black hole of the stairway, so far away.

Her body tensed. She heard her breathing, faint wisps of air blowing across the covers. She caught her breath and held it. There was no other sound. Despite the warmth of the blanket she was cold.

The night-light from under the door beckoned to her, promising safe passage to the bathroom. But an undefined feeling of warning kept Jenny locked in her bed.

All of a sudden she sensed eyes on her. There was someone else in the room! A presence in the darkness!

Someone was watching her! The feeling washed over her. Shadows crossed the wall. Footsteps shuffled.

More than watching her. Scrutinizing her. Devouring her.

She pulled the blanket up over her head, so she couldn't see what was there. So whatever was there couldn't see her. She dared not peek out.

A sound. Creaking. She didn't know where it came from. The closet door! Her body trembled under the blanket as she waited for something to happen. She pictured the marionettes coming out of the closet, searching for her.

Seconds passed. An eternity.

Nothing happened.

She slowly let out her breath and lowered the blanket down to her chin. Her eyes combed the room, expecting to see the marionettes. But there was no one there. No one in the room. No person. No puppet. And the closet door was still closed. She had imagined it all.

A car passed outside, its tires whining against the blacktop. Jenny froze.

But still nothing. She breathed easier and smiled nervously in relief. She was a big girl with her own room, and she wasn't afraid of noises in the dark, shadows that weren't there, or staying alone when her parents were out.

As she closed her eyes and tried to bring back sleep, she couldn't shake the eerie feeling that *something in this house didn't like her.*

CHAPTER 19

The next morning Rufus awakened first and stretched. The sun streaming through the half-drawn curtains caught him square in the eyes, and he closed them to escape the glint. He felt tired and was in no rush to move from the warmth of the bed.

Mickie was sleeping on her side. Rufus freed her hair from under the blanket and started to gently stroke it, moving down to the nape of her neck, gently tracing lazy circles on her. She stirred and rolled onto her back.

Rufus propped himself on his arm and watched her sleep, her chest rising and falling almost imperceptibly. He touched her forehead with the tip of his index finger, traced down her nose to her mouth, prickled her lips, followed under her jaw line until he trailed along her neck. He played his fingers against her nipples, flicked them with his tongue. He watched her mouth. A smile played across her lips. Her eyes were still closed, but he knew she was awake, enjoying his touch. He felt himself grow hard as he worked his fingers lower, past her stomach to the soft mound of blond pubic hair, a shade lighter than the hair on her head. He felt her body shudder. She threw her arms around him and drew him close to her. He readily responded. He raised himself up and their bodies met. Tension flowed from each of them and they relaxed.

"*Mmmmm,*" Mickie purred and finally opened her

eyes. She looked at Rufus with surprise and confusion. "You?"

Rufus picked up the game. "Who were you expecting, my dear? Al Pacino?"

"Damn!" she said with a smile. "I have to be more careful about who I bring home. Or at the very least open my eyes before you open me." She hugged Rufus so tightly he thought his bones would crunch under her crush. Their lips and tongue met. Mickie finally let him go and he rolled back to his side of the bed.

"I wish I could call off my office hours today."

Mickie shook her head. "No go. I promised Jenny I'd take her shopping this morning. She needs some new clothes for school, and this is the first chance we've had. And don't forget," she added, "you promised that you would play with Todd this afternoon. It's important, Rufe."

"Right."

"You'll finish early today, won't you?"

"I'll certainly try, Mick," Rufus said. "But if I can't—"

Mickie put her finger across Rufus's lips to silence him. "Try," she said simply. She laid her head down on Rufus's chest, slid her hand between his legs, and she heard him sigh. He began to respond again but her eyes went to the night-table clock. She moaned. Time to get out of bed. Jenny would be downstairs waiting for her. "Hold that position, Rufe," she said, and laughed as he promptly lost it.

Todd and his friends were playing a game of touch football in the school yard when a group of bigger boys, Rick Webb among them, asked if they wouldn't mind vacating the court. Rick had asked so nicely—by taking Todd's football and tossing it over the fence and into the street—that the boys couldn't help but oblige. For a second Todd thought about using the power on Rick but decided against it. He wasn't certain if he had perfected it as yet, and besides, it wasn't time to show what he could do. He felt comfortable, though, knowing that he had the power. Like Clark Kent.

They retrieved the ball and Jeff and Greg decided to bicycle back to Todd's house because he had the biggest yard.

After they had been playing for a while, Todd saw his mother and sister come home. A few minutes later Cara came over, and then another little girl. There were still plenty of cars in the lot and Todd knew his father was running late. But he didn't mind because at least his friends were there to play football with him.

Until Jeff got bored. He caught the ball, collapsed on top of it in the grass, and rolled over onto his back.

"Come on, throw it," Todd yelled from across the yard.

Jeff waved for them to come in. "No, I'm tired of this. We've been doing it all day."

Greg flopped down next to him. "So what do you want to do?"

"We can go fishing," Todd suggested. "Stream's just out back."

"Nah—I don't want to go back and get my pole. Hey—" Jeff's eyes widened with interest. "Let's go back down the cellar. We didn't finish looking around the first time. Remember, Todd, you found that knife and almost killed me—"

Todd winced. Boy, did he ever remember that! He was lucky Jeff wasn't hurt so badly that he had to call his father. He would have been in trouble for sure.

"That's a good idea," Greg agreed. "We can feed Todd to the griffin."

But Todd shrugged the idea off. His parents were both in the house, and he didn't want to do anything to antagonize his father. He had promised not to go back into the cellar, and he didn't want to get caught breaking the promise again. "No. It's too nice a day to stay indoors."

"Come on," Jeff said and got up. "I'll bet there's lots more to find down there."

Greg got up too and followed Jeff toward the house. "Coming, Todd?"

Todd didn't know what to do. He didn't want to disobey his parents, and he didn't want to have to tell his friends why he couldn't go down. "No," he said. "I don't want to."

"Why not?" Jeff challenged.

" 'Cause it's a nice day." But his words weren't convincing.

"Hey, you are chicken, aren't you? Why? What's down there you're afraid to see?"

"I'm not chicken," Todd protested. "I went down with you last time, didn't I? And I went first!"

"*Woo!* I'm impressed," Jeff said. "He went first!" And he and Greg laughed.

"Hey, guys, cut it out. I don't want to go and that's all."

"Tell us why not, Todd. We're your friends."

Todd hesitated but then blurted it out. "Because my folks don't want me down there, and I promised I wouldn't go."

Jeff and Greg exchanged glances and then Jeff broke into a wide grin. "*Oooo,*" he mimicked Todd. "Because your parents don't want you to. Why not? Is the bogeyman down there?"

"Cut it out," Todd repeated glumly. He felt about six inches tall and didn't want to have to sit through this.

"Or because they're afraid you might get all dusty and dirty?" Jeff continued. Greg, enjoying the spoof, doubled over.

"Knock it off, " Todd growled. He was missing the joke altogether.

But the boys, like sharks surrounding a floundering victim, moved in for the kill.

"What are you afraid of—your mommy?" Jeff challenged.

"Go to hell," Todd muttered.

"He is afraid, Greg," Jeff said, but Greg saw that Todd was getting angry.

"Let's do something else, okay, Jeff?" he suggested, and then said. "Forget him, Todd. He's just fooling around. He gets this way a lot. Knock it off, Jeff—"

But Jeff was having too much fun riding Todd. He made baby sounds. "Baby Toddy afraid of mommy . . .?"

"Just drop it!" Todd ordered, and he felt the tension flow into his muscles. But Jeff remained oblivious to Todd's mood.

"Well, I'm going down anyway, and I don't care if you come or not, Todd. I'll tell your parents that you did anyway."

As Jeff started to walk toward the house, Todd screamed, "No!" and charged after him, knocked into him on the run, took him down in his leap. The boys rolled on the grass, struggling for supremacy, trading punches and kicks, arms locked around each other. But Todd was much bigger than Jeff, and Jeff was soon in trouble.

"I was only joking, Todd," he sputtered as he came up for air. "Can't you take a joke, man? Let me up."

But Todd kept punching wildly, as though he didn't hear his friend.

"You're crazy, man!" Jeff screamed and managed to get up and run. But Todd jumped him again, took him down. Jeff groaned as he crashed to the ground. Todd kept punching as Jeff tried to protect himself.

The fighting boys attracted attention from the parents and children in the waiting room, and soon Rufus burst out of his office and strode across the yard. He grabbed Todd around the waist and lifted him off Jeff.

Jeff stumbled to his feet. Heaving, he faced Todd, who was restrained by Rufus. Todd struggled to free himself, but Rufus tightened his hold. Alerted by the commotion, Mickie came running out of the kitchen door.

"You're weird, man, you know?" Jeff sputtered, gasping for breath. "I was only joking. I didn't want to go down into that cellar anyway. It's probably weird down there. Like you. You're not my friend, Talman, you know that?" Angry, hurt, and embarrassed, he picked up his bike and sped off down the road.

Greg started walking away, turned, and faced Todd. "You didn't have to hurt him like that. Couldn't you tell he was only putting you on?"

"I couldn't—" Todd said. "I thought—" But Greg, too, was gone.

Others started to drift back to the waiting room. The show was over, there wouldn't be any more blood. But Rufus still felt their eyes on him. Children. Adults. They knew he couldn't control his son. Todd had humiliated him again. He knew he had promised to tread easily, but he couldn't stop the rush of anger that surged through him. He spun Todd around forcefully, pulled him over to the side, out of earshot of the others.

"Where the hell do you come off hitting your friend like that?" His face was beet red.

Terrified by his father's tone, Todd tried to pull away from him, but Rufus held his arms.

"Rufus, find out what happened," Mickie pleaded. "Don't jump to conclusions!"

Rufus pointed his finger at her sharply. "No, Mickie! You stay out of this. It doesn't concern you. I don't care what happened! Todd is much bigger than Jeff, and he heard him asking to let him up! That's all that matters!" He shook Todd's arms with each of his words.

Todd wrenched himself free of his father. "You leave

me alone!" he screamed at Rufus. "You're always yelling at me, telling me I'm wrong." Tears streamed down
his face, blinding him. "Jeff wanted to go down into the
cellar. I didn't want to break my promise to you. But
I can't seem to fucking do anything right around here!"

Mickie saw the rise of Rufus's hand, felt the slap
against Todd's face as if it were her own.

"Never talk to me like that again, young man. Do
you hear me!"

Todd recoiled from the slap, but he wasn't going to
show his father he was hurt. He felt Rufus grab him,
shake him again. Violently he pulled away, his raw
emotion pouring out like lava flow. "I hate you!" He
screamed at the top of his lungs. "I hate you!"

"Todd!" Mickie yelled. Immediately she stepped between them, separating them. "Okay, the two of you,
stop it! I want no more yelling from either of you.
Todd—you apologize to your father right now!"

Todd looked from her to his father. His face
flushed with confusion, as he realized what he had said.
"I'm sorry, Dad," he said. His voice choked with tears
of shame. "I didn't mean to say what I did."

"Rufus, you too," Mickie ordered. "Apologize to
Todd for yelling at him and hitting him."

"God damn it to hell, Mick. Just God damn it to
hell!" he said. He grabbed Todd by the arm and
stalked back to the house, dragging Todd along with
him, almost lifting him off the ground. "I am tired of
apologizing!"

"Rufus!"

"Up to your room, Todd!"

"Rufus, we have to talk."

"I have a waiting room full of patients. I don't have
time to talk to you." When they got inside the house, he
let Todd go. He pointed a finger at him. "I want you to
go upstairs to your room, young man, and stay there. If

you so much as leave that room today I will beat you to within an inch of your life. Got that?" Then he pointed a finger at Mickie. "And I don't want you going to him, Mick."

"You go to hell, Rufus," she spat out.

Todd ran upstairs to his room. He slammed the door shut behind him with a fury, hoping to shake the whole house. His skin was crawling, he wanted to escape from himself, run away from the pounding inside of him, the terrifying swirl of sound. He clamped tense hands over his ears but couldn't block it out.

There was only one way he could free his mind.

And this time it took no thought, no effort, no preparation. It was natural. It was right.

The test tubes on his worktable crashed to the floor in a jangle of broken glass. The books on the shelves flew across the room as if forcibly ejected from behind. The night-table lamp clattered to the floor. Pictures fell off the wall, games jumped out of the closet, along with clothing and shoes. The dresser drawers sprang open, shirts fell out. The microscope spun to the floor and bent out of shape.

"Watch me clean my room, Dad!" Todd screamed.

And then exhausted, he slumped to the bed. His breathing eased, his head cleared, tension flowed out of his body.

The sound and fury was over, the room suddenly quiet.

Jenny, Cara, and Ivy were playing in the toy room. When they heard the fight break out, they ran to the window to watch it. They saw Rufus charge out of the house and drag Todd back. Now that it was quieting down they went back to playing with the dolls and antique doll houses.

"Your brother's strange," Ivy said to Jenny.

"Crazy," Cara agreed. "Like the old ladies who used to live here." She made a circular motion with her index finger to her temple.

But Jenny felt a rush of concern for Todd, and confusion at how her father had been acting. He could have been hitting *her* if she had done something wrong.

"Todd is not strange!" she said loudly, defensively.

The other girls looked at her and Jenny was sorry that she had said anything. These girls were her only friends up here. She didn't want to argue with them. And Todd *had* been acting a little strange, she thought, as she remembered what he had done to her last night with the puppet. "Well, maybe a little," she conceded, and glanced at the puppets along the wall.

Todd finally calmed down and stopped crying. He sat hunched into a ball on the bed, knees pulled up to his chest, chin resting on his knees.

It was clear that his father hated him. Nothing he did pleased him.

His father hated him and wanted to kill him. The thought was oddly soothing, and he pictured the scene in his mind: his father held the knife he had found and chased him from the toy room on the second floor, down the stairs, across the living room, the kitchen, through the cellar door. Looking for a place to hide, Todd stumbled through the cellar. He pulled open the door to the cellar bedroom and was cowering in a corner when his father raged in. He came closer and menaced him with the knife. "No, Dad," Todd begged, but without thought or hesitation, his father plunged the knife into him, stabbed Todd over and over. Todd grabbed his guts and imagined the blood spurting out of him, his life waning, and the satisfied grin on his father's face.

But he became frightened by his thoughts and

blocked them out. Once again he was a little boy who did not understand.

He climbed out of bed and picked up the microscope and tried to bend it back into shape. He hoped it wasn't irreparably broken.

CHAPTER 20

Mickie stared out the car window at the Vermont countryside. Her arm was propped up, palm supporting her face. Her cheek pressed against the glass, fogging it with her breath. Her eyes were distant and glazed. She half remembered seeing this same view on their first trip to Vermont to look for a house.

Somehow that trip seemed so long ago.

She and Rufus were going to the mall. Not that she really needed anything; she just wanted to keep him away from Todd.

Anticipating what Mickie was going to say, Rufus spoke first. Mickie heard the defensiveness in his voice. And the regret. "I feel badly about what happened, but I don't think I said or did anything that was out of line. Todd was beating up a kid smaller than himself. You didn't like it when Rick Webb beat him up. I had to punish him."

"You could have just pulled them apart," Mickie said gently. "Boys are going to fight."

"I just overreacted, I guess."

She turned to look at him, straining against her shoulder harness. "But you're not one to overreact. And you've never hit him before."

"No."

"What's the matter, Rufe? Talk to me. Do you miss New York? Regret moving? Aren't you happy here?"

"No, I'm happy, Mick."

"I really thought Vermont would bring us all closer together, you know? But it hasn't. Do you realize we haven't done anything together as a family in the weeks we've lived here, and except for a few minutes here or there, you haven't spent any real time with the children. Maybe Todd got into that fight because he's looking for attention. Maybe he failed his test up here for the same reason. Even with your limited time back home you used to do more together. I would have expected you two to be out jogging every day in this country air. You can make the time, Rufe. For things that are important we always do."

"We were jogging in Central Park one day," Rufus said slowly, reflectively. "Right after we made the decision to move here. I told Todd how guilty I felt because I wasn't giving him more of myself. It's easy to get lost in your work, let things slide . . ." He patted her hand contritely. "I will, Mick."

"Good," Mickie said softly. She took his hand. "And if we ever have to discipline the children, I won't be divisive. I'm sorry."

They rode in silence until the mall turn-off. Then Rufus spoke. "I just had an idea. Jenny's birthday is coming up. Let's make her a big party up in the toy room. Invite all her new friends from school. Don't you think she'd like that?"

"She'd love it; it's a wonderful idea. But please, Todd first. He needs you more now."

"I know she'd love it."

"Just don't leave Todd out, Rufe."

"No, Mick. Of course not."

But Rufus didn't talk to Todd that afternoon. As soon as they got back he disappeared into his office. Mickie didn't know what to do about it so decided to do nothing. This was *his* problem with Todd, and if he didn't care, then neither did she. She had knocked on

Todd's door, but he told her he wanted to be alone, and
she left him. At least in this house there was plenty of
room for each of them to be alone; back in New York
it would have been harder. Talk about mixed blessings.
It all had to blow over sooner or later, she realized.
Father and son couldn't remain angry at each other forever.

Todd didn't come down when she called him for dinner and she didn't push it. Jenny was nervous at the
table, eyeing her father strangely. But Rufus smiled
warmly and put her at ease.

"We have a little surprise for you, Jen," he said.
"Mommy and I have decided to give you a birthday
party for you and all of your friends. We'll have it up in
the toy room, and I'll put on a puppet show for you . . ."

Jenny's eyes opened wide with delight, and she
clapped her hands together.

"How old are you going to be?" Rufus asked, pretending confusion.

"Eight!"

"That's right. So we have eight candles on the cake."

"No, Daddy. Nine," Jenny said. "One to grow with."

"Of course. How could I forget."

The kitchen door swung open slowly. Todd walked
in. His head was down, eyes on the floor. Mickie knew
it had taken a lot for him to come in there. Silently he
took his place at the table.

"Hi, Todd," she said, forcing enthusiasm. "We're
planning a birthday party for Jenny and her new
friends." She put a chicken leg and a spoonful of vege-
tables on his plate. But Todd wasn't listening to her. He
opened his mouth but nothing came out. His face contorted as he worked his thoughts. Finally he was able to
blurt out the words.

"I'm sorry, Daddy," he said to Rufus. "I didn't mean
to say what I did today." He held out his hand.

"Put it there, pal," Rufus said, taking his hand,

pumping it. "All square between us?" Todd nodded. "Good. Now you just sit there and eat. Jenny and me— we have a party to plan." He rubbed his hands together excitedly and turned his attention back to Jenny.

Jenny smiled; her father and brother were friends again. But Mickie stole a look at her son. He was idly picking at his dinner. There could have been more warmth from Rufus than just a formal handshake, and she knew that Todd had hoped for more too.

"Let's see," Rufus said slyly. "What else do we need?"

"Ice cream," Jenny prompted. "And cake."

"And what about presents?" he asked with a smile.

"Presents!" Jenny yelled happily.

With a squeal of the chair Todd pushed himself away from the table. "May I be excused?" he asked. "I'm not really hungry, and I want to do some studying now."

"Sure," Mickie said and saw the pain that remained in his eyes. She glanced at Rufus but his attention was still on Jenny.

"How about a clown? Would you like that?"

"I'll bring you some dessert later, Todd," Mickie said before he left the kitchen.

"Not really hungry, Mom," he repeated.

"Jen? A clown?"

"Just a puppet show, Daddy, that's enough," she said, feeling guilty for being the center of her father's attention, her eyes drawn to the swinging door.

Mickie brought Todd a piece of apple pie with a large scoop of ice cream. When he didn't respond to her knock, she opened the door. He was face down on his bed, shoes still on, head buried in the pillow. *Here we go again*, she thought.

"Todd?" she said softly.

"Go away."

"No. I want to talk to you." She sat down on the bed

and patted her son. "Come on. Don't cry." She pulled a
tissue out of her pocket and wiped his face dry.

"Not crying," he said, and tried to turn away from
her.

"Blow."

He blew.

"I didn't mean what I said today," Todd said.

"I know you didn't. And so does Daddy."

"Then why does he still hate me?"

"He doesn't hate you."

"Is he coming in to say good night?"

"I don't know," Mickie said softly. Then she patted
him gently. "It's all going to be okay. I promise you. By
tomorrow it'll all be over between you. Daddy shook
your hand, didn't he?"

"Yeah," Todd said glumly.

Mickie met Rufus coming out of Jenny's room.

"We've got six girls on the guest list so far," he said.
"This is turning into the social event of the season. I'm
getting another cup of coffee. You want to join me?"

"No. I want to say good night to Jenny. I'll wait for
you up here."

"I might be awhile. I have a little work to do."

"I'll be up."

As Rufus reached the head of the stairs, Mickie
called after him softly. "He's right in there. Waiting for
you. He's made his move."

"Oh, Mickie," Rufus dismissed it jokingly. "We're
good buddies." But as he walked down the stairs he
didn't know what was keeping him from his son.

Todd lay in bed staring at the ceiling. He followed a
snakelike crack until it blurred out of his sight. His father wasn't coming to say good night; he was probably
never coming to see him again. He wasn't stupid. He
understood what was happening. Despite all that his
mother said, his father still hated him. All of his love

was saved for Jenny. That's why he was planning this birthday party for her. *Why can't you be more like Jenny, Todd?*

Jenny.

His lips curled in resentment and fury as he said the word out loud.

He suddenly felt very small and very alone.

Everyone hated him.

His father.

His friends.

Everyone except—

His thoughts turned to the boy who was his only friend. He fixed on the shadowy image in his head—the clawed hand, the gnarled fingers. Someone out of a horror movie. But he was his friend, the one who gave him the power.

And he wanted to use the power right now, make things move, send them flying across the room, crashing to the floor. He grinned broadly and turned to the lamp to concentrate on it.

But fear crept through him. Suddenly. Stealthily. Like a black mist swirling toward him, tightening around him like choking fog. What he could do was wrong. *The power was evil*, the thought streaked through him, frightening him more. All he could see were the fiery pits of hell waiting for him, punishment for his dealing with the devil.

His stomach felt hollow and his fingers trembled. His right arm twitched spastically. He projected the thought and barely moving his lips, whispered the words. "I don't want the power."

Once the thought was uttered, he shivered, afraid the boy had heard and would come and hurt him. Fear and shame washed over him.

The night was quiet. Against the blackness beyond his window he saw his reflection in the glass as curves of light and shadow from the lamp next to his bed. He stared at himself and the rest of his room outside the window, a murky mirror reflecting back darkly the objects cast upon it. He rose from his desk and walked toward the window. He was suddenly out of the lamp-light, his face thrust into darkness.

His fingers brushed against the glass, making scratching sounds. He looked down at them. They were gnarled and curved. He stumbled back to the night table, frantically searching for the light switch. He found it and clicked it off, plunging the room into darkness. His reflection disappeared from the window and all he saw was the country night.

The moon hung in the sky, full, mocking, the light of darkness, the evil eye. Or, the thought raged through him, the eye of God, staring down at him in condemnation and damnation.

No—he thought wildly, almost desperately. He had done nothing wrong. He was afraid of God, afraid of the boy, and was filled with the cold dread of helplessness.

He quickly pulled off his clothes, slipped into his pajamas, and dove under the covers.

He lay awake in bed, unable to close his eyes, expecting something to come out of the night and take his soul. The night wind whined through the trees, and the shadows on the wall were heavy and dark. Monster shadows. Demons coming to get him once he weakened and lost himself to sleep.

He didn't know how long he had been in bed when he heard the party sounds. The girls were calling to him to come to the party.

Curious, he threw off the covers, got out of bed, and followed the noise. He knew he wasn't asleep. This wasn't a dream; it was real. There really was a party, Jenny's party, and the girls were really calling to him.

In the hallway the sounds were louder. A rush of voices, bursts of children's laughter, sudden squeals and screams. "Come to the party, Todd. Come," the children were saying.

Todd stopped. A swirl of fear spiraled through him. He remembered when he had last gone to the toy room. The girls threw things at him and called him names. *Monster. Devil.*

He hesitated. But this time it wasn't a dream, and now there was nothing wrong with him, no reason for them to call him names.

But when he pushed open the door, the sounds disappeared. And by then it was too late. He saw the children; a picture frozen in time.

He held his breath. He tried to scream, but no sound escaped from his constricted throat.

The moon was playing tricks, he needed to think, but it wasn't the moon playing tricks, it wasn't shadows he was seeing.

The children were dead.

His eyes roamed the room. A half-dozen girls.

Dead.

Todd wanted to turn from the room, run back down the hall to his bedroom, and forget what he had seen, pretend he had never come down here. But instead he walked farther into the room, drawn by an unseen power. The toy room door creaked slowly closed behind him, the latch catching.

And there he stood, transfixed, surrounded by death.

The toys were in their places: the puppets and marionettes affixed to the walls, bearing silent witness, the carousel horses frozen in horror. The wooden animals and dolls were strewn about the room, the Noah's Ark toppled over on its side, wedged under the ankles of one of the girls who had fallen over it.

He didn't know why he had come into this room. His brain tightened as he fought to remember. He had heard the party sounds, the girls calling to him. But they hadn't, really. It had been a terrible illusion, a lure. He had been deceived, purposely brought here. He stood silently in the center of the room and said to the boy, *I'm here. What do you want?*

His only answer was a thin breeze carrying the lingering smell of death. The room was quiet, the girls splayed out, figures on canvas, locked in time.

Todd heard a sound. His name. One of the dead girls had moaned his name. Which one? His gaze went quickly to each of them, their lips silent, blue and cracked with death.

Another whispered sound. It came from behind him.

He felt the touch on his shoulder.

Instinctively, Todd twisted around to see what had landed on him.

The marionette's hands were cold against his neck. He tried to free himself from its hold. His hands grabbed the wooden wrists of the puppet and closed around them, pushing them away from him. Desperately. Frantically. The puppet's arms didn't feel like wood at all.

Like flesh.

Then he saw the eyes and heard the voice again.

"Todd! Stop!"

His mother's voice.

His mother?

Todd looked at his hands, clasped on wrists, pushing the marionette away from him.

"Todd!"

—His mother!

The voice was louder, more forceful. Hands closed around his arms, tightening their grip on him. He ceased his struggling. He wasn't fighting a marionette. It was his mother. She had come into the room.

He held her at arm's length and stared at her, wide-eyed, then collapsed into her waiting arms, buried his head in her chest. His body shook, he sobbed softly. His mother patted his back reassuringly. He didn't hear her words, but her tone was soothing. His breathing eased.

The dead girls!

Surely his mother saw the dead girls!

Todd broke free from her hold, spun around and looked at the room.

It was the toy room. Like it should be. Nothing else. *There were no dead children anywhere.* Only the toys in their places, the marionettes watching him.

He looked at his mother, confusion and fear wiped across his face. *Where were the girls?*

"Todd, what are you doing in here?"

What *was* he doing in here?

"I heard—" *A party,* he started to say, but stopped. There was no party either. There hadn't been one. He had dreamed about the party, dreamed the sounds. Like the first dream.

But it had been so real!

He swallowed and faced his mother.

His father came up behind.

"What's going on?" Rufus asked. His glance went from Mickie to Todd to the puppets on the wall.

"I don't know, Rufe," Mickie said. "I got out of bed . . . " Something intuitive had woken her up, made her look in on her children. Jenny was asleep. Todd's bed was empty. Somehow she knew to go to the toy room, that's where she would find her son. How could she communicate that to Rufus? "I found Todd in here," she said simply.

"Playing?" Rufus asked, not angrily. Concerned.

Todd shook his head. "I—" He stopped, not knowing what to say. How could he talk about the party, about dead girls. Everything had been a dream, he knew, the party sounds, the children—

But he was here in the toy room and not in his bed. And his head hurt. He thought about the boy, the power.

"I don't know why I came down here," he said, shrugging, tossing it off as lightly as he could. "I guess I couldn't sleep. I wanted to go for a walk."

"A walk?" Mickie looked at him queerly.

"More like a hike," he said, forcing a smile.

"He didn't hear me when I came in," Mickie said to Rufus, worriedly. "I even called to him and he didn't answer. I touched him—" She broke off, remembering the struggle until Todd realized who she was.

"Well," Rufus said calmly. "I think the best thing now is for Todd to go back to sleep." He smiled at his son. "Why don't you just hike back to your room now, and we'll talk about this in the morning."

"I didn't do anything wrong, Dad," Todd said nervously.

"I know you didn't, son," Rufus said and patted Todd's head reassuringly. "Go on, now."

"I'll go with him," Mickie said.

She walked Todd down to his room. Rufus watched them, poised at the toy room door. Something made him look in again. He scanned the puppets on the wall. The head of the Punch marionette was tilted loosely toward him, its mouth open, exposing jagged teeth set in a perpetual grin. He stepped back into the hallway, dimly lit by the night-light at the other end, and let the toy room door slip shut behind him.

CHAPTER 21

Mickie sat down on the edge of her bed and covered her face with her hands. Rufus stood across the room watching her. He knew she was upset.

"He was only sleepwalking, Mick," he said softly.

Mickie's mouth fell open. "*Only* sleepwalking?"

"It's not abnormal for children to sleepwalk," Rufus answered patiently.

"It is not normal for Todd to sleepwalk!"

Rufus tried to be clinical. He was talking to the distraught mother of a patient. He was explaining, comforting, helping her to understand there was no danger to her child.

"Mickie, sleepwalking only represents some sort of antisocial behavior. What he can't do during the day preys on his mind and is acted out at night."

Mickie looked at her husband blankly. "What are you talking about, Rufus?"

"I'm talking about sleepwalking, Mick."

"Rufus, it's four o'clock in the morning. Our son was walking in a trance. I don't want a lecture from you."

"I'm not—"

"Todd was in a trance!"

"Will you calm down, Mickie!" Rufus's voice was sharp. She looked at him, rubbed her eyes.

"Okay, Rufus. I'm calm."

"Thank you. Now listen to me. There is nothing dangerous about a child's sleepwalking. Todd's angry about something, and he's expressing this anger in his sleep."

"Of course he's angry!" Her fist pounded against her leg. "All you seem to do is yell at him, and when he wants to make up with you, you rebuff him for some childish reason or other."

"Yeah," Rufus said guiltily and ran his hand over his neck. He sat down next to her. Her hands were in her lap. He reached for them, took them in his. They were cold to his touch and he stroked them, warmed them. "It's just one episode and it's over. There won't be any others. I promise you."

He got up from the bed. The mattress creaked as the extra strain on the one side was removed from it. He walked around to his side, flipped off the lamp on his end table, and climbed into bed. He opened the covers for Mickie. "Come on," he said. "Let me hold you for a second."

Mickie heard him but didn't answer. She was staring across the bedroom toward the windows. There was a slight breeze blowing into the room and the curtains waved gently. Her hands were in her lap again, and she was twisting her fingers unconsciously.

"Mick," Rufus repeated gently. "Come to bed, please. You'll feel better tomorrow morning."

Mickie nodded distantly. She reached over and turned off her light. She crawled under the covers feeling like an old woman. Rufus drew closer to her. He put one arm under her neck and swung the other over her chest. She felt him shiver as he touched her icy legs.

"I love you," he said softly.

But even with Rufus's body on hers she was cold and feeling alienated from him.

She shifted. He could not read her mind, did not know why she had turned from him. She felt him move closer to her. He nuzzled her hair. She felt his warm breath on the back of her neck. Usually she loved his touch; tonight she found it irritating.

Rufus's breathing told her he was asleep.

Gently she extricated herself from his hold. She wasn't comfortable with his weight on her, but wasn't it more? Rufus awakened momentarily, then curled up on his own side of the bed, snuggled against his pillow and fell back to sleep.

She wasn't a psychologist, but something that Rufus said disturbed her.

Todd's expressing his anger in his sleep.

That didn't make sense.

If he was angry at Rufus, why didn't he barge into their bedroom here? Instead of going to the toy room?

Mickie's eyes opened wide. Why were her children always ending up in the toy room?

First Jenny.

Now Todd.

She could even hear what Rufus would say to that. *Jenny thought she heard music, Mick. She was new to this house, confused. Todd was sleepwalking and not aware of where he was going.*

Is it possible, Rufe, that they know about the tragedy in the toy room and are drawn to it?

She hated when her mind grew suddenly active at three, four in the morning, churning, sifting with worry.

She was overtired. A cup of milk would relax her.

The kitchen was silent. She listened to the faint, almost imperceptible hum of the overhead fluorescent lights, the groan of the refrigerator motor. She steadied her shaking hand.

As she warmed the milk in a saucepan, she looked toward the cellar.

That's what had frightened Todd.

That's where she found the suicide note.

What else was down there? What horrors? What secrets?

Only the cellar door kept her out, but at four in the morning she knew damn well she didn't have the courage to open it. Whether her fears were real or imagined, the cellar was hallowed ground this late at night when she was alone and susceptible. And she would not disturb it.

She went into the children's bathroom, washed her face, and gulped two aspirins. She didn't want the running water in their bathroom to wake Rufus. All else aside, he needed his sleep; his workdays were long up here. From early morning to dinnertime, with only an occasional break for lunch. Longer hours than either had anticipated. He was almost as busy as he had been in New York. How ironic.

Mickie dried her face and looked at herself in the mirror. Her eyes were puffy, tired. She felt she could sleep comfortably now.

Ironic, yes.

They had moved to Glendon so Rufus would have an easier time of it, and the entire family would draw closer together.

But Rufus was still working too hard, harder than was good for him.

And her family had drifted farther apart than ever.

Their move to Vermont, she thought ironically.

Just what she had wanted.

It was all going to work out, she told herself as she slipped back into bed.

Rufus.

The children.

This house.

It had to, she repeated. Because if it didn't, what would they do?

But these fears would stay with her, would not dissolve with light.

* * *

Todd slept fitfully. His eyelids were fluttering; he was dreaming. More than dreaming, he was receiving, experiencing. All of his senses observing, absorbing.

The boy was helplessly trapped. A prisoner in the tiny room in the cellar, lying on the bed, hidden by the covers. Todd felt the boy's confinement, the agony of his loneliness, the terror of his endless isolation. He understood. And he knew intuitively that the boy's father hated him and had locked him down there.

Just like him, it registered. *This boy was just like him.*

Then he felt the scratch of the wool against his chin and *he* was under the covers, *he* was the boy in the room.

He was hunched on the top of the dresser, staring out through the tiny dirt-streaked window, watching them play.

A man and a girl.

His father and Jenny.

Laughing. Running. Spinning in the grass.

All the while knowing he was there, locked in.

A vicious jealousy swept over him as he stared at his sister, her blond hair waving in the autumn breeze, the look of joy across her face as his father picked her up and swung her around.

Resentment flooded through him. Anger. *She* was the one his father loved. *She* was the one he played with when he was endlessly locked up in this room. *She* was the one whose birthday party he planned.

Then he heard the girls. Their voices were faint at first, but then grew louder. They were calling to him to come upstairs, to come to the party.

And Todd was sneaking out of the cellar room, climbing the stairs to the kitchen, to the second floor, walking down the corridor to the toy room. He pushed open the door, and there was his father—holding the knife!

Terrified, Todd turned and ran. Back down the stairs, down to the cellar to his room where he felt safe. All the while his father crashed behind him, screaming, swearing.

Todd cowered in a corner of the room. His father advanced toward him. The blade of the knife was pointed directly at him.

He saw his sister standing in the doorway.

Jenny, help me, he pleaded. *Don't let him kill me.* He held out his hand to her in supplication, and they both saw it—his devil hand and fingers.

And Jenny was screaming at him in madness. *Monster!* she shrieked. *Kill him, Daddy! Kill him!*

No! Todd screamed as his father stood over him, rage and insanity in his eyes. Todd saw the knife in front of him, clamped his eyes shut, and tensed himself to receive the fiery pain.

His final thoughts were of hate.

He hated his father; he hated his sister.

And when he came out of sleep, his body taut and drenched in sweat, the dream was as vivid and clear as if it had really happened.

Mickie awoke with an undefined feeling of dread and her mind drifted to thoughts of her husband and son.

Rufus was sleeping next to her, and she could see him in the growing light as dawn slanted in. His morning stubble shadowed his face, and his hair was tousled across his forehead. He meant so much to her, and she prayed she'd never have to choose sides. Because her children were her life.

She couldn't fall back to sleep; she never could when she awoke this way. She would toss and turn, her mind would heave. She would eventually nod off fitfully as hidden worries surfaced, and she would awaken more tired than when she went to sleep. She lay awake in bed, her eyes wide, listening to Rufus breathe, resenting his comfortable sleep when he had robbed her of her own. She grew fidgety and time was endless.

She threw off her covers and shivered in the chill of the dawn. The sun hadn't yet poked above the horizon and the air was still cold. She drew her robe around her. She decided to do some work.

A new manuscript had been delivered Saturday morning. It wasn't due back for another week, but she would get started on it now. With coffee at her side, she began to edit the manuscript, a post-Civil War saga. A family, torn apart by the war, was picking up the pieces and moving to London.

A family torn apart, she thought ironically. Now here were people she could identify with, and she applied herself to her work.

Her eyes grew heavy, and she was half dozing, reading and rereading lengthy descriptive passages when the words came to her. They crept into her mind like an unwanted tune, or a line of poetry from a forgotten high school class which trips into the head unsummoned and triggers memories.

The words Mickie thought of suddenly were ominous ones. A sentence that played over and over within her: *He will return and kill again.*

Were those words she had just read in the manuscript? She looked back over the novel she was working on to see if the phrase appeared anywhere. But in all the pages she had worked on that morning, the sentence did not appear. Nor could she imagine why she would think them.

He will return and kill again.

She frowned. Then something clicked. The words were vaguely familiar from another context. Immediately she knew where she had seen them before.

Her fingers grabbed for the Longfellow volume and struggled to free it from the tightly packed bookshelf. She almost broke a nail in her haste, and she dropped the book. She knelt down, fumbled through the pages to find Laura Cuttings's suicide letter. She couldn't unfold it. *"Damn!"* she muttered to herself and almost ripped the letter to separate the folded halves.

She scanned it quickly, looking for confirmation. There! The last sentence. The same words. *But I fear his hatred is still too strong, and he will return and kill again.* She read the words out loud in horror, felt them thump within her like a heartbeat.

He will return and kill again.

Why had she thought about *those* words?

She was upset, she reasoned.

Upset over her discoveries.

The tensions of the previous day.

She was tired and her subconscious was sneakily at work.

And she knew exactly what Rufus would say: given her state of mind, her subconscious had sent her a warning message to feed her fears.

For a second she relaxed; that was all it was.

But the feeling in her stomach told her it was more.

And Mickie wasn't aware that at that very same moment Todd was in the cellar retrieving the knife he had stashed away. Then he climbed back upstairs, hid the knife in the toy room, under the long flowing gown of a princess doll, and returned to bed.

CHAPTER 22

"Laura Cuttings is warning you, Mick? Is that what you're saying?"

"Yes."

Rufus stared at her uncertainly, then decided she was serious. He was propped up in bed, barely remembering Mickie shaking him awake. He rubbed his eyes to clear them of sleep, glanced at the clock on his night table. "Mick, it's seven fifteen on a Sunday morning." He weighed his words. "Couldn't she have picked a more convenient time to warn you?" If looks could kill, Rufus knew he was six feet under. "I'm sorry," he said and smiled weakly. He reached for her hand but she pulled away from him.

"No, Rufe. Don't apologize. Don't do anything." She walked to the window and looked out. But she couldn't see anything beyond her anger at his insensitivity.

Rufus threw his legs over the edge of the bed, mumbling to himself, "Aren't you a little distraught, Mick?"

She turned and faced him, a hot flush of anger reddening her face. "Of course I'm distraught. I'm a regular crazy woman. Haven't we already established that? Breaking into mausoleums, creeping through cellars."

"Calm down, please."

"No! I refuse to calm down, Rufe!" She screamed each word at him petulantly. "I refuse to calm down!"

"All right, so don't calm down."

There was a tension pause between them. Each waited the other out. Mickie broke. "Okay, Rufe."

"Mick, I hear you and I sympathize," Rufus said softly. He was struggling with himself to give her what she needed. "But it's your own subconscious talking, that's all. You were half asleep. Maybe fully asleep. Or in some nether region. You've been upset. *I* upset you, I know. I don't know what more to say to you except you brought those words up from the depths yourself."

"Can we afford not to accept the possibility? To ignore what could be a warning?"

"It's not a warning!"

"How do we know that!"

He eyed her for a moment, then calmly asked, "All right. Call it a warning. What do you propose we do?"

"I don't know. But I'm worried. You can see that. There is something here which I fear is beyond our control."

"You're making yourself crazy, Mick," he said and tried to ring compassion in his voice. "Believe me, there are no warnings."

"My vision of Laura handing me the knife."

"Don't use words like vision, okay? That's just *your* word, nobody else's. Your interpretation. People don't get visions. Saints get visions. Instead say 'your dream' or your 'daydream.' Either. Both. You fell asleep in that cemetery, Mick. You had a fantasy. Why can't you have normal fantasies like getting laid?" He tightened his lips. "Mick, there is nothing to talk about anymore. You're lost in these other-world machinations and plots of yours, of madmen coming to kill the children. You have been since you found that damn suicide letter whether you know it or not. I had hoped you had buried all that like you promised, but apparently you haven't. Well, our children are safer up here than they have ever been in their lives, and you know that as well as I do." He dove back into the bed and pulled the covers

over his head to stifle more converstion. Annoyed,
Mickie watched him, then she opened the door and ran
out of the room.

She sat at the kitchen table and stared at a piece of
toast. She picked up a knife to spread some butter,
thought of Laura Cuttings, thought of suicide, then decided she wasn't hungry.

When she looked up Todd was standing in the doorway, rubbing his eyes. Mickie summoned a smile.

"Up early?"

"I couldn't sleep, Mom."

"Neither could I," she admitted. "Breakfast?"

Todd shook his head. "Not hungry."

Mickie tossed the toast back onto the plate, scattering crumbs. "Me either."

Todd sat down opposite her. "What are you worried
about, Mommy?"

Mickie forced another smile. "I'm not worried,
Todd. Just a touch of insomnia."

"Is it Daddy and me and what happened?"

Todd's eyes looked so searching. "I always worry
about you and Daddy." But that wasn't answering his
question, she knew. She knelt down next to him. "I
want you to know something, hon. None of what happened is your fault. Daddy is having a rough time these
days. It's been a big move for him. A big cut in income.
He's worried about taking care of us, and maybe that's
why he's been a little more critical with all of us." *And
me of him*, she thought to herself.

"I don't want you to fight over me, Mommy."

Todd must have heard their yelling in the bedroom,
Mickie realized, and now he needed confirmation that
he wasn't the cause of their strife.

"We won't, honey," she swore to him and silently
prayed she could keep her vow.

"Good," he said, and there was an awkward moment.

"Do you like it here, Todd?" Mickie asked, fumbling at the sash on her robe to pull it more tightly around her.

"I guess. Why?"

"No reason in particular. A little survey."

A shrug. "It's okay."

"Do you miss New York?"

"I miss my friends. The guys up here are okay—" He twinged. Jeff and Greg had walked away from him. He had no friends. He brushed aside the thought. "Why, Mom? Aren't you happy?"

"I am, hon. But I want to make certain that you and Jenny are." She looked at Todd closely and saw the hint of sadness behind his eyes. "What is it, Todd?" she asked softly. "Daddy?"

Todd shook his head and looked uncomfortable. "I had this dream, Mom."

"What?"

Then he sloughed it off. It was just a reaction to what had happened with his father. "Nothing."

"Well, if you ever want to talk, I'm available."

"Like a shrink, huh?"

"Like a mother."

"Yeah. Okay. I'm going to do some reading now. I'll play with Jenny when she gets up, I guess."

"Good idea," Mickie agreed.

He walked over to her, threw his arms around her, and squeezed her. He took her hand in his and gazed into her eyes. "I love you, Mommy."

"I love you too, Todd." He pulled away from her and started to leave the room when Rufus came in.

"Hello, Todd," he said and rubbed his son's blond hair.

"Hi, Dad," Todd said.

And then there was silence. Father and son had nothing to say to each other.

"See ya, Dad."

"Yeah, Todd. See ya." Rufus walked closer to Mickie. "Mick," he begged. "Please, please don't make anything out of this. It's not healthy for anybody."

Mickie nodded, and Rufus turned and went back upstairs. He hoped he had gotten through to her.

Todd didn't really want to play with Jenny. He should have been playing with his friends, but as they didn't seem to want to have anything to do with him, he was sort of stuck with his sister.

But it was more than that. There were things about Jenny that were bugging him. The way she tossed her head to clear hair out of her eyes, the way her eyes roamed searchingly around the room or narrowed as she thought to herself.

"What do you want to do next?" he asked with little enthusiasm.

It had been raining since nine o'clock, and they were confined to the house. Cabin fever was setting in. They had already gone through the board games in Todd's room and had been in the toy room for the last hour taking turns on the rocking horse, although Todd felt a little too big to be doing something like that and crawled with inner embarrassment. Well, none of the guys could see him . . .

"You want to play some catch in the hallway?"

Jenny shook her head and crinkled her nose.

He hated that about her too.

"I have an idea. I'll put on a marionette show for you."

"I don't know," Jenny said, feeling a little uncertain. She still didn't really feel comfortable around the marionettes. She let her eyes roam the room; they were watching her from their pegs along the wall. If she didn't know better, she might have thought there was an amused look on the face of the witch marionette which she didn't like at all.

"Come on," Todd prodded. "I'll give you the old razzle-dazzle."

She caved in. "Okay."

"Good."

Todd pulled the clown off the wall. Jenny made a face. It was probably her least favorite of the marionettes. Its eyes were expressionless, seemingly innocent, but Jenny still watched it with caution. Things tended to happen when that clown was around. It was ridiculous, she knew, but she almost thought of the clown as their leader.

"Now you sit right there," Todd said, positioning Jenny with her back to the wall. "Let me think for a second about what I'm going to do, and—" He snapped his fingers. "Got it!"

He sounded a fanfare, pulled the proper wires, and the marionette suddenly sprang to life.

"Hi, Jenny," Todd said out of the corner of his mouth in a falsetto. The clown tilted its head in her direction. "How are you today?"

"Fine," Jenny giggled in spite of herself; Todd was making her laugh.

"Do you like it here in the toy room?" The clown's voice was wooden and funny.

"Yes."

"Would you like me to dance for you, Jen-ny?" the clown asked, and Jenny detected an odd sneer in Todd's voice when he said her name. And when she looked at the clown now, she wondered if it was only in her imagination that the button eyes of the marionette seemed to grow smaller and harden—on her.

Todd jerked the crossbar and both arms and legs of the marionette moved spastically up and back. The clown jiggled from side to side in a twisting motion, pretending to dance. Its baggy silk pants made a whispering sound as its legs brushed against each other.

Jenny clapped with amusement, her lips spread into

a wide smile. From her sitting position she flopped her arms in sync with the clown, moved her head with his.

The marionette drifted closer to her, its legs kicking, its mouth opening and closing.

"Do you like my little dance?" the clown asked, and Jenny nodded that she did.

"Can I hug you, Jen-ny?" and Jenny again noted that strange sneer when her name was said. Without waiting for a response, the clown widened its arms stiffly and moved closer to Jenny, jutting its head toward her. It danced face to face with her; their noses touched. She was eyeballing the clown and the marionette winked at her slyly. Its hand brushed lightly against her neck, and suddenly she didn't like it. She shuddered and tried to pull away from the clown as it tickled her.

"Stop it, Todd," she said and pushed the clown back from her face. The soft touch of the silk was irritating. But still the marionette remained, dancing in front of her, its arms and legs and body all over her face, touching her, covering her eyes, blocking her vision.

So she didn't see the witch marionette off to the side as it drifted closer to her. Nor did she see that its hands were clasped around a knife.

"Todd—" she whined.

"What?" He sounded annoyed. "What is it?"

"Move the marionette away. It's scaring me."

She was suddenly lost in a jumble of the marionette's arms, legs, and manipulating wires.

"Please, Todd." She put her hands up in front of her face to push away the clown.

"It likes you, Jen. It only wants to kiss you."

"No. I don't want to kiss it. Take it away. Take it away." She waved her arms wildly in front of her, as if to scare away the marionette. She tried to edge away from it, but the clown stood its ground, gave her no breathing room, pushed ever closer, and threatened to cut off her air. She tried to stand, but her arms were now entangled in the marionette's wires and without leverage she couldn't get up. She was trapped. She felt the marionette's icy lips on her.

"Todd!" Real fear in her voice.

"Oh, all right. If you don't want to have any fun."

At first she wasn't certain what had happened. At the limits of her peripheral vision she could see another puppet, then a gleam above her eyes, and the clown collapsed in a heap in front of her.

Then she saw the witch marionette and the knife it was holding. Immediately Jenny knew what had happened. The knife had sliced through the manipulating wires, separated the clown from the crossbar, and killed it. That was the gleam she had seen—the knife motion slashing in front of her. Her mind whirred in confusion. The witch had been on its peg across the room. She remembered seeing it when she came in and remembered how it leered at her. How had Todd gotten the witch while he was still manipulating the clown in front of her face?

Now the clown was a motionless heap on the floor, its head twisted and looking up at her with one wide accusatory eye. She was responsible for its life-giving strings being clipped. Then Jenny twisted with a start and saw the witch hanging in midair.

Where was Todd?

Who was manipulating the witch marionette?

She looked wildly around the room but Todd was gone.

And the witch was there!

She was alone with the witch!

"Todd, where are you?" Confusion and terror flashed across her face.

The marionette floated closer to her, and Jenny could clearly see its features, its ghost-white face a horrible mask: a bulbous nose that hooked downward at the tip, wrinkle lines that crossed its forehead giving the appearance of age, eyes that were pools of blackness, a mouth half empty with missing teeth twisted in a grimace. And it was holding the knife prayerlike in front of its face. The tip was pointing at the ceiling.

"I don't like this game, Todd," Jenny said, and she didn't recognize her voice.

Not taking her eyes from the witch she started to get up. The marionette moved in front of her, blocking her. Its hands changed position suddenly, stiffly, as if wires had been pulled, and it was now pointing the knife directly at her. Jenny moved to her left; so did the witch who seemed to stay with her whichever way she turned.

"Don't move, Jenny," the witch warned in a wrinkled voice that she still recognized at Todd's falsetto. But where was he? Her eyes widened desperately, but all she could see was the tip of the blade in front of her, and the wide mocking eyes of the witch. She did not understand what was happening.

"Todd?" she cried out fearfully, her voice cracking. "Stop it. I'm frightened."

No answer. Just a slow, deliberate wink of the witch's eye.

"I don't want to play anymore, Todd," she said angrily, searching the room, looking for her brother.

"*I don't want to play anymore, Todd,*" the marionette mimicked her in its high falsetto voice. Its mouth flipped open. Its eyes glistened with life.

"Todd, stop!"

"*Todd, stop!*"

It was no longer a game.

The witch started to dance spastically in front of her, its arms and legs doing crazy jumping jacks, the knife in constant motion wielded over its head.

"No," Jenny mouthed. Her head quivered in disbelief and she looked like a living marionette.

"I have to hurt you, Jenny," the witch said, and there was a new coldness to the voice; it was also deeper. "Just like you hurt me."

"I didn't hurt you," Jenny cried. Her breath came furiously with her fear.

"You killed me," the witch said, drifting closer. "You wanted me dead."

"No," Jenny hissed, terrified. Her voice built within her. "I don't want you dead."

"Yes, you do."

"No—" and her voice came out a moan that was swallowed by fear.

The knife hovered in front of her face, a swinging pendulum. It was hypnotizing. She could sense the coldness of the blade, almost feel its touch. She covered her eyes with her arms and buried herself in the bend of her elbow. She tensed and awaited the inevitable.

She heard a fluttering noise and peeked out. The clown marionette had come back to life, springing up in front of her, attacking the witch, seeming to wrestle with it for possession of the knife. Mesmerized and terrified, Jenny was frozen in place, unable to move, unable to scream. She could only watch as the two puppets battled against each other.

The knife clattered to the floor as the clown wrested it from the witch's hand. The puppets went at each other in a tangle of arms and legs and wire. There were the grunting sounds of a hideous struggle.

Finally both marionettes collapsed on the floor and were silent.

For long moments Jenny didn't know if she should move. *The knife. She had to get it.* It was on the floor but still within reach of either of the puppets. She was afraid that if she made a sudden move for it, one of them would jump up and grab it first. Hesitating, Jenny reached out toward the blade. Frightened at its touch, she pulled her hand away, leaving the knife where it was. She hunched into herself, her back to the wall, trying to make herself smaller.

"Todd?" she whispered.

No answer, dead silence in the room.

The two marionettes were motionless, their arms locked around each other in final death grips. Jenny slowly slid up the wall until she was standing. She edged her toe under the body of the witch and pushed it. Quickly she jumped back, afraid of a reaction. But there was no life to the marionette. It lay on the floor where she had moved it. The danger was over.

Had she been dreaming? Had she fallen asleep?

She didn't think so. Because the knife was there, where it had fallen.

It was Todd! He had played a terrible trick on her!

Suddenly furious she flipped the witch over so it was face up, separated it from the clown. She stamped down on its body, its head, to kill it more, make certain it stayed dead. The limp body offered little resistance as she ground it into the floor.

Finally convinced it could no longer hurt her, she stepped over it, to go to the door to find Todd.

She was barely over the witch marionette when she felt a tug on her leg. The witch was alive. It had grabbed her. It hands were tightening around her, working their way up her body. Its eyes brimmed with new life, murder in its expression. It was crawling up her leg, its right hand already touching her crotch.

Jenny shrieked, tripped over a toy, and slipped to the floor. Todd helped her up.

"What's the matter, Jen?" he asked.

At first she didn't know who he was. Then it connected. She stared around wildly. There was no puppet clawing at her, none even on the floor. Her eyes went to the wall. The clown marionette and the witch were in their positions, their arms supported by the pegs, legs hanging limply. Their eyes were unmoving, staring dead ahead.

But they had wanted to kill her! Stab her with the knife!

Although now there was no knife on the floor.

Jenny didn't know what to say or do. She felt twisted in different directions. Like the marionettes.

"Where did you go, Todd?" she asked in maddening confusion.

"Go? What are you talking about, Jen?"

"Go!" she repeated loudly, angrily. "You weren't in the room when the clown and witch were fighting!"

Todd screwed up his face in confusion. "What are you talking about?"

"The clown. The witch!" she said, almost screaming. She knew what she had seen.

Todd pointed to the wall blankly. "There they are, Jen."

"No. They were here. Fighting."

"Dancing. The clown was dancing. I was making it dance for you."

"Fighting!" she insisted and accentuated the word with a tightened fist. "The marionettes wanted to hurt me. To kill me!"

"Jenny, no," Todd said. "I was playing with the clown. We were finished, and I put it back on the wall."

"No, Todd! You did those awful tricks to me with the marionettes. With the knife." She charged after him with her fists, beat against his chest. Todd caught her by the wrists and held her.

"I didn't like those tricks, Todd," she screamed. "I don't know why you did it to me. It was wrong!" She was sobbing uncontrollably now, her fear still alive. "You scared me. And the puppets *were* fighting. I don't like it in here. I never want to be in here again!"

And she was past him, heading for the door, not wanting to turn around and see this terrible room again. She raced down the stairs to her mother, not knowing what she was going to tell her.

Todd stood alone in the toy room as the door slowly shut behind his sister. He was suddenly tempted to run after her and tell her it wasn't a trick, *that none of it was a trick*. But instead he got on the hobby horse and rode back and forth, back and forth, the squeal of the runners the only sound in the toy room.

Todd was in his room reading when Mickie knocked once and entered.

"Todd?" she questioned. "Jenny is very upset and she says you scared her with the marionettes."

"I know. That's what she said. We were . . . you know, dancing with them and then all of a sudden she got hysterical and started to hit me. Then she ran out crying."

"And you don't know why?"

"No, Mom. I swear."

"Nothing else happened? You were just playing."

"What could have happened?" he shrugged. "I was dancing the puppets close to her, but that isn't scary, is it?"

"I don't know, Todd. You didn't hit her?"

"Mom—" he said.

"Do you have a knife, Todd?"

"Not a real one."

"What do you mean 'not a real one'?"

"Well, I got my gag one. The rubber one. The one you guys got me in Disneyland."

"Where is it?"

"In the toy room, Mom. I was playing with it. One of the puppets was pretending to duel with it. Jenny was there. She saw it."

"Todd, something upset Jenny terribly, and I'm

trying to get to the bottom of it. She said the knife was real."

"Uh uh." He vigorously shook his head back and forth. "Well, it looks real. You want me to show you?"

"No. I know what it is," she said. "You never left Jenny alone in the toy room?"

"Nope."

"Then what could have scared her like it did?"

"Maybe she thought she saw something?" he asked, trying to help.

"Maybe," Mickie said and shook her head, not knowing what to think. "Well, if you remember anything else, let me know."

"Sure thing."

Mickie hung by the door. The toy room again, she thought with bitterness and anger. That room was making her skin crawl.

CHAPTER 23

Mickie was downstairs in the living room thumbing through a magazine. Jenny was sitting near her quietly reading the next offering in the Bobbsey Twins series. After listening to Todd, she explained to Jenny about the rubber knife and was able to calm her down, both agreeing that Todd hadn't been nice to her. But Mickie was aware that she still didn't know what had happened up there. They had played with the rubber knife, that was evident, but how had Jenny mistaken it for a real one? From the very start it seemed like the room had spooked her, and perhaps she had mistaken and misread innocent play for something more sinister and threatening. It would be best to keep her out of the toy room awhile, at least not let her play in there alone. During the birthday party, with a roomful of girls, she would feel at ease.

Rufus was making rounds at the hospital, checking the children he had operated on earlier in the week, and it was just as well he hadn't been there to listen to Jenny describe what had happened to her upstairs. He would have inevitably jumped down Todd's throat, even if Todd was as innocent as he claimed. The peace between father and son was tenuous and anything could snap it.

She hadn't called her mother in almost a week, and it occurred to her that now might be a good time to do it. She reached over and rubbed Jenny's head. "You want to talk to Grandma?" she asked, and Jenny nodded that she did. She'd let Jenny talk for a minute, then she'd finish the call upstairs in her bedroom, out of earshot.

Jenny's part went smoothly, and as she talked, Mickie made it upstairs to the extension. "Okay, hon, that's enough," she said when she clicked on. "Let Mommy talk for a while, okay?"

She waited for the hang up and felt sudden butterflies in her stomach. She didn't know what she would say.

She encouraged her mother to talk first. Tessie filled her in on what she was missing in the city—a brownout, new subway crime statistics, a robbery in her old building *on her floor*, and an extremist group planting another bomb. None of it seemed as terrible to Mickie as it might have only months before when she was clamoring to leave New York.

"And how are our little refugees from the city?" Tessie finally asked, turning the conversation over to her daughter. "Is it all like the fantasy promised?"

Mickie had been only half listening to what her mother was saying about New York, searching for ways to tell her that there were problems. Real ones with her family. Uncertain ones with the house. But when she got ready to voice her fears, she had to stop and think for a moment. She didn't want to mention anything about the house's tragic past, and what could she really say—that a dead woman was giving her a warning?

"Mick? Are you still there?"

"Oh, things are okay, Mom."

"Rufus all right?"

"Fine."

"Todd?"

"In his room."

"Is everything all right, Mick? You don't seem as talkative as usual."

"Everything's fine," she said a little too breezily. "Well, Todd had a run-in with one of the neighbor boys, but it's nothing to be alarmed about." She hated herself for lying to her mother.

"He's at that age," Tessie agreed. "Hey, are you ready for a visit from Grandma? I'm dying to see what you've done with the house. And aren't the trees turning about now?"

"I think it might be a little too soon, Ma. We're still finding our way around up here, and I couldn't be as gracious as I'd like to be." She couldn't even think about bringing her mother up to the house yet, at least not until the family was a unit again.

There was a slight hesitation before Tessie asked. "Everything's okay between you and Rufus, isn't it?"

"Of course," Mickie said.

"No strains or problems from the moving or new environment?"

The door to the room swung open. Jenny was there.

"Everything's fine, Ma, believe me. Look—I've got to run, Jenny needs me. I'll give you a call later in the week. After eleven when the rates change. Okay?"

"Send my best to my grandson."

"Will do. Bye." She hung up the phone and turned to Jenny. "Grandma says hi to Todd."

"Good," Jenny said with little enthusiasm, then added, "I didn't need you, Mommy. You didn't have to stop talking to Grandma."

Mickie opened her arms to Jenny, who ran into them. "Well, I need you, hon, okay? And don't ever forget that."

Todd was suddenly in the doorway. Jenny imperceptibly tightened her hold on Mickie's hand and Mickie couldn't believe that Jenny actually was afraid of Todd. They were usually so close that it saddened her to see Jenny like this.

"Are you coming to apologize to Jenny, Todd?" she asked in a tone of voice that demanded a positive response.

"I guess," he shrugged. "I'm sorry, Jen." He held out his hand for her to take.

"No," she said, shaking her head back and forth, putting her own hand behind her, hiding behind Mickie's back. "I don't want to."

"But Todd is here to apologize to you," Mickie said.

"No. He was mean to me. He wanted to hurt me."

"I was only joking, Jen. Fooling around. The knife wasn't real."

"It looked real—!"

"Jenny, please," Mickie said. "Todd has never done anything mean to you before, has he?" Jenny thought for a minute. She was about to say "yes—he scared me with the marionettes another time when you weren't home." But Mickie continued, "Of course he hasn't. So we can be a big girl and forgive him this one time, can't we?" *Please, Jen,* she said to herself, *I don't need another problem now.*

But Jenny shook her head no.

"Eh, I don't care anyway," Todd said, and he started out of the room.

Jenny watched him go, uncertainty washed across her face. She looked from her mother to the closing door, then back to her mother. "Wait, Todd," she finally said and ran after him.

Problem averted, Mickie thought, but she still wondered what had happened upstairs.

The rain had stopped and Mickie sent the children outside to take a walk together. She watched them from the upstairs hall window. Todd, his shirttail hanging out, his hair rustled by the breeze, taking his sister's hand and walking with her across the yard and to the woods.

Her children—God, how she loved them.

She sat down and tried to continue the work she had started on this morning when Laura's words had interrupted her. It now all seemed so very long ago. She pulled out the suicide note and reread it, letting her glance linger on the last line. *He will return and kill again.*

"No, he won't!" she said out loud and crumpled the note into a ball, tightening her fist around it as if trying to choke the evil out of the words.

It was only her subconscious that had sent her those words she repeated to herself. That's why she had said nothing to her mother. The power of the subconscious, she thought respectfully. It can trigger horrendous guilt-ridden dreams. It could manifest real ailments with physical symptoms and pain. It could repress a terrifying past event. Or it could send a message to feed fears. She could be her own worst ememy, she knew, and if she looked for problems, she was going to find them.

But how did her subconscious explain what happened in the toy room with Todd and Jenny?

It couldn't, and that was why she had to take positive action. For herself. For all of them. Close up the toy room, sell the toys, or give them away, destroy them. Anything—just get rid of them. Those toys were witnesses to the massacre of the girls, and she wanted them out of the house. Jenny had lived for seven years without them, and Todd had no need for them. They could throw out all the antiques and buy a whole new set of toys, set up a new toy room. In another room if they wanted—God knew they had enough of those.

Mickie inhaled deeply and suddenly felt better, like a giant weight had been lifted from her shoulders. She had solved a problem. The house had no stranglehold on them. Now all she had to do was get her husband and son to patch things up between them and life could go on normally.

* * *

The children made it through the trees and down to the stream in seconds. It was a glorious fall day. The air was cool and teased with winter, the sun had broken through and now only a few clouds floated loftily by. Leaves fell in kingly displays of reds, oranges, rusts, and burnt umber, dying in a brilliance of color, each with a different hue. One final burst of individuality. The water flowed among the stones and boulders that peppered the stream. Todd held out his hand to Jenny.

"Come on. Let's go across."

Jenny held back. The water wasn't too deep—she could see bottom—but the smoothed rocks looked slippery. She was afraid she might fall.

"Come on," Todd pressed. "It's fun."

"You go, Todd. I'll wait here."

"I'll help you," Todd said. He reached out to take her hand.

"No, I don't want to."

"I won't let anything happen to you. Don't worry so much."

Jenny hesitated. She remembered the toy room. He *had* let something happen to her there. "Come on," he prodded again, and she decided it was okay. Before he had been fooling around, but here there was real danger, and he had never let anything happen to her before. She put her hand in his and let him guide her toward the first rock. Todd stepped easily and surely onto the second.

Jenny wobbled, uncertain of herself, her weight suspended between dry land and the first slippery rock. For a split second her center of gravity was over the water. She held on tightly to Todd's hand and then landed securely on the rock.

The water swirled in eddies around the stones beneath them. Another dozen rocks led to the other side and the tree-lined bank. Tiny fish darted through the water. Without letting go of Jenny's hand, Todd crouched low on the rock, reached down, cupped some of the stream water, bringing it to his mouth. He smacked his lips. "Better than back in New York. You want some?"

Jenny shook her head. She just wanted to get over to the other side, then deal with getting back. She suddenly regretted having started doing this; she wasn't as brave as Todd.

Todd moved to the third rock and helped Jenny advance one. The house poked through the trees, and he could see the gabled roof and window on the second floor. Cloud shadows drifted lazily across the back of the house.

Jenny was having trouble balancing, her sneakers not grabbing on to the rocks as well as Todd's hiking shoes. Todd used leverage to steady her as he gently guided her forward.

"The secret is to do this quickly," he said and made a quick move to the next rock.

"I want to go back, Todd," Jenny said, a note of fear rising in her voice.

"We're almost there, Jen," he said, and tried to pull her forward.

She yanked her hand away from him. "No!" she cried, and threw him off balance.

Then his foot slipped.

He teetered back and forth on the rock, his shoes sliding off, refusing to grab the wet surface. Jenny screamed at him. "Todd, be careful!"

His balance went. He knew he had lost it. At the last moment he instinctively threw himself forward, so he would not fall back and risk hitting his head on one of the rocks. But he did land painfully on a rock, banging his knee.

He stood up in the water. His knee hurt where he had fallen on it. He rubbed his knee, trying to massage out the pain. Blood was trickling out from his open wound.

"Todd, help me, please." Jenny's voice was small. She was afraid she might fall too.

"Sure," he said, once again helping his little sister. Slogging through the hip-deep water, he led Jenny back to shore and hoisted himself out of the stream.

"I'm sorry I made you fall, Todd," Jenny said. "But I was afraid and didn't want to go across."

"Hey, no sweat. You didn't know I was going to fall. Race you back to the house, okay? I better get out of these wet clothes before I catch it from Mommy for sure." And as he ran back to the house and pulled open the screen door, he thought to himself, *Old Super Todd wasn't invincible after all.*

CHAPTER 24

On Monday morning Todd wasn't looking forward to going to school and seeing his friends again. He could still remember what happened on Saturday word for word, moment by moment. He cringed at some of the things he had said and done. And starting that fight with Jeff—No, he was not looking forward to going to school. Rick Webb was at the bus stop when Todd got there with Jenny—a less than auspicious beginning to the day.

"Hi, Todd-y," Rick sang as he eyed Jenny critically. "Need your mother to bring you to school?" He threw a fake punch at Todd, who flinched as the bus pulled up. Todd pushed Jenny on in front of him. They slid into their seats, and Rick sat down behind them. He snapped his fingers against Todd's ear. It burned.

"Cut it out, Rick," Todd said, brushing it off.

Rick did it again. "Cut what out, Todd-y?"

"Knock it off, damn it!"

The bus stopped. Riley and Biff got on. Rick winked at his friends. "You want to see old Toddy get angry?" He buzzed Todd's ear again. Todd stood up and turned to face Rick.

"I told you to leave me alone."

Rick stood to meet him and puffed out his chest. The games were over. "Yeah? Well, what are you going to do about it, Talman?"

Todd's face reddened. "Don't you mess with me,

Rick," he said coldly. "You don't know anything about me, what I can do."

"Yeah?" Rick challenged, but Biff was touching Rick on the shoulder. He had seen something in Todd's eyes, something marbly and hard, that chilled him.

"Hey, Rick, cool it. He's just a kid. Leave him alone."

Rick feigned a punch at Todd, purposely pulling up short. He laughed.

"Cut it out, I said," Todd said coldly.

"Rick!" Biff said. "Knock it off."

"I want to knock the crap out of that guy and nobody's going to stop me," Rick sputtered, suddenly turning on his friend.

Biff shrugged. "Your funeral, Rick," he said, without knowing why.

Around them the bus grew quiet. The other children wanted to see what was going to happen. Nobody had ever stood up to Rick Webb before.

Todd balled his fists, ready. "Come on, Rick. Take me on."

"What's going on back there?" the bus driver called. He had been watching the two of them in his rearview mirror and decided it had gone far enough. "Talman. Webb. Sit down before I stop short and send you both through the windshield."

Rick grumbled, took one more fake shot at Todd, and then sat, laughing it up with Riley.

Todd sat down and calmed himself. He unclenched his fists. He would save it for another time.

Todd felt a tap on his shoulder.

"Just thought I'd tell you again, Todd-y," Rick said softly. "I may not get you today, and I may not get you tomorrow, but when I do, it'll be a fate worse than death."

"We'll see," Todd said simply, and hid a smile.

* * *

In homeroom Todd greeted his friends with a weak nod, and they returned his greetings just as weakly. They wanted nothing to do with him. Todd took his seat and buried himself in a textbook, pretending to study.

He joined them at their table for lunch, slid his tray in front of an empty chair, and sat down. He pointed to the food he had ordered.

"Is it dead?" he asked shakily, forcing a smile which he hoped rang true. His friends just grunted. "At least the Coke is okay," Todd said and took a sip from the cup. "They can't screw up Coke."

Silence around the table. Todd barely tasted his meat. Finally he said, "Look, guys, I feel shitty about what I did on Saturday." He met Jeff's eye and they both quickly looked away.

"Yeah," Jeff said simply and turned to Greg. "You catch the playoffs yesterday? Think the Red Sox will do it?"

Greg grimaced. "Playing like a bunch of girls."

"Hey, guys," Todd tried. "I want to show you something. Watch."

A girl was approaching the table. She was carefully balancing a lunch tray in one hand and her schoolbooks in the other, all very precariously.

After only a glance from Todd the cup of soda on his tray sprang into the air and splattered all over the face of the girl. Surprised, she dropped her lunch and books. The tray clattered to the floor amid resounding applause from the other students. She glared at the table, her face dripping with soda.

"Who did that?" she shrieked at them.

Jeff and Greg stared at Todd. He had done it, they knew. But *how*? He had never touched the cup or the table. Nothing.

"It was an accident," Jeff mumbled. "We didn't mean it."

"Who's going to pay for my lunch?" the girl demanded.

"I'll pay," Todd said. "I guess it was my fault." He tried to smile. "Sorry."

"Well, all right," she said, snatching the money. "As long as it was an accident." She turned and stalked away from them.

Todd beamed at his friends. "Wasn't that neat?" he asked.

"How did you do that, Talman?" Jeff asked seriously and looked closely at Todd.

"It was a trick. I can do a lot of things. Want to see something else?"

"No," Jeff said strongly. "I don't want you to do anything. You hear me, man. Nothing." He got up. "Just stay the hell away from me, Talman, okay?"

"I was just—" Todd protested.

"Okay!" Jeff repeated loudly and stalked away from the table. Greg got up to follow him. He turned back to Todd.

"Do whatever you want, Todd. Just don't do it around me."

Todd stared after his friends as they threaded their way through the cafeteria and out the double doors leaving him alone. A spiral of fear shot through him. *His friends had left him,* he had no friends, and he felt a terrible loneliness sweep over him. *No friends.* He choked on the thought.

But the boy had no friends either, he knew. The boy in the shadows, the one they had locked in the cellar.

And that made him just like the boy, and that was a pleasing thought.

Because the boy gave him the power.

And with the power no one could ever hurt him.

Not Rick Webb.

Not his father.

A boy at the next table was leaning against a chair.

Todd stared at the chair, toppled it out from under the boy and sent him reeling to the cafeteria floor.

At dinner Rufus gave Jenny a gift-wrapped box. Happily she ripped apart the colored paper and ribbons. It was a pair of stuffed rabbits, hugging each other, their noses and lips pressed together. *The first toys for the new toy room*, Mickie thought.

"They're beautiful, Daddy," Jenny squealed. "Thank you."

"Did you get anything for Todd?" Mickie asked.

"Todd? No—not this time. I got him the microscope, remember? Hey—you ever play with it, Todd?"

"Yeah," Todd answered as he watched Jenny holding the rabbits. "Sometimes."

Rufus and Mickie were alone in the living room after dinner. Rufus was thumbing through a paperback novel, his face so serene in the firelight that Mickie hated to disturb him. But she wanted to voice her feelings and make them official.

"Rufe—"

"Mmm?"

"I had a thought. What do you say we get rid of all the old toys upstairs and start a new toy room with more modern things. You can get an electric train set for Todd. I'm sure he'd love that."

"*I'd* love that," Rufus said. "What boy wouldn't? I still remember my old set of Lionels. Hey, we can even use one of the empty rooms to lay it all out in. But why get rid of the toys that are up there now?"

"I don't know. Because I don't think Jenny really likes it in there."

"Of course she does."

"She doesn't, Rufe. Remember the night she thought she heard the carousel, when she couldn't open the door and get out? She hasn't really felt comfortable in there since. And—" Mickie stopped short of telling Rufus what happened between the children on Sunday morning.

"That was a long time ago, Mick. She's used to the house sounds by now."

"And Todd—?"

"The sleepwalking? Don't remind me. That was a terrible night."

"We threw out everything else the old ladies left. We might as well get rid of the toys too."

"But why? They're probably valuable."

"So we'll give them to a toy museum. There must be a good tax deduction there. And we'll get our names printed on little brass plaques. Donated by Dr. and Mrs. Talman."

"The toys belong here, Mick," Rufus said flatly.

"What do you mean 'belong here'?"

"They've always been here; they'll always remain here. Where's your sense of history and tradition? And if we ever sell the house—or if Todd and Jenny ever sell the house—the toys will stay right where they are. Countless children have enjoyed them and I'm not going to disturb them."

Countless children? Did Sarah Cuttings and her friends? Did Essie—?

"I'm sorry I brought it up, Rufe. Let's not talk about it until after the party."

"Let's not talk about it at all. Those toys were a very attractive part of this house when we bought it and will be when it's sold. And unless you can give me a pretty good reason to give them away, I'd like to keep them."

Mickie exhaled but then Todd walked into the room and she decided not to pursue it now. There was time enough and she'd figure something out.

Todd flopped down on his stomach in front of the fire, opened a comic book and started to read.

"Where's Jen?" Mickie asked.

"I don't know, Todd said, his head buried in the comic book. "Maybe playing with her bunnies somewhere."

"Did you finish your homework, Todd?" Rufus asked.

Todd shrugged, crossed his legs, and bent them up at a 90-degree angle to his body so his father was staring at the soles of his feet.

"Todd?" Rufus repeated and when he got no answer a second time repeated "Todd" once more. He closed the paperback, put it on the couch beside him, and leaned forward over his son.

"Answer me, Todd," he said, his voice rising. "Did you finish your homework? I don't want you falling behind and failing another test."

Todd turned a page in the comic book and didn't answer.

"Todd!" Rufus repeated sharply. "You're about to lose your new skis."

"I did what I had to do, okay?" He turned another page.

"No, that's not okay. That does not answer my question."

"Rufus, please," Mickie said in a low voice.

"I want to see your homework, Todd."

"No," Todd said casually, although tightly, testing his father. He didn't look behind him.

"Todd!" Rufus demanded.

Still no answer.

"I want to see your homework right *now*, young man," he sputtered on the rise.

Todd twisted around and faced his father. "You don't own me!" he flared. "You hear me? You don't own me!"

"Rufus, Todd . . . " Mickie said hoarsely and

touched her husband's arm. He brushed her off. He was reaching for his belt. She could see anger blazing in his eyes, sense the blood pounding through his temples.

"I have never taken the strap to you, Todd—"

Rufus was almost on top of him when Todd sprang to his feet. His skin flushed. His arms were tensed at his side, fingers tight and twisted.

"I gave you an order, Todd! You hear me! And I want it obeyed!"

Father and son faced each other.

"And what are you going to do if I don't!" Todd screamed at Rufus. "Kill me?"

"Enough!" Mickie yelled. "Rufus, you sit down. Todd, unclench your hands."

For a second nobody moved; the scene was frozen.

"Todd!" Mickie repeated. "Unclench your hands."

She heard his heavy breathing, saw the pain in his face, the tension in his arms, the struggle in his hands.

"Todd!"

Tendons stood taut on his arms, and Todd stared down at his fingers, straining to concentrate on them. They were stiff and refused to relax.

"Todd! Unclench your hands!"

Todd strained, the anguish visible in his eyes, and finally screamed "I can't!" and stormed out of the room. Mickie started after him. Rufus put a firm hand on her shoulder stopping her.

"Leave him alone!" he said, and there was a new fury in his voice that frightened her. But she pulled away from him, started up the stairs. He caught her by the arms and turned her around to face him. "I said to leave him!"

"What is that . . . an *order*?" Her voice oozed with sarcasm. "What is it, Rufus?" she spat out. "You've decided all of a sudden that you don't want a family? Well it's a little late for that. It's—"

"Shut up!" he yelled and shook her.

"Get your hands off me, Rufe," she hissed. "Get your God-damned hands off me! You don't own me either!"

Rufus's teeth clenched tightly and he stared at his wife. His arm raised, bent slightly at the elbow, palm stiff as if he was going to slap her. She followed the rise of his arm and looked at him scornfully. "What are you going to do, Rufe? *Kill me?*"

He dropped his arm. A sneer crossed his face. He stepped aside contemptuously.

"Go! Go to your son, Laura!"

Mickie broke away from him, then stopped and stared at him. "What did you say, Rufe?"

"I—" He shook his head.

"You called me Laura." Confusion suddenly replaced anger. "That's the name of the woman who committed suicide."

"Hey—" he smiled weakly and tried to slough it off. "I guess the name sort of stuck in me."

"I guess," Mickie whispered, shocked, and hurried up the stairs to her son.

CHAPTER 25

It wasn't until ten thirty when Mickie awoke. She had slept twelve hours and needed it. She glanced out the window and saw the lineup of cars in the parking lot; Rufus was open for business as usual. The rest of the house was empty, the kids apparently having left for school. A look at the kitchen revealed that nobody had eaten anything, and she felt a stab of guilt. This was the first time, except for being sick, that she had missed making breakfast for the children.

When she was watering the philodendrons in the living room, trying to keep the leaves from yellowing and dying, she noticed the pillow and blanket on the couch. Obviously Rufus had slept down here last night, and she had never even noticed.

Why hadn't he come upstairs to bed?

Was he too embarrassed? Ashamed?

Or was it something else?

The ring of the phone startled her.

"Hello . . ."

"Honey, I'm driving up to Montreal to spend several days with Bill, and there's no reason I can't leave a day early to visit with you too. Vermont is on the way to Canada, isn't it? Bill wanted me to fly, but I've never been up that way, and the leaves are turning now, and I do want to see you and that mansion you've moved into—"

Mickie always knew when Lois was happy; she talked nonstop. She admired her breath control.

"What do you say, Mick?"

"Hello, Lois, how are you?" Just hearing her friend's voice was lifting Mickie's spirits. Lois was a touch of home, a reminder of when things were . . . better.

"Do you have to ask that question, Mick?"

"I guess not." Mickie smiled into the phone.

"Bill wants me to meet his parents . . . and first wife. Only kidding."

"Sounds like it's getting serious."

"It's *gotten*. You haven't been around to hear the day by day. But I'll tell you all about it when I get up there. I already have the directions, and if I start early in the morning, I should get to you by four, so we can have dinner and the evening, and I'll leave for Montreal the next morning and," she continued without catching a breath, "how are you?"

"I really could be better." Mickie sighed.

Lois paused, drew a breath. "You need a shoulder?"

Mickie let the smile come into her voice. "More than a shoulder."

"Rufe?" she asked hesitantly.

"And other things too."

"You do sound exhausted. Now that I've stopped blabbering I can tell. You should have stopped me before. I feel dreadful. What's the matter?"

Mickie told her friend everything she couldn't tell her mother. And now there was even more to tell because even when she thought things were calming down between Todd and Rufus, there was the explosion last night. After some hesitation, she also told Lois about the suicide note and her intuitive feelings about Laura Cuttings. When she finished Lois took a deep breath and said, "And I thought I talked fast."

"Lois, I'm sorry," Mickie said. "I didn't mean to burden you with all of this."

"Knock it off, okay?"

"Okay," Mickie agreed readily.

"Look, I can still come, can't I? You wouldn't be adding fuel to anything by having me? Maybe Rufus wouldn't like the idea."

"Right now I don't really care what Rufus likes."

"Got it," Lois said.

Mickie started to falter. "Lois, I feel like I'm being twisted in so many different directions at the same time. The problems between Rufus and Todd, then my crazy worries about this house. Sometimes I don't know which problems to address myself to first, because something worse always seems to be surfacing. Even when I think there might be a little improvement, zowie! I'm hit with something new." Mickie noticed she was twisting the telephone wire as she talked, aware of the tension in her hands. "I just can't shake the feeling that there is something evil in this house. Am I being silly, Lois?"

"No. Not silly. If it's concern for family, it's never silly." She heard Lois take a breath. "Mick, I heard everything you said. It's all a little jumbled, but I understand. I'm not a shrink. I'm a friend. So I can only give you a layman's opinion. I don't think you have ghosts in the house delivering messages to you—and I say that seriously, with no condescension because I understand what you're going through. And I don't think you should be spending any energy in that direction."

"I honestly don't know what any of us has done to make Rufus act like he has."

"From what you've said, I don't know either, Mick. But it *will* work itself out. And it's not going to be something you do or don't do. Rufus will discover on his own that he's been an absolute shit to his son— pardon my French—and go out of his way to bring it all back. Guarantee it. I'll send you my bill in the morning."

"Hey, speaking of bills," Mickie said suddenly; "this call is costing you a fortune. You're not crosstown anymore. I'll see you on Monday. Stay as long as you want, and Lois—thanks."

Mickie held the phone an extra second before she replaced it in the cradle. It was like a security blanket she hated to give up.

Mickie chattered on at dinnertime, not really knowing, or caring, what she was saying, just trying to be distracting and pull everyone in. The tension between Rufus and Todd was still obvious, and Mickie tried to overlook it. It would all work itself out, she told herself. Like a virus.

The children quickly left the table as soon as they were finished, and Mickie made no move to stop them. She wanted to talk to Rufus, to ask him—

"Did you sleep on the couch last night?"

"Yes," he nodded, playing with his coffee cup.

"Why? There was plenty of room upstairs."

He shrugged sheepishly. "I thought you were mad at me. I was a little loud last night."

"I was and you were."

"I'm sorry I carried on like that. Todd got defiant and I guess I just met him head on."

She said nothing more, waited for Rufus to continue, but after a long pause, he pushed himself away from the table. She would have given anything to know what he was thinking at that moment, why he was so distant.

"I'm going to make a fire," he said.

"Okay, Rufe."

He was sitting on the couch with Jenny on his lap when Mickie came into the living room. Todd was slumped in the Barco-lounger, staring at the fire which

Rufus had built up to a roar. Mickie sat down on the far end of the couch.

"And we have to have invitations," Rufus was saying to Jenny. "We can either have them printed up or write them ourselves. I think it's nicer if we do it. How many friends do you want to have?"

"I don't have that many yet. But maybe if I can get Cara and Ivy to bring some of their friends, I can make more."

Todd snorted. "Friends," he said, and thought about not having any.

"Is something the matter, Todd?" Rufus asked, and Mickie looked up. Todd turned, brushing his hair out of his eyes and smiled at Rufus.

"No. Nothing's the matter, Dad."

"Lois called today," Mickie interrupted, hoping to head off more tension between father and son.

"How is she?"

"She's seeing someone seriously now. You met him at the party. But you'll have the chance to ask her yourself. She'll be here Monday night."

Rufus looked up surprised. "Here?"

"She's driving up to Montreal, and she's stopping here on the way."

"Aw, Mick. We're so busy—"

"It's just one night, Rufe. And besides, I've invited her."

"Check with me next time," he mumbled, and turned away from his wife, back to Jenny, when all of a sudden a smile broke out on his face. "How about a week from Friday, Jen? If you want, the girls can bring their pajamas and sleeping bags and stay over. Would you like that?"

"Can I, Mommy?"

"Hey," Rufus said in only mild rebuke. "Daddy said you can."

"It's okay, honey," Mickie said.

"Pajama party," Todd spit out and picked up his comic book. When Rufus looked over toward him, he casually said, "No problem, Dad. Don't sweat it."

Rufus and Mickie were in the kitchen having a cup of tea. Jenny was on the couch reading, and Todd was still in the Barco-lounger, having read and reread the comic book to the point of boredom.

He was roaringly pissed. Nobody had paid him any attention tonight, the last several nights. Except to pick fights with him. It was bugging him beyond words that his father and sister were so locked into that Goddamned birthday party of hers, you'd think it was the end of the world.

A look of disgust crossed his face as he stared at his sister, the object of all their father's attention and love. *Why can't you be more like Jenny?* He heard his father's words echo within him and his resentment of his sister grew.

His eyes seared the back of her neck. Then his line of sight shifted; he was drawn to the fireplace. He stared at the fire, the waving flames sucking him into it hypnotically. He saw nothing else as he concentrated on the alluring patterns of the flickering flames and he thought how satisfying it would be to watch Jenny burn.

He stared at the flames, imagined what it would be like for Jenny to be on fire, for the heat to scorch her skin. He envisioned the flames teasing her, licking at the flesh on her arms growing hot and red, and Jenny trying to pull herself away from the fire that was swirling about her, billowing up and around her head, finally surrounding her. Within him he saw Jenny's flesh blistering, her eyes bubbling, melting. He could hear the scream rising out of her throat and then being cut off as her vocal cords burned to cinders. Then he saw her face engulfed by the inferno and reduced to a shapeless black pulp.

He watched his sister burn with a curious mixture of horror and . . . pleasure. With Jenny dead his father would have to pay attention to him.

And suddenly in the midst of Todd's fantasy, it started to happen.

The flames had life. They shuddered and breathed. They left the fireplace.

Todd watched as long, twisting fingers of flame snaked outward from the hearth, spitting, cracking. He was held by them, mesmerized by their movement. The fire sought Jenny out. It wanted to burn her. Just like he had imagined.

He was responsible for what was happening!

Jenny! He tried to warn her, but he couldn't get the words out. His vocal cords were paralyzed, useless. He couldn't make a sound as the snarling flames arced closer to her.

He wanted to jump from his chair to snatch Jenny away from the fire, but he couldn't move either. His hands dug into the wide armrests as he tried to propel himself forward. But all he could do was watch helplessly as the fire raged closer and lapped at Jenny's face.

Why didn't she see it? Feel the heat on her body? Jenny!

Suddenly he knew what to do.

He trained himself on the fire to will it back into the fireplace. His mind totally fixed on the fire, his body tensing. He saw the fire surge closer, bathe Jenny's face in flickering red orange light. His eyes burned. They wanted to blink. He strained to hold them open. The fire twitched and heaved as Todd pitted his will against it. Then in a final burst of concentration the flames started to recede.

It was at the same moment that he found his voice, and the word locked in his throat finally escaped. "Jenny!" he screamed.

Startled, Jenny jumped. "What, Todd?" she asked, alarmed.

Todd struggled to catch his breath. He squeezed his forehead to break the pain. He stared at the fire back in the fireplace, as though it had never moved.

Never moved?

"What, Todd?" Jenny insisted again.

"Nothing," he said. "Nothing. " And he took in deep breaths of air to wash away what must have been a dream.

Mickie appeared in the doorway. "Is everything all right?"

Todd wheezed. "I just thought I saw something. I thought—" And he looked again at the fire which was now almost mockingly calm.

CHAPTER 26

Mickie couldn't get the conversation with Lois out of her mind. It was as if finally sharing all her fears of some unknown evil in the house gave license to explore it.

They were all acting so strangely. It seemed that everyone who had ever lived in the house had fought. The old ladies argued constantly. The suicide note said that Jonas Cuttings beat his wife. Essie's parents didn't get along, Nina had said. And it seemed that they themselves were always on edge—snapping, antagonizing, bullying. Perhaps there *was* a negative force in the house that somehow affected everyone who lived there.

Rufus's words of the first day came back to her: *Mickie, I am so convinced we have found the place for us. It's like there's this little voice inside of me saying "buy me, buy me."*

Now you're hearing voices, Rufe? she had asked, and now wondered if her words had been prophetic. In a rush she thought about the suicide note, her dreams, fantasies, the *warnings*. And Rufus had called her Laura! There had to be something there that was beyond them.

She raised her eyes and stared at the ceiling. She balled her hands into fists and shook them above her. "I'll defeat you, I swear I will," she yelled to the empty house. "You will not take my family."

She repeated the words in the toy room, her eyes

resting on the marionettes hanging limply, motionlessly, along the wall.

Shocked at her uncontrollable fury, she pulled on her sweater and ran out of the house into the cool, fall air. Looking up at the house, from the road she shielded her eyes and squinted into the sun. Somehow it didn't seem as ominous as she was making it out to be. The sun caressed it softly, in innocence. There seemed to be nothing frightening about it at all.

Calmer, yet anxious to find some company to help her bury her confusion, she walked next door and rapped on Nina's door, but nobody answered. She decided to take a walk to sort through her own thoughts and clear her head.

But her mind refused to rest, and as she walked up Route 17, she started to hum the calliope tune from Jenny's music box.

Then she was in front of the Union Christian Church.

And cemetery.

She did not realize she had walked this far.

The sun glinted off the tombstones, and Mickie felt she could almost see through the trees to the far end of the cemetery and the Cuttings mausoleum. It was claiming her . . . beckoning her . . . telling her to look inside Benjamin Cuttings's coffin.

Her eyes widened in surprise, and with some amusement she marveled at what a frightened mind could conjure. Then she shuddered coldly. No. She certainly wasn't going to break into anybody's coffin.

Not today. Not ever.

She was turning to leave when she saw Mr. Jenkins coming toward her—

"Hello . . ."

—And decided that she was hoping he'd be there.

"Hello," she said and smiled.

Mr. Jenkins tipped an imaginary hat. Just his presence was making her feel more at ease.

"Lovely day," he said.

"It is," Mickie agreed.

"Great day to be alive, or"—he looked sadly around him—"not." His eyes went from Mickie to the Cuttings mausoleum. "You feel them in your house, don't you?" he asked sagely. "They've brought you back here."

Mickie nodded slowly, then asked the old man, "Mr. Jenkins, are you afraid of anything?"

"Dying, maybe. Once. But I've made my peace."

"Do you feel there's anything that can hurt you?"

Jenkins looked toward the mausoleum. "You mean them?"

Quietly. "Yes."

"They're dead."

"That doesn't answer my question."

"Memories hurt," he said. "Regrets. Missed opportunities to say I love you to someone. Lost, wasted time that you could have better spent. But I can't expect someone of your tender years to understand that. I've barely started to learn it now. Only moments perhaps before it's too late." His eyes passed around the cemetery.

"I'm afraid, Mr. Jenkins," Mickie said quietly, "things are happening to my family. Unexplainable things. There's turmoil when there shouldn't be any." She bit her lip, then asked, "Do you believe evil can remain in a house?"

"Shakespeare did. 'The evil that men do lives after them,' he said. 'The good is oft interred with their bones.' Yes," he said. "I do believe there's evil that never dies. Waiting for something to bring it out." He smiled sadly. "Sometimes it doesn't take much."

Mickie shuddered. Her eyes went to the mausoleum. She could almost feel the stone exterior. It was cold, like she was. *They were in there. Exerting influence over her family.* Her family who had never done them any harm, anyone any harm, whose only misfortune was to move into a house. The wrong house.

"I sense," she started slowly, "that there's something in there that I have to find—"

Involuntarily, she started for the mausoleum door. It was like she wanted Mr. Jenkins to stop her. He did, with a restraining hand on her wrist. "No," he said. "There's nothing in there for you. Don't even think it. You must solve your problems another way. And you will," he added with a smile. "I'm certain you will. Good day."

Mickie watched him walk slowly back up the cobbled path toward the church and road. From the back he looked hunched over, older suddenly, and she had to suspect, a little frightened by what she had suggested. Leaves shuffled underfoot.

And then there was oppressive silence in the cemetery.

Mickie stood torn, suspended. So close to the mausoleum. A grab of the handle, a twist of the knob. She'd already been inside. All that was remaining was to lift the lid of the boy's coffin. That was all.

All! She recoiled in horror and disbelief at what she had even thought of doing.

"No"—she said out loud. She resolutely refused to accept there was a lasting evil strong enough to destroy the love in her family. She was just making herself crazy again, and she tried to laugh in relief and didn't succeed.

Todd got the note to report to the principal's office. When he got there he was surprised to see Rick Webb was also waiting. The principal told them the bus driver had reported them for fighting, and he wanted to make certain there would be no more trouble. "A little warning," he said. Next time would mean detention for

Todd, and for Rick, a constant troublemaker, suspension. "Now shake hands," the principal said, and Todd took Rick's with a glint of a smile that the bigger boy couldn't understand. The principal ushered them out of his office, confident he had solved another school problem.

The handshake was forgotten as the boys went their separate ways down the corridor. Todd felt Rick's eyes bore through him as he rounded the corner, but he wasn't worried.

He didn't have to be.

A light bulb in the fixture over Rufus's desk blew and he was standing on his desk to change it. But the electrician who had installed the jar-shaped fixture had tightened the screws to excess, and Rufus's fingers slipped over the ridges of the screws without making any progress in loosening them.

"Damn," he muttered to himself. "Need a pair of pliers."

Rufus kept his tool chest in the trunk of his car. Although tool chest implied a little more than was actually there: two screwdrivers, a hammer, three unused wrenches, and some rusty pliers. As Rufus walked out to the car, he smiled to himself as he thought that about all he had ever done around the house was hang pictures and change easily accessible light bulbs. For anything else, a stuffed-up sink, an overflowing toilet, anything with molly bolts, he had called the super.

But the smile left his face when he saw the driver's side of the car. At first he thought it was a trick of the setting sun, casting shadow lines of pine needles across the doors and side paneling, but when he got closer he saw what it was.

Angry, wavy scratch marks were etched deeply into the metal, all the way down to the paint. Not surface scratches that could be touched up. All four panels would need sanding and total repainting. At least three hundred dollars worth of repainting. He ran his thumb along one of the scratch marks, feeling the rough edges. It had been done deliberately. No sideswipe would have made marks like that. It was like a thin piece of metal had been scraped against it. A key perhaps or a stone. The other side of the car was the same.

He went back into the house. Mickie was sautéeing onions to serve with the broiled liver for dinner.

"Did you see the car?" he asked.

"The car? No—why?"

"You drove it today, didn't you?"

"Just to the store this afternoon." She put the cover on the frying pan. "Why? What's wrong?"

"The sides are all scratched."

"Scratched?"

"About a half dozen lines from end to end. Both sides. It was done deliberately."

"No—"

"I just saw it, Mick," he said louder.

"All right, I'm not saying you didn't. I had the car at the market. I couldn't have been inside more than a couple of minutes. Maybe somebody did it in the parking lot, but I don't remember seeing scratches when I got out. But I was carrying packages . . ."

"These you would have remembered, Mick." Then he knew. "It wasn't done at the market." He was out of the kitchen. "Todd—" he bellowed from the bottom of the stairs. "Come down here."

Mickie was beside him. "Rufus—wait."

They heard Todd from upstairs. "I'm studying, Dad."

"I said come down here!" Rufus demanded again. Then he said, "Never mind," and started up the stairs. Mickie ran up after him.

Rufus burst into Todd's room. Todd was sitting at his desk, looking at a math textbook.

"Todd, did you scratch the car?" Rufus asked. He stood right next to Todd, towered over him.

"Scratch the car?" Todd asked.

"Did you scratch the car?" Rufus repeated louder. His eyes were small and blazing, his breath short, explosive.

Todd shook his head again but didn't say anything.

"Rufus, *please*," Mickie hissed in an undertone.

"Why did you do it? Because I yelled at you for not doing your homework? Were you trying to get back at me by destroying the car."

"I didn't, Dad, I swear."

Rufus stepped toward him. Mickie saw unjustified rage in his face. "I want you to admit it, Todd. I want you to admit doing it."

"I didn't," Todd repeated again in a small, scared voice. He backed himself into a corner of the room. He was aware he was trapped, his father closing in on him. Behind his father in his line of sight, Jenny stood in the doorway, watching. "I didn't, Daddy. Don't hit me," he begged. He shrank smaller into the corner, trying to disappear into the walls. He raised his arms to protect his face.

In one motion Rufus removed his belt and raised his hand over his head. Mickie stopped his arm in midair.

"Rufus, what do you think you're doing! Todd didn't scratch the car. Maybe the marks *were* there when I got out of the store, and I just didn't see them."

"The marks weren't there, Mickie. You couldn't have missed them. Not these marks." He turned his attention back to Todd. "You've done it this time, Todd. I am just sick and tired of all of your bullshit, and I am going to—"

"Rufus, Todd says he didn't do it!"

"Well, who else would have done it!" Rufus demanded.

"Maybe it was Rick Webb, Rufe," she blurted out.

"Maybe it was Rick getting even for what Todd did to his car. Or one of his friends. Or someone else altogether pulling a prank! Did you ever consider any of those possibilities?"

"I—"

"Did you, Rufe?" Mickie said with new strength. "Did you before blaming and hitting your son!" And she was aware she was yelling as loud as Rufus had been. "Did you!"

The anger drained from Rufus's face, replaced suddenly by confusion, then contrition. No—he hadn't considered any of those things. It had to be Todd who had done it, getting back at him for yelling . . .

"No," he said softly. After a lengthy pause he looked from Mickie to Todd to the belt in his hand, thinking about what he might have done. "I'm sorry, Todd," he said quickly, and pushing past Jenny, left the room.

Mickie extended her arm toward Todd who was still hunched in the corner, frightened, confused. She slowly drew him out. But she had nothing she could say to him and she, too, turned and left the room.

Todd stared at the closed door. He took deep breaths, calmed himself. And smiled. He didn't have to be afraid of his father anymore.

Rufus was lying in bed reading a detective novel. The blanket had fallen down to his waist baring his chest, and as Mickie came out of the bathroom drying her hair, she stared at him silently. Despite her denial in the cemetery, the thought of evil in the house continued to plague her, and especially after the incident tonight, she needed to share it with Rufus. In fact, she almost hoped it was something supernatural rather than her husband turning away from his son. She sat down on the edge of the bed and gently lifted the book from Rufus and rested it next to him.

"Hey, I'm almost finished," he protested.

"Rufe," she started slowly, summoning strength. "I want to talk about the problems that seem to be here." She was nervous.

"There aren't any problems," he answered, automatically reaching for his book.

"I don't know how you can say that," she said, her hand stopping his. "And I may sound like a broken record, I know, but you've been yelling at Todd, hitting him, the two of you have been snapping at each other like never before. And tonight, what you accused him of! Where did you come off thinking that Todd would—?" To Mickie her voice sounded as brittle as her words. "Perhaps," she continued stronger, and struggled to keep her voice steady, "what has been happening in some way ties into the past of the house. What if there is something in the house, something we have no control over, that's causing the tension. We know that other people who lived in this house fought with each other. Perhaps we're all victims of something."

"Victims of *what*?" he asked her.

"Rufus, I don't know!"

He looked at her for several moments, and she watched nonacceptance cloud his face.

"Won't you at least consider it as possible?" she asked suddenly feeling exposed and a little foolish.

"What? That there are evil spirits here in the house making us fight with each other? Is that what you think?"

"Yes! That's what I think. Do you have any better explanation for what's been happening? Why you've been yelling at Todd."

It was evident that Rufus was forcing himself to be patient with her. "I have been yelling at Todd because he deserves to be yelled at. And for no other reason. I am not yelling at Jenny because she's been good. So you see, if there was any truth at all to your theory, she would be drawn into this too. Once Todd gets rid of his smart-alecky attitude, then there won't be any reason to yell at him anymore."

"Why has it only been since we've moved up to this house that he's been smart-alecky!" she flared. "He wasn't like this back in New York."

"*I* can't answer that question, Mick. Ask *him*!" He met her intensity with his own. Then he lowered his voice. "Todd will change. He'll see he can't get anywhere by being fresh, and we'll all get back to normal. But there are no ghosts here, no devils, nothing is possessing us."

"That doesn't answer my question, Rufe."

"Then it can't be answered. It will remain a mystery."

"Fuck you," she spat out.

"And that really helps the situation."

"And was it Todd's smart-alecky attitude that made *you* think he scratched the car—?"

"I thought . . ." Rufus started.

"You thought," Mickie said with a breath of contempt. "I want to bring a psychic into the house."

"What? A mind reader?"

"No. A sensitive. A medium. Someone who can tell us if there's a spirit present here. Somebody who knows."

"Mickie, this is not Amityville."

"Rufus, why are you fighting me like this?" she pleaded.

"Because I don't want you to make yourself crazy."

"I've already done that. The purpose of the psychic is to relax me."

"And what if he tells you there's something spooky here?"

"Then we have the common sense to get out of here."

"And what if he's wrong?"

"I don't know."

"The old ladies lived here for how long, Mick?"

"About twenty years, I guess."

"Twenty years and nothing happened. And then we move in and all of a sudden the house is haunted. Come on—"

"Don't say *nothing* happened. We don't know. They fought all the time."

"They're old. Crotchety."

"And Laura and Jonas Cuttings. And Essie's parents. And God knows who else."

"No, Mick," he said forcefully. "I don't want any so-called psychics in the house telling you what they think you want to hear."

"Rufus, I have to do it."

He exhaled slowly, deliberately. "Fine. Do it. I'm sure you'll find a good one in the yellow pages. Only don't do it when the children are home. I don't want you to upset Jenny with your nonsense." He reached for the paperback and started to read again. "Possession," he sneered, leaving her standing over him.

With a sudden spurt of energy she didn't know she had, she wrenched the book from his hands and flung it across the room. "Damn you, Rufus. We have a real problem here whatever the source. Don't you laugh at me. Don't be condescending and don't treat me like a child."

"Mickie, you can't truly believe what you're saying—possession?"

"Just don't treat me like a child and tune me out," she repeated. "Okay?"

"Fine. I won't."

Mickie was suddenly calmer. Yelling wasn't going to get them anywhere. She took a deep breath. "Rufus, why are you turning your back on me like this? I need your help now. I'm upset."

"I see you are, Mick. But when you throw possession and devils at me, and you're not willing to hear any-

thing else, I just don't know what to do. That scares
me a little about you too." He shifted on the bed and
moved closer to her. "Look, I am not unaware of
what has been transpiring between Todd and me. And
I don't like it any more than you. Yes, I have been
yelling at Todd, he has been yelling at me. I'm tense.
He's tense. We both have adjustments to make up
here. New tensions. New friends. And that's what it
is. Yes, I overreacted tonight and jumped to errone-
ous conclusions. But you are looking to find evil in
perfectly normal, although unpleasant, father-son problems—all prompted by your accidental finding of a
hundred-year-old suicide note. Face it, what if you
hadn't found that note? Would you be thinking any of
this?"

"I don't know," she said. "But what if it wasn't by
accident that I found it. What if—?"

Rufus cut her off. "Mick, enough. Enough." He
reached up and pulled her down to him. He kissed her.
"I love you, Mick, and I promise you, I am not pos-
sessed and everything here is fine. And it's going to remain fine. And I will do everything I possibly can not
to yell at Todd. I don't want to see you upset. Okay?"

Mickie nodded slightly, her lips in a thin, expressionless line. There would be no breaking through. He
wasn't going to give her an inch. "Okay."

"You're sure."

"No."

"Be sure, Mick. *Please*."

"Okay, Rufe. Enough for tonight."

"Good. Thank you. Now may I please have my book
back?" he asked calmly. His eyes were on her as she
retrieved the book and brought it back to him. "Thank
you," he said and buried himself in the novel.

Mickie stared down at him, dry-eyed, suddenly emotionless. She felt drained. Her breathing was even, yet
her heart was racing. No, she wasn't okay, and she

didn't know what would make her feel any better. Even though what Rufus said made absolute sense, and it was what she wanted to hear, still nothing had been resolved. They still didn't know the origin of the problems and were no closer to finding it. Except that she now knew she would be watching everything closely. She *would* look to find evil in perfectly normal father-son problems.

Although she didn't know where it all would lead.

CHAPTER 27

Lois arrived late in the day, barely in time for dinner. "Two flats. Can you believe it?" she asked, hugging Mickie. "Ooo, it's so good to see you." She knelt down and hugged the children. "And you. And you."

"How are you?" Mickie said excitedly.

"Love is all you need," Lois sang happily. "I'll summarize it for you. Unless I spill soup on Bill's parents or do something equally gauche and unforgivable, we're going to be married in December."

"That's wonderful!"

"Mick, I haven't been this happy in years."

"Can I come to the wedding, Aunt Lois?" Jenny asked.

"You bet. And—I also remembered somebody's birthday—" She offered Jenny the present. "Not to be opened until," she cautioned. "Or else it self-destructs."

"Thank you, Lois," Jenny said and kissed her.

Rufus came in from his office.

"Well, here he is now," Lois said. "The mad pediatrician of Glendon, Vermont."

"Hello, Lois," Rufus smiled and kissed her lightly.

"I expected you hours ago," Mickie said. "We'd better get into the kitchen before the roast turns three shades of color. All black."

"Without first seeing this castle of yours? No way. One quick look. I like my meat well done anyway." She held out her hand for the children to take. "Lead the way."

They entered the living room first and Lois was immediately taken by the fireplace. "This alone is worth the price of the house, isn't it?" She marveled at the display of Mickie's Waterford along the mantel.

"We've been building a fire almost every night," Mickie said. "It gets rather chilly up here now and a fire is so romantic." She winked.

"It also saves on the cost of heating oil," Rufus said. "One man's romance is another man's fuel bill."

"And now up the grand staircase," Lois suggested. "You should give guided tours of this place, you know. I want to see the room with the toys first."

All five of them stepped into the toy room. Lois scanned the wall of marionettes and saluted their staring faces. "Hi, guys," she said, then frowned and turned to Jenny. "Don't they speak?"

"Only when I make them." Todd grinned. "Right, Jen?"

Jenny nodded without conviction.

Mickie led the way to their bedrooms, opening up the several rooms they had closed off.

"You can house an army up here," Lois observed. "Planning on having any more children?"

"Are you kidding?" Mickie asked. "We're having enough trouble raising the ones we have now—" She met Rufus's eye and immediately regretted her flub. She had meant the words as a joke, but then she realized this was not an area for humor. She opened the door into their bedroom. "*Ta da!* Where his and her majesty sleep."

"Nice," Lois said and then amended her statement. "What nice? It's terrific. It's bigger than my first studio apartment in New York. And the view—!"

The sun was setting over the Vermont mountains, the sky a rich purple with slashes of light between the clouds. The evergreens huddled together against the coming night.

"Mick," she beamed. "This whole setting—the house, everything—is just so utterly fantastic. I envy all of you."

"Thanks," Mickie said, a bit distantly.

"Come see my room now, Aunt Lois," and Jenny tugged at her arm.

"You mean you have a room too?" Lois teased. "Well, lead the way."

Jenny's room was scrupulously neat. After living with Todd and his clutter for her entire life, she had resolved never to have an item out of place. A pink coverlet lay across her bed which Jenny had spent the better part of an hour tightening to perfection. A matching bolster was propped against the headboard, with Snoopy sitting grandly on top. "Lovely," Lois said, and Jenny giggled happily.

"She's absolutely perfect, isn't she?" Rufus beamed and hugged Jenny to him.

"Now shall we see the little prince's room?" Todd shrugged. There really wasn't much to see. "Well, boys aren't really expected to be neat, are they?" Lois said when they stepped in. "I think we should call this the Oscar Madison Memorial wing. Somewhere in here there's a bed I'm sure." Clothing was strewn across the chair and bed and sporting equipment lay scattered about the floor. It seemed like there was more out of the closets than in them. Rufus's exhale was heard by everyone.

"I thought you promised to clean up in here, Todd."

"I did, Dad, but it keeps getting dirty again," Todd shrugged innocently and smiled at Lois who ran her hand through his hair.

"Responsibility, Todd," Rufus said. "Remember our talks." His voice was calm, but with a whisper of tightness. "Your room doesn't have to look like this." Then he smiled at Lois and offered her his arm. "Well, shall we eat? I think we're having what used to be meat for dinner."

Silently Mickie muttered thanks that there hadn't been a blowup.

At dinner Lois noted that Rufus was trying to be pleasant and mask any discord in the house. But there was no mistaking the undercurrent of tension over the meal. Nothing overt, just a quiet, subtle strain. Todd was quiet and brooding and no conversation passed between him and his father. Occasionally Lois caught them eyeing each other suspiciously. It upset her to see them like this, and it upset her for Mickie as well. She recognized Mickie's discomfort and her own tension, and helped keep the conversation lively with small talk about New York and life in Glendon.

After dinner Lois and Mickie stayed in the kitchen to clean up and catch up. Mickie put on a pot of coffee, and they helped themselves to a second piece of applesauce cake that Mickie had made that afternoon.

"Now you see what I've been talking about?" Mickie said. "And it doesn't seem to be getting any better. At first I blamed Rufus for not making the effort—Todd seemed to be willing. Now nobody is willing. The other night Todd goaded Rufus into yelling at him again. Rufus just asked him a question and instead of answering it civilly, he made a whole to-do and brought Rufus into a screaming match. And you saw that room of his. He knew it would make Rufus angry. Maybe they're getting some perverse enjoyment out of all this. I don't know. Or maybe it *is* something else altogether," she added.

Lois touched her hand. "Mick, I just don't think so, but I also don't think I should make you try to accept that. You have to figure this out on your own."

Mickie smiled. "I seem to be in the minority around here, don't I?"

"Look, Mick, I'm not going to tell you what I think you want to hear, and I'm not going to try to change your mind."

"Why is it so much easier to hear this from you than Rufus?"

"Because it's a second opinion, maybe. Or because you see me as totally objective."

"Yes," Mickie said softly. "That's it. And believe me, I'm working on this. I know I'm my own worst enemy. A regular looney sometimes."

"No, you're not," Lois said.

"Just don't think of me as too much of a crackpot."

"Of course not, hon. I love you." There was a thoughtful silence, then Lois asked, "What about Jenny? How is she coping with all of this?"

"Basically all right. She and Rufus are closer than ever. The farther Rufus seems to pull away from Todd, the closer he gets to Jenny. Then she sees what's happening between her father and brother, sees herself benefiting from it, and doesn't know what to do. She's loving the attention, but there's strain now between her and Todd. He's jealous, probably, and I'm sure he's taking it out on her. Bothering her. Frightening her sometimes."

Lois smiled sadly. "You know, I had saved up a whole wad of country bumpkin jokes, but I don't think they'll go over big tonight."

Mickie matched her smile. "No, we don't do much joking anymore. Unless there's sarcasm. We're very big on sarcasm."

Lois reached over and touched her hand. "Mick," she said. "It's only temporary. They are father and son. They'll get over it."

"I can't get through to him," Mickie said. "If he would make a move, Todd would have to respond. I'm sure Todd wants to, and all he's doing now is fighting fire with fire, responding to Rufus in kind. But I can't

get Rufus to budge. He wants Todd to change his behavior first, and Todd is, but the wrong way."

"Can you take the children away for a couple of
days?" Lois suggested. "Everyone could blow off his
own steam that way. Leave Rufus here. I'm sure Todd
will be happy to get out of here."

Mickie shook her head. "I don't see how. School."

"A long weekend then. Leave Friday. Come back
Monday. Why don't you go to New York and visit your
mother? It'll give you a chance to breathe. Let Rufus
get this out of his system. By the time you get back,
they'll have missed each other, and it will be all over."

"It's a good idea," Mickie agreed.

"Better than pulling open somebody's coffin?"

"A lot better," Mickie said.

They moved into the living room where Mickie apologetically set Lois up for the night on the convertible
couch. But neither was ready to end the evening. There
was so much left to talk about. The fire was still blazing, and they sat in front of it talking about everything
and everyone. Neither mentioned Rufus or possession
again.

When she got upstairs, Rufus was already asleep.
She would talk to him in the morning and insist that she
take the children for a long weekend back home. Home
was still New York, she thought ruefully; she couldn't
call this house home yet.

She pulled on her nightgown and climbed into bed
next to Rufus. Impulsively, tenderly, she kissed his
cheek, letting her lips linger an extra second. An unexplainable feeling of relief passed through her. Rufus
stirred slightly, but did not awaken.

Downstairs, the fire was out, the last dying embers
glowing. Charred wood and paper remains dusted the
fireplace in piles of gray and black. The thermostat had
been turned down, the doors and windows locked, the
lights switched off except for the night-light in the sec-

ond floor hallway, a forty-watt bulb which cast a dim, orange light. Outside, the night wind whined through the evergreens. Rufus and Mickie and the children were sleeping upstairs and Lois huddled on the couch downstairs. The house was closed up, silent in the night.

Rufus struggled in bed, trapped somewhere between sleep and wakefulness, fighting thoughts that penetrated his almost conscious mind. Thoughts about Lois.

She knows about him and the boy.

Knows his secret, knows what's going to happen.

Knows about the room in the cellar.

Wants them out of the house.

But he couldn't let her stop it from happening.

It all had to happen.

Just like it had before.

Then he groaned and twisted, and his covers fell back.

A creaking sound woke Lois.

Creaking . . . ? She was puzzled. The sound of a door opening and closing.

It wasn't one of the night sounds that Mickie had warned her of, the whirring sound of the boiler, the sudden click of the furnace turning itself on and off, the moaning of a settling house. It was a slow and painful creak. It had to be a door.

Could Mickie have forgotten to lock the back door? Lois wondered, and was the wind brushing it open and closed? She turned over, pulled the covers over her head, and tried to ignore it, but felt uneasy. The creaking sound grew more insistent, demanding.

She threw the covers back and eased off the couch. She grabbed her robe which was draped over a nearby chair and slipped it on. She shivered in the cold room and wished they had thrown extra logs on the fire to burn well into the night. She looked hesitantly upstairs, the stairwell faintly illuminated by the night-light. "Mick—?" she mouthed, but she knew her voice wouldn't carry upstairs. She would go close the door herself. She crossed the living room and swung open the kitchen door and flipped on the light switch. The flood of light blinded her momentarily. She shut her eyes and when she slowly opened them and adjusted to the light, she saw that the back door was closed and chained.

Yet still the creaking sound persisted from the other side of the kitchen.

The cellar door.

It was only open a few inches, but it was not latched, and a breeze from downstairs was blowing it open, then withdrawing and allowing it to close.

She walked to the door, intending to shut it, latch it.

She saw something move. In the thin line of blackness behind the door. The movement drew her to it; her response wasn't conscious curiosity, just reflexive.

She pulled open the cellar door and jumped when she saw the figure standing in the dark shadows behind. And in one split second, she understood that Mickie had been right. The house *was* a house of the damned.

And when she saw the hand that reached out toward her, she was already beyond fear. And as she was flung full force down the cellar stairs to the concrete floor below, she thought about Bill, waiting for her in Montreal. Then she wasn't thinking about anything at all.

CHAPTER 28

Mickie didn't know what prompted her to open the cellar door. For a moment she stared in bewilderment; the scene wasn't registering. But then her eyes telescoped down the stairs toward her friend's body sprawled out on the floor. Lois was lying on her side, her head twisted at an awkward angle. Her arm was pinned under her, her hand sticking out, palm open, as if pleading for help. Her neck was apparently broken. Mickie ran halfway down the steps and stopped, uncertain whether to continue or not. Lois's eyes were open and staring at her in accusation. Her mouth was twisted and grimaced in final pain. There was no doubt in Mickie's mind that Lois was dead.

She had come downstairs before Rufus to put up coffee for them, knowing Lois wanted to get an early start. The covers were on the floor next to the couch, the sheet was rumpled, the pillow scrunched up and balanced half off the couch. Lois wasn't in the downstairs bathroom or kitchen. She must have gone outside for some country air.

Then something had moved her to open the cellar door.

"Rufus!" she shrieked and then thought about the children. She raced up the stairs and slammed the cellar door behind her. Todd was in the kitchen.

"What is it, Ma? What's wrong?"

"Nothing, Todd—" and she crossed the kitchen.

"Rufus!" She turned around and saw her son. "Todd, stay away from that door. Todd, no!"

But Todd opened the door and looked down the stairs.

"Mommy!" he screamed, terrified.

"Close that door, Todd," Mickie ordered, but Todd was already slamming it shut. "Get out of here right now. Don't let Jenny come down here. Keep her upstairs. I'll be up soon. Rufus—!"

Rufus ran down the cellar stairs. He looked in Lois's eyes, held her wrists, and checked her pulse. Went through the motions. Mickie stood in the middle of the staircase.

"She's dead, Mick," he said softly.

As though her tears had been waiting for the formal pronouncement, they now came in an hysterical flood. Rufus led her back up the stairs and sat her down at the kitchen table. He poured her a glass of water and put it to her lips. Her hands were shaking too much to hold it herself.

"Dead, Rufus?" Mickie asked blankly, unbelieving. As if all of a sudden the word had no meaning to her. Just last night Lois had been in here, making plans to be married. Now . . .

Dead

"I have to call the authorities."

"The authorities?"

"The police."

She nodded weakly and got to her feet.

"I'll get the children dressed and out of here. They shouldn't be here when the police arrive."

"No, Mick," Rufus said gently. "The police will want to talk to them too. Maybe they heard something last night. Saw something . . ."

"What could they—?" she asked. She had to get her children away from this house.

"Mick," he repeated gently, and clasped her firmly

by the wrist, restraining her, easing her back into the chair. "I'll call the police and dress the children. You wait here."

Mickie eyed the cellar door.

"No, Rufe," she said firmly. "Not here."

The children were told what happened and the police duplicated many of the questions Rufus prepared them for. No. They hadn't seen anything or heard anything. *None* of them had, Mickie shook her head vigorously. There were no signs of forced entry by an intruder. Nothing missing. Lois must have gone into the kitchen for a glass of water, got confused, walked through the wrong door, didn't realize where she was, tripped on the top stair, and fell . . .

No, they didn't know her to be disoriented or suffer from vertigo, epilepsy, walk in her sleep. But Lois was the kind of person who would never make her short-comings be known. She wasn't on any medication that they knew, and a quick look through her suitcase and purse revealed nothing stronger than aspirin. It was just an honest to goodness accident.

"Oh, God," Mickie said, her face in her hands. "If she hadn't come up here . . ."

Family? No parents. An ex-husband in New York. A fiancé in Montreal. A sister out west somewhere— Tucson, Albuquerque. Yes, they knew the ex-husband, and he would know where the sister lived.

And then they carried her upstairs. Mickie stood anchored next to the sink as the body came through the cellar door, covered with the sheet that Lois had slept on last night. They put her on the stretcher and wheeled her outside to the waiting ambulance.

Rufus would accompany the body to the morgue until the proper arrangements could be made. He would be back as soon as he could . . . after the necessary people were informed and things were in order.

Mickie wanted to go with him and felt that somehow she was responsible, but Rufus wouldn't let her go. She was in no way responsible, he repeated strongly, and she should stay here. In case someone called. Would she put a sign on his office door saying an emergency had called him away? The patients could wait or come back later.

The state troopers were grateful that Dr. Talman had been so helpful. There wasn't the slightest bit of suspicion of anything other than an accident.

Rufus and the others were gone and a deathly quiet settled over the house.

Mickie ran upstairs to be with her children. Todd was in Jenny's room staring out the window at the police car that was speeding away, red light flashing. Jenny was familiar with death because her best friend's father had died recently, and she had shared the girl's grief with her. But here it was more real. It was Aunt Lois who had died! In their house!

It was a terrible tragedy that had occurred, Mickie told them, and the best place for them now was in school. Maybe tomorrow they would take a little vacation in New York, without Daddy, who was busy up here. Would they like that? Jenny was all for it; Todd more reluctant. She had expected him to jump at the chance to get away from Rufus, but instead he just shrugged and said if that was the decision he would go along with it, but he would just as soon stay there. Mickie thought his reaction strange, but she said it was only an idea she had and hadn't even talked with Rufus about it. She suggested they keep it among themselves.

They had missed the bus so Mickie drove them to school. They were better off there than anywhere else right now. Mickie wished that she had someplace else to be.

After returning home and parking the car, she really

didn't want to return to the empty house. Being there would be too painful for her. She started up the road again, hands thrust deeply into her pockets, eyes toward the ground. She passed quickly by Nina's house. She didn't feel like talking to anyone.

Poor Lois. Poor, poor Lois. Mickie started to cry. She could still hear Lois's joking words, her mile-a-minute patter from just the night before.

Haven't been this happy in years.

And suddenly without reason or warning it's over. Stupid, stupid accident! Mickie pressed her tight-fisted hands against her eyes to arrest the flow of tears.

She had known Lois for over twenty years. They had attended college mixers together, dated, compared notes and rated their boyfriends even before it was fashionable. They had both married doctors and had been in each other's wedding parties. Then Lois's gynecologist husband had run off with a twenty-year-old patient. Lois had taken it very hard. She had loved David and he hurt her badly. Mickie had seen Lois through the separation, the divorce, and the painful aftermath. And every day she had thanked God for Rufus. Knowing that even though the strains were there, they were insep-arable. She wondered if that was still true. All those years she hadn't lost him to another woman, she hadn't lost him to his work, and now she wouldn't, she vowed, lose him to this house. She would fight against anything that threatened her marriage, her life. Anything alive . . . or dead.

She had walked along Route 17. She was now stand-ing in front of the Union Christian Church. Across the road from the cemetery. Her feet—*no*—*her mind* had drawn her here.

She had to laugh. It was a nervous hollow laughter that was forced. She crossed the road, pushed open the crossbar gate, and walked into the cemetery. She was there.

She felt torn. Yet driven.

She walked forward, trying to decide what she should do. She was out of sight of the roadway, past the Jenkins grave, almost to the back of the cemetery. She was alone. The day was cool, overcast. She had left the house without taking a sweater, and now with the sun hidden behind the clouds, she shivered. But her goose skin was coming from something other than the wind.

The harsh call of a black crow shattered the cemetery silence. Mickie jumped and stared up at the tree limb. The crow seemed to laugh at her, daring her to proceed.

The mausoleum stood out starkly against the gray light of the cloud-ridden sky. She eyed it uncertainly and silently asked Laura Cuttings for guidance.

She could almost hear the voice within her, urging her forward.

And Mr. Jenkins's voice as well. *There is nothing in there for you. You must solve your problems another way.*

"What other way?" Mickie questioned out loud. She felt all alone. Except for Laura.

She circled her hand around the brass handle.

Then the door was open and she was standing in the entrance, daylight displaced the darkness of the tomb. Tentatively, she crossed to Benjamin Cuttings's coffin.

Nothing in there for you . . .

There was a scream behind her.

Jenny! her mind whirred.

She spun around.

Not Jenny . . .

Just the crow who had landed in the doorway. He seemed to eye her curiously, his head cocked at an angle, wondering what she was doing in *his* cemetery. He was the guardian, she the intruder.

She chased him away, and with no further hesitation

or thought knelt down next to the boy's coffin and started to raise the lid.

She caught her finger on a burr.

"Damn!" she spat out, as blood surfaced and dripped onto the rotting wooden coffin. All of a sudden she understood the horror of what she was doing. By taking this awful irrevocable step, she was acknowledging that she *believed*. There was no longer any doubt. She—and all her family—now were part of it.

Tuesday afternoons instead of last-period gym, Todd had service in the chemistry lab. He would wash the test tubes and beakers, wipe off the electrical balances, and clean up from the demonstrations of the day. It was slave work, but he didn't mind ducking out of gym. He was cleaning the countertop when through the glass classroom door he saw Rick's friend, Riley.

Riley saw him too, stopped, and tried the door. Open.

The chemistry teacher had gone down to the office to punch out and gather up her mail. Todd was alone in the lab room.

"So this is where you hide out on Tuesday afternoons, huh, Todd-y?"

Todd said nothing. He kept wiping off the counters, although a ghost of a smile crept on to his lips.

Riley walked closer, pretending to look at the bottles of chemicals—sodium hydroxide, potassium bromide, hydrochloric acid.

"You and me got nothing going, Riley," Todd said.

"Maybe. Maybe not. But Rick'll be happy if I flatten you." He took a step closer to Todd. Todd saw that he was leaning with his palm on the counter, close to the bottles of acid and base.

Todd thought about an old movie he had seen over and over again—*The House on Haunted Hill*. He would never forget a scene where one of the characters tripped and fell into a tremendous vat of acid under a trap door in the basement of the house. All that was left of the girl was a trickle of bubbles that floated to the surface. It became a source of horrid fascination to him. To be killed by concentrated acid. What would it feel like? Would the skin simmer? Burn? Disintegrate? Would there be pain or would it all happen too quickly? Would the eyes sizzle? Did the person drown in the acid or did it bubble away face and brain and lungs and tissue well before that. Did only skeleton bones remain, if that . . .

His curiosity would soon be appeased. He knew what to do, and it happened quickly.

The acid bottle tipped over and fell onto the desk behind Riley. The glass stopper flew out and the acid spilled out across the counter.

"Look out!" Todd cried. "That's acid!"

But before Riley could react, the acid flowed under his hand and burned him.

Riley shrieked. His hand was on fire.

"The water!" Todd yelled. "Put it under water."

Riley dove for the sink, turned the faucet on full, and let the cold water wash over his hand. The acid was dilute and had scared him more than hurt him, but his hand had already started to blister.

Riley looked at the countertop. The acid had spread across it and was dripping onto the floor. Some of it had gotten onto his pants and was eating at the material. Todd still stood across the room.

"A message for Rick," Todd said, his eyes cold and intense. "You tell him to stay the fuck away from me. Or"—his mouth curled upward in a smile—"it'll be a fate worse than death. Now get out of here."

And Riley got out and did not look back.

A hundred *Twilight Zone* episodes ran through Mickie's head. She steeled herself for whatever horrors lay inside. She had no idea what to expect when the light streamed into the coffin.

She was prepared for anything—a skeleton, a decayed corpse, a putrid, century-old odor. Anything.

What she wasn't prepared for was nothing.

She stared in disbelief at the empty coffin as tension ran out of her body. She had to laugh out loud. Nothing! My God!

She looked again; the coffin was empty.

No, not entirely . . .

She had been looking for a corpse so almost missed the piece of paper. It was yellowed and stuck to the bottom of the casket. She reached for it, lifted it so it wouldn't tear, and sensed its fragility, its importance . . .

She slammed the coffin shut and quickly left the mausoleum without looking back. She wouldn't be returning there again.

Outside she squinted at the paper. The ink was faded, barely readable.

> No one ever knew of his birth and no one shall ever know his whereabouts now, save the worms and insects that burrow through his rotting corpse. He was born with a twisted, cloven hand, the mark of a demon. In a fit of rage I killed him, and became no better than he. Knowing that is my punishment, my regret was that it was not done sooner, and that first others had to die.

She could barely make out the faded signature of Jonas Cuttings.

CHAPTER 29

"You did *what*, Mick?"

He wasn't listening to what she was saying.

"Rufus, will you just read—"

"You actually opened somebody's coffin?" He clamped his hand against his forehead. "My God. I don't believe it!"

"Jonas Cuttings killed his son!" she said loudly, angry and frightened all at once. "With everything else going on around here, doesn't that mean anything to you?"

"What am I supposed to be afraid of?" Rufus bellowed. "That he's coming back to kill *our* son—?"

"No, Rufe. Don't you understand. It's *you* who's going to—" She broke off as she met his incredulous stare.

"Are you out of your mind?" he asked horrified.

"What the hell do you think you're saying? This is real life, Mick, not some Stephen King novel. Don't you understand that?" He pushed her away from him.

"Rufus, you don't see it, because it's happening to you." She took two steps away from him and rubbed the back of her neck. "Whatever it was that happened to Laura and Jonas Cuttings is happening here. God, I'm so afraid right now. I'm shivering." She closed and opened her hands, tried to get the circulation going to warm them. "Rufe, you read Laura Cuttings's suicide note. Look—see what it says—" She fished the wrin-

kled piece of paper out of her pocket and thrust it at
him.

"I thought you threw that out—"

"Well, I didn't! Here it is. Read it!"

"I know what it says."

"Then you remember this—" Her hands shook as
she pointed to the words. *He will return and kill again.*
"It's going to happen, Rufe. Through you!"

"You're out of your fucking mind!"

"Maybe I am. Maybe. But can we afford to take that
chance? Listen to us. We're screaming at each other.
The same way Jonas and Laura fought with each other.
There is something in this house that's causing this and
you can no longer deny it. Are we just going to wait for
something to happen? What if it's going to happen tonight? How will we know when it's coming on? How do
we stop it?"

"Stop *what*?"

"The possession!"

Disgusted, Rufus threw up his hands at her and
turned away. He started to walk toward his office. "I've
had it with you and this possession crap, Mick. There
is no possession here, nothing supernatural or demonic.
But you've been on this for a month now, and I just
can't listen to it anymore. Go call a psychic, if you
want. Call a priest. Call anybody. Just leave me out of
it."

He was almost at the door when she reached him,
grabbed his shoulder, forcing him to turn around to
face her.

"Don't run away from me! We have to deal with this
together. This house has already killed Lois and what if
it isn't finished!"

It was automatic. A reaction to her hand on him,
spinning him around, her one-track mind.

"Mickie, shut up!" he screamed at her. "Will you
just shut up!" He slapped her hard across the face.

And then as if he had lost his control and suddenly found it again he reacted in horror to what he had done.

"I'm sorry, Mick, I'm sorry. Jesus—"

He moved toward her, to quiet her, to hold her.

But frightened, Mickie started to back away.

"I am getting out of this house," she said. "The children and I are not spending another night here."

Her fear of him, of the moment, eclipsed the sting of the slap.

He ran around her, blocked her. "Mickie, please. Stop. Listen."

"Get out of my way," she sputtered. "Because *I'll* kill *you.*"

"Mick—"

"I'll kill you," she screamed and stamped up and down like an hysterical child.

He let her pass. She was halfway up the stairs when he called after her.

"You won't take the children, Mick."

She stopped, turned to him. Her back was rigid.

"What?"

"I said you're not taking the children anywhere. If you try, I'll take you to court, have you committed. You hear voices, break into mausoleums, pry open coffins. Snatch children. You're not a fit mother. Go prove your possession. I'll win them and you'll never see them again. I swear it."

"You'd do that?" she asked incredulously.

"If I have to."

She stared at him for what must have been five agonizing minutes and then slumped onto the stairs where she stood, bones and muscles refusing to support her. She didn't even have the strength to stand. Her world was collapsing around her. She sobbed into her hands. She couldn't believe he would do this to her.

Rufus climbed up to her and sat down next to her.

He took her hand in his and stroked it lightly. She was only vaguely aware of him as she looked out through a wall of tears.

"I don't want to do anything like that, Mick. And I don't want you to leave either."

"I have to," she said absently, not looking at him. "You hit me, Rufe. Like Jonas Cuttings. Can't you understand? It's not going to stop."

"Yes, I hit you," Rufus said softly, contritely. "And I'm terribly, terribly sorry." His words came out in whispers. He caught her eye, saw her desperation, and looked away from her, embarrassed. "I've never done anything like that before. You made me so tense and crazy with your incessant talk of possession. I didn't know how else to quiet you. I lost control."

"Rufe, we have to get out of this house before you lose control again and really hurt me or Todd." Again she thought of the note in the coffin, of Jonas Cuttings killing his son, and finally of Lois. Rufus saw her eyes and knew what was crossing her mind.

He shook his head fiercely from side to side. "Don't even think it. It was an accident. She opened the wrong door and tripped in the dark."

"No," Mickie said fearfully, pulling away from him, crowding against the wall so he wouldn't even be touching her.

"I—did—not—kill—Lois!" he repeated.

"What if you didn't know? What if that's part of the possession?" She threw herself into his arms. "Oh, Rufus, I'm so frightened. I don't know what I'm saying anymore. Of course it was an accident. I didn't mean— But you must see what we're doing to each other— screaming, fighting, hitting—" She buried herself in his shoulder and fought back the tears. "We've got to get out of here," she repeated in a whisper. As if the house could hear. "Before it's too late. Before something more happens."

"Nothing's going to happen," Rufus said soothingly, stroking her head.

"You keep saying that!" she said and didn't care that her voice was growing loud. "But I've been watching what's going on here. Let me just take the children away for a while." Rufus could see the terror in her eyes.

"And tell them what?" he asked softly. "Frighten them so they won't want to live here anymore? Is that what you want? All three of you will be looking over your shoulders for shadows in the night. Don't do anything to hurt us, Mick. We love this house—"

"I hate it."

"We love it," he repeated firmly. "And we have a life here now. And responsibilities. A mortgage. Everything we own is tied up in this house. We can't just pick up and leave because Todd and I are feuding with each other."

Nothing is forever.

"We can, Rufe! There's nothing holding us here, nothing stopping us."

"No, Mick, no!" he said sharply. Then he drew her close to him. "*We'll* go away," he whispered. "Just the two of us. A long weekend. We'll drive down to the Cape and rent a beach house. There won't be many people out there now. We'll be alone. We'll talk. We'll listen to each other. And we won't argue, I promise. We'll try to understand each other. Sort things through, see what makes sense and what doesn't. We'll talk about me and Todd, you'll help me make up with him. I just want you to trust me that it's all okay here. Honey, please," he begged.

"I don't know," Mickie said, her mind confused like never before. "I just don't know . . ." She tried to sift everything that had happened through in her mind but she only became more confused. Her frightened mind was unable to focus on anything—to make sense—to convince Rufus . . .

She turned away from him and stared at the fireplace, at the piles of gray-black ash and soot that needed sweeping. Rufus wanted her to trust him, and that was what it all came down to. Did she trust his judgment (which might be clouded by possession) or did she follow her instincts, grab the children, leave this house. She looked at him, his face warm and serene, his blue eyes almost glowing. He looked more himself than the entire time they'd spent in this house, she thought. Was it only a deception, the calm before the storm? No!

Maybe she was only making herself hysterical with coincidence, she thought with a rush of giddy relief. Looking to find things, make something out of nothing, mountains out of molehills. That's what Rufus had said over and over. And Lois, too, with all of her objectivity. She knew she could easily talk herself into or out of anything. And she also knew that she didn't want to believe any of this!

Getting away alone with Rufus was a solution, she realized, however temporary. As long as Rufus was out of the house and he and Todd were separated, nothing bad could happen. So she could go away with him, try to work things out. *God, how she hoped she wasn't making a mistake.*

But her mind was made up.

"Mother will be thrilled to sit with the children," she said quietly. "I'll tell her you're tired and need a rest. And we'll have to cancel Jenny's birthday party."

"No, don't do that," Rufus said. "Jenny needs her friends here, and we need a sense of normalcy in the house. Your mother can handle a half-dozen girls. She'd love it."

Mickie shook her head, her palms wiping the tears

from her face. "It's not fair to the other mothers. They think I'm going to be in charge."

Rufus smiled. "You'll call them. See if there's a problem. I think they'd be happier with Mom, anyway," he winked. "She doesn't hear voices and rob graves."

Mickie forced a tentative smile. "Not funny, Rufe, but all right. I'll call them. If they don't object, the party stays on."

Rufus opened his arms to her and she let herself be enclosed by them; she needed him. For the moment she let her mind block out the problems, block out everything except Rufus, his touch, his warmth. It was all too much to handle now. She was too confused. When they were away and alone they would talk, understand.

Rufus rested his head on her shoulder and out of the corner of his eye he caught Todd. He was at the top of the stairs, on the landing, leaning against the wall and watching them.

Jenny was very understanding when they told her they would miss her birthday party.

"Daddy's been very tired lately," Mickie explained. "And we thought we'd sneak away for a quiet weekend. We talked about postponing the party, but it's all set up, and Grandma is eagerly looking forward to chaperoning. And then when we get back, we'll have a private party just for the four of us with some surprises that we'll buy at the Cape. So you'll really have two parties, all right?"

Jenny nodded; it was all right with her. There was even a hint of excitement that her parents would be away. Grandma was not as strict, and they could probably get away with more.

Nina was sympathetic as well. "God, yes, take him for a vacation, Mickie. I think the only time he's taken off was the night you came to dinner. I've never seen that lot with fewer than five cars. Don't worry about the kids. I'll be on the alert if your mother needs me, and I'll even pop in every once in a while to take a look. Even though Cara will be mortified, I'm sure."

None of the other parents objected either, so the party remained as scheduled.

That night Mickie stayed in the shower for longer than usual with the water hotter than usual. She let it pour over her head to wash away the day's cares. It had been a long, exhausting, emotionally draining time for all of them. In bed she clutched Rufus to her, half afraid that if she let go of him for even a second the house would swallow him up. They only had to get through the next two nights without incident, when they were all still in the house, and she half hoped she could remain awake all night on vigil.

Dinner had passed easily. Rufus and Todd talked pleasantly to each other, with no friction, no tension. As if inexplicably they had been brought back together. Father and son the way they should be, the way they used to be. And when she and Rufus went upstairs to tuck the children in, she was more than surprised to see that Todd's room had been immaculately cleaned. Why, she wondered, but then had to berate herself for looking for evil in their reconciliation.

The curtains were up, and she stared out the window at the watchful moon and tried to relax. A wave of guilt passed over her when she realized she had not really thought about Lois all day, except to assure Jenny that Lois was in heaven watching over all of them.

"Did you speak to Lois's sister from the morgue?" she asked Rufus. "God, what a word," she shuddered, and then added, "I should call her."

"I called Dave," Rufus said. "He's arranging for the body—" He met Mickie's eyes, faltered, choked on the word. "The *body*," he repeated, "to be sent to a funeral parlor in the city. One of the local homes dispatched a hearse to take her."

"When's the funeral?"

"Tomorrow. When Cheryl gets in from Tucson or wherever."

"It's all so unbelievable, Rufe. So very unbelievable. From one moment to the next. She's talking about getting married and then she's gone. I feel so responsible."

"Don't, Mick. Please . . ."

"I want you to put a lock on that cellar door."

"I will, hon," he promised.

"Tomorrow."

"I will."

"Freak accident." She shook her head angrily. "What happened? Why did she go through that door? It's so cold down there—she should have known immediately."

"Don't do this," Rufus repeated quietly.

"I just can't understand."

"No more today, Mick," he said. "It's only going to make things worse."

"I know," she said. "I won't." Her eyes clouded over with tears. "So many things to cry about, this is the first time I'm crying for her. I loved her, Rufe. Like a sister." Briefly she thought about Nina Wallace losing her best friend, Essie, in the house. Now she had lost hers here as well.

"Mick," Rufus stroked her hair. "I love you, okay?"

"Yes," she said softly. "It is okay, and I love you too." They fell asleep holding each other, partially because she loved him, and partially so she would wake up if he moved and left the room.

CHAPTER 30

Tessie arrived the following afternoon. Mickie picked her up at the Greyhound station.

They stopped first at the A.&P. to buy food for the party and weekend. Tessie would be left without a car, but Mickie would supply her with a list of telephone numbers in case of emergency, grocers that delivered in case of shortage, and she introduced her to Nina should she need any help with the girls. Tessie assured her that everything would be okay; she had taken care of children before.

Mickie apologized to her mother for inviting her up for the first time and not staying to entertain her, but Tessie told her it was all right; she understood. She also realized that there had been something unsaid, something urgent in Mickie's phone call.

They talked about Lois, how terrible the accident was, and what could anyone have done to prevent it. Mickie had phoned Dave that morning. The funeral was set for late in the day, and Bill was flying down from Montreal to bury his fiancé. Mickie wished that she could attend but knew it was impossible.

She didn't tell her mother any of her fears.

Then came the reunion with the grandchildren. Hugs. Kisses. Gifts. Grandma was a favorite and a chronic spoiler, sometimes rescinding punishments meted out by Mickie and Rufus.

"I did all right with you," Tessie would say. "So it proves I know how to raise children."

Mickie could never get angry with her and looked forward to the day when she would have grandchildren so she could finally be the good guy.

Mickie gave her mother a tour of the house. Tessie couldn't get over how it had changed from the stark "before" pictures she had seen. They had truly made it into a home for themselves.

She especially liked the toy room and couldn't understand Jenny's reluctance to play in there. But finally she was able to coax her in.

There wasn't a problem until Tessie tried to manipulate the crossbars of the clown marionette. Then Jenny pulled away from her, hunched into herself, and watched her grandmother with suspicion. Tessie couldn't imagine what was frightening Jenny. Nor could she miss the overall fear that seemed to permeate the house. She sensed Mickie's fear as well. The way she talked, reacted, watched Rufus and the children. Part of her need to get away for the weekend, Tessie reasoned, and prayed that she and Rufus would find whatever it was they were looking for.

The girls had elected Cara as their speaker. They all gathered around Jenny at the lunchtable as she did the talking. She and Ivy had been telling the others the stories about Todd. He was weird; he scared them. And the bottom line was that none of them wanted to come to Jenny's party if Todd was going to be there.

That night Jenny curled up in Rufus's lap, wound her hand in his, and told him what her friends had said. Rufus assured his daughter that when it was time for the party, even though he and Mommy weren't going to be there, he would make certain that Todd wouldn't bother them.

Then he winked at her and told her not to mention anything to Mickie. He would take care of it all.

Thursday afternoon Todd was late in coming out of the locker room. His looseleaf notebook had sprung open and a month's worth of notes had scattered over the locker room floor. By the time he had gathered the papers up, piled them so their holes were all on the same side, and slipped them back into the binder, the other boys had all cleared out.

The empty gym seemed larger than it did when filled with boys, and Todd's footsteps echoed loudly against the wood. The custodian hadn't yet come to close the windows and wash the floor. Todd heard movement, then saw that someone was doing revolutions on the high bar. Rick Webb.

Rick jumped to the mats, landing expertly with feet together, knees slightly bent to absorb the impact of the fall. He wiped his hands together to clear them of the excess chalk he had used to dry his palms and secure his hold on the bar. He started toward Todd who for a moment froze automatically. But then amusement lit up his face as he watched Rick come closer.

"Heard what you did to Riley," Rick said, as he grabbed the rope and started to pull himself up.

Todd shrugged noncommittally.

Rick palmed the ceiling and started back down the rope. He swung it back and forth and made Tarzan cries. Halfway down he stopped and met Todd's eye.

"Riley's scared of you."

"Didn't know that."

"Riley's a pussy," Rick said, dropping to the mats below the rope.

"If you say so."

"We're all alone now, Toddy." Rick grinned and slapped his hands together. "No daddy and no teachers to save your ass." He took a step closer to Todd. "Let you run if you want."

Todd shook his head. "Don't want to."

Another step.

"I catch you, I kill you," Rick warned and he showed teeth. "Last chance."

"No, Rick. It's time."

"Right." Rick smiled. He pounded his right fist into his left palm. He would wipe the floor with this kid. He couldn't believe that Riley was actually afraid of him or thought that from across the room he had somehow trip-wired the acid bottle. Well now there was nothing around that could hurt him, except the kid himself, and that wasn't going to happen.

The sound of his fist hitting his palm echoed throughout the empty gym. He hoped the school was deserted now, so no one would hear the kid's cries. He was taking a chance doing it in the school, but there they both were—

"Throw down your books, Todd," Rick said. What was the matter with the kid? He wasn't ready to fight. One arm was still around his schoolbooks, the other hung limply at his side.

He was about fifteen feet away from Todd and eyed him strangely. It must be the sun, he concluded, shining through the wire mesh screen outside the gym windows that was casting a strange light across the gym floor, across Todd's hand which suddenly looked deformed to Rick.

And as he closed in on Todd, his back was to the hanging rope.

So he didn't see it twist and come to life behind him, the frayed end brushing the floor as if electrified.

Todd smiled. "I may not get you today, Rick," he said with icy calmness as he echoed the bigger boy's words.

The smile on his face and the marblelike quality to his eyes suddenly scared Rick.

"And I may not get you tomorrow . . ."

The rope wound itself loosely around Rick's foot. He felt its tug against him, didn't know what it was and looked down. He was more than surprised to see the rope snaking up his body. He wasn't afraid though, because he still didn't know what was happening, but as soon as the rope slithered up his leg and across his stomach, Rick's blood froze.

"Todd?" he questioned uncertainly.

Rick grabbed at the rope to try to pull it off him, but like a python it wound itself more tightly around him.

"Todd!" he screamed sharply. *Jesus God, Riley had been right!*

Rick was lifted off the floor and the end of the rope wound around his neck.

"But when I do . . ."

"Todd, please," he begged as his fingers clawed frantically at the rope.

"Todd, no—!"

And that was all he could get out before the rope closed his windpipe and blocked his air. His eyes bulged, and his tongue dropped out of his mouth. He gurgled and sputtered and gave it up.

"It'll be a fate worse than death," Todd finished with satisfaction.

Rick Webb's body dangled halfway between the floor and ceiling. His hands were chalk white and matching his face which had drained of blood. Urine trickled down his leg and dripped to the floor. His eyes were open, still staring at Todd in terror and bewilderment.

The custodian had snuck home early that day. They would thank him for leaving the gym windows open to air out the odor, and nobody would notice or care that the floor had not been washed and waxed.

So Rick's body would not be discovered until the next morning when the first-period boys burst through the double swinging doors.

Rick Webb never knew what it was that had killed him.

The only one who would ever know was Riley.

And he certainly wouldn't say anything.

Thursday night across the town of Glendon, second-grade girls were preparing for bed.

Karen Ames was sitting under her covers in flannel pajamas watching *Happy Days* on television, laughing at Fonzie, who had locked himself in the garage and couldn't get out. Ivy Blake was having her hair washed by her mother and was feeling more grown up as the days went on. Pretty soon her mother promised her she could use nail polish and then even makeup! Shelly Johnson was yelling at her twin brother, Eric, who had put a frog in her bed and hidden in the closet to await the expected results. Joanne Tribble was saying her evening prayers, praying for her father's full recovery. Jonathan Tribble lay thirty miles away in the Rutland Hospital with a broken back and collarbone from tumbling off his roof, as he tried to reslate it himself to save a couple of bucks. Sally Richards had just jumped into bed with her golden retriever, Clancy, an elegant dog bigger than she with the softest bite and gentlest touch. Clancy found a comfortable position with his head resting on Sally's legs and within minutes was asleep. And with her hand on Clancy's head, Sally also fell asleep, dreaming about the man she would one day marry and the children she would have. Cara Wallace was staring out her bedroom window at the shimmering stars that filled the sky. Angel lights her mother had called them when she was very young. The angels were watching over her and she felt safe.

And Jenny was going to bed happy. Daddy had the

Todd situation well under control. Her friendships were assured.

But before getting into bed, she looked into the closet, made certain it was empty and the door securely closed. She tested the knob so it could not spring open by itself. Then she walked around her bed and looked under it.

When she was satisfied that there was nothing in the room, she climbed into bed.

Then Rufus came in to share a special good night moment with his little daughter. The next day was Friday, and he and Mickie would be away.

Across the hall Todd was already asleep.

CHAPTER 31

As Friday wore on, Todd grew more and more keyed up without knowing why. Sounds roared through his head like wind rushing by the windows of a speeding car. He couldn't calm himself, and when he came home from school, he burst into the kitchen, scooted around, and got underfoot.

Mickie was putting the finishing touches on Jenny's cake, icing roses and letters. She still had to pack for the weekend, although she had already mentally laid out what she would take along. It was too late in the year for swimming, but she expected them to do some beach-combing and spend a lot of time together in the motel room. She would pack—or not pack—accordingly. She was still on edge, but she wouldn't even let herself think about yesterday—it was over. She and Rufus would face their problems together this weekend. They *would* come together again. . . .

Todd buzzed past her, brushing against her, jostling her arms, almost making her smudge the lettering.

"Todd!" she scolded. "Will you just go upstairs and let me prepare for Jenny's party?"

"Jenny's party," he spat back contemptuously.

"Yes, Jenny's party. Tonight is Jenny's night, and I don't want you spoiling it. Whenever you want you can have your friends over for a party too."

"Friends," he sneered. "That'll be the day." He

darted under Mickie's arm, flicked a fingerful of icing off the cake, and squashed a rose.

"Todd! she screamed. "Will you go upstairs now!" She pushed her hair back out of her eyes and smeared frosting across her forehead.

Todd bounded out of the room. Mickie shot her mother a look which telegraphed "I hope you know what you're getting into." Tessie smiled, as she removed a tray of gingerbread men.

Rufus came into the kitchen and buried his head in the refrigerator. "Still have three kids out there, but I desperately needed a glass of juice." He winked at Tessie. "Actually I desperately needed something stronger, but I'm still on duty and we have a long drive ahead of us." He lifted the Tropicana container to his lips and drank. Then he asked, "Hey—did you hear the news about Rick Webb? One of the mothers just told me."

Mickie looked up from her decorating. "What happened?"

"Hanged himself on the gym rope. Either suicide or accidental. They don't know yet. The police were questioning some of the kids."

"I don't think they talked to Todd," Mickie said. "At least he didn't say anything. I wonder if he knows."

"I'm sure he does," Rufus said. "Must have been some prank that went bad." He grew thoughtful. "I remember a guy I went to high school with. One of the young toughs of the neighborhood. Like Webb, I guess. Stuck a shotgun in his mouth, saying, 'It takes guts to do this' and pulled the trigger. Turned out the gun was loaded. Maybe Webb was trying a stunt like that." He shrugged. "Anyway, see you in half an hour. I want to get out of here as soon as possible. Forget dinner. We'll grab a bite on the road."

Mickie looked around the kitchen littered with baking pans, mixing bowls, and doughy blobs. "Believe me, Rufe. I've forgotten."

But when she was certain Rufus was back in his office, she ran out of the kitchen and called upstairs. "Todd?"

"Yeah, Ma."

"Come down here, will you?"

"You told me to go upstairs."

"I'm telling you to come down now," she said, a bit impatiently, and then caught herself. She was leaving the house in less than an hour and wanted no trouble between now and then.

Todd came sliding down the banister. "*Wheeee!*"

"I'll overlook that for now, Todd," Mickie said sternly. "But don't do it again."

"What do you want, Ma?" he asked, a casual toss to his head that bothered her, a fearlessness in his eyes she didn't like.

"Did you know about Rick Webb?" she asked.

"Yeah. Cops all over school today." And his smile widened from ear to ear. "Great, huh?"

"No, not great," Mickie said. "The boy is dead."

Todd shrugged noncommittally.

"What do you think happened? Was he fooling around?"

"Must have been, I guess," Todd said, and Mickie saw a sudden flickering in his eye, a momentary shifting away from her that suggested guilt, and she suspected he knew more than what he was saying.

"Well, when things like this happen, I worry, Todd. Just be careful, okay?" she cautioned. "Don't play any games that might be dangerous or get out of hand."

"Don't worry about me, Ma," Todd said and grinned broadly. "Nothing can happen to me."

And he was up the stairs, around the landing, and out of Mickie's sight.

She had no love for Rick Webb for what he had done to Todd, but she still couldn't help but feel sadness at his death. Such a waste. A stupid accidental death, she thought, and then realized that there had been two accidental deaths in as many days.

Jenny was in her room trying to decide what to wear for the party. Half of her clothes were laid out across the bed. She was modeling a candy-striped pinafore in front of the mirror when Todd burst into the room. He charged to her bed and started to throw her clothes around.

"Todd!" Jenny screamed. "Stop it!"

Then he picked up one of her good white dresses, draped it over his head ghostlike, stretched his arms out in front of him, and advanced toward her stiff-legged, moaning as if in hellish pain.

"Todd!" Jenny yelled, suddenly angry with him. Then her eyes widened as she saw something very peculiar.

She stepped back away from him, her breath caught somewhere between stomach and throat. She didn't know what had happened, what was wrong with Todd's hand! She watched horrified as he reached out to touch her.

He was making sounds: growls, gurgling . . . shrieking, Jenny lunged for the door. Her perspiring fingers groped desperately for the knob, which slipped through her grasp. She kept gaping over her shoulder to see Todd coming closer to her. When his hand touched her shoulder, her fingers at last gained a firm hold on the doorknob and twisted it. She raced out into the hallway, directly into Rufus's arms and buried herself hysterically against him.

Rufus strode into Jenny's room. His eyes were on fire. Todd was standing defiantly, fists clenched at his side, and chin jutted forward. Waiting for him.

"What did you do to her?" Rufus demanded. He grabbed Todd's arms and shook him. "I said what did you do?"

Mickie appeared in the doorway. Rufus looked at her.

"Don't say anything, Mick!" He shook Todd again, hooked his fingers firmly under Todd's armpit, and pulled him out of the room. "You're coming with me, young man." He half dragged, half carried Todd down the stairs and through the kitchen, almost lifting him off the floor. He yanked open the cellar door.

"Rufus, what are you doing to him?" Mickie cried.

Rufus pushed Todd ahead of him and down the cellar stairs. Todd almost stumbled but regained his balance on the railing.

"I promised Jenny you wouldn't bother her party tonight, and I'm going to keep that promise."

Mickie saw where he was taking Todd. He flung open the door and pushed Todd inside the room, then slammed the door shut. Horrified, Mickie ran to it, tried to pull it open. Her eyes opened in surprise. The door was locked. She looked at Rufus. He was holding the key, starting back toward the stairs.

"Rufus, you can't leave him down there all night!" Mickie cried, following him into the kitchen.

Rufus gave the key to Tessie. "You will let him out only after the girls have gone home tomorrow. Not a minute before. Do you understand?"

The intensity in his eyes and fury in his voice paralyzed her. She numbly nodded.

"Rufus, what do you think you're doing?" Mickie yelled.

"Giving Jenny a chance to have some friends."

"By locking Todd in the cellar! Mom, give me that key."

Obediently, Tessie handed the key to Mickie. Rufus opened her hand and took the key away from her.

"I said no, Mick," he hissed and their eyes locked. "And this is one time I don't want you undermining me."

Silence took hold. Tessie slipped out of the room.

"What did he do to Jenny?" Mickie begged, feeling her knees sag under her.

"He's been scaring her and her friends. She was afraid he would disrupt her party and frighten the girls away. And I have no idea what he did to her just now. I'd better go upstairs and see how—"

"Wait, Rufe." She stopped him. "Please don't do this to him. We can send Todd to a friend's house for tonight."

"Todd has no friends," Rufus said. "And he's jealous because Jenny has, and he's alienated all of his. That's why he's been rough on the girls. Let him cool his heels down there. Nothing's going to happen. It's just like I sent him to his room, but this way we're certain he'll stay put." Mickie started to open her mouth in protest, but he stopped her, silenced her. "Go upstairs and pack, hon," he added. "I just have to make some phone calls and I'll be ready."

Tessie joined her daughter in the kitchen when Rufus left. "You should stay home tonight," she said. "Don't leave Todd like this."

At first Mickie agreed with her—they *should* stay home. But then she realized that they had to go. She had to get Rufus out of the house, had to separate him and Todd. *My God, if she didn't, something could happen tonight!* They would get away and she would talk to him, convince him that it *was* happening, just as she said it was. And this time she knew she'd be successful. Surely after what had just happened, Rufus couldn't possibly deny . . .

"No, Mom," she said quietly, avoiding her mother's probing eyes. "It's better this way. Todd'll be okay. Just trust me." *Trust me.* Those were Rufus's words.

And with Todd downstairs he and Jenny would be separated too, and there would be no conflict there. She didn't need Todd's jealousy to flare up at his sister when all of her friends were over.

"And please leave Todd downstairs," she said softly. "Like Rufus asked. Until the other children are out of the house."

"I will, Mick, but—"

Mickie held up a finger to quiet her mother. "Mom, please," she said. "I know what I'm doing."

And she hoped to God she did.

"I'm going to run down and see Todd now," she said.

Tessie gave her the key. Todd was lying on the bed, hands clasped under his head, staring blankly at the ceiling. He barely moved when she came in.

"Hey," she said with a crooked half smile. "How ya doing?"

Todd shrugged. "Okay, I guess."

She sat down on the bed and brushed the hair out of his eyes. "It's just for tonight. We're afraid you might bother Jenny's friends. I hear you've been sort of rough on them."

Todd shrugged indifferently, did not deny it. But it didn't make Mickie feel any better for what she was condoning here.

"It's not so bad down here, you know?" she said and took in the room. It was next to the boiler and comfortably warm. Light slanted in from the setting sun. But there were no other lights and in minutes the room would be plunged into darkness. "You want me to sneak a television down? A reading lamp?"

"Don't have to, Mom."

Mickie cupped his chin tenderly and smiled at him. "Do it for Jenny, okay? For me, too." She hoped her eyes would communicate her thoughts. *Just give me the time to be alone with Daddy and convince him to move out of here. Then everything will get back to normal. And the next house we buy won't have a cellar at all.*

"Yeah, okay," he said, as if reading her mind.

"Good," Mickie said softly. "I'll make this up to you. I promise."

"Don't sweat it, Mom," Todd said.

Mickie put her hand into his. "I love you, Todd," she said, the pain she was feeling visible in her eyes.

The voice came from upstairs.

"Mickie, come on. I want to get out of here. Pack already, will you?"

"Coming, Rufe," she called up and kissed Todd good-bye.

It was either carelessness or an unconscious gesture, but Mickie forgot to relock the door when she hurried out of the room, responding to Rufus's insistent call and her own inner conflict.

CHAPTER 32

Mickie was packing quickly, carrying clothes from her dresser to the suitcase, which lay open on the bed. Rufus was already packed and impatiently pacing the length of the bedroom growling for her to speed it up.

"I want to get there tonight, Mick," he said.

"I'm coming, Rufus, I'm coming," she said. She, too, wanted to get out of there as soon as possible.

Every time she passed near the dresser she couldn't help but glance at the family portrait anchored in a standing frame on top. It was a formal picture, taken two years before, when they realized they didn't have a picture like that and felt they should. Mickie hated her too wide smile and felt Rufus was standing too stiffly, his back bent slightly, unnaturally. His hand rested on her shoulder, and Mickie could remember the clamminess of his palm against her in the hot lights of the photo studio. Only the children seemed at ease, as only children can, their hair falling naturally, their faces bright and full of life. And that was why they kept the picture.

Now she tried to keep her mind off Todd, who lay in total darkness down in the cellar.

Tessie finished the preparations for the party, hung the balloons, and stacked the party hats. She carried the cake up to the toy room. She, too, tried to keep her mind off Todd. She had never directly meddled in the children's upbringing and certainly wasn't going to start now. She prayed that Mickie knew what she was doing.

Rufus was piling the suitcases by the door when Jenny appeared at the landing and came floating down the stairs. He ground to a halt as he gazed up at his daughter, preparing to host her first party. She had selected the white dress that Todd had draped over his head. Its front was ruffled and was tied at the waist by a rope belt. She looked like an angel walking on air. Obviously she had put the incident with Todd behind her and composed herself into a perfect young lady.

"How do I look?" she asked and her face glowed. She twirled around for Rufus's benefit. He extended his hand to her which she took graciously and curtsied.

"A heartbreaker," Rufus said, and drew her close to him. She had even sprayed on some of Mickie's perfume. He held Jenny for an extra second before finally easing her away.

Mickie sailed downstairs. "I'm ready," she said and caught her breath as she saw her grown-up daughter. She knelt down next to Jenny and adjusted the neckline of her dress. "Don't you look marvelous, honey."

Tessie, carrying a tray of gingerbread men, remarked that she knew who Jenny got her good looks from.

"Me," Rufus said, puffing out his chest and everyone laughed.

Nobody mentioned Todd.

The doorbell rang and the first of the children arrived. Ivy and Shelly had come together, and Mickie hurriedly greeted Shelly's mother, trying to hide the suitcases that were so very evident and seeing a note of scorn in her smile. *What kind of mother would run out on her daughter's birthday party?* That was an easy one, Mickie thought, with a grim half smile of her own. *The kind of mother who wanted to keep her family alive.* And suddenly she was no longer bothered by her actions, no longer cared what others might think. The end would justify the means.

Then Nina arrived with Cara. The little girl was clutching her gift and looked lovely in a new tartan skirt and ruffled blouse. Mickie helped her off with her coat.

"Well, is everything under control?" Nina asked Tessie.

With only a glance at Mickie out of the corner of her eye, Tessie smiled. "I think we'll manage," she said.

"If you need anything at all," Nina offered, "you know where to find me."

"I taped the number right next to the phone, Mom," Mickie said.

Nina knelt down next to Cara. "Have fun. I'll see you tomorrow, okay?"

"Okay, Mommy," Cara said. She turned and ran up to the toy room, to the party. Nina looked after her daughter as she rounded the landing and disappeared from sight.

"Well, you two have fun, too," Nina said and smiled. "I envy you your weekend away. Bye."

"Bye," Mickie said, and then thought, *If only she knew.*

Rufus took the suitcases out to the car while Mickie said final good-byes to her mother.

"Let's synchronize our watches," Tessie said. "Then you can call me at nine fifteen, ten fifteen, eleven fifteen and—" She caught Mickie's puzzled expression and said, "Only joking." But neither of them laughed.

In the toy room Cara climbed onto the rocking horse and Ivy pulled a puppet off the wall.

"Where's your brother?" Cara asked and made a face.

"Don't worry about him," Jenny said. "He won't bother us tonight."

And the girls giggled into their hands.

* * *

The car slipped out of the driveway and into the Vermont night. Rufus turned right onto Route 17 and headed toward the Interstate. Mickie twisted around in the seat to look back at the house partially hidden by a line of trees. The downstairs lights were ablaze, as well as several on the second floor. A thin trickle of smoke spiraled out of the toy room chimney where Rufus had built a fire before they left. As the car took a curve in the road and was about to leave the house behind, she thought of Todd, alone in the cellar, draped in darkness.

There would be guilt for a long time to come over this, Mickie knew.

She glanced over toward Rufus. His eyes staring straight ahead, while he concentrated on the dark road. She watched them narrow as they were assaulted by headlights from oncoming cars. In the flickering light of approaching headlights she could see he looked more at ease than he had over the last several weeks and that perhaps just knowing he was out of the house had lifted the almost demonic possession from him.

She wanted to talk; there was so much they had to say, discuss, plan. But there was also something welcome and comfortable about sitting silently next to Rufus. She would let the silence hold them for a while longer, allowing the tension to drain from their pores, from around their eyes.

They drove past the Union Christian Church. The light from a lone streetlamp was cast upon it. It seemed as if the cemetery behind was trying to shrink back from the flat yellow glare. It would not take too much imagination, she thought, to conjure ghosts rising from the shadowed and silent graves. In fact, she thought ruefully, she already had.

Mickie idly twirled her hair and gazed out the window at the passing countryside. The gentle hills of the Southern Vermont ski areas were now only dark shapes rising on both sides of the valley.

She turned back to her husband and took his hand. She knew intuitively it was all going to turn out well.

Todd lay spread-eagle on the bed. The room was completely dark and he had nothing to do. He had already worked up to holding his breath for a count of seventy-five seconds, although he wasn't certain if he had been accurately ticking off the time, and he knew he had speeded up at the end to break his own records. He vaguely wondered if you could hold your breath until you died. He had never been as aware of his breathing as he was now. In. Out. In. Out. Fifteen times every minute. Then do it again. Slowly. Meticulously. Consciously.

They all hated him, Todd knew. *His father. His mother. Jenny. That's why they had locked him in the cellar.*

Just like they had hated the other boy and locked him in the cellar.

Benjamin.

And he hated them all in return.

Like Benjamin had.

He was a prisoner of war in solitary confinement. They were trying to get him to crack, to reveal top secret information. They had already beaten him, doused his body with acid, plunged his hand into boiling water, and pulled out his toenails. But he had not talked. He would never talk.

Now they had locked him in total darkness, wanting to drive him crazy. But he was stronger than they thought; he could withstand anything they did to him.

He imagined how they would torture him next. He would be tied to a post, arms and legs twisted behind him and painfully tied. The branding iron would be in the fire until red hot. The torturer would wave it in front of his nose, so he could smell the heat . . .

But then his thoughts were abruptly pulled from him

as he heard the party sounds drifting down from upstairs. Just like before.

The carousel spun in a show of color and sound. The calliope tune filled the toy room as the girls played with the puppets and dolls. The fire glowed warmly and made Jenny's first birthday party in the new house a resounding success. Except for cutting and serving the cake and leading a chorus of "Happy Birthday, " Tessie had left the girls to themselves.

"Who wants more cake?" Jenny called and stood next to the cake tray, holding the knife, poised and ready to slice a piece. The wooden handle of the knife interested her. It was ornately carved in a pattern of crisscrossing X's. She ran her finger through the grooves and thought it looked familiar, but then Ivy asked for another piece, and she cut an end slice with a rose and put the knife back on the tray, forgetting about it.

"Open the presents," Cara yelled, and Jenny sank into the pile of packages. Blouses. Pajamas. A scarf. Jenny modeled everything and could not remember being this happy in a long, long time.

Low-hanging evergreen branches framed the road and gave Mickie a safe, cocoonlike feeling. Through the windshield she hypnotically watched their dim, shadowy reflections and felt her eyes grow heavy and drift closed. She opened them abruptly when she felt Rufus's hand on her leg.

"Sorry," he said and smiled sheepishly. "I feel like I've just woken you up to tell you to take your sleeping pill. Tired?"

"Dreamy," she said. "Comfortably spacy."

"Take a nap. We'll stop for dinner in about an hour."

"No—" she straightened up. "You shouldn't have to drive alone."

"I like it," he said. "It's relaxing. Lets me think I own the night."

"Tonight it's ours," Mickie said and entwined her fingers in his, enjoying the pressure of his squeeze. She put her other hand on his inner thigh and felt his body shudder. She gazed out the window. They were passing a diamond-shaped lake. A row of swamp maples grew out of a tiny island in the center. Picture postcard Vermont. She sighed contentedly.

What events spiraled together to bring her to a certain place at a given moment? What pyramided on top of what, what lines converged to bring them here tonight to this dark, country roadway, passing this tranquil lake?

They had taken trips like this when they were first married and didn't have the money or time for extended well-planned vacations. Stolen Saturdays and Sundays when Rufus found himself with unexpected free time. They had had only the vaguest notions of where they were going, no idea where they would end up. Reservations? Never heard the word. There was freedom. Excitement. Life.

Now they were running away again, this time from a house that wanted to claim her family.

She leaned against Rufus's shoulder and let her mind drift with the motion of the car. She was on the verge of sleep when suddenly she remembered she had forgotten to lock the door to the cellar room. But even if Todd came upstairs, she rationalized, what harm could there really be. He had learned his lesson by now, she was certain and, in fact, would think she left the door open for him to get out.

CHAPTER 33

Todd was able to discern individual voices. Jenny. Cara. Others. But the words were unclear. Just a distant murmur of sounds, spurts of girlish giggles, singing, sudden shrieks and calls. How was he able to hear so clearly? The window must be open, he concluded, and the sounds were coming out and drifting down. There was a hazy familiarity to the party sounds. There were flashes of dreams he couldn't quite recall, lost somewhere in dark, seldom used channels of his mind.

Then through the jumble of sounds he heard his sister's voice as clearly as if she were standing right next to him.

"Todd," Jenny was saying. "Come to the party." Her voice was sweet and pleasant, he could imagine her smiling.

And then all of the other girls were calling to him, inviting him upstairs.

A sudden surge of loneliness came over him when he realized that he had no friends. And here were the girls inviting him upstairs. But he was afraid. His father had told him not to bother Jenny, not to disturb the party. His body grew tense from the nervousness of having to make a decision.

It was made for him.

"Todd!" Jenny's voice was louder, more insistent. "Come."

And then the darkness of the cellar room closed

around him. It was confining, suffocating. It clogged his nostrils, layered over his skin.

"Todd . . ."

"Coming, Jen," he said out loud and his voice sounded hollow in the empty room. He sat up and remained motionless for a minute. His feet dangled over the edge of the bed.

A passing car flooded the room with momentary light, then grew dark again.

"Coming, Jen," he repeated, more to himself, making up his mind with the words. He got up from the bed and crossed the blackness to the door. He ran his hands along the wood, searching for the knob, and finally found it. Surprisingly, it turned easily.

The cellar was a shade short of total darkness. There was a faint light source from somewhere. Outside. Upstairs. He could make out the forms of cellar objects; work tables and cartons, piled furniture, and the coal black eyes of the griffin statue which fell on him as it charted his progress. If the kitchen light was on, there would be a sliver of light under the door where it did not fully meet the floor. He knew the cellar well enough to find his way.

He no longer heard the sounds of the party, but he could picture the girls as they must be. Rocking on the horse, dressing the dolls and puppets, working the marionettes, spinning the carousel.

He saw the slender line of light and walked up the stairs. He eased the kitchen door open. The light momentarily blinded him, and he shrank back into the comfortable darkness of the cellar. Then he looked again and adjusted to the light.

His heart was thumping, his pulse racing. If he had taken it now, he would have found that what had been seventy in the calm of the cellar was now well over a hundred. He was experiencing an excitement like never before.

Something was about to happen.
In the kitchen light he looked at his hand.
It was as he expected.
Twisted. Clawlike. Just like the boy's.

Mommy.
It was Jenny's voice, shaky and frightened.
Mickie was in the upstairs corridor, running toward
the toy room. The hallway carpet was a treadmill; her
feet were moving but getting nowhere, growing tired,
weighty. Her breath came harder in short gasps. She
couldn't take a deep breath, couldn't fill her lungs. Her
hand closed around the doorknob at last.
Help me, Mommy!
She burst into the room.
Jenny cowered in the corner, hunched over, pointing
toward the opposite corner where the firelight did not
reach.
He's going to kill me, Mommy, and her words were
chopped off, strangled deep in her throat. Her mouth
was open but no more sound emerged.
No, Mickie whispered.
The boy started forward.
*Leave us alone. Go away. Go back to the dead where
you belong.*
She saw the knife in his gnarled hand. His face was
still hidden in shadow.
Don't hurt my daughter.
She tried to move toward the boy, but her legs buck-
led beneath her and she toppled to the floor.
The boy walked slowly, silently.
Please don't hurt her, Mickie moaned and extended
her arm out in front of her in supplication. The knife
tip was inches from her, but it was pointing past her,
toward Jenny. *No,* Mickie hissed and summoning all
the strength she could, rushed toward the boy. *Take me
instead.*

And as the knife found its mark and plunged into her, too late she saw the boy's face. *He was born with a twisted, cloven hand, and mark of a demon.*

It was—

Todd! she screamed in recognition and realization and slumped at her son's feet.

The knife made a slurping sound as he pulled it out of her.

Todd, no. It's Jenny. Jenny! Mickie gesticulated wildly. She felt herself slipping, dying. *Run, Jenny,* she screamed, but blood was gurgling out of her mouth, mixing with her words. She would die, she knew, without knowing if her sacrifice had saved her daughter's life. She reached up to try to grab hold of Todd's leg to stop him. But her weakening fingers barely pulled at his shirt. Easily Todd shook free of her. Her eyes closed.

She was being sucked through a long dark tunnel. At the end of it was a brilliant, blinding light. Words echoed in her ears, faintly at first.

He will return and kill again.

Louder.

He will return and kill again.

A woman came toward her out of the light, her face twisted in anguish, arms over her head, blood pouring from her wrists, down her arms, her body . . .

Laura—!

And her words ringing deafeningly in the tunnel.

He will return and kill again.

It all came together in her sleeping mind and in the moment between sleep and wakefulness she understood.

There had never been a madman who had killed those children.

She had misunderstood Jonas Cuttings's letter—

My regret was that first others had to die.

It was Benjamin Cuttings who had killed!

And now all the girls were in danger!

But there wasn't any danger, she sighed. Todd was locked in the cellar.

No one will ever know of his birth, and the words made sense—the boy had been locked away in the room in the cellar. That must have been what it was used for. Put away from birth until he had gotten out and—

Her eyes bulged in heart-stopping realization.

Now Todd was in the cellar as well.

Just like the boy.

And she had forgotten to lock the door.

"Rufus, stop!" she gasped, and did not recognize the naked voice as her own.

The six girls sat in a circle. The lamps were all turned out and only the firelight bathed their faces. Each held a different hand puppet. They were constructing a Romeo and Juliet play, shadow dancing the puppets against the wall with exaggerated movements of arms and heads. Two of the puppets loved each other; the strict parents didn't want them to get married. Jenny played the young man's father, her phony deep voice reminding her of her own father when he talked sternly to her. She was sitting with her back against the wall. Above her the marionettes hung from their pegs. From time to time Jenny would glance up and look at them; they made her feel a little uneasy. But surrounded by all of her friends she knew they couldn't hurt her.

She turned her attention back to the playacting. Now she was the girl's father.

"No, you can't marry my daughter until you have a good job." And she nodded the puppet's head up and down angrily, paced him back and forth as she had seen her own father walking the living room when he was displeased about something. The other girls clapped and laughed; this was fun.

Jenny looked up at the wall again at the clown marionette. Its head seemed to bob as if saying she was doing a good job at the game.

She blinked and thought the marionette had winked back at her.

Todd pushed open the swinging kitchen doors and entered the living room. His grandmother was dozing in the lounge chair, her glasses slipping off the bridge of her nose, a magazine propped on her lap. Todd didn't want her to catch him. He thought his grandmother's loyalties would be with him, but he didn't want to chance it. He tiptoed toward the staircase, careful not to make a sound. His back against the wall, he eased up the stairs. A floorboard creaked. But his grandmother didn't awaken. He continued to take one careful, silent step at a time. Then he was beyond the landing, out of Tessie's sight.

He was on the second floor and heard the party sounds again.

"Dunk for apples," someone yelled.

"No. Pin the tail on the donkey."

"Me first. Me first."

"Let Jenny. It's her party. Get a blindfold."

Smiling, Todd started down the corridor.

Rufus kept the car up to speed. He did not stop, despite Mickie's pleading.

"Now it's *Todd* who's going to kill?" he asked incredulously. "Give me a break, will you? It was only another dream, and you've had so many of those. No warnings from beyond. We've been through all this before. We'll call your mother when we get to the diner. I'm not going home now just because of some Goddamn dream of yours. You're the one who wanted to get away. Now you're desperate to get back again?"

She stopped listening to him. Even if she would

never be strong with Rufus again, she had to be now.

"Rufus, turn this car around!" she ordered and felt like she could explode through her skin. Her fists were clenched, nails digging into the fleshy part of her hands, leaving red half-moon indentations. Her knuckles were pasty white as if she had been rolling a pastry dough.

But Rufus's face remained a tight mask and he did not respond. She even sensed him push harder against the accelerator and felt the car speed up.

Images whirred kaleidoscopically in front of her. Visions of a gnarled hand, blood dripping from a wrist, Laura Cuttings's anguished, dying face offering her the knife. Jenny hunched in a corner of the toy room. Visions? Reality? Nightmares? Warnings? Insanity?

She had to get out of the car, back to the house. She grabbed for the door handle, her fingers slipping off the antitheft lock. If Rufus wouldn't stop the car, she would jump out and hitch a ride with someone else. Would anyone pick her up, she wondered with black hysteria—an incoherent woman babbling about her son who was going to kill a party full of children.

Rufus slammed on the brakes. The car skidded with an alarming shriek, crossed the solid white line, and ground to a halt, stalling out. The sudden silence was deafening.

Mickie was exhausted. Her hair was wet and matted across her forehead. Her eyes were wild with fear.

"If only to prove to you that nothing is wrong," Rufus growled and started the car again. She hated the sneer that crossed his face and briefly wondered how she had ever loved him. It took two tries for the engine to catch, Mickie dying a thousand deaths in between. "And maybe some time next year we'll be able to get away for a weekend," he added angrily.

"Thank you, Rufe," she said calmly, hiding any anger from her voice. "Just hurry, will you?"

They were silent for fifteen minutes. She watched the

sweep of the dashboard clock and couldn't imagine anything moving slower. They were still miles from the
house. She glanced over at Rufus and saw that he was
seething, his teeth clenched, jaw set and hard. She
sensed the tension in his fingers as he grasped the
wheel. But she didn't care. She prayed that there would
be nothing wrong when she got home and hoped that
Todd was still unaware that the room downstairs was
unlocked.

She stared blankly out the window. They were passing the diamond-shaped lake, but Mickie could barely
see it through her tear-filled eyes.

The party sounds were clear to Todd as he stood outside the toy room door. He hesitated for only a fraction
of a second before he pushed it open a crack and
peered in.

The girls were all standing. Jenny was blindfolded,
being spun around by the others. She held a stickpin
and donkey tail in her hand. The fire was lapping at the
top of the hearth, throwing shadows of the girls against
the wall, suggesting some bizarre sacrificial ritual. The
cake was half eaten, the knife coated with chocolate
frosting. Todd recognized the knife with its carved handle. The marionettes along the wall nodded to him, invited him in. Todd walked into the toy room.

Cara Wallace was facing the door and saw him first.
Her mouth hung open as she stared at him. Then she
screamed.

The party stopped. The other girls turned to Cara,
who was pointing toward the door. Their hands flew to
their mouths, their eyes.

"Monster!" Ivy yelled loudly, her voice rising above
the others, ending in a high-pitched wail.

"Animal!" howled another. Then all of the girls
were screaming.

Jenny ripped off her blindfold. It was Todd, but why

did his hand look like that— She looked away in horror but her eyes met the face of the clown marionette. It was moving back and forth; its eyes were glowing red in the firelight, its mouth wide with laughter. But any sound it might have emitted was drowned out by the screaming girls.

"Jenny?" Todd asked fearfully.

Why were the girls screaming at him?

Jenny narrowed her eyes and stared at her brother.

But she couldn't react quickly enough and wouldn't have time to stop it.

The first apple that was thrown hit him square in the chest. He winced from the pain. Then other things were thrown at him. Apples. Party hats. Presents. Garbage. He angled his body away from them so nothing would hit his stomach.

Girls screaming at him, calling him names, trying to hurt him.

There was a foreknowledge to these acts like it had happened before.

Jenny stood stock still eyeing her brother uncertainly.

But then frightened by the reactions of the other girls she started to scream as well. And that was the last hope that any of them would have. She picked up a hand puppet and threw it at Todd, the hard-molded head bouncing painfully off his. Todd held up his hands in front of him to protect his face.

The girls were all throwing things at him, hating him.

He covered his ears to try to block their awful cries.

"Stop!" he yelled, but his own voice only intensified the cries of the girls.

Jenny ran past him to summon her grandmother.

The others would not get out.

The voice raged through Todd.

See how they hate you! They never wanted you to come upstairs. They want you dead. Kill them! Kill them like I did! Like I taught you.

Then there was no more thought or confusion. Todd knew what to do.

He concentrated.

They would never get home, Mickie thought. She was nervously spinning her hair through her fingers, pulling it into little knots. Traffic had picked up. There was a line of cars, the lead car going no more than thirty miles an hour on a posted speed road of fifty. Cars were coming from the other direction, making it impossible to pass. They were fifth in line. Mickie reached over and leaned on the horn. The blaring sound seemed out of place in the peace of the Vermont night. It only made the lead car slow down more out of spite.

Maybe she was only being hysterical for no reason, she tried to calm herself. It was only a dream she had had. Like the others. No reason to panic. And now *everything* that had frightened her—Rufus, Todd, *possession*—took on a distant air of utter ridiculousness. Mickie ran the scenario through her head. They would get home. Her mother would be surprised to see them. She would have to make up some excuse as to why they returned. She would look in on the children, go down to the room where Todd was, test the door, see if he was still inside, and tell him Mommy had come home, she missed him. And then laugh at her foolishness and try to make it up to Rufus some other way. She prayed that would be the scenario, prayed it wasn't just her defenses marching to her aid.

But now she was experiencing the utter helpless feeling of not knowing. Maybe they should stop, call. But what would she say to her mother?

"Pass them, Rufe," she hissed.

Rufus looked at her and shrugged. "Your funeral, Mick," he said and took the whole line of cars.

Drivers stared in bewilderment as the Rabbit shot

past them toward an oncoming car in the opposite lane. The car blasted its horn, then veered off the road and let Rufus pass. Mickie looked behind her to see that they had not caused an accident.

Dear God, she silently prayed, *please make everything be all right*. She repeated the words again and again until they blended into each other and lost all meaning. She tried to close her eyes, but every time she did the vision reappeared: Todd stepping out of the shadows, the knife in his deformed hand. And now it was more real, more clear than ever before.

Todd concentrated on the fire. It heaved and shuddered and surged to life. It left the fireplace, curled into a twisting hand, separated into long, searching fingers and reached out toward the girls. Ivy stood closest to the fireplace; her back was to it. Shelly saw it happening, at first detached, unbelieving. What she was seeing had no grounding in her reality. She was unable to react. Like watching someone step off the curb into the path of a speeding car. One portion of the brain intuitively knows what's going to happen, the other portion shuts out the event, detaching the observer from his environment, and the fraction of a second before the impact seems to last forever.

Then it happened. The flames caught Ivy's hair, billowed around her, and burned her face. Screeching, she ran madly around the room, fanning the flames and within seconds she was completely ablaze.

There was only a split second of hesitation before the girls understood the danger. Nothing could be done for Ivy, they realized, with thousands of generations of instinct ingrained in their young minds. There was a mad rush for the door. A stampede. They forgot about Todd, about Ivy, about everything except escape.

Sally Richards reached the door first. It had slipped shut after Jenny left the room. Her hand closed around the knob, but before she could pull it open, she felt the weight on her back. Like a small animal had taken a flying leap and—

She snapped her head around. Her neck muscles creaked as if whiplashed. She saw eyes. A wide smile. It was the dancer marionette she had seen on the wall.

A gasp of surprise fought its way to her lips, and they puckered slightly. But no sound emerged as the marionette's hands closed around her throat and her air was cut off.

Cara Wallace ran to the window. She could see her house right next door, the lights burning in the living room and her parents' bedroom. Her own bedroom light was off, but that was right because she was here and her mother had always told her to turn off the lights when she wasn't in her room. And now her lights were out and everything smacked of normality. Her mind had closed and refused to accept what her eyes were seeing, her ears hearing. It was time to go home; she would just call to her mother and her mother would come and take her away. The birthday party was over.

But with only a glance from Todd, the cake knife flipped into the air, twisted parabolically end over end as if thrown at a human target in a carnival sideshow. But instead of missing by fractions of inches to the wonderment of the crowd, her fragile body offered little resistance as the knife found its mark and imbedded itself deeply into Cara's back. It made a faint squishing sound as it ripped her flesh and muscle tissue; the kind of sound made when a honed knife cuts into a ripe tomato. Blood flowed through the open wound and pooled on the floor. Cara's mouth wrenched open and twisted downward in horror and pain, a strangled death cry, her eyes alive with terror and confusion. The little girl couldn't understand what was happening to her, why she was feeling what she was, the reason for the terrible, searing pain that sent fiery needles up and

down her back. But perhaps that was best. Cara fell
into her own blood, her arms outstretched above her,
streaking the window red in a desperate attempt to hoist
herself up to reach the lock. The light in her bedroom
was off, everything was as it should be, she had done
nothing wrong. Why were her parents allowing her to
experience this terrible pain? Why weren't the angels
watching over her?

She was dead before her cheek touched the floor,
and her mouth fell open expelling final blood. She
never knew that thirty years before, her mother's best
friend, Essie, had died in the house as well.

It wasn't over.

The Noah's Ark shot across the room hitting a girl in
the neck, snapping her spinal cord, killing her instantly.

It was as if the hobby horse had sprung to life. It
lurched forward, knocked another girl down, pinned
her under its front runner as it rocked back and forth,
back and forth, crushing her windpipe, muffling her
scream.

Marionettes surged forward from their pegs along the
wall, as if a spring released them, alive, demonic, an
army at war, their faces screaming masks. Their cloth
bodies swarmed against the girls, covered their noses,
their mouths. Their manipulating wires wrapped snakelike around the girls' necks, pulled taut, tore tender
skin, severed arteries, closed off windpipes, and strangled and mutilated their defenseless victims. The girls
pulled at the wires, pushed against the puppets in a desperate tangle of arms and legs and string; their shadows, cast by the firelight, cavorted madly, grotesquely
across the wall. But Todd held his concentration, and
soon the girls stopped their struggling, and one by one
slipped to the floor in their blood and urine.

Quickly it was over and the room was oddly silent.
Todd's fingers opened; he was suddenly calm. He
stared at the girls, and a nervous half smile crossed his

face. They were playing with him, his defenses told him. Only seconds before they had been screaming, now they lay silent, unmoving. They were playing the statue game! On a given signal they had dropped to the floor and froze in position.

But they weren't statues, his mind whirred, as it searched for meaning in what he was seeing, his gears grinding, looking for their proper groove, for *sense. It was only the dream again!* That was it. He remembered the night he had sleepwalked. The girls were like this then too. He hadn't known it was a dream and thought they were dead. But then his mother had come and he had woken up.

Cold realization slithered over him like a creeping python and his defenses slipped away. This wasn't a dream and his mother wasn't coming. This wasn't an illusion, nor a joke. It wasn't the moon playing tricks, toy shadows—

The girls were dead!

It took only a fraction of a second before his mind opened his mouth, and he shrieked in understanding, in madness. *They were all dead!*

The fire was only now going out on Ivy's body. Where there should have been a face, there was nothing but oozing blackness; the sickly, pungent odor of burned flesh filled his nostrils, overpowered him.

He was terrified beyond comprehension—*because he could not understand*. Where was Jenny? What had happened!

Tessie pushed open the door. She saw her grandson in the room, then everything else. Jenny was behind her in the hallway crying uncontrollably.

"Todd!" Tessie screamed hysterically. Then fear drove her from the room, pushing Jenny ahead of her.

Pain radiated from her chest to her arms and back again. She clutched her chest, her eyes closing to absorb the pain. She didn't see the staircase.

She tripped on the top step, sprawled down the rest. Her glasses flew off and clattered to the floor beneath her.

Still not believing, not trusting what her eyes had seen, she looked back through hazy, distorted vision and dimly saw the boy at the top of the landing.

"Run, Jenny," she ordered, the word gurgling up in her throat, mixing with her own screams of pain.

Then in a moment of final, disbelieving terror and anguish Tessie's heart stopped beating, and she slumped to the stairs, dead before her head fell against the wood.

CHAPTER 34

Blind with fear, Jenny raced to the front door. Her fingers closed around the brass knob. She pulled and pulled but the door refused to budge.

She was trapped!

Todd had trapped her in!

She kept looking over her shoulder to where her grandmother lay in a folded heap at the bottom of the stairs. Her eyes were open, but she wasn't blinking, wasn't moving. She was dead, Jenny comprehended. Like Lois was dead. Like the other girls were dead.

And then she saw Todd standing on the landing. The frigid knot in her chest was like nothing she had ever experienced before. Once again she tugged at the door with all of her young strength, and when she turned around again, Todd was one step closer. He was walking down the stairs!

To kill her too!

She pounded on the door. Tears were streaming down her cheeks, and she was no longer aware if she was screaming or not. Breathless, she turned and faced Todd.

Her back was to the door. Her shoulders heaved spasmodically. Her eyes darted in desperate search for escape. She couldn't run across the living room to the kitchen door because she had to pass the staircase, and he could get her. He was already at the bottom of the stairs.

His arms were outstretched in front of him.

Like the marionettes that had wanted to choke her!

Todd stalked her, almost with kaleidoscopic slow-motion stop action. Jenny blinked, trying to will the image away. But still he came toward her. Her knees started to buckle. She felt herself slumping against the door in resignation. There was no doubt in her mind that he would catch her and kill her like he did the others.

Then something within her memory clicked. She remembered the bolt lock. Her grandmother had thrown it into place when the last girl arrived. New York City paranoia, her grandmother had said, and Jenny had laughed too, even though she wasn't certain what paranoia meant. She wasn't trapped after all. The door was only locked!

Todd was only a few feet away, his eyes blood red.

Her fingers grabbed at the bolt. She twisted the lock. She heard the metallic snap and that was what told her she was no longer screaming.

She felt Todd's touch on her shoulder, his breath on her neck, and at the same moment she yanked open the door. The cool air assaulted her immediately, and gave her new life. She flew down the porch steps in utter, utter terror.

Not knowing where to go she turned toward the back of the house. She would run into the woods and hide from Todd there. He would never find her among the trees. Exhausted, she stumbled across the grass, already damp with dew. Mud and grass stained her white dress and smeared her legs.

Todd, his shadow framed against the light of the doorway, watched Jenny run around the side of the house. For a moment he was confused. Then the voice sounded within him.

She must be caught. You have to bring her back. We must kill her like the others.

Todd took off, down the steps, around the house. He saw Jenny pick herself off the ground where she had skidded on the wet grass and disappear into the woods.

Jenny's breath pounded heavily. Twigs snapped as she ran through the woods, slipping and sliding on piles of wet leaves that formed a soft, uncertain mat beneath her feet. Her hands waved almost spastically in front of her face to protect it from low-hanging tree limbs, monster arms waiting to envelop her, to *cut off her head*! She shrieked as a branch caught her across the neck, scratched her skin. The limb was wet and slimy, with burrs and prickles; there might have been blood, but she didn't know. All she knew was that she had to keep running, or else Todd would hurt her, kill her. She could barely see where she was going. The night was dark and only minimal light filtered down from the moon; everything else was swallowed up by the dense trees. She was trapped in the woods, a finite universe that closed in around her. She tripped on a spidery root and knocked painfully into a tree trunk. She steadied herself and continued running.

She had made a terrible mistake, she suddenly realized. She should never have gone into the woods. She could fall, slide on the spongy leaves, a branch could snare her, strangle her. Todd would find her. And even now she heard him tramping loudly behind her, calling her name. She should have run toward the road, a neighbor's house, to Cara's mother.

Jenny.

Todd's voice boomed behind her.

There was the stream back here too. She couldn't get caught near it. He could push her against the rocks or drown her. She had to make it back to the road. Abruptly, she stopped, darted around in a V arc, and started back to where she thought the yards and houses must be. She tried to remember which way she had entered the thicket of trees. She would have to run away from there; that was where Todd was coming from. She had to stay away from Todd.

He had to find her, the voice screeched within Todd. And Todd saw his dream flash through him—his father was holding the knife on him, and Jenny was standing in the doorway screaming gleefully for their father to kill him. *She hated him. Like the others. She had to die.* His mouth thinned out, neither smile nor sneer. Just determination. He would find her. She couldn't hide from him.

Jenny stopped to catch her breath. Above the fierce pumping of her heart she heard the sounds of the Vermont night: the stream rushing over rocks, only yards from where she was it seemed, and all around her, the lone, mournful cry of an owl, and the faint rustling of dying leaves in the night breeze. She strained to hear human sounds. Nothing. No Todd. Apparently he had stopped too, which made her all the more vulnerable. Todd could be anywhere, waiting for her to move first. In the silent night he would hear her, know where she was. Panicked, she understood what it was like to be hunted, defenseless, terrified. Her nostrils flared wide like a trapped animal, trying to sense the danger, see through the darkness, and locate its attacker.

Then she heard breathing. Her own gasps and wheezes as she struggled to calm herself, find her breath. She tried to take air in slowly, silently, not betray her location. She tried to gauge where she might be, which way was the house, the road.

She felt it against her face. "No!" she gasped and flailed her arms. But it wasn't Todd. A falling leaf had brushed against her, and in her susceptible state anything felt like it might be—

More breathing.

She couldn't catch her breath, couldn't inhale fully,

fill her lungs. Her breath was shallow and short; a faintness came over her.

More breathing.

A blackbird sounded above her, harshly, hoarsely, disturbed from its sleep. With fluttering wings it lifted itself high into the air, above the treetops, out of sight. *If only she had wings to take her away from there,* Jenny lamented.

More breathing. Heavier now.

This time not hers.

Aware of the new sound she jumped.

He was there.

One hand touched her neck; the other grabbed her arm, holding her.

"Todd!" she cried. "Don't. Don't."

In a thin band of moonlight that caught her brother's face she witnessed a momentary look of puzzlement, and it was enough. Instinct took hold; it was her moment. She yanked herself free from him and broke away, almost slammed into a tree trunk but side-stepped it in time. Then he was after her again.

Through the trees she could see the lights of the house. That was where she was heading.

She broke into the clearing. She was almost completely out of breath. Her heart and lungs strained against her chest cavity. She had only felt this way once before, when she had tried jogging with her father and Todd. Pain raged through her, like a knife was twisted into her side. She wanted to fall where she was. Give up. Nothing was worth this.

"Jenny!"

But she pressed on. If she could only make it to the road, to someone else's house. They would know what to do. She looked behind her and screamed again.

Todd was also in the clearing. And he was gaining on her.

* * *

The car turned into the driveway. From first glance it seemed like nothing was amiss, the house was as they had left it, and Mickie felt a fiery, cleansing rush of relief.

But the feeling was short-lived.

Mickie saw the front door of the house wide open, light streaming out almost wastefully into the night.

And then she heard a scream.

Her eyes were pulled to the sound as if on a wire suddenly drawn taut. Jenny came running out of the darkness into the headlights of the car, looking as if she was spotlighted on a stage.

"My God!" Mickie gasped and was out of the car before it rolled to a stop.

And then they saw the other figure.

The boy ran briefly into the light, then darted out again. From the size, build, and coloring there was no mistaking it was Todd. Were they too late, Mickie raged. Had it happened? It couldn't have, it was too unbelievable, too—

"I'll fucking kill him!" Rufus sputtered. He turned off the car engine and bolted out.

Seeing his father vault out of the car, Todd turned and took off for the house. Jenny ran straight toward Mickie and without slowing down barreled into her, almost knocking her over, as she buried herself in her mother's chest. Mickie felt her daughter's body tremble as if she had a raging fever.

"They're dead!" Jenny shrieked. "Dead!"

"Who?" Mickie gasped, and while a part of her already knew, the rest refused to acknowledge it had happened. All she wanted was to shield her daughter from all pain, all terror, and bundle her into the car and get her away from here.

"Todd killed them. All of them. And Grandma!"

Mickie looked up toward the house. Rufus was already inside, seemingly swallowed up by a house pulsating with death and tragedy.

"Dead!" Jenny repeated louder, uncertain if she had gotten through to her mother, uncertain if she, herself, knew what the word meant anymore.

"No, honey, no—" Mickie started to say, when suddenly she remembered another piece of the puzzle. Something she had learned from the courthouse records of the Cuttings family. Benjamin Cuttings had died the same day as the girls he had killed. And when she collated the information she understood.

"Todd!" she screamed. "Rufus!"

Frantically, she knelt down next to Jenny. "Don't move from here, okay? Lock the doors and don't move until I come outside and get you. Don't go into the house."

"Don't leave me, Mommy," Jenny said in a tiny voice and started to cry again. But she didn't know why she was crying. Was it for the other girls? Or herself?

"I'll be right back," Mickie said. She had to get to her son. Somewhere there was a terrible mistake. It felt like she was just thrust into a vacuum, and her head was exploding outward. "Don't move," she repeated, and felt herself suddenly torn, off-balance, undecided whether she should stay with Jenny or go into the house. Then she took off toward the open front door. She disappeared into the house leaving Jenny sitting alone in the front seat of the car.

Rufus raged into the house. He knew what he had to do—he had to kill the devil child. Kill him like he had before. Sounds roared through his head like brush fire. In a flash he was across the living room, heading toward the stairs. He had not actually seen Todd go upstairs, but never questioned why he was choosing that direction. There was something within him telling him that was where he was supposed to go. If he noticed Tessie still slumped at the bottom of the stairs, he did not react. He had only one purpose.

"I'll kill you!" he bellowed, and the words rebounded throughout the house. Then he was up the stairs and in the toy room.

Todd was across the room, his shoulders hunched and stiff. Rufus saw nothing else in the room. Not the toys. Not the girls. Only his bastard son.

And the cake knife.

It was thrust into the back of a child. Showing no understanding of where it was or what had happened, Rufus's hand closed around the handle and jaggedly he wrenched it free. Blood dripped from the tip back into the open wound. Rufus wiped it crosswise on his leg, staining his pants red with Cara Wallace's blood. He balanced the knife in his palm. It felt good, comfortable. Familiar. He held it out in front of him.

Todd saw the gleam of the blade as it caught the firelight. His father started toward him.

The sight of his father menacing him with the blade was familiar to him. He knew it had happened before.

It had happened to the boy.

To Benjamin.

Then his father took a step closer.

Mad with terror, Mickie ran into the house. The pungent odor of burned flesh assaulted her immediately. Why had her mother been cooking meat, she wondered insanely, then gagged when she realized what the odor was. Vomit rose high in her throat, and she tasted it, bitter. She choked it back and then saw her mother. Falling to her knees next to Tessie, she knew before touching her that she was dead. Her eyes were protruding, glazed with shock. Reading into those eyes Mickie imagined that they were frozen in condemnation of *her;* as a mother, Mickie had failed. Mickie closed her mother's eyes, suddenly weary, feeling as if all her insides had been wrenched from her body.

"I'll kill you!" she heard echoed from upstairs.

The scream jerked her forward, and Mickie stumbled up the stairs, hands on the steps above her, stooped over, like a bear cub walking on all fours.

She was expecting the worst, but still she wasn't prepared for what she saw when she pushed open the toy room door.

She took it all in. What she was seeing couldn't be real. She was somewhere else, watching a horror movie, sleeping. A thousand other possible explanations because this certainly had no footing in reality.

She couldn't scream out, cry. All she could do was stare mutely as a strangled moan tried to escape through her lips, and she made a sound as if someone was choking her from the inside. Her entire body trembled.

The last flames lighted the faces of the girls who lay on the floor. It was a room of death. A holocaust. The odor of burned flesh was stronger here, but that was just one more sensation that did not register. Another girl's face was blue and bloated. The manipulating wires of the Punch marionette wound innumerable times around her neck, her skin a deep purple where the wires dug in and stopped the flow of blood. Mickie looked away and scanned the walls, met the button eyes of the marionettes that suddenly seemed strangely red, victorious. For a moment she wondered why her mind didn't relax into madness and leave her alone. But instead the thought streaked through her mercilessly: She was responsible. Like Laura Cuttings.

Then she saw her husband and son eyeing each other, feinting left and right, two alley cats, streetfighters, each afraid of the other, hatred flaming in their eyes.

Rufus held a knife. He was stalking Todd. A rabid animal, playing with its intended victim. Mickie struggled to find her voice but phlegm kept filling her throat.

Rufus took a step toward him, and a grin that wasn't quite human opened broadly on his face. The room was alive with the thrill of the hunt, the scent of death.

"Rufus!" Mickie cried out, her first sound since coming up the stairs. It was a deep, desperate animal cry that had no impact. Rufus didn't hear her; or if he did, he ignored her.

"Stop!" she screamed. She raced toward him, to tackle him, but he roughly pushed her away and she fell backwards, stumbling over the body of a dead child. She struggled to her feet, her palms red with the girl's blood. She saw the possession behind her husband's eyes, which were now blind and cold and stony hard. There would be no breaking through to him, she despaired.

Then in a leap Rufus lunged toward Todd who sidestepped him, tore past his father, and darted out of the room.

"I'll kill you, you son of a bitch!" Rufus screamed and turned to follow him.

Mickie tried to grab at her husband, who was already halfway to the door, swearing at his devil child.

Then she heard a muffled rush of sound behind her.

"What?" she gurgled.

She felt something on her leg.

Suddenly off balance she crashed to the floor. What had tripped her? Then she saw the clown marionette gripping her leg; its macabre head tilted upward, its hideous smile claiming final victory. *God*. The word formed on her lips. She tried to push the marionette off her, shake herself free, but her legs lay twisted and useless beneath her, paralyzed; she had no control over them. A wooden hand reached higher up her thigh, its almost human nails digging into her as the grinning marionette tightened its hold on her leg. But the smile was deceitful; there was a deadly seriousness behind its painted, savage eyes. She tried to crawl forward and drag herself out of the room. Her palms scraped painfully against the hardwood floor and splinters burrowed under her skin, but still she wasn't able to move.

"No! God, no!" she cried and pounded at the marionette in desperation. She didn't know how to kill it. But now the clown was inanimate. Just a puppet. Just a toy. *That refused to release her!* And Mickie suddenly recognized the very first of her terrible dreams: she was trapped in the toy room, unable to move.

CHAPTER 35

Even with the car windows rolled up, Jenny shivered, and she didn't know how to put the heater on. She thought she remembered her father pushing buttons on the dashboard, but now when she tried it, nothing happened. Another button and another and then the headlights went out and the night closed in around her. Quickly she pulled the button out to turn the lights back on. She didn't want to be in the dark.

Her white party dress was stained with grass and dirt from when she had stumbled, ripped from being caught in the brambles. She had lost the rope-belt somewhere in the woods, and her dress hung formlessly around her. Her face was streaked with dirt, muddied by her tears. She trembled and wrapped her arms around herself, rocked back and forth to try to get warm. She was all alone.

She could hear nothing from the house. She had no idea how long it was since her parents had run in after Todd. She started humming to herself, but all she could summon was the calliope tune from the music box— *their* song. She tried to banish the eerie melody and the vision of the marionettes, but it tauntingly played over and over in her mind. The more she tried to stop it, fill herself with something else, counting by fives, multiplication tables, the louder, more insistent, the music became. It was telling her that even out here she wasn't safe. *They knew where she was.*

A car screeched past the house, and suddenly there was silence; the tune had come to an abrupt end. Now the night was hauntingly still, all sound and movement suspended. No breeze to rustle trees. No birds. No people. No cars. What she thought she had wanted, but she still couldn't find any peace.

Because now she sensed she was no longer alone. She had been humming to herself, had not been alert. She should have watched the distant parade of trees, listened for danger. The feathery hairs on her arms rose and prickled. Something had snuck up on her. She drew in her breath and held it, as if the extreme silence would reveal whoever, or whatever, was out there. It was a hideous game of hide-and-seek and everyone was looking for her. To tag her. To kill her.

There was a low rustling outside the car, a scratching against the metal. *No.* The word came out as a helpless whimper. She tried to ignore the sound, convince herself she hadn't heard anything, because if she didn't acknowledge it, it wouldn't be there. But it sounded again, louder, and hysterically she swung around, trying to see out all four sides of the car at the same time. There was nothing, but then she knew: something was hovering just below the window, ready to spring up and get her.

She shut her eyes and prayed that it would come and kill her, and it would all be over. Death was preferable to the awful fear of the unknown that she was experiencing. She remembered a story her mother had once told her about a mouse who was being chased by a cat. It was sheer terror that had killed the mouse. Its heart had given way from fear before the cat caught up with it. Jenny tensed and waited for the inevitable to happen—for her own heart to explode through her body, mercifully, painlessly, killing her instantly.

She had no idea how long she held her eyes shut, but her eyelids were lightly balanced now, pushing to open.

She opened her eyes slowly and from mere slits they sprang wide in horror.

A pair of eyes met her own through the windshield of the car. They were large, circular, ringed with black circles.

Marionette eyes!

Jenny screamed. The eyes moved. And then she saw it was only a raccoon disappearing into the blackness of the woods. But even that knowledge couldn't calm her.

She had to get out of the car. Her trembling fingers slipped on the handle, but finally the door swung wide, and she ran toward the house, not wanting to be caught outside alone in the dark.

She entered the living room, purposely not shutting the door behind her, instinct telling her to leave an escape route open.

She heard sounds from upstairs. Voices. Footsteps. Screams. Her father. Her mother.

Then Todd was racing down the stairs.

Jenny tried to shrink away from him, so he wouldn't see her. Her father was behind him, chasing him, a knife in his hand. They were through the living room and into the kitchen. She heard the sobs coming from upstairs. Her mother was up there. She was hurt!

Jenny hesitated. She wanted to go to her mother but was afraid of the toy room.

She had to find her father. He would know what to do. He would help Mommy. Both of them.

Summoning her courage, she pushed open the kitchen door. It was empty. The cellar door was open, a gaping hole. Feet were pounding down the wooden boards.

Jenny stood in the cellar doorway for only a second. Then she, too, started down.

Todd crashed through the cellar. He jabbed his knee against the leg of a discarded chair that ripped his flesh and drew blood. But he didn't even feel it as he ran from his father toward the room where he would be safe.

Just like Benjamin.

Dim light filtered back from the foot of the cellar stairs, but Todd knew his way more by feel and instinct now than anything else.

His father was close behind him as he pulled open the door. He raced across the room, he would hide in the corner. Rufus appeared in the doorway. He was blocking the light, his face lost in shadow. His eyes adjusted to the darkness of the room, and he searched out the child. He poised the knife in front of him.

It was just like his dream! Todd shrieked, where his father had chased him, and tried to stab him. He shrank smaller into the corner, tried to disappear.

Another step closer; a smile opened on Rufus's face. "Bastard," he sneered. "You're not my son. You're the devil. I'm going to kill you."

The words echoed within Todd. *I'm going to kill you. Like Benjamin had been killed.*

But suddenly Todd was no longer afraid.

He knew what to do.

What Benjamin had taught him to.

He stepped away from the wall and stood, shoulders high, and met his father. He showed no fear.

Then he concentrated.

On his father.

On the knife.

Rufus's eyes widened in surprise. His hand started to quiver, tingle, as if an electric current were passing through it. "I'm going to kill you," he hissed, but he sounded less sure of himself. Pain was radiating from the knife to his hand. The knife was on fire! No! It was his hand. He tried to open his hand, drop the knife, but he couldn't. It was paralyzed. His other hand tried futilely to open his fingers.

And then his shaking hand was turning by itself. Rufus couldn't control his muscles. His wrist twisted abnormally, turning the knife inward. The tip of the blade was pointed at his chest. Confusion exploded over Rufus's face.

"Todd?" he questioned and saw his son for perhaps the first time. His face was contorted into an almost unrecognizable mask as he concentrated. "No!" Rufus screamed. "Todd!" But he couldn't break through, his fate was chosen.

"Oh, dear God!" he whimpered. "Mickie—!" he shrieked. She had been right all along; there was possession.

The knife moved closer to him. He watched it move, his eyes flitting frantically from the knife to his son. A smile crossed Todd's face. He was toying with his father, taking his time. Rufus felt the forced tension in his arms, saw the tautness of his tendons, the stiffness of his elbow. With all of his strength he strained against the movement of his arm, tried to twist his body out of the way. To resist! But still the knife moved fractionally closer; his mind, his muscles were being controlled from without. Would this be considered suicide, he wondered. Or murder.

"Todd!" he howled.

But Todd was only hearing the voice within him, telling him to kill their father. To exact revenge.

The knife tip broke skin. Rufus watched it, almost curiously detached, as it entered inch by inch. The knife punctured his chest, stabbed downward, ripped open diaphragm and stomach. Pain surged through his body and almost instantly blood spurted out through the open wound. Rufus weakened, stumbled to his knees, and clutched his stomach, still trying to pull out the knife. But Todd waited until Rufus fell to the floor before he allowed him to loosen his grip. The tension of his hand on the handle of the knife had stiffened his fingers into a curled position. It was only the briefest of thoughts, but his hand reminded him of an animal's claw. Blood dripped from the corners of his mouth. He looked up at his son and said, "I forgive you, Todd. Forgive me."

His body jerked as death took hold, and Todd eyed his father with satisfaction.

Released, Jenny screamed and part of her was surprised there was even voice left within her.

Todd heard her and looked up sharply. She was standing in the doorway.

He knelt down next to his father and withdrew the knife from his body. Blood exploded out, splattered Todd's clothing, covered his face like war paint.

Jenny saw Todd start after her. The knife he held dripped with blood. She ran from the room, back through the cellar, knocking into boxes and furniture. She scampered up the stairs. She didn't even consider running out of the house. There was only one place she could go. Her mother would help her.

Jenny ran toward the toy room.

Mickie heard Jenny's screams. They were getting louder. Closer.

"Dear God!" she cried. Jenny was in the house. Coming up the stairs.

The marionette's cold hands were clamped around her leg, pinning her to the floor. Her eyes raced around the room. What was here that was allowing this lunacy to rage?

"Jenny!" Mickie screamed. "Don't come up here. Get out of the house!"

Jenny heard her mother, stopped, hesitated on the landing. It was too late. She heard footsteps behind her. Todd was coming for her. She was trapped on the stairs; she couldn't go down.

"Mommy!" she cried.

Mickie heard the footsteps too. She tried to kick free from the marionette, but she was unable to move.

"Jenny, you have to hide. Don't come in here!"

But who was following Jenny? Rufus? Todd? Something else? Her eyes met the grinning, mocking face of the clown.

Then Jenny was in the room running toward her. She threw her arms around her mother and hugged her chokingly, as if it might be the last time she ever held her. Jenny was sobbing, babbling. "Todd . . ." she was saying.

And then Todd was there. In the doorway.

"He wants to kill me, Mommy," Jenny screeched, and there was familiarity to the words. Jenny was clutching at her mother, desperate for Mickie to help her.

Mickie saw Todd's hand—gnarled, deformed—and the knife! With all of her effort she threw Jenny toward the corner of the room, away from Todd. And slumped on the toy room floor, as she had been in her nightmares, Mickie prepared to meet her son.

"Where's Daddy, Todd?" she questioned, and tried to make her voice as strong as possible.

Then she saw the tip of the knife was red with blood and Todd's clothing was splattered.

Todd made no sound. He was walking closer to her, one even step at a time. Toward Jenny across the room. He never took his eyes off his sister, never acknowledged his mother. His right toe nudged the body of one of the girls. Almost like a blind man he stepped over it. Mickie saw the haunted, dead look in his eyes.

She struggled again to lift herself from the floor, but the clown gripped tighter, knotting her flesh in its hands.

"No, Todd," she said in a terrified whisper. "It's Jenny. Jenny," she repeated louder as if the word alone

would break through whatever barrier was surrounding
him.

Jenny remained in the corner, eyeing her brother,
knowing he wanted to kill her, knowing as well that her
mother couldn't save her. She was all alone, helpless
against the knife. She knew now she had made a terrible mistake in coming up here.

Mickie's lips formed words soundlessly. *Take me instead. Let me sacrifice myself for my child.*

The dream cascaded within her. In a burst of
strength she had risen up, flung herself toward Todd in
self-sacrifice, taken the knife into her as surrogate for
her daughter. And then she had fallen dead to the floor,
not knowing if her sacrifice had saved Jenny's life.

She now understood the meaning of the dream. This
was not what she should do.

She had to get through to Todd.

Reach him somehow.

Crack the wall of possession that surrounded him.

"Todd!" she wailed. "It's Mommy. Mommy!"

Todd walked forward. He was listening to the boy's
voice telling him to kill his sister as he had killed the
others. Jenny hated him. She wanted him dead.

But off in the distance he heard another voice. It was
trying to break down a door.

Todd

He strained to hear it.

Todd

His mother's voice. Where was she?

Kill her the much stronger voice bellowed within
him.

Todd took another step toward Jenny.

Then the other voice found a way in. He let it in. It
grew stronger. His mother. Calling him. Telling him to
put down the knife.

He hesitated.

The pain surged through him. Like an electric current pulsing across his temples. The boy was hurting him. Todd begged for relief from the pain.

I will take away the pain, the boy promised, *if only you will kill your sister.*

Kill Jenny? The words struck like hammer blows.

He couldn't!

His mind heaved and shifted in maddening confusion. His face screwed up in anguish. He saw his terrified sister in front of him, hunched in the corner. And his mother, her arm outstretched pleadingly toward him. He tried to open his fingers and drop the knife. But the pain closed in around him, forcing him to clamp his fingers shut.

"No!" Todd yelled and Mickie saw her son's face contort in agony. She could only imagine the pain raging through her son, but somehow she was getting through to him, splintering the possessing hold of Benjamin Cuttings, finding her son beneath that hold.

Todd's fingers shook spastically as he struggled to open his fingers and then with a spurt of sudden energy he was successful. The knife fell from his hands and clattered to the floor. Mickie reached out and grabbed it. She twisted around and faced the clown marionette, triumph streaking across her face.

"Todd." She sighed and reached out to him in embrace.

But her rush of victory came too soon.

The witch marionette sprang from the floor and wrapped its wires around Jenny's neck.

"Jenny!" Mickie cried helplessly. *Oh, God,* she thought. She was going to watch her daughter be choked to death.

But Todd saw what was happening and knew what to do.

Jenny was frantic. Her fingers clawed at the choking wires, drawing blood on her neck. Her eyes bulged wide, her mouth open to gulp air.

Todd concentrated. He strained against the forces that were on his sister. He could do it, he knew.

He sensed the boy within him, a mask of hate, death. New agony surged through him.

"No!" Todd shrieked and his mouth grimaced with the word.

The voice roared within him.

She must die. We must get revenge. You must kill her like we did before!

"No! I don't want her dead!" Todd screamed. And with the one small part of his mind that was still his, he fought the pain, tried to block the voice, the vision of the boy.

I'm your friend, Benjamin Cuttings taunted. *I taught you to concentrate. I gave you the power to be like me. But you're like all the other children who hated me. I'll kill her myself and then you too!*

"I'm not your friend!" Todd screamed back at him. He balled his fists and shook them at the ceiling. "And I'll stop you!" he swore. "I'm as strong as you are!"

Mickie watched her son struggle with the unseen enemy, saw the lines and strain on his face, heard only his side of the verbal battle with the ghost child.

"Todd . . ." she gasped. Jenny was weakening. "I love you, Todd!" she called to him desperately.

The pain continued to pulsate through Todd like a buzz saw, severing nerves, arteries, and brain cells. But with all of his will trained on the choking wire, he concentrated. Like he never had before. He could only redeem himself by saving his sister.

The marionette wires loosened around Jenny's neck. She was able to fling them wildly off her and cast the marionette into the fireplace. Ashes swirled and the fire immediately caught the cloth and wood and burned afresh. From across the room Mickie saw the punch marionette, sensed it was about to spring from the wall.

"Run, Jenny! Now!" she screamed, and in her moment of freedom Jenny didn't hesitate. At the doorway she turned, tears of helplessness in her young eyes. She couldn't save her mother.

"Go!" Mickie hissed and Jenny was out of the room, the door closed, the marionettes crashing against it in flutter and fury. Mickie didn't know if she would make it out of the house or not.

Because it still wasn't over.

The knife was clenched tightly in Mickie's fist. She stared at the flat of the blade, still red with her husband's blood. She gripped the carved handle and stabbed the blade into the body of the clown marionette, ripped the clothing, and scattered the stuffing underneath until there was nothing left of the puppet.

Todd was exhausted. Concentrating had left him weak. The pain throbbed through his skull. It felt as if his head were cleaved, with one hand grasping each side, both hands twisting in opposite directions. He knew he could not endure much more.

He staggered toward Mickie. She opened her arms to him, but then saw that his hand was quivering, reaching out toward the knife she held.

"No!" she shrieked and thrust her arm behind her, the knife away from him. "Fight it, Todd! Fight it!"

But Todd's hand closed around hers. He struggled for the knife. Mickie wouldn't relinquish the handle. Todd grabbed the blade. It sliced deeply into his palm. Blood flowed to the floor but it was as if he couldn't feel the gash.

"Fight it, Todd. You did it before!"

But helplessly Mickie watched him take the knife from her, saw the blaze of new possession in his face.

The knife arched high over his head. Mickie followed the rise of the blade. *He was going to kill her*, she thought wildly.

"Todd, no!"

And then he would go after Jenny and get her too.

"Todd, no!" she repeated in a voice choked with final desperation.

But even though Todd heard the voice, he no longer had the strength or power to resist the command within him. He started to bring the knife down.

Horrified, Mickie shut her eyes, tensed, and waited.

But when seconds passed and nothing happened, she opened her eyes again and saw what Todd was about to do. His eyes were locked hypnotically, almost reverently, on the tip of the blade.

"Dear God!" she gasped in understanding and screamed the words to the room: "Take me instead! Let me sacrifice myself for my child! Whoever you are! Take me!"

But the knife swept downward in a smooth, unbroken curve and plunged slowly into Todd's stomach. Only a slight grimace on his face, a tic beneath his eye, was his acknowledgment that it had happened.

"Todd—" Mickie sucked in her breath and lunged toward him in a feeble attempt to stop the inevitable. But the knife twisted jaggedly into her son, and she felt the pain as if it were her own. She turned away, unable to watch. "God forgive him," she murmured.

And then, with the coming of death, Todd relaxed. All tension drained from his face; his innocence reappeared. "Mommy . . ." he said faintly and extended his arm toward her. But it weakened, fell to the floor, and their fingers never touched. For only a second, his eyes searched out Mickie's and then closed. He slumped to the floor, falling on the knife, which pushed farther into his body.

"Todd—" Mickie said blankly, and for one hysterical second wondered if the knife was a rubber one and her son was joking.

Mickie would not know how long she lay on the floor looking at Todd. Todd's blond hair was washed across his face; he was seemingly only asleep. She wanted to reach out and push his hair out of his eyes, like she had done countless times before, but it was the slender trickle of blood running from the corner of his mouth that cried out the truth, and she understood there was nothing more she could do for him. For any of them. Except—

Jenny.

Was her daughter all right?

With a pained cry from deep in her soul Mickie struggled to her feet. Her legs were stiff from her cramped position, and she half stumbled, half ran, half crawled to the toy room door and down the stairs.

From the road Jenny saw her mother emerge from the house. Arms wide she ran to her. A mad look of survival blazed across her young face. They had been victorious. They had lived. She did not ask about Todd.

Mother and daughter embraced in the cool Vermont air that suddenly chilled their bodies, now exhausted, defenseless, drained. They started walking up the road, not knowing where they were going: Mickie's arms were wrapped around her trembling daughter.

A state trooper would pick them up later. They would be frightened, disoriented, and he would remark later, strangely emotionless. In shock, he imagined.

But alive.

EPILOGUE

It seemed as if there would be no end to the media coverage of what was called the Glendon Tragedy. Television covered the removal of the bodies and was followed by extensive interviews with neighbors, townspeople, teachers, and parents. It would be months before the town relaxed, years before it recovered. The parents of the slain girls, of course, never would.

"It was only a birthday party," Nina Wallace repeated numbly, not comprehending what could have gone so terribly wrong.

It was Simon Stoneham of the Southern Vermont Historical Society who revealed the parallels of the tragedies of the Cuttings family of a hundred years ago and of Essie Webster, the girl who had been accidentally hanged by the marionettes. "Nobody would ever be expected to buy that house again" one reporter wrote in his story, and another made reference to the Amityville Horror and the resultant tragedies there when the family had tried to challenge the demonic. Whatever, all agreed that the Talman house was marked for life. And Simon Stoneham sadly filed away all the newspaper reports.

It was days before Mickie came out of shock and was well enough to talk with the police. During those first days there was a constant wild fear in her eyes for the safety of her daughter and a need for them to be together. Understandable after the terrors they had endured and survived. The media kept a twenty-four-hour vigil outside of her hospital room.

When finally coherent enough to answer questions about what had happened, Mickie just shook her head vaguely and muttered, "It was a madman. I didn't see him. We came back unexpectedly." It would then be pieced together that Rufus Talman had evidently surprised the madman during his brutal acts, chased him downstairs, and was killed in the room in the cellar.

Jenny kept repeating something about her brother,

Todd, but doctors and police dismissed her hysterical accusations. Obviously the shock had confused the little girl.

Mickie would never allow herself to be hypnotized to try for an accurate description of the murderer. She was too terrified of what she might see and remember; as it was, the entire incident was wiped from her mind.

So the crime would remain open; the madman never found.

Months passed. The seasons changed. The snow came. Except for those directly affected by the tragedy, life continued in the town of Glendon, Vermont.

It was deep into a January night, four months after the deaths. It was closer to dawn than to midnight, the time when darkness seems denser, cold more intense, and when familiar objects loom suddenly larger and strangely unfamiliar, and everything seems ominous. Especially for a child. Outside. Alone.

Timothy Evans desperately wanted to join the Night Raiders, the newly formed club at the Glendon Elementary School. It was a group of the elite; if you were a Raider, you were someone. Timothy Evans wanted to be part of the "in" crowd.

His initiation rite was simple—go into the Talman house at night and come out with a marionette.

Timothy Evans snuck out of bed, quietly dressed in parka and ski pants, and without turning on a light or making a sound, slipped out of the house. His father would skin him, he knew, for being out of the house alone at night. Especially going to the Talman House. It never occurred to Timothy that all he really had to do was buy a marionette at the local toy shop; his friends would never know the difference.

From his vantage point across the road, the house loomed high in front of him. Silent, dark, foreboding.

Although it seemed oddly calm as well, deceptively innocent, sealing the unknown behind its closed doors.

Timothy's hand tightened around his flashlight, and he tried to remember when he had changed the batteries. It would be ghastly if the light should go out when he was somewhere in the house.

He quietly crossed the road and approached the house.

He made his way up the Talman driveway, through snow knee deep. No one had bothered to shovel it out. There was no need to. Nobody would be going there, and neither Mickie Talman nor her daughter would ever set foot in there again.

The flashlight quivered in Timothy's unsteady hand, scrambling the thin beam of light. He made his way up the porch steps and stopped in front of the door. He reached out and tried the knob. *Locked.* A dizzying sense of relief surged through him and a bit of self-ridicule. *Did he really expect the door to be open for him?*

But he knew the Night Raiders had already found a cellar window that opened. That would be how he could get inside. He broke a path to the side of the house, crawled under the veranda, and found the window. He tested it. It moved and squealed on its hinges. He propped it up with a piece of wood and shined the flashlight in. He stiffened, not knowing what might be silhouetted in the darkness. It was a room. Against one wall was a bookcase, a chest of drawers. Beneath the window was a bed. Rumpled covers were on the bed. He could just ease himself into the room, land on the bed, and make his way through the house and up the stairs.

For only the briefest moment Timothy wondered if he could possibly go through with this operation.

But he knew he had to. If he didn't, not only would he miss his chance to join the Night Raiders, but everyone would know he had chickened out.

He slipped into the cellar. His flashlight picked up the stains on the floor. Blood, he knew, and shuddered. This was where the father had been killed. Hurriedly, he found the door and left the room.

The heavy blackness of the cellar immediately engulfed him. The flashlight broke a narrow path in front of him as he found the cellar steps and walked upward. The darkness was strangling. The old wood creaked loudly beneath him. He paused, his hand resting on the kitchen door. He pushed it slightly and shined the light through the narrow gap. He thought he heard sound behind him and turned around. But it was only his heartbeat booming in his ears. He tasted terror on his tongue . . .

And pushed open the kitchen door.

His eyes were wide, unblinking, rapidly darting to and fro not to leave an angle unobserved. His eyes searched for the staircase.

Hesitating, his hand on the banister, he started up. Then he was aware he was humming to himself. The song was insistent, distracting. He couldn't stop humming the hypnotic tune. A circus song.

He reached the landing and knew he was on the second floor.

With a sweep of his flashlight he illuminated the hallway in a swirling circle of yellow white light. The hallway was empty.

The toy room was at the far end.

With a swallow that refused to go down his throat he started toward the toy room door. He turned to look behind him every few steps lest something be sneaking up on him from out of the darkness.

He wanted to turn, to run, to get out of there. But he

had come this far. He couldn't leave now with nothing
to show for it.

He stood in front of the toy room door.

*No such things as ghosts, no such things as ghosts, no
such things as ghosts,* he repeated to himself. He
hunched forward and slowly elbowed the door open a
sliver, pushing the flashlight through. He cringed, not
knowing what he would see.

The door creaked open painfully, and he shined the
light into the room. The room where the children had
been killed.

The marionettes were back on the wall, resting silently on their pegs. There was a carousel in the center
of the room with horses seeming to chase each other.
Puppets were on the floor, and dolls and other toys.

There was a faint odor in his nostrils. Like something
was burning.

All he had to do was go into the room, grab a marionette off the wall, and be out of there before anyone
would know it. Fear surged through him. He felt the
pounding in his temples, the burning knot in his chest.
His breathing was heavy and rasping, audible to himself—and anyone else, he knew. He eyed the marionettes suspiciously.

No such things as ghosts, no such things as ghosts . . .

The witch marionette was the closest to the door, the
easiest one to pull off the wall.

Taking deep breaths of air, he steeled himself and
burst into the room.

He didn't hear the door slip shut behind him.

He grabbed the witch and raced back to the door.

It was closed!

His fingers closed around the brass knob and
yanked.

Locked!

The door had locked itself!

He was trapped! He tried to scream but fear had completely stolen his voice.

It was then that he heard the flutter of sound. He shined his flashlight on the wall of marionettes.

He let out a strangled, muffled moan.

And then all was silent.

He wouldn't be found for two days. His parents were frantic, and it was only when Johnny Werber, president of the Night Raiders, came forward to tell about the initiation plan that Timothy Evans's father and a group of local men went into the Talman house. They found Timothy dead in the toy room. His arm was stretched out above him, seemingly trying to claw his way past a door which opened easily. The flashlight was still clutched in his hand—Death Grip—as the newspapers would call it, the Eveready batteries still operating.

There were no markings on the boy and an autopsy was run.

It was determined that fear had killed him; terror had stopped his heart.

Like a mouse—a mother had once told a child—that was being chased by a cat.

BLOOD ROOT

by Thomas Mordane

For centuries the inhabitants of Hubley's Gore had tilled the soil, eking out a living from the harsh land. Bound together by time, by ties of kinship and by their battle against the savage elements, the silent, dark secret held sway over them. Ancient and powerful, it commanded the very elements.

Now Laura and Mark Avery have come to the bustling little Vermont village, have given up their frenetic city life to have their child. They are not superstitious but as the seasons turn, as the full moon rises, people begin to die in Hubley's Gore.

A DELL BOOK   10411-4   ($2.95)

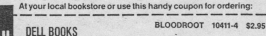

Who is Baby? A gift from God? Or a hoax? Whoever—
or whatever—Baby is, she has changed the lives of
those who know her. Doris, her mother: a fifty nine
year old "virgin" who thinks she is dying, gives birth
to a child who sings. Shockley: an aging professor,
feels it is his mission to spread the word of Baby's
gift—at any price. Jacobsen: the hustler's hustler, will
manage the child's "career." Irina, beautiful but desperate, will kidnap the child for a huge ransom. Will
Baby's song remain angelic after all this foul play?
BABY is powerful, moving—and the story of a haunt-
ing and rampant greed.

"Astounding. An unconventional novel by a spell-
binding storyteller."—ALA Booklist

A DELL BOOK   10432-7   ($3.50)

BABY

by Robert Lieberman